I0788403

Run With the Hunted
Second Omnibus
Books 4-6

For Jim

Run With the Hunted
Second Omnibus
Books 4-6
Jennifer R. Donohue

Run With the Hunted 4: VIP

Chapter One

Nobody at this party matters, but I thought it would be amusing to attend anyway. I've been to the club hosting it before, and know the degree to which I should dress. No red soles tonight; far too showy and that would strike the wrong note with other guests. I needn't draw *too* much attention, and not the sort which would generate resentment.

The lighting is dim, kind to everybody's faces even before things become drink-blurred. Drink-blurred for them, that is; I have a firm grip on sobriety, sometimes in spite of how much alcohol I've consumed. Some genetic luck, though if I'd been the type to *want* to imbibe to excess, it would certainly be a burden; instead, it was a boon in my earlier days, when every penny counted. But there is a distinct benefit to being the most sober one in the room, or at a table, especially if deals are being made, or if the people with you have nefarious intentions. Which isn't to say that I always assume the worst of people, you understand, it's just necessary to keep your wiles about you while also matching the proper mood for the environment.

They have champagne so I have a champagne cocktail; there's just something about the aesthetic of holding a champagne flute that is so compelling. There is some small talk to be had, in the way of these things, and at about the middle of the evening, if my estimation is correct, I find myself standing next to a man who really doesn't seem as though he fits well here.

"What are we celebrating?" he asks me, nodding to my champagne flute. It's another reason I almost always get champagne, it gives people a chance to ask me that and feel clever.

"I'm not certain yet," I say, with my head tilted just so. He is handsome, and his suit fits him particularly well. There's something about how he holds himself, though, that tells me a suit is not his preferred manner of dress. "I simply had the impulse."

"Maybe you're celebrating our meeting," he says, a little bold I think. But his demeanor says that he doesn't do this often, and he is trying very hard to be earnest, so I think I will give him the benefit of the doubt for now.

"I suppose that remains to be seen," I say, and smile. As I take the next sip of my cocktail, I drop my eyes to his shoes, which are cowboy boots made of some exotic leather; I'm not entirely sure, with this lighting, but my guess is ostrich. Oh very interesting; something to tell Dolly about later, when I'm making the girls listen to my tales of the evening, if I have any tales of this evening. I did not, until this point.

"I suppose it does," he says. "Well let me grab my own whatever that is...?"

"Ask them for a champagne cocktail."

"A champagne cocktail, and then we can go to one of those tables there, and we'll see how things progress?" He smiles a little quizzically, as though the champagne cocktail were not simply called that, but one could excuse him for not knowing. I'd guess that he prefers beers, probably lagers. Maybe stouts.

"Perhaps you'd prefer a black velvet," I say. "There *is* still champagne involved, I promise."

"Perhaps," he says, like he's tasting the word. "I'll be right back with one of those then. Do you need a top off?"

"Not right now, thank you." He moves easily through the crowd, comfortable with himself despite the suit, and has the kind of presence where people kind of move for him, he isn't jostled or jostling. I watch his face in the bar mirror; he smiles easily for the server, slides a cash tip across the bar when he receives his drink, also giving a little nod. When he turns back around, he meets my eyes across the room and raises his glass a little, champagne with stout layered on top. Then he nods towards the tables, and we each cross the room to meet there; I pause briefly to speak with somebody I recognize from a previous party, and when we part I have a mental note to drop a missive to Marquis. Sooner or later, they're going to soften again; it just isn't in their nature to make me keep *groveling*.

"Thank you for the drink recommendation, miss," he says. He'd sampled it by the time I reached the table, the layers starting to lose their distinction. "Just champagne is definitely a little too sweet for my taste."

"You struck me as a beer aficionado," I say. "I'm pleased I was right."

"What gave me away?"

"Your boots."

"My boots?" He's the sort of man who's cultivated an easy smile in place of a whole myriad of emotions, such as surprise and disappointment and confusion. "My best boots outed me as a beer drinker?"

"They are western boots. Ostrich western boots."

"They are at that." He leans back in his seat a little, straightens his leg out to admire them. "You don't see a lot of these in places like this, I guess."

"I do not." I don't see many ostrich leather accoutrements in general, or perhaps not in North America, but I needn't inform him of that. "They suit you, though. You're obviously comfortable."

"Well thank you, I am." We nod at each over the rims of our glasses. What an interesting flirtation this is, because he does not seem actually interested in flirting, but he has something he is working around to. He sets his drink down, starts to lean his elbows on the table, just in repose, but something that isn't manners hitches him up and he thinks better of it. Which is not to say I think he's unmannerly, but it's a physical inhibition, new or he wouldn't have forgotten it.

"Except for that," I say mildly, and there's that smile again, a rueful tilt of the head.

"Except for that." He considers a moment, shakes his head. "Alright, I might as well just lay things out, I'm not good at social games. I've got kind of a proposition, and I'd like you to hear me out." He sees my face and holds up his hands just a little, right above the table's surface. "Proposition's the wrong word. It's a job offer."

I take one last sip of my champagne before I set it down, rearrange myself slightly in my seat. "Perhaps, before I hear you out, we ought to ascertain just who you think I am?" I was not expecting a job offer, nor had I heard of this man from any of my contacts, and I feel certain I would have, were they sending him my way. The chances of a job just dropping from the heavens into my lap at rather a boring, inconsequential party were...low. Goodness, have I just been mistaken for an escort? "Just to keep from wasting your time, of course."

He repeats the raised hands gesture, like he wants to gentle the situation. "I hope I haven't offended you, I saw you and thought I recognized you, but I don't really know where. Like maybe I'd seen your face in the paper for a local theater concern that just wrapped up production."

"And you'd like to hire an actress privately?" He doesn't seem to be lying; nor does he seem to be telling the truth, and I am amused and intrigued.

"Actually yes. It's real weird, and a little complicated, and I don't blame you one bit if you say no."

"Well now I absolutely *must* hear you out," I say, smiling. "Though lest I mislead you further, I am not said stage actress, and I daresay we've until this point never shared a space."

"Oh," he said, actually crestfallen, the darling. "Well I'm sorry to have bothered—"

I reach out and touch his wrist as he starts to get up. "You haven't bothered me, this is one of the most dull parties I had ever been to until you approached."

"Really?"

I nod. "Cross my heart."

He has some more of his drink, maybe to collect his thoughts after having been so swiftly derailed. He is clearly used to other, perhaps more physical, kinds of challenges. "I find myself in need of a wife," he says finally, and I get the sense that he had a different sort of speech planned. "And I'm not in the business of propositioning beautiful women that I meet in clubs, and I'm not interested in making women do anything they don't want to. But I was in different circumstances, which have changed, and I have a legal deadline coming up, so I don't have the time to do things the right way."

I certainly had not expected anything of that sort. "So in order to meet this legal deadline, you wanted to hire an actress to be your wife?" I ask. "What sort of a legal deadline?"

"One my parents set, for a trust. See, me and my brother were both happy to just do our own thing and live on a stipend and get married on our own time." Oh a *trust*. There are such fascinating rules surrounding those. I don't know many lawyers, but at least one in my acquaintance has been a trust lawyer, and the *stories* he could tell.

"You said your circumstances changed, though. What were you and your brother up to?"

"Bull riding, actually," he said, and that's where his easy physicality comes from. I'm not certain I've ever known a bull rider, and Dolly's escapades at bars with sawdust on the floor do not count. "But I wrecked my shoulder and elbow just about for good pretty recently, and can't do that anymore, but my brother still can."

"So you were going to both just take the stipend, but since you cannot continue with what you were doing..."

"I thought I'd make a go of it, yeah."

"May I ask what the trust is...regarding?" I'm not even certain how to phrase it.

"Oh yeah, sure. My family's one of the biggest ostrich farming concerns in North America."

"Oh I see." I could just imagine Dolly's excitement. A bull rider *and* an ostrich farmer, she will be simply obsessed. She'll throttle me, if I turn this down. A business marriage, so a man who can no longer bull ride might access his family's fortunes. "And how long are you envisioning this whirlwind courtship and subsequent marriage needing to last?"

He laughs, open and honest; he's amazed and relieved that I haven't thrown my drink in his face and huffed off to have the bouncers remove him. "Oh I don't know, we don't need to break any records like the movie people. The trust doesn't go away if divorce happens."

"Do you have staff that you need to maintain this ruse for?" I have a sudden horror of needing to keep up appearances under the very close scrutiny of his own Mrs. Danvers, and then another thought follows swiftly on the heels of the first. "Besides, I won't do this alone, you understand. For safety's sake."

He frowns a little, but picks up his drink again. Settling into the conversation, the idea that perhaps he has been successful. "I don't know if I follow."

"Well if I'm to be your sudden mysterious and unexpected bride that you might step in and claim your ostrich fortune, I must have my bodyguards with me." I'll have to do something about their clothes, of course, but I do believe it's possible I can get both Bits and Dolly to adopt nice suits in lieu of their riot gear, for this situation. Everything as reinforced and dragonscaled as can possibly be, of course.

He pauses with his drink midair. "You...have bodyguards?" He looks around, but no bodyguards appear.

I smile indulgently, finish my cocktail. "It's all the rage nowadays."

The poor man looks even more out of his element, but I'm comfortable waiting for him to work through his thoughts. I look out across the room, but the people gathered have become no more interesting in the interim, and no familiar faces have turned up. "There will be some house staff, but nobody's a personal servant, if that's what you mean. And the master suite has enough rooms where behind closed doors, nobody needs to know who's sleeping where."

"That does sound suitable." I study him for a moment; he is a handsome enough man, if a little rugged for my tastes. "How is it that you never found love before now?"

He shrugs. "Just didn't stop long enough, maybe. And not every lady is interested in a bullrider. It's dangerous, and they don't want to go through not knowing if he's going to walk out of the ring at the end of the day." He's been asked this time and again, it seems.

"And your brother is the same way?"

"He's maybe more inclined to accept the advances of a buckle bunny here and there than I ever was, but yeah, I've never yet seen him inclined to settle down. And he knows I want to do this, there's no feud going on."

I raise my eyebrows. "Buckle bunny?"

He clears his throat, hitches in his chair a little. "Slang for women who follow rodeos. Like groupies, but girls of a certain type getting notches on their belts."

"I see." Every industry has its own language, it's just fascinating. And nearly everybody has their own way to denigrate women.

He shakes his head. He's uncomfortable, but I think only because he doesn't want me to think badly of him in that way. "Like I said, I don't get in with all that. And it won't matter anyway, I'm not asking you to perform maritals, just be my wife on paper for long enough to get those things settled. A couple of weeks, probably."

"That seems reasonable." I'm honestly delighted by the whole charade, and he does seem as though he'll behave in a gentlemanly manner. Especially with my 'bodyguards' about; I have seen Dolly put much larger men in their place, when it came to that. But, I cannot accept without consensus, unless I'm also willing to just do the job alone, and I'm not entirely certain that I am. I consider the intersection of bull riding people and ostrich ranching people, and all of that money. "We would need to hash out the events and appearances you anticipate, so that I might be adequately prepared for them. And I need to speak to my associates before I can give you a firm yes, of course."

"Of course," he says. I think he is perhaps marveling that this has worked. I hesitate to speculate what his backup plan may have been. "I'm R.J. Sutter, by the way."

Which of my aliases might be suitable for this? I should have considered sooner. "Madison," I say, and we shake hands, and he looks right into my eyes as we do. He has a warm, firm grip. "May I ask, though, what does the R stand for? I'm not in the habit of calling people by their initials like that."

"If I tell you, does that mean you'll be calling me that?"

"Likely, yes." R.J. *indeed*, my goodness. He very much does not like that, and I can see in his face that he's second guessing everything.

"Rafael," he finally says. "People used to also sometimes call me Rafe."

"Oh darling, that isn't a terrible name at all. I thought you were going to tell me *Ryan* or *Richard* or something." I smile and he laughs, shaking his head.

"No, not Richard." He looks like he wants to ask me something, and I get out my phone before he arrives at a decision.

"Now let's exchange contact information, and I'll tra la la on home and talk to my bodyguards, and I'll be in touch. How does that sound?"

He gets out his phone almost automatically when he sees mine, nodding. "That sounds good."

"Besides, it gives you time to reconsider." His eyes dart up to mine from our screens.

"I'm not sure I can," he says.

Chapter Two

We three don't always live together, but in this particular instance, we've rented a spacious three bedroom apartment on the top floor of a repurposed brick building that used to be I'm not sure what. It isn't quite dire enough for a school or factory, and my curiosity regarding it has only run so deep. There is parking and ensuite laundry and a close proximity of many restaurants which deliver, just beautiful hardwood floors and french doors to let all the light in. I do think Bits has literally boarded the windows in her room, judging from the way she sometimes seems to shrink from the light when she emerges, but Dolly doesn't seem perturbed either way.

Dolly is on the couch with the robot dog when I arrive, watching something which contains a lot of fire and explosions. "Hey Bristles," she says. "I wiped it down first, don't worry. No floor crud on the couch."

"I'm not worried, though perhaps I am concerned. Did you have a security shotgun when you were little, instead of a blanket?" It's difficult for me to understand the robot dog, perhaps because I don't favor animals in general, but also due to its complete lack of physical comfort. One does not *cuddle* a robot dog.

She grins at me. "Doesn't everybody?"

"They do not." I know that she's only needling me, it is her way, but Dolly is astonishingly good at pressing buttons. "I didn't have a security blanket either, I should add."

"No? What'd you have, a security handbag? Actually, I kinda like that, it makes sense. You can whack somebody with a handbag."

"Mmm, no, not that either." I look at her movie, but I don't recognize it, and have no way to assess if it will be over soon. "So I may have a job. Of course I wanted to consult with you girls before accepting out of hand, but I think it sounds both lucrative and interesting. Perhaps a little unusual for us, but we might be able to work an angle."

Without warning she yells "Bitsy! Family meeting!" and turns off the TV. "Bristol, what did you do?"

"*Nothing*, I just told you." Well, if she's already going to be up in arms about it... "I know you've objected to, how do you put it, 'Dolly dress up' in the past, some of it might be required. For both of you. Suits, though, not dresses."

She huffs out a breath while looking at me, and nodding a little, and Bits shuffles out with her hair sticking every which way, VR goggle marks on her face. "We call these family meetings?"

"Got your attention, didn't it?" Dolly grins. "Okay first off we're gonna need suits."

"What? What kind of suits?" Bits blinks at Dolly, blinks at me.

"Dolly, would you please allow me to explain before you hare off on some wild fantasy?"

"You *said*," she says, grinning even more, and I can't help but laugh. She is so incorrigible.

"Yes, I did say suits, but that's only a piece of the job."

"We have a job? Did we talk about this already and I forgot?" Bits sits on the end of Dolly's couch, and the robot dog swivels its head to look at her.

"No, it was brought to me just tonight if you'll let me speak!" I give a little stomp for emphasis, and Dolly sits up straight and folds her hands in her lap. Bits runs a hand through her hair, taming some of its unruliness, and does not comment further. "I was at an otherwise very boring party when a very handsome man asked for my temporary and fraudulent hand in marriage because he has to make an upcoming deadline for a family trust."

Bits blinks some more, and Dolly actually clasps her hands. "This is even better than I could've imagined."

"And I said that I could never take such a job without my bodyguards, and that I must speak to them about it before saying yes."

"And this was a totally normal like, just alcohol party? You didn't have any funny brownies or anything and then read a pulp paperback in a drugstore with a scantily clad lady and/or gentleman on the front before toddling back home again?"

"I had a single glass of champagne," I say icily.

"Just checkin', you understand." I look at her with raised eyebrows and she holds up her hands, not unlike Rafe not so long ago. "Okay, go on. What kind of a trust? Why the hurry, if he's so handsome?"

"Evidently he and his brother were both content with the bull riding circuit, but he's sustained an injury that prevents him from continuing."

"Wait, wait, what's this guy's name?"

I roll my eyes. "He calls himself *R.J.* and I told him that would absolutely not be what I—"

Dolly sits bolt upright. "R.J. Sutter?"

"Oh you know who—"

"And his brother Gabe is having a real good season. Oh wow, Bristles, you've really outdone yourself. Are you even kidding me? R.J. Sutter and you just have no idea."

"And here I thought you'd be pleased that the trust was to do with ostrich farming."

She frowns quizzically. "Why would I be pleased by that?"

"Never mind."

"Look, your husband-to-be—"

"Fake husband-to-be," Bits interjects helpfully. She looks more alert now.

"Thank you, Bitsy. Your unlawfully wedded husband is a two time PBR champion, and for one of those rides, he had 95 points. Actually, I think he got special recognition for that? Maybe the bull got some award that year."

"Okay." Honestly, with all of her vehicle knowledge, and weapons knowledge, and familiarity with both casual and formal violence, I had no idea that Dolly had room for further interests. "This means we would like to accept the job then?" I ask sweetly.

"Hell yes, we would. Right Bits?" Bits nods, reaching over and taking Dolly's popcorn. "Do you think his mechanical bull has a face?"

The rich inner workings of my companions, honestly. "Dolly, darling, I'm sure I have no idea what you're talking about."

"Don't worry about it." She's grinning at her own joke and it's best to just let her have that, I think. I'll call Rafe in the morning to tell him we'll be accepting; it simply wouldn't do to appear too eager. "Okay so you're going to be his mystery bride, people're gonna go *nuts*, the bodyguard idea is a good one actually. We'll have to find somebody who can fit us up in Secret Service dragonscale I guess. I imagine you'll be on that, Bits?"

"Yeah, I'll contact a few people." She looks at me, a little wide eyed. "You're sure this is something you want to do? Fake engaged is one thing, but you'll be really married."

"And then really divorced, yes. It will be fine, it's simply a business arrangement."

"Careful you don't fall for him," Dolly says, taking her popcorn back. "There's movies and country songs and everything about stuff like this."

"Oh goodness, country songs," I say with an elaborate shiver.

"It's a whole culture, Bristol. Keep that in mind, and our body-guarding'll be easier than not."

"Well, it's a very good thing that I have you to educate me then, isn't it?" I ask, and she makes a face at me as though she realizes, fully, that she invited that. Then another wicked smile surfaces.

"Y'know, it is. And I'm gonna find a bar with a mechanical bull in it so that you're acquainted."

"That will not be necessary..."

"I still just can't get over this. Yeah, I remember now, their family was one of the early adoptors for the ostriches. They used to have I don't even know how many head of cattle before they started reducing, for the carbon, you understand." I nod, because I can follow, but I mostly have no idea. "I think some of the bulls the league uses might still come from their breeding, but that always depends anyway. You said he got hurt?"

"He mentioned a shoulder injury. Shoulder and elbow."

"Ah yeah, that's shit luck. Bullriding wrecks you, if it don't kill you."

"Well thank heavens he escaped that," I say. It has been less than three hours, and already I have thought more about rodeos than ever before in my entire life. Their danger had never occurred to me.

"You're bored already, aren't you?" Bits asks, as Dolly takes the popcorn back.

"I am not!" I protest. "Perhaps *rodeo* things aren't going to be my interest, but the society that we'll be briefly dipping into is new and interesting."

"Oh yeah! You'll get to rub elbows with both rodeo people and ostrich barons!" I suppose I should be pleased that Bits is somewhat indifferent, and Dolly is this enthusiastic, but Dolly's enthusiasm can be a chaotic ingredient. All in all, though, it is better than them preferring not to take the job at all.

"Well that's settled then," I say. "I'll call him in the morning and get all of our particulars ironed out."

"Sounds good," Dolly says. She offers me the bowl of popcorn, and I look at it for a moment, then lean over and take a handful.

"Thank you."

Chapter Three

I wasn't even aware that we knew somebody who tailored dragon-scale here, but in the morning, Bits and Dolly are leaving without me peculiarly early, perhaps hoping to escape my scrutiny.

"We know how to dress ourselves," Dolly says and I very pointedly look her up and down. Ripped jeans, what I'm certain is a man's white undershirt, black bra, the same boots she always wears, and a canvas jacket over it that might be surplus and might actually be fashion, it's just that close sometimes. Bits snickers, and I look at her cargo pants and t-shirts, because she's wearing a long sleeved shirt under a short sleeved one. "We aren't *naked*," Dolly says, as though the two statements are equivalent.

"Can I at least send you with specifications, if you'd prefer to escape my watchful eye?" I sigh. I do dearly want to attend a suit fitting for these two, but there are other things on my to do list.

"Yes, give us some examples," Bits says, and waits for me to text her. "It's a more solid cover if we're to Bristol's specs," she says, and Dolly rolls her eyes elaborately, but she's smiling.

"Sure, sure. Today it's suits, you just wait and see what she does to us next time, now that she's got her foot in the door." Dolly's still going as Bits pushes her out the door ahead of her.

Once they're gone, I do a little bit of light searching on society pages, and gossip streams that I favor, to see what they say about Rafe and his family. To see how ostrich-y I can expect the property to be, and thus inform my clothing decisions. He and his brother have really been *very* rodeo focused for a number of years, and yes, his brother does run around a little and Rafe has not, that I can see. His brother's looks are flashier, but both of them are very handsome gentlemen. What a distinctly odd situation this is; was there ever a time I just wanted a rich, handsome man to take me away from all this? Perhaps years and years ago, when I'd just started out.

I call Rafe, and he answers hastily, eagerly. "I was starting to think you'd reconsidered," he says, laughing in an effort to cover how serious he is.

"No, I am *quite* intrigued, and my colleagues have agreed that the job is a compelling one," I say.

"Didn't take much convincing, I hope?"

"One of them is evidently a fan," I say.

"Does that make this easier for you or harder? I'm still real embarrassed that I just walked up to you at a party and—" My goodness, I can imagine him rubbing the back of his neck, squinting a little, abashed. What striking luck our encounter was.

"No, it's a fantastic meet cute."

"A what?"

"The story that we'll tell of how we met. I caught your eye across the room at an otherwise unremarkable party, and we hit it off immediately. I told you about a cocktail you'd never had before, and you're tall, dark and handsome, just the way the fortune teller always said I would marry."

"The fortune teller?"

"Perhaps I'm getting a bit nostalgic. Though don't all fortune tellers always say that?"

"I've never been to a fortune teller." He sounds interested and a little baffled. The more he talks, the more I enjoy his voice, and have a sense of the clothing that I'm packing.

"Oh you *must*," I say.

"Well if you say so," he says, bemused. "Is that just a thing you can do online?"

"I'm certain you can, but I find it's best to do so in person." That seems like excellent tabloid fodder indeed. Washed-up bullrider and his mysterious fiancée consult mystic. "I'll see if there are any local that are of good enough reputation that we should consult them, or if we'd have to go elsewhere."

"Is there a ratings website for that? Like how they do for restaurants?" He sounds amused. He does seem like a very nice man, and I do hope that continues to be the case for our several weeks of association. Otherwise, it shall be such a chore.

"We may be getting away from the construction of our narrative." I hold up a dress to myself in the mirror, consider whether it's too city-suited. "Who is it that you'll need to convince most, that this engagement and marriage isn't a sham? A lawyer?"

"My Great-Aunt Gertrude. She's still the executor of the trust. Maybe executor isn't the right word, but you get the gist."

"I do indeed. And what is Great-Aunt Gertrude like? Is there anything that she absolutely can't abide?"

"I think she hates gardenias," he says, without much of a pause. "Honestly, she probably won't be a concern but..."

"I'm sure she just wants her dear nephew to be happy." I put the dress back in my closet. "I do think that I'm going to need to go shopping."

"The girls do that a lot, so you'll be right at home. Maybe it'll be a bonding experience for you."

"The girls?"

"Yeah in the neighborhood. Well, I guess you wouldn't call it a neighborhood, but it's the group of our houses closest together I guess, in the scheme of things. Some family, some friends. They're people we'll see a lot, so we need to fool them too." Does he sound just a little disheartened?

"Just for a little while," I remind him. "I shall do my utmost to make certain this goes smoothly."

He laughs a little. "I believe it."

"Now when shall our second date be? And where? Have you selected a ring yet?"

"A ring?"

"Yes, darling, an engagement ring. Do you want to do a public proposal, or shall I just be suddenly wearing it from one appearance to the next?"

"I confess I hadn't given it that much in-depth thought." I wait him out, selecting shoes. While I have a variety of boots, cowboy boots are not among them. Perhaps they have charms of which I was not aware? "There's a family ring," he says finally. "I can get that from the bank."

"Only if you're certain. I wouldn't want you bringing out an heirloom for a farce."

"Well it isn't doing anybody any good where it is." I do approve of that sentiment. Fancy and special things are to be appreciated, not locked away; otherwise they might as well not exist.

"I will take the utmost care with it, of course."

"I appreciate it. So your, uh, bodyguards were on board?"

"Yes, they're settling their attire as we speak."

"Fair enough. I'll make sure my staff knows to loop them in and everything."

"Perfect."

"Is it weird that I'm looking forward to this?"

"I wouldn't say so, no. I'm sure it will be very interesting, and perhaps at least a little bit fun."

"There'll be plenty of parties, I hope you're ready for that."

"It's as though I've been training for it," I say with a little laugh. He laughs with me, and I do hope that after our faux engagement and marriage ends, he ends up finding somebody to spend his time with. He seems like a very nice man indeed, and I'm rarely wrong in these things.

Bits and Dolly come back not long after, wearing their new suits, and also cheap plastic sunglasses they must have procured at a convenience store, and fedoras, which I have no earthly idea where they would have gotten or why. From the same person who did the suits, presumably. Bits' pants are perhaps slightly too long; I assume she intends to fix that with different shoes.

"It's dark and we're wearing sunglasses," Dolly says, grinning.

"Yes, you are," I say, mystified.

"Aw, come on Bristles, I thought you loved old movies."

"Why yes, I do, but I don't get this reference, darlings, I'm very sorry."

"It's fine," Dolly says, pulling her sunglasses off and tucking them into the suit coat pocket. "Do we pass muster, ma'am? What are we calling you?"

"I went with Madison this time," I say. "And yes, that is as close to what I envisioned as I can expect."

"Well that's a great endorsement," Bits says, opening a bag of snacks she produced from I know not where.

"You *did* say that—"

"*Any*way," Dolly says. "Do we have a move-in date? Do we need a vehicle for that? We should probably have something that's 'ours,' right?"

"I hadn't thought of that. Yes, I expect we must." There's always some vehicle or other Dolly procures for our operations, but whether it's appropriate for the sort of persona that I am putting forth varies wildly. Our current vehicle is not. "I leave that to you, of course."

"Of course," she says, grinning. "Don't you worry, Miss...what's Madison's last name? You haven't used her in awhile."

"You're correct, I haven't, which is why it makes sense to do so now. Calloway."

"Miss Calloway," Dolly says.

"And the two of you…?"

"Well we talked about that, and figured we'd keep it simple with Darlene and Beth."

"Simple enough," I say. "It seems like we've made some preparations, but probably not nearly enough. What are we forgetting?"

"I'm making you a panic button," Bits says.

"Pardon?"

"To add to your bracelets. So that if it isn't really possible for you to talk at the moment, you can hit it and we know to bail you out."

"Yeah, you can put it with your…actually you don't use a bracelet phone anymore, do you? I noticed but I didn't notice." Dolly cocks her head, a little perplexed.

"Those fell out of vogue," I say.

"Oh of course, what was I thinkin'."

Bits sighs. "But anyway, that makes sense, right?"

"Yes, it absolutely does, thank you."

She finishes her chips, and then she and Dolly go out again, to car shop.

Chapter Four

I'm not entirely certain how much property Rafe's ostrich farm comprises; Bits could tell me, as without a doubt she's looked it up, but I prefer to discover it, or not, on my own. We come up the drive at the appropriate time, Dolly driving, Bits in the front with her. They came up with a sleek and subdued black sedan which may or may not have been some manner of auctioned law enforcement vehicle, or a seized vehicle auctioned by law enforcement. I'm not entirely certain of that either, other than the knowledge that those auctions are frequently cash, and I can just imagine Dolly's smug joy at walking through such a transaction and coming away with the now-legitimized merchandise.

Rafe is on the front steps of a tastefully rambling two-story affair, the original house of which was probably built quite a long time ago, and then added on to as the family required. I wonder if he's been hoping I wouldn't show up. Or was he pacing nervously in anticipation, pleased to be taking this step in acquiring his family's fortune, regardless of the subterfuge? I could ask, but it is more fun to guess for myself.

He opens the car door for me mere moments after Dolly has put it into park, and hands me out. I catch a glimpse of people in the doorway, but don't have the time to parse whether they're staff or family or friends, as he is on one knee in front of me and that requires my full attention.

"I'm sorry I didn't have this for you the other night," he says with a smile. He's rehearsed the line, but the smile is genuine, I think. While I haven't purposefully rehearsed being proposed to, this is certainly not my first one.

"Rafe, it's just beautiful," I say breathlessly, but audible to our audience. The ring slides perfectly onto my finger as though it were sized just for me, and I'll assess later if I think it's the heirloom one or not. Then he clasps my hands as he stands, and it's the right moment for it, so I lift my chin and he leans down to kiss me. So far as first kisses go, it is more than adequate.

When we separate, there is a smattering of applause from the audience, and they come down the stairs to us. "R.J. said you were just a doll," a brassy blonde woman about my age says, taking me by the arms and looking at my face. She's wearing quite a lot of jewelry. "We were all very surprised!"

"I imagine you were," I say. "I was a little surprised myself."

"You'll have to tell us *all* about it," she says in a conspiratorial tone, and then lets me go so the next woman can greet me, a shorter brunette.

"We thought for sure that R.J. would just be a bachelor for life," the brunette says.

"You haven't even let me introduce her," Rafe says, gently interposing. "Madison, this is Paisley, and this is Rosalie. Ladies, this is Madison."

"We're sorry, we were just very excited," Rosalie, the brunette, says. Paisley sort of makes a little mouth, her eyes gleaming, intent; I can see who runs the parties, unless I'm missing my guess. There's something else, though. Oh, this will be interesting.

"We're hardly overwhelming," Paisley says. The men hung back a little, but they come and shake hands now, Ned and Paul.

"Maybe I'm feeling protective," Rafe said, chuckling. "I didn't even have the whole crew over, just you."

"We feel very privileged." Paisley smiles up at him. Oh yes, there was something else. "He even let me organize lunch," she says to me.

"Did he indeed?" I glance over my shoulder at Bits and Dolly, standing by the car. "Would it be possible for you to tell my people where to park, and where to bring our bags?"

"Yeah, don't worry, Gerald's going to take care of them for you." I raise my eyebrows at Dolly, who nods. It's quite alright for us to separate, we've all got our tiny, cunning earbuds.

"Perfect, thank you."

"Shall we?" Paisley asks. She seems determined to get me away from my supposed fiancé and finally he lets her, going over to talk to Dolly for a moment as another man, presumably Gerald, appears. "We'll get a mimosa in your hand and show you around a little on the way to the brunch table."

"That does sound delightful," I say. Mimosas and brunch are certainly a route to my heart. The entryway is as expected, with a sweeping staircase to the second floor, and a large gilt mirror in the front hall. It is hard to resist a mirror like that, and I comfort myself by thinking I'll revisit it later, but then Paisley has my arm again and we clack over there in our heels; the floor is polished tile. Standing next to each other, we're of about the same height as well.

"We're like sisters," she says, beaming. "You'll fit right in with the family!"

"I think I need to learn everybody's connections," I say carefully, and she laughs. She doesn't exactly seem like a cousin.

"You will! We're just all so cozy here in the neighborhood, you'll figure out who's who in no time." She gives me a conspiratorial little smile, and I smile back.

"And you're here to help me, of course."

"Of course!" Just a split second too slow, but I think she's still trying to work out if she's going to like me or hate me. I think she had intended to hate me on sight and is perhaps surprised that isn't the case." We wives need to stick together!"

"That we do," I say. My earbud clicks then, Bits letting me know that everything is proceeding smoothly. I assume she's making sure the suite is suitable, both for comfort and privacy. I assume Dolly has already cowed and then befriended all the rest of security. We each have our strengths. Do I wish I was prowling the estate and familiarizing myself with its nooks and crannies? Getting a sense of the staff? Yes, I do. But I'm also wildly curious about this little neighborhood clique of very wealthy individuals.

"Let me admire the ring," Paisley demands, and she has my hand before I can offer it, but also lets it go with only cursory examination. "He's definitely serious, that's the Sutter ring alright."

"Did anything suggest he wasn't serious?" I ask innocently.

"He's never brought anybody home other than—" Rosalie is silenced with a cutting, eloquent glance. "Not since just after high school," she recovers.

"I see. We didn't discuss any of that, I'm afraid."

Paisley's eyes darken a little, but then she pulls up another smile. "Of course you wouldn't! Why waste time talking about past flings." She does seem to have forgotten the notion of a preliminary tour, though.

The others are already seated in a very nice and airy room, one wall of which is entirely glass, allowing the morning sun to flood in. I'd somewhat expected the furniture to be gaudy or tacky, or even careless and too utilitarian, whatever a former bull rider would have an assistant fill his house with, but the table, chairs, and sideboards are all very nice and understated wooden pieces, perhaps antiques. Maybe this was purchased six generations ago, before their ostrich barony days and when they only had cattle, and has been in this room ever since. That seems distinctly possible.

The guest couples are arranged at the sides of the tables, Paisley and Ned, Rosalie and Paul. Rafe is at one head and I am at the foot, as is proper. Of course, there's probably a finishing school or at least manners lessons that each one of these individuals had, in addition to a debut ball, I'm certain. Now that I have names, I can look. Or have Bits do it, but why should she have all the fun? She won't see the significance in the same details that I would.

"Shall we toast the happy couple?" Paisley says, nearly the moment that we're seated, picking up her flute of mimosa. Rafe looks a little uncomfortable; I'm certain he doesn't prefer the formality of this setting. Perhaps he's unused to lying in general, and more specifically, to this inner circle of his friends.

"Don't let's make a big deal out of this at every meal," I say with a little smile. "I'm sure there are other opportunities on the horizon!"

"You've got that right," Rosalie says, with a bigger laugh than I was expecting. "This is just the everyday bosom friends, you're going to be hip deep in Sutters pretty soon here."

"Will I?" I ask, and raise an eyebrow down the table at Rafe.

"Only because you aren't as tall as me," he says with an easy smile. "Some extended family, yes. Not a circus like Rosalie is saying. Great-Aunt Gertrude. My older cousins who don't brunch, but live down the road a piece."

"It all depends on what you call a circus, R.J., your lady love might have a different definition," Paisley says sweetly, and then we have crepes suzette in front of us and our mimosas are refreshed, and the conversation becomes a bit less adversarial. By accident or design, the men are all at the one end of the table, and 'us wives' at the other, and we carefully navigate our getting to know you small talk and my earbud clicks again, a double-click.

//These're nice digs, Madison// Dolly says quietly. //Bitsy didn't find anything wrong with anything, and I can't either. I'll walk you through the exits once we're all reunited, but you can just relax right now I think. They're letting us hang around in the hallway outside and offered us coffee and everything.//

"Oh, splendid," I say to Dolly, but also to Paisley, who has just said that dinner will be at her house tomorrow evening, so I needn't worry about it at all. I hadn't been; this house has a staff, I'm certain I won't worry about dinner at all. My party planning prowess mightn't be called upon at all, more's the pity.

At the other end of the table, R.J. is talking about the revenue or return on ostriches or some such; the business side of it definitely sounds like he's still getting comfortable with the words in his mouth. The livestock handling aspects, though, he's clearly a natural at.

"Now I'm unclear, do you all ranch ostriches? Is that even the proper word to use?"

"We do, yes. All this land used to be Sutter land, and when they cut back on the cattle, on account of the ostriches, other families were able to move in and take part in the same types of concerns. It's just plain luck that we kids all got along so well, isn't it Paisley? Well maybe sometimes we all fought like cats and dogs, but that's part of growing up." Rosalie seems to be a creature without guile, and it is refreshing. I do think it means that I need to be all the more wary of Paisley's hidden claws.

"It certainly is, and I'm sure it makes you all that much closer now that you're adults."

"What about your family, Madison? Will we be meeting any of them?" Paisley asks.

"My family? I'm afraid I'm tragically orphaned," I say, sipping my mimosa. The panic button that Bits made me blends quite nicely with my other bracelets. I suppose some technology related skills extend to other disciplines. "It's just myself and my bodyguards, no more and no less."

"Your...bodyguards."

"Yes, we've worked together ever so long now, they're practically my sisters."

//Who share the profits// Bits mutters.

"But you don't have *any* family at all?" Rosalie asks, wide eyed. Her shock is very touching. I'm sure, were she to know the truth, that I walked away from a quite living family in order to make myself a better, if entirely fraudulent, life, she would be entirely beside herself.

"You're such a darling, don't be sad for me. I'm quite used to it."

"Does that mean your half of the church will just be your bodyguards?" Paisley asks, and Rosalie gapes at her.

"Paisley, you can't just ask somebody that."

"We're all family here," Paisley says, eyes glittering. "Or we're close enough now, isn't that right?"

"It means I won't have a side of the church," I say, and then pause, smiling sweetly. "Though perhaps we'll elope, and dispense of the need for such things"

Paisley laughs as though I've said something very foolish and impossible, and Rafe casts us a quizzical look from the conversation at the other end of the table. "Elope? Great-Aunt Gertrude would never stand for that!" She shakes her head. I maintain my smile, though.

"I suppose she'll just have to sit, then." There is just the *slightest* of pauses, and then Rafe laughs, and the rest of our guests follow suit.

Chapter Five

Our brunch guests stay for an interminable amount of time. They're Rafe's friends, so clearly he does not feel as though he is entertaining them; they've just always been there. They take me all over the house, and eventually, Dolly trails us at a near remove. I assume Bits has decided to remain in the suite and traipse about in the ranch's cyberspace. I'm certain Dolly wants to get a broader sense of the property, and of the staff. Perhaps also Rafe's friends, though I'm confident that I have Rosalie's measure. Paisley, I shall need a little more time with. From her attitude, though, it seems I'll have ample opportunity.

There is quite the expansive gym setup, but Rafe doesn't take us in there. I see Dolly craning her neck, presumably to catch a glimpse of the mechanical bull, if there is one. It's only the first day, we'll find out.

Rafe keeps my arm comfortably threaded through his, and matches my pace as we go. He looks at my shoes more than once, especially when we venture outside, but seems to have decided that if I don't say anything, he won't either. The other ladies are wearing lower heeled sandals. Well, the other *guests* are, Dolly is wearing some manner of combat boots. I don't need to even look to know that's true.

"R.J. who *is* that?" Paisley asks eventually, catching sight of Dolly at one point as she turns to say something to her husband.

Rafe glances, barely; he'd already noticed, clearly. "She's one of Madison's bodyguards," he says easily, as though this is a completely normal occurrence. I think, after our first meeting, I hadn't expected his complicity in his own scam to be quite so polished.

"*One* of Madison's bodyguards?" she asks, eyebrows and tone climbing.

"Come on, I keep telling you, don't screech around the ostriches," Rafe says, smiling, and he glances at me. The ostriches in question are not at the very picturesque fence, but rather further out in their field. I assume they don't care much for human companionship, they aren't pets.

"I wasn't screeching," she says petulantly, but with her tone adjusted. "Why does Madison need bodyguards? More than one bodyguard?"

"I guess she likes feeling secure. Why are we talking about Madison in front of her like she ain't here?"

"Oh don't say ain't," I say before I can stop myself. I'd given up correcting Dolly's periodic usage, I was not prepared for Rafe's. I smile apologetically, and he laughs.

"Yes, dear," he says, and pats me on the hand, very natural. I suspect perhaps he overstated his guileless nature. I catch Paisley's reaction just barely, from the corner of my eye; I wonder when they were an item, and for how long. And what Ned thinks of their history. Maybe he thinks Rafe was a fool to lose her.

I wonder if she one day thought that the Sutter ring would again be hers.

The ostriches remain disinterested in us, despite Paisley's screeching, to my relief. I am more than a little surprised at just how large they are. I knew, of course, but had never seen them even this close previously. I don't find birds particularly engaging; to me, they lack the cuteness that a puppy or kitten does. I suppose I am in general simply not an animal person, as Dolly was more than happy to prove to me during our Macau adventure.

By the time our guests finally get into cars and depart to their respective neighboring homes, Rafe seems to have settled very comfortably into the deception. He isn't too demonstrative, but just enough. Thoughtfully so, without being too touchy. We wave from the front steps as though we're doing the end-credits scene for our very own reality show, and then he sighs, loosens his collar, and turns to Dolly.

"Nice to meet you..." he says, extending a hand.

"Darlene," she says, and gives him a firm enough grip that he's surprised. "The other one's Elizabeth, not sure how often you'll see her."

"Fair enough," he says. "Do you do this kind of thing often?"

"Not really," she says with a grin and a shrug.

"Our jobs together have varied," I say.

"Fair enough," he says again. "That went okay, right?"

"I think it went very well indeed."

"Good, good." Now that we're all here, he doesn't seem to know what to do about that, exactly.

"Do we have a schedule of upcoming get-togethers, so that I know when they are and how to dress for them?"

"I think Paisley sent me a thing, yeah."

"She always arranges your parties, then?" Dolly grins but clearly keeps from laughing.

"Yeah, she's great like that." He looks up at me from his phone. "Oh, though I guess you would normally be taking that over, wouldn't you."

"Normally, yes. Given our plan, though..." Rafe sends the information to my phone, and I scroll through brunches that are just me and the other women, a larger friends and family party, some dinners. He's paying us well and I do enjoy parties. Then a thought strikes me.

"Oh! I'll have to go wedding dress shopping."

This time Dolly *does* laugh, and Rafe slowly blinks. "I...I guess you will."

"Obviously, you won't be attending that. But I should invite Paisley and Rosalie, yes?" Or perhaps not, given the history...

"I'm sure they wouldn't want to be left out," he says slowly.

"And they can tell me where their wedding dresses came from, it's a perfect bonding opportunity."

"I didn't think you'd be so eager to—"

"Nonsense, it's certainly under the umbrella of what we discussed. I can't spend all my time by the pool, I have my complexion to worry about."

"Right."

"Just let me know if there are any topics I should avoid? Or areas of the house?"

"Nothing I can think of." That's a relief; I didn't expect him to be a Bluebeard, especially not with a former bride visiting at will, but boundaries are important.

"Okay, good. I'll text them about it this evening. Is there anything else you'd like me for today?"

"No, you more than earned your keep already." He makes a face, and suddenly seems all too aware that Dolly is standing nearby. "That feels like the wrong thing to say."

I laugh, and lay a hand on his arm. "It's all right, I know what you meant."

"I'm glad." He smiles and shrugs. "But no, you can do whatever. Use the pool, I know what you already said. Use the training room. Just be careful of the equipment, don't want you to hurt yourself."

"Oh, Darlene is well aware of the workings of mechanical bulls, from what I understand," I say airily, and he raises his eyebrows and looks at her.

"Are you really?"

"Just from a casual, drunk at the bar perspective, yeah," she says, laughing. "But also, I know who you and your brother are."

"And Madison didn't." He grins at me.

"I don't know who *any* sports figures are," I say. "I can't be expected to."

"I suppose not." His phone rings and he looks at the screen and looks at me. "Anyway, enjoy your day. You know how to get a hold of me, if you need me. And any of the staff can help you with meals or whatever you need."

"Thank you," I say, and step away so he feels comfortable taking his call.

"Well ain't he dreamy," Dolly says with a wicked grin, and we fall into step as she takes me to the suite.

"You knew that already," I say, perhaps more impatiently than I feel. He is a very handsome man. He seems kind, and unusually emotionally perceptive.

"More than you."

"To my advantage, n'est-ce pas? He isn't looking for just another...buckle bunny." What an awful, if illustrative, turn of phrase.

"Nah. It also means you'll probably feel bad if we lift anything from here. Family jewels, wherever those are. Antique guns from the Alamo. The golden spike from the transcontinental railroad."

"Oh, that's in a museum in the Bay Area," I say. "It's best if we don't 'lift' anything from this property, correct."

"*This* property," Dolly says. "So other places we visit..."

"Let's just be discreet, shall we? We're already getting a payday out of this situation. I'm certainly not *against* getting a bonus, but—"

"Readin' you loud and clear, boss," Dolly says.

Chapter Six

There was a time I would have confidently said that of course every girl has imagined her wedding dress, but then I met Bits and Dolly. Their wedding aspirations, or lack thereof, aside, I have certainly imagined *my* wedding dress. And I confess, I have had a running file for a number of years, containing designers and styles which have caught my fancy.

The issue with marriage in my particular line of work is I've been enjoying my freedom so thoroughly, I'm uncertain about stopping, and settling down, regardless of the nest egg I have built for myself, and the hotel in Morocco that still waits for me, run by efficient staff whom I pay handsomely. I've spent so little time there, even though it is truly a life's dream come true. Maybe somebody else would have stopped and settled down, but it seems so early to do so. There's so much *time* left.

Paisley has a shop in mind, with a seamstress and designer who she went with, and so Dolly and Bits drive me there to meet them that Tuesday afternoon. "You sure you don't want us to hang around?" Dolly asks.

"Quite sure. You can occupy yourselves nearby, and I'm certain your services and supervision wouldn't be needed anyway."

"Aw, you don't want my opinion on dresses? I'm really hurt, Bristles."

"I'm sure you are," I say, rolling my eyes.

"There's a surplus store down the street," Bits says. "And I'm honestly not sure what I'd bet on taking more time, you in a bridal shop or Dolly in a surplus store."

I laugh. "I'd say I'm insulted, but I'm not sure either."

Dolly shrugs. "Depends on what I'm lookin' for."

"Do you have something you're looking for?" Bits asks.

"No, but I can always look." Dolly grins at me in the rear view mirror, and Bits shrugs an eloquent 'see what I mean?'

"That works out perfectly," I say after a moment.

"Sure does. I didn't really want to hang out and watch you get loaded anyway."

"Pardon?"

"Don't they have champagne and stuff for these things?"

"I hadn't considered that, but yes, probably. I'm *highly* unlikely to 'get loaded.'" It is with effort that I don't make a little face at that.

"Maybe not you, individually. Collective you, the other rich girls." We pull into the parking lot; Paisley and Rosalie are standing out front waiting, Paisley in a wide-brimmed hat and large sunglasses, Rosalie smiling and bareheaded, waving when I got out of the car. Rosalie is very sweet; I can just imagine the two of them in high school, maybe as cheerleaders. Would the Sutter boys also have done something like football, or would they have concentrated on rodeos even then? It's so delicious and unusual for me to know so little about the main interest of a social group. "You have fun now," Dolly says, like a movie mom dropping her child off at the mall.

"I'm certain we'll do our best," I say.

"I'll be listening in if you need us," Bits says quietly. "And you have your panic button."

"I do and it will be *fine*." I close the car door, laughing a little. The idea of that sort of trouble at a bridal shop is simply absurd.

"I'm so surprised your bodyguards won't be lurking with us," Paisley says, managing to keep her smile just short of a smirk.

"You don't think we'll need them here, do you? I'd only just convinced them that it would be safe enough..." I trail off and make a show of turning to watch the car drive off.

Paisley laughs. "Honey, I don't think you'll need them at all, is my point."

"Oh, I see." They are just wild to know more, for me to explain, and I don't think that I will. "Let's hope not!"

Inside the shop is both airy and cozy at the same time, a cultivated intimate boutique experience. There are comfortable chairs and a low coffee table by a three-paneled mirror that one ascends a small dais to stand before, and little plates of single-bite hors d'oeuvres, along with presumably chilled cans of sparkling water and champagne. The woman who greets us is dressed so simply that her clothing probably cost more than the car that Dolly drove me here in, unless she is indeed the designer at this establishment.

"A Sutter bride, at long last!" she says, after air-kissing both Paisley and Rosalie. "It is my honor to do a showing for you today."

"I appreciate your hosting us at such short notice," I say.

"Oh the pleasure is mine." She extends both hands and takes mine. "Now let me look at you. I have examples of what previous Sutters wore, and some things in the shop which are a modernization of that aesthetic. Get yourself a drink, and let me take some measurements."

This isn't my first fitting, of course, though it is my first wedding dress fitting. It would be more poignant if it wasn't all fake, but it is great fun all the same. The other girls had their turn here, on the same little dais, in front of the same mirror. Though I do wonder if Paisley had *two* turns; I'm very, very certain that she and Rafe were previously an item, though I cannot say at this point what I think broke them up, nor why she would still be so chummy with him. Unless she is still holding out hope, that's very possible. Which makes her welcoming grace towards me quite a herculean feat; I almost wish that I could reassure her that I am not here to stay, but this is such a temporary arrangement, it's really unnecessary.

The dresses are lovely. They aren't couture, of course, but I wasn't expecting that. The canned champagne is a frugal choice, but there are many passable brands that package like that nowadays, and I'm not turning my nose up at it. The proprietress, Leah, who also designs and does some of the alterations herself, is very good; knowledgeable, but with her own vision, which I can respect. And she does indeed, in the smart mirror, show past Sutter brides, both early century and also back in the twentieth. She can put me in those dresses, and we have a great deal of fun preening in period dress, though I do notice Paisley getting tense about one or two of the designs.

"Won't you girls tell me what your dresses looked like?" I ask sweetly, stepping off the dais.

"I thought you'd never ask!" Rosalie says, popping up off the couch. We're all a little pink from the champagne, I think. "I got it here, of course."

Leah pulls up the image in the mirror. "Her church look was this, with the veil, and the overskirt." She taps the screen. "And then for the reception, both of those came off, and she had this mermaid tail skirt." A couple of more taps and Rosalie, in the mirror, has her hair and makeup done, and is adorned with jewels.

"How delightful!" I say, clasping my hands. "And you were radiant."

"Aw, thank you." She smiles, open and happy. "Paisley, you show her!"

Paisley is a little more reticent, but she takes her place. For a wicked moment, I'd like Bits to be listening in and working her magic, so that I know what the dress Paisley picked for her wedding to Rafe looked like. But I do not ask, and that does not happen. Paisley's dress is the sort of subtle that makes it flashy, in addition to a train that drips off the dais and stretches partway across the room.

"The train came off for the reception," she says, eyeing herself critically. "So it went from peacock length to just floor length." Leah shows us, and I'm sure to match my delight to what I showed Rosalie.

"It's perfect, it suited you so well! I hadn't considered that many add-ons and takeaways, I do love the tea length gowns so much." The less hampering of my movement the better, but those *trains*... "Perhaps an extravagant veil, to make up for it?" I ask, turning to Leah.

"We do have many options, even with your short turnaround."

"You're an angel," I say, and Paisley cracks open another can of champagne.

"So you decided, then?" she asks.

"Yes, this tea length one with the lace detailing," I say. "I have just the necklace to wear with that neckline."

"Is that your something old?" Rosalie asks. "Ooh, we need to get all that figured for you. What should you borrow? A purse? And what's *blue*?"

"I thought blue shoes might be delightful," I say. "I hadn't given a thought to the rest of it." That isn't entirely true, but I do want to see what they'll say.

"Your something old has to be the Sutter jewelry," Paisley says. "It's tradition. R.J. has it in a vault at the bank. And you'll borrow something from one of us, of course."

"You have just been so welcoming, I can never thank you enough." At the bank, that would make sense. I wonder when last anybody wore that jewelry. Did Paisley get to try it on? I will have to have Bits gather up the information on that for me, I simply won't have any time to do the sorts of society pages searches I might otherwise delight in carrying out.

"It's how we are," Paisley says, and her smile is *just* warm enough. "I'll have you over to look at my things this week." She pauses. "Tomorrow maybe? My, things are moving fast aren't they?"

"Well I could..." Rosalie starts shyly, but she stops before Paisley can cut her off.

"That's sweet, honey, but I think we're closer for hair and complexion."

"You're right," Rosalie says, with a doubtful little quirk of the lips that I'm not certain Paisley catches.

"Oh I'm sure I can borrow something from each of you," I say. It's wicked of me to disrupt their dynamic, I won't be here forever to maintain any changes that I effect, but I simply cannot help myself. But Rosalie brightens.

"You could! One of the parties is at my place the day *after* tomorrow, you could look then."

"See? Perfect." I smile, and Paisley finishes her champagne.

Chapter Seven

B its fills me in when she and Dolly pick me up. "Paisley and R.J. were high school sweethearts, and she even travelled the rodeo circuit with him for awhile? He proposed to her from the ring after some award winning ride and—"

"Oh, now that you say that, I remember watchin' that livestream," Dolly says. "They put her on the jumbotron and everything, and then brought her down bawling into the ring."

"Had he planned it, or was it the euphoria of a...seventeen second bullride?" I cannot for the life of me remember the span of time they consider significant, just that there is a span of time that they consider significant.

"He had a ring in his pocket, so it had to be planned," Dolly says, then glances at Bits. "Sorry to interrupt."

"It's okay. I don't really know what broke them up, though. They were doing this long engagement with parties thing, your society type columns are really great for getting that information, and then just one day a week before the wedding, the whole thing was called off. He still paid the caterers and everything, but there was no wedding, no party, and then he went away for the next rodeo circuit and she stayed here."

"And then when did she marry Ned?"

"They announced their engagement that year and got married the next."

"That's kinda weird isn't it?" Dolly says.

"It is indeed." There is an obvious answer, of course, but it would have been mentioned by now, I would think. "She wasn't—"

Bits shakes her head. "Nope, no baby. No indication anywhere that she cheated or he cheated or anything. General speculation is she didn't want to be a rodeo wife, and R.J. wasn't willing to give up the rodeo life."

"I can understand not wanting to be a rodeo wife," I say. "What business is Ned in?"

"He's an accountant. It looks like he runs the books for his family's properties, which are some animals, some feed. They've got a patent on some kind of newer corn."

"New corn, Christ Jesus," Dolly says, and pulls out her ecigarette. We drive in silence for a few moments.

"So an accountant's wife, a bit more stable, a bit less glamorous."

"Boring as hell, I'd think," Dolly says. "Your accountant husband's life is exciting, you got the wrong kind of accountant." She exhales sugar cookie-smelling vapor.

"Or the right kind, if you're bored," Bits says.

"And is Paisley bored?" I get a text notification and pull it up. It's Rafe.

//We're invited out for dinner tonight with some shareholders. I said yes, but you don't have to come.//

"Her husband's boring and she's bored. She mostly just buys things and bullies her housekeeping staff, though. And plans parties."

//It's perfectly fine, I'll freshen up and be ready when you need me// I text back. //Where are we going?//

"What does Paisley like buying?" I ask. Bits blinks at me.

"Paisley has a couple of different things she collects. A certain pattern of china that was discontinued thirty years ago, glass figurines from an Italian company, and watches."

"Watches? Wristwatches?" I'd noticed Paisley wearing a watch, but it didn't seem particularly distinct. Or nicer than mine, which is a trinket-y little darling that I picked up in Johannesburg last winter. It hasn't got a single smart piece in it, it is purely mechanical, and it's certainly made me think that perhaps I might want to start a mechanical watch collection. When I actually retire for good and simply relax into a life of leisure.

"Yeah, wristwatches. She collects smartwatches, from vintage to modern. Different styles and functionalities, and even OSes. It's a little weird."

"If *you* think it's weird…" Dolly says.

"Well if she was into coding or VR or anything it wouldn't be weird, but she doesn't seem to be. Their house doesn't have any kind of equipment that reads like that, and while she's an always online kind of person, it's the social media type, not the swimming in code type. She livestreams making lemonade."

"Lemonade livestream," I say.

"Yeah, she's got one of those granite countertop kitchens," Bits says. "Gray and white and chrome everything else."

"Oh, *that* type." Dolly catches my eye in the rear view. "You know the type, Bristles."

"I'm certain I do," I say. "But I'm very interested in what you think about that type."

"Oh, you know," she shrugs. "There's just a certain kind of white lady that's like that." Bits is nodding and I can't help but laugh.

"Yes, I do know," I say. "Oh, Rafe says that we're invited out to dinner someplace tonight, so I suppose you two can lurk at your leisure, or remain—"

"At the ranch?" Dolly asks, and I sigh somewhat.

"Yes, at the ranch. At least it doesn't really *smell* like a ranch."

"Do you know what a ranch smells like?" Bits asks.

"While this is my first proper ranch experience, I assure you, I have seen animals before in my life."

"Sure you have," Dolly says, eyebrows climbing.

THE SHAREHOLDERS ARE dreadfully boring and ridiculously rich. After the introductory niceties, they in general talk business in a way that does not require my input, and Bits is a great help in keeping me occupied, by continuing to research the Paisley-Rafe romance that failed, and reading occasional items of commentary into my ear. Winning prizes for her at the little county fair, going to an exclusive club at the nearest big city, her being seen on shopping sprees, her at the hospital after each of his injuries. Maybe that was the reason why; she just couldn't stand seeing him hurt over and over, and not knowing if he would recover each time.

At one point, once we've finally reached coffee and cigars, some of the men are talking to each other and Rafe leans over, squeezes my hand, and says in my ear "I'm sorry this is so boring, I'll make it up to you."

I smile at him, a little startled. It's the perfect time for him to steal a kiss, and he does.

"We shouldn't be taking time away from the lovebirds," one of the men says. No check has come, and I'm not certain who arranged this or how, but there is a flurry of handshakes all around and that is that. One of them palms some folded bills into my hand and gives me a wink, and I wink back just slightly, smiling, and slip the money away without looking at it. Perhaps it isn't real money after all, but rather religious tracts; I've seen that more than once, what a dreadful trick people play on waitresses and the like.

"I hope that wasn't so bad," Rafe says, holding the car door for me.

"No, it wasn't so bad at all," I say, smiling. "And well within the scope of our agreement."

"I think you're lying, but it's hard to tell." He starts the car. "Well, let me show you something. Maybe it'll make things up a little."

"Rafe, honestly, there isn't anything to make up," I say, but he doesn't turn back towards the ranch.

//You okay, Bristol?// Dolly asks. I don't know if she's actually stayed at the ranch this evening, or if she followed me at some remove.

//I do think so, yes// I say.

//Well okay, just say the word if you're not.// I have never, in fact, had to say the word. It is a comfort knowing it's there, though.

We start to pass signs for historic attractions, and Rafe's surprise is ruined directly when I say "A carousel?"

"It's more than a hundred years old," he says. "Not originally from here, but moved here from someplace else and restored. And then it's weathered a bunch of storms. It's not normally open this late but, I know a guy." He gives me a sidelong glance and smiles.

We make a final turn, and then there it is, golden and lovely under the starlight. It begins its rotation as we get out of the car, the calliope playing merrily. I think there's a river nearby, or perhaps a lake, though I can't see it for the dark, just feel the breeze off the water. "It's beautiful," I say.

"I hoped you'd think that. You want to go for a spin?"

"Of course."

There is an attendant in the little booth, and Rafe stops and has a quiet word with him. I'm a bit surprised that it isn't automated, but I suppose an antique wouldn't be. I'm not certain many people are making modern carousels, what a shame. Bits would know.

The carousel slows, and we step up to select our animals. I have a moment of delicate indecision, next to a white rabbit with flowering wreaths serving as its saddle and bridle, and consider my dress. "Perhaps I ought to simply choose one of the benches," I say, indicating one which looks like a Roman chariot.

He laughs, then steps close. "Just ride sidesaddle," he says and, looking into my eyes, lifts me by the waist, as though performing a dance move, and sets me up on the rabbit in a way which allows me to modestly arrange my skirt.

"Why, you clever man," I say, and with the ease of ten thousand rodeos, he swings up onto the creature next to me, a beautifully rendered griffon.

The carousel picks up speed, the world beyond it smearing into a band of bright lights. I feel as though I ought to know the carousel melody, as it seems all carousels share the same one, but I can't place it even as it grows in volume, making conversation impossible. I wonder if Rafe ever brought Paisley to the after-hours carousel, and if this is a standard means by which he charms women. He is indeed *very* charming, which makes me wonder a bit at the necessity for our arrangement after all. But a deadline is a deadline, and once we've done our work, he'll be free to pursue a genuine romance.

The carousel slows again, the music growing gradually quieter, and Rafe helps me down again, still smiling. I lean on his arm when we step to the ground, delightfully dizzy. "Oh darling thank you ever so much, it's been ages since I've done that," I say, enchanted despite our arrangement.

"You're welcome," he says, and we pause in the golden puddle of light cast by a street lamp and he kisses me briefly, gently. When we step apart, I can feel myself flushing, just a little. "I hope that was okay to do." He sounds as though he isn't used to being confused on this point, despite having kissed me twice prior. It's within our arrangement.

"It was the perfect thing to do," I say, but as he leans in again, his phone rings, breaking the enchantment. He sighs as he pulls back, steps away to answer it. I turn to look back at the carousel, maybe see if I can spot lights reflecting off the water I think is nearby. It wasn't quite so cool at the restaurant, but here, the breeze raises goosebumps on my arms.

"Sorry about that," he says, coming back. "It's hatching season."

"Is everything all right?"

"Yeah, I was just ignoring their texts, so they wanted to be sure I was okay, and that I knew. It's my first real one, as it were." He looks at me, shrugs out of his jacket and puts it around my shoulders. "Here, I shouldn't have kept you out here like this."

"Oh, thank you." Hatching season; I've never given a moment's thought to the life cycle of the ostrich. Certainly I've never seen a baby ostrich in any of those posts of cute baby animals.

"Thank you, for being so patient with all of this. It's kind of embarrassing."

"Luckily for you, I very much enjoy parties."

"I sensed that about you, when I first saw you across the room."

"You didn't, but it's nice of you to say so." We walk back to the car, and the carousel lights stay on until we drive away. "Do you show that off to all of your dates?" I ask.

"You're the first," he says, and this time, I do think he's telling the truth.

BACK IN THE SUITE, Dolly is sprawled fully dressed on the still-made bed like she's been there the whole time, her boots hanging off the edge. So maybe she wasn't at a sniper's vantage the entire time I was out. I don't know what she was watching on the television, as she turns it off the moment I walk in. Bits is reclined on a chaise longue in the corner, her VR headset pulled down.

"You clever man," Dolly says with a grin, and I laugh.

"There isn't any harm in stroking his ego," I say.

"No, I guess not," she says. "Plus you got a jacket out of it." When Rafe dropped me off at the entryway, I *did* try to return the jacket and he demurred, so I'm still just wearing it around my shoulders.

"I did, what do you think?" I do a little spin.

"Brings the whole outfit together," she says, but I'm not certain she's even looking.

"What did you buy at the surplus store? I'm so sorry that I didn't ask before dinner, but I didn't have the time."

"Oh, the usual sorts of things. A new ghillie suit, for the local flora. Boot laces."

"Is that all?" I take off Rafe's jacket and put it on the chair nearest the door, slip off my heels. What a full day it's been.

"Bitsy got some vintage binoculars, I didn't really follow why they're special. Some kind of smart but not smart tech? Oh and they had a display of stuff *for the ladies*, so I got you one of those pepper sprays that looks like a perfume."

"Goodness, you didn't have to do that. Thank you." Upon examination, it is a *very* tacky spray bottle, but that adds to the fun of it. It also makes absolutely sure that I wouldn't mistake it for one of my actual perfumes, were I reaching into a purse or pocket for it.

"Seemed like your kind of thing." Dolly swings off the bed and stretches. "Okay if we go off duty for the night, ma'am?"

"Of course, your time is your own. Honestly, you're taking this bodyguard thing far more seriously than I thought we discussed."

"Just keepin' up appearances," Dolly says, and kicks Bits' chair leg.

"I'm not asleep," Bits says.

"Didn't say you were."

"You could've said you were going to bed."

"I could've, but am I?"

"Are you?" Bits pushes up her headset and blinks up at Dolly, and then over at me.

"I am," I say. "I'm simply exhausted."

"There see, let's clear out so Bristles can do her rituals."

"You make it sound like witchcraft, I'm just washing my face and toning and moisturizing."

"Rituals." Dolly shrugs, grinning. "Anyway I'm gonna go play poker with some of the guys on staff, but you know how to get a hold of me."

"It didn't take you long to settle in," I say.

"Never does." Dolly winks and goes out the door to the hall, and Bits gathers herself and trails into the adjoining bedroom.

Chapter Eight

Dolly brings me around to Paisley's the next morning, and leans whistling against the car as I am greeted and brought inside. "Where's your other one?" she asks, still perturbed that I have bodyguards, but wanting to know the details in spite of herself.

"She had some technical things to go over. I don't know all of the particulars." The house seems to be an older one, I don't know what vintage I would say necessarily, but has very elegant architecture, and high ceilings. When it is very hot, it probably remains fairly cool in here, even without the addition of central air.

"Isn't it a little weird, that you don't know?"

I give a little laugh. "Oh, heavens no! That's what I pay her for, so I don't have to keep track of the technical things."

//It's very artful, the way Bristol lies// Dolly says in my ear on the little groupchat we three nearly always share. //There's some truth in it, more often than not.//

//It isn't fair to bait her while she has to talk to a mark// Bits says.

//It's the best time to bait her.// But she desists.

"I guess that's fair," Paisley says, laughing with me, though she's a little mystified. She takes me to a cozy little craft room that contains many shelves of materials, a very nice desk on which to organize those crafts, or perhaps letter writing, as there is stationery there as well. Regular pens and fountain pens and sealing wax, of all things, and an engraved brass lighter. "Can I trust you to keep a secret?"

"Of course you can," I say, and of course that is a lie that perhaps does not contain any amount of truth. But she seems satisfied, and removes a frame from the wall that contains a mosaic of photographs of herself and Ned, perhaps on their honeymoon. A little chrome safe is set in the wall behind, with a spinning dial combination.

"I keep the good stuff in here," she says. "The things I don't wear all the time."

"Very smart."

She spins the knob this way and that, and I don't pay too much attention to it. It is a little shocking, how easily she is trusting me. There has to be a reason, either security she has that she won't think I'm aware of, or just that level of carelessness. Or perhaps she thinks me so harmless, a threat only in that I'm taking Rafe away from her. Perhaps I should be more on guard, lest she turn with a gun in her hand and simply shoot me dead.

But of course what she turns with is a little carved wooden box of assorted trinkets, and the glimpse I get of the safe behind her is mostly of small boxes, manila envelopes, and the glint of what might well be a tiny private gold store that so many people of a certain demographic maintain, 'just in case.'

"The Sutter jewelry is a necklace and earrings, so you could borrow one of these rings, or a bracelet, or I have these doodads for in your hair," she says, opening the lid and turning the blue velvet interior towards me.

The bracelets are not precisely to my taste, and also don't go with my current assortment, which of course includes my panic button. I'd resolved myself to be amenable to her suggestions, and am relieved that the hair 'doodads' are some rhinestone combs that seem very vintage in appearance, and are wearable under the veil but will go quite well with the reception look. "You're sure this will go with the Sutter set?" I ask, resting my fingertips on them. "I don't want to upstage them, or look as though I'm not taking them seriously enough."

"They're perfect with them," Paisley says, her voice and smile a little brittle at the edges. She swiftly turns to find a box for me to transport them in.

"Thank you again for all of this, the parties, and welcoming me so readily. I really didn't know what to expect when I came here," I say.

"I'll bet you didn't, whisked off your feet like that by R.J.," Paisley says. I still can't see her face, quite, as she fiddles with tissue paper, but her tone is a bit recovered.

"It's very unlike me," I say. "To be swept up in that manner. And you and Rosalie have just been so wonderful in helping me acclimate..."

"You and your bodyguards," she says, handing me the hair combs in their neat little package.

"Oh please don't tease me about them," I say, making a very pleading face, and she laughs.

"Tease you? I would never..."

By the time I ask after Rosalie, we've moved to Paisley's screened-in porch to have some lemonade. Dolly talking about white ladies with granite countertops floats through my mind.

"I'm surprised Rosalie wasn't here this morning," I say, to avoid talking about lemonade.

"It must just seem to you like her and I are joined at the hip," Paisley says, smiling but not.

"I haven't had such a close friend in ever so long, I might have been the teensiest bit jealous," I say in a confessional tone, and watch the surprise flicker in her eyes. If she thinks so little of Rosalie, why does she keep her around? Proximity?

"Other than your bodyguards, which I am absolutely not bringing up to tease you."

"Absolutely not," I say, and we smile at each other and sip our lemonade.

"Miss Rosalie had a doctor's appointment this morning," Paisley says.

"Nothing serious, I hope?"

"Well it might be serious, but it isn't *bad*, if you know what I mean." I blink at her for a moment, as I don't know what she means.

//She's talkin' about *babies*, Bristol// Dolly says.

Oh, of course. "Oh, she must be excited! Hopeful, perhaps?"

"Hopeful, definitely." That hangs in the air between us, and I consider that Paisley's household seems childless. "We've all got our schedules for things like that, and she's felt like her clock was ticking."

"Well the best of luck to her then," I say. I wait a moment, and then ask "And you?"

"Ned and I haven't started trying yet. I couldn't imagine having a baby in my twenties, I still feel like a baby." She looks at me intently. "Have you and R.J. discussed it yet?"

"*Babies?*" I'm more than a little aghast, but then I rapidly consider that she must know what his designs on continuing the Sutter line are and are not, and I don't. However, his focus has shifted considerably in his new post-rodeo world, and I would guess that even if he was not previously amenable to children, he likely is now. "We aren't in a hurry, to be sure."

"As opposed to your wedding," she says, but I don't rise to the bait. She must know about the trust deadline, and after a moment she flashes a smile. "Was just checkin' to make sure I wasn't planning a baby shower already as well."

"You would be among the first to know," I say. I can't say why I think that little detail doesn't ring entirely true, but of course young married women talk about babies all the time. I'm a little embarrassed that I needed Dolly of all people to prompt me. "After all, you and Rosalie are the best friends I've made here."

"I'm so happy to hear you say that."

DOLLY AND I ARE PART of the way back to the Sutter ranch when Marquis calls me. "I *know* you aren't getting married to some rodeo man without inviting me," they say when I pick up.

"Oh darling, of course I'm not. Or I am, but it's strictly business."

"Bristol..."

"His family trust has a date by which he is to be wed, or else it disburses elsewhere. We met at an otherwise dreadfully boring party, and hashed out the details."

"Of course you did. Where are Bits and Dolly in all of this?"

"They're acting as my bodyguards," I say.

"Bodyguards? And you aren't inviting me? This is ridiculous. An awful insult, I will never forgive you."

"I promise you, it is not the sort of fun to which you are accustomed."

"She's tellin' the truth," Dolly says, raising her voice. "Lotta dumb parties, lotta driving around."

"Engagement parties, I'm sure. What does your dress look like?"

"I'll send you a picture. But darling, how did you find out?"

"You aren't keeping up with your magazines," they say, and when I send a pair of wedding dress pictures, one with the veil and one without, they send me a link to a gossip column about R.J. Sutter's mysterious bride.

"Oh how *sordid*," I say, a little bit delighted, a little bit scandalized. Of course they don't have a single good picture of my face, I'm very careful about that, between clothing and makeup. But of course Marquis would recognize me, we've been thick as thieves for years.

"And you're right, I'm woefully behind in my reading. Is there anything else I need to catch up with?"

"Not that can't wait until after your nuptials." We both laugh. "Is the plan also a splashy divorce, then? You're getting a good paycheck out of this, I hope, for the girls' sake if not your own."

"Yes, we're getting paid handsomely for this, I promise you."

"Good, I'm glad. I'll let you get back to your cowboy glamor, then, and you must visit me and tell me all about it once you're done."

"Of course I will, darling."

There is another vehicle parked in the drive, that Dolly stops behind. "Huh," she says, but doesn't continue the thought, as Rafe and another man come out the front door as though they've anticipated me, or were just well timed.

"Madison, this is my brother," Rafe says.

"Gabriel, I've looked forward to meeting you," I say, and he pauses in the middle of shaking my hand, a pained look on his face.

"Oh hell, at least call me Gabe? I heard you're calling R.J. Rafe."

"I certainly am, I absolutely will not call my fiancé something like R.J. And noted, of course."

He smiles, and we finish shaking. "Well okay then." He glances at Rafe, who shrugs in a classic 'I told you so' manner. "I guess we don't have to worry about you keeping up." Even as he says that, though, his eyes drop to my high heels and he raises an eyebrow.

"No, I don't think you do," I say.

"Madison, I told Gabe the whole thing, you don't have to pretend around him."

"Pretend what, darling, that we're madly in love? But what if it's the truth?" I smile wickedly, and they both laugh.

"I didn't think R.J. had it in him, to be honest," Gabe says. "Especially not after what went down with Paisley."

"Gabe..."

"You didn't tell her? She's gonna get an ice pick in the back and have no idea why." Gabe turns to me, shaking his head.

"I know they used to be an item," I say. "I was unsure of the breakup, but given how friendly they still seem..." trailing off, hoping Gabe will pick up the thread, and he does, bless him.

"Oh yeah, they're still real chummy. But you watch your back around her, she's still carrying a torch, and she'd drop poor old Ned if R.J. would only say the word."

"She'll be able to continue carrying that torch, we already have my graceful exit planned. I'm not interfering with her in any way." I think of how avid she suddenly was, in the baby conversation. "Though I don't envy your continued handling of her."

"Paisley's Paisley," Rafe says with an uncomfortable shrug.

"Isn't that the truth," Gabe says. "Now I'm starved, are we having lunch or not?"

I KEEP WAITING FOR Great-Aunt Gertrude to become a concern, but she remains a bogeyman. She would have been to visit sooner, or we to visit her sooner, but she has had some minor medical complications arise, and so while Rafe still visits her, and Gabe does, they don't want to tax her by introducing a stranger. There is discussion whether she'll be able to make the wedding, but that remains up in the air.

Still, I have Bits research things about her, that I'm adequately informed should we suddenly meet. She is, or was, a member of the local chapter of the Daughters of the American Revolution, and has been active both with her local church and also a number of both social and charity organizations. Quilting and soup kitchens and the like. Very community minded, is Great-Aunt Gertrude.

I do think that some of my interest is in maintaining the most flawless facade possible in our little charade, which has been some of the most active diversion that I have had in some time. I do also think that I am fascinated by this family, these blood related people who all have a certain genuine care and fondness for one another. Seeing the manner in which they operate is foreign to me, and different from how my own family functioned, before I left them. Perhaps if they had been more like this, I would have been less inclined to leave. But no, that environment was simply unbearable; we were not born into fortune, in the way the Sutters had been. They rather put me in mind of Dolly and her brothers, when we've had occasion to work with them, though Dolly and company were also not born into fortune. People are always the most interesting puzzle of them all.

Chapter Nine

I do have some very short unscheduled time on my own, which is not caught up in the whirlwind of extravagant wedding planning or Paisley's neighborhood social calendar, and on one of those afternoons, I have Dolly and Bits take me to the charming little downtown so that I might look into the possibility of getting cowboy boots. Part of the reason is just to get away on one of my favorite diversions, but also I know it will be a crowd pleaser, both amongst the locals and Dolly, should I trade out my footwear for something more environmentally appropriate.

She in fact can hardly believe it. "You're giving up the black velvet combat boots?" she asks.

"I am not. Different situations call for different footwear."

"Oh so you're tired of wearing high heels all day on an ostrich ranch."

"I didn't say that either. Dolly, honestly, you're ridiculous. I thought you'd be happy." Perhaps I'll get a blue pair, for the wedding. No, that's too ridiculous.

"I'm ecstatic, Bristles. I didn't dare dream that one day it would come to this. Did I, Bits?"

"Nope." Bits doesn't move from her position of recline in the back seat.

"Bits, I'm so sorry, are you dreadfully bored? Dolly is obviously in her element, but you..."

"Bristol, I don't need to be physically anyplace in particular to be in my element," she says. "But I appreciate you thinking of me. It's interesting, seeing the different levels of internet security the different households here are using, and whether it extends to their devices or not."

"I hadn't considered that." Bits indeed always has her own puzzles.

"And at Rosalie's house, all of her appliances are online, and the refrigerator orders certain things when they're running low, and the thermostat is linked up to some health app she has that's—"

"None of our business, Bits, though I do know digital privacy is one of those things," I say a bit hastily. Of course they already overheard the baby talk, but it doesn't mean we need to rehash it. "We haven't been to Rosalie's house, Bits, why would you—"

"She's one of the people you've spent the most time with here, and there keeps being suggestion that we'll be at her house eventually. Though keeping you away is just another one of the ways that Paisley is exerting what control she can over the situation."

"She's a real piece of work," Dolly says. "Princess gets-her-own-way."

I laugh a little. "Dolly, honestly."

"I don't trust her."

"Yes, darling, you've said." She gets out her ecigarette instead of arguing further. "Okay, you can drop me here. I'll let you know when I'm done."

"Whatever milady wants," Dolly says.

"Surely you don't want to come *shopping* with me."

"Don't call me Shirley." I frown at her and she grins. "No, you're right. I'll park and be nearby, though. Have fun. You gonna get ostrich boots to match the mister's?"

"I'll have to see what they have available," I say, closing the door behind me. It's something of a relief, to be standing alone for the moment. We three do not normally spend so much time in such close quarters, even though I've spent mornings by the pool and Bits can make herself nearly seem like furniture with very little effort.

I stop in a little touristy boutique first, simply for the sake of it. It's the sort of shop which could exist anywhere in the world, except by the register it also includes a little spinner of local postcards, and a small display of items from local artisans. In their display of synthetic silk scarves, I think I see a pattern that I recognize Paisley as having worn, and it is unkind of me to judge her for shopping locally, but I do, a tiny bit. It is tiresome to be fair all the time. Our days here are numbered, but I select some postcards to send Marquis; we share a fondness for receiving physical mail.

I step back outside and orient myself towards the boot shop, and then I hear a familiar voice from across the thoroughfare, and I freeze, not unlike when Bits had her difficulties some time back and did what, in her lingua franca, she called rebooting. I hear my old name and I reboot. What an odd feeling to have, so unexpected, just a span of moments with no thoughts, no words.

Then I recover and the world comes swimming back to me but by then it's too late to fade into the crowd and become somebody else, somebody that Lorraine doesn't recognize, who she hadn't ridden the train into the bright city center with, pooling our grubby dollars between us for a cover charge as I learned to wheedle our way past the bouncers, the velvet ropes, the lines of undesirables that we were so close to being, except for a certain je ne sais quoi that I finally cultivated, fully, and she fell short of and so when I left I shed her as part of that old life, old self, my outgrown chrysalis. And now she is here and she recognizes me and I have to take care of her or else quite a lot will be ruined. Bits hasn't said anything in my ear yet, nor Dolly, who I'm sure is watching this grisly tableau unfold, but I can hear the emptiness, the pause of their bated breaths. And they're certain to snicker about it later, those wicked girls.

"Stephanie? Oh my god we thought you were *dead*! And then *feds* came around looking for—" she's saying as we rapidly close the distance between her as if to embrace, me dipping my hand into my purse for the taser that I've carried off and on since Dolly got them for us in Macau, cutting off as my left arm goes around her shoulders and the taser in my right hand makes contact with her belly and she's out like a light, sagging against me, but now I can't just *leave her*, after what she's said. What feds? How did they track me back *home* after Bits spent all her due diligence erasing all of us. Oh drat. Oh darn.

"Dolly, darling, I do think we need to talk to her," I say quickly and quietly, holding my dear old friend up, as though we are conspiratorially whispering together and will part again soon with promises to call each other lately, to go out sometime, to have dinner.

To her credit, there is no laughter in her tone, just business. "Understood, be there in a sec."

I stagger Lorraine to a bench and get us both sat, careful not to drop any of her belongings. I never, ever thought that I would see her again, and am entirely unprepared for how I might feel about it. Luckily, now is not the time to feel anything, but rather to handle the situation which has arisen. Boots will have to wait another day, though. She isn't entirely unconscious, but she isn't actively awake either, and it's a relief when Dolly walks up, still smoking her ecigarette, grinning casually like we meant to meet here. She gives Lorraine a cursory check-over, feeling her pulse as we prepare to change locations, and doesn't seem outwardly perturbed by what she finds.

"You've just had a fainting spell, darling, but the car is just here," I say, just slightly too loudly, so that any passers-by who decide to take inopportune notice will have an explanation that allows them to return to their lives, satisfied that nothing sinister is happening.

"Okay," Lorraine mumbles, and I think of times she was drunk but I was not, and we got ourselves to the bus or train, and back to our shabby abodes. I *never* think about the past, or at least not that far past. Oh this is dreadful. We're of very similar height and build, and always were, and so it is surreal to see Dolly handle her so easily back to the car, giving the impression that Lorraine is helping far more than she is.

Bits, double-parked, is in the driver's seat, her VR headset hung around her neck, and I get into the front seat and Dolly slides into the back seat with Lorraine. "Where to?" she asks, pulling back into traffic once the doors are closed.

"Gimme a sec." Dolly opens Lorraine's purse, makes a face, hands it to me. I look inside, open the hidden zipper in the side, and pull out her wallet. I don't think her ID is a real one, but it does say her local address, and I show Bits.

"We're just taking her home?" she asks.

I arch a brow. "What else would you suggest?" She shrugs, and drives. Dolly is notably quiet in the back seat, as is Lorraine. When I glance back, Lorraine is belted in, her head lolled back against the headrest. "Is she okay?"

"Probably never been tased before," Dolly says, rather than saying she doesn't know.

"I'm certain that's true." I certainly had not, before my association with Dolly. Then I remember that I am the one who tased Lorraine and feel an unaccustomed pang of guilt.

Her apartment building is a predictable sort, square and tall and with dubious security measures at the front door that simply require us to wave her phone at them. She's still a bit stunned, but more able to walk, and by the time we're at her apartment door, she's able to take her purse and get out the keys, though not field the lock, and Dolly grabs her wrist and guides the key home into the lock, a solution I had not considered. Inside, Bits goes to the kitchen and I hear the tap run, and Dolly deposits Lorraine on a nubbly looking couch that I'm certain is made from recycled plastics and probably came with the lease.

Lorraine looks at me, and her eyes fill with tears, and I drop onto the couch next to her and catch up her hands. "I'm so sorry to hurt you like that, darling, I just had no idea what you were saying and couldn't—"

But she interrupts me. "I'm so glad you're okay. You were *gone*." Two tears break free, tracking down her cheeks and dripping onto the couch between us, and I'm so startled that I tear up as well, dropping her hands in surprise. I am entirely unprepared to have any sort of feelings about deciding to leave my old life; what's done is done. But Lorraine is here, and if I've ever had the slightest semblance of regret, it was leaving her in the gutter that I climbed out of.

"I'm so sorry," I say again, and not for the taser this time.

"You wanna clue the rest of us in?" Dolly asks.

I take a brief moment to compose myself. "This is my very dear friend Lorraine. We grew up together." Dolly and Bits both have similar expressions of wide-eyed shock on their faces. "We used to dress up and go to clubs together, when we were old enough." I pause, and amend "*nearly* old enough, we had fake IDs of course."

"Even without the IDs, Stephanie could get us into almost anywhere," Lorraine says. Bits hands her the water, and she takes it, drinking automatically. "Clubs that actual rich people went to. We saw celebrities, sometimes. She just had that face. Has that face. You look *great*."

"Thank you," I say. "Honestly, darling, so do you." People used to mistake us for sisters; we didn't always correct them. Oh, this is dizzying. "What are you doing here? And what do you mean, people came looking for me?"

"Well, I figured if I was going to be poor and have a shitty job, I could do that anywhere. So I came someplace different. Plus the rodeos are fun." She drinks some more water, looks at Bits and Dolly. "You really knocked me for a loop, I didn't really see your friends. Like, I know all of you helped me get here but..." she trails off.

"This is Bits and Dolly," I say after the slightest hesitation. "I work with them."

"You work with them? What do you do?"

"Acquisitions," Dolly says, smiling easily, but I see her taking in possible exits, I'm not certain what else. Which piece of furniture to barricade behind in case of gunplay? How to most quickly and quietly incapacitate Lorraine if this should take a turn. A further turn. "Though right now we've been relaxing with some rodeo folks."

"That sounds nice," Lorraine says, sounding a little unsure.

"It can be," I say. "But what were you saying about people looking for me? Feds?"

"Well, they didn't really say who they were, but they seemed like feds. Shiny shoes. They had a few pictures, not many, and they said they were looking into you as a missing person. Which was really funny, because we were the ones you were missing from first." She laughs a little, drinks some more water. She seems more alert now, more normal. "Kind of a younger guy, blondish hair. A woman and another person, those two didn't say anything though."

"I can't imagine they learned anything useful."

"They didn't, they were really frustrated about it. I still have the guy's card, though." She looks around for her purse, and Dolly picks it up from the coffee table and gives it to her. She rummages for a moment, comes up with one of those little metallic business card holders, and I can't help but smile. She gets enough business cards, or intends to, to keep a holder like that. "Here."

It's plain white, good thick matte cardstock, and says Will Scarlet, of course. I wonder who his companions were, and if we met them in the course of the diamonds debacle, or if they're from elsewhere in whatever agency it is he works for. There's a phone number, and an email address, and that's all. I pass it to Bits, who looks at it a moment, and then hands it back before pulling out her phone.

"Don't *call* him," Lorraine almost squeals, and Bits blinks at her, surprised.

"I'm not. I'm tracking him."

My phone pings, with a message from Rafe. //Sorry to cut into things, but Great-Aunt Gertrude is going to make an appearance tonight. Real brief after dinner, when we're doing the cocktails by the pool thing.//

//That's quite all right, thank you for letting me know.// I reply, then look at Lorraine. "Darling, we're going to have to go. Here, I'll take your number, now you have mine. This rodeo stuff is very intricate, but is only for the next week or so. We'll be able to catch up after that, does that sound agreeable?"

"How do I know you won't just disappear again?" she asks, a dig that surprises me a little, but is more than fair.

"I suppose you'll just have to take my word for it," I say. "I have no way to make it up to you, or assure you in such a manner that you'll believe me, but I also can't take you with me."

"I didn't ask you to take me with you," she says. The unspoken 'this time' hangs between us. This, and I have to go meet Great-Aunt Gertrude. I'll have time to compose myself.

I hug her, surprising both of us I think. "I will call you," I say firmly, standing up. "Do you feel okay? Do you need anything before we go?"

"No, I think I've recovered from my electrocution," she says dryly, and Dolly laughs, then stops herself.

"This one's pretty okay," she says. "Not stuck up like your other friends."

"Well thanks." Lorraine smiles crookedly, and follows us to the door to close it behind us. "Talk to you soon. Maybe."

"I promise," I say, and she closes the door. It latches a moment later.

We ride the elevator to the lobby in silence. And then go out to the car, Dolly in the driver's seat, Bits in the passenger seat, headset on already, hot on Will's electronic trail, I presume. I just know Dolly is going to— "*Stephanie?*"

"You can *imagine* why I might have changed it. So dull. Though none of us go by our real names, after all."

"Oh, I do."

"You cannot *begin* to convince me that your given name is Dolly."

"Oh it ain't, it's short for Haunted Dollhouse."

"It is *not*." I was so foolish, not even five minutes ago, thinking I would have time to compose myself. Or she's doing this on purpose, as a distraction.

"Wanna bet?" She's grinning at me in the rear view.

"I am not *betting* you..."

"Not a big bet. Just a dollar. A thousand dollars? For fun."

"Please pay attention to the road." I sigh and try to look to Bits in appeal, but she's still in her headset and oblivious to our nonsense, accidentally or on purpose. "And how are we to know the final answer? Do you carry your birth certificate, that I'm to assume is undoctored?"

"Nah, you can call Butler."

It is with great effort that I keep from rolling my eyes. "He's sure to back up any ridiculous story you tell."

"If *you* call him, he won't know I'm involved."

"You are entirely impossible. And of course he will, why else would I call him?"

"Aw, it'd hurt his feelings to hear that, but suit yourself."

"He carries that torch for *you*, Dolly, he never gave me a second glance."

"Yeah, maybe." But she lets it go, for the moment, and I'm relieved. Dolly can be exasperating, but normally, there is only so much that her banter and teasing gets to me. This has not been a normal day.

Chapter Ten

Paisley is already at the ranch and whisks me away the second I set foot out of the car. "Did you hear that Great-Aunt Gertrude is coming for like, five minutes?" she asks.

"Yes, Rafe messaged me. You're so sweet for coming to help set up, but he said her arrival would be after dinner?"

"Yes, exactly, so I've made it so you don't have to worry about dinner at all. But we need to get you dressed."

"Thank you," I say, a little mystified. I haven't yet worried the slightest bit about dinner. "Does she have a particular cocktail she likes? Oh, I'm so thoughtless, is she even able to drink?"

"If she was, you'd never be able to separate Great-Aunt Gertrude from what she wanted, but no, she'll just want a lemonade. I brought that too."

"Paisley, you're a godsend." There is no earthly reason she should not want me to fail spectacularly to gain Great-Aunt Gertrude's approval, and yet, here we are. Maybe she failed to garner that approval herself.

"Aw, you're sweet," she says. In the suite, I allow her to throw my closet open and examine what I've brought. "You have such a lovely complexion for this shade of pink," she says, pulling out one of my favorite dresses which is just dressy enough for a party and just casual enough for broader wear. "Definitely wear this one."

"I think I'll step in the bathroom and freshen up a little," I say, waylaid by a memory of having similar conversations with Lorraine before a night out. I am not one given to nostalgia, this really must stop.

"I'll leave you to it, then. Just call me when you need me." And she flits off again.

By the time Bits comes to the suite, I've changed, washed my face, and applied a new face of makeup. "So that was weird," she says.

"I'm afraid you'll have to be more specific."

"Mostly the Lorraine thing." I look at her in the mirror as I put my earrings in. "What are the chances, right?"

"Astronomically low, one would have thought. And yet."

"And yet." She hesitates a second, chewing her bottom lip. "Are you okay?"

"Yes, thank you." There was a time in our association when things didn't get so emotionally messy all the time. "Were you able to find anything about Will? That wasn't the same number he used back when—"

"No, it was a different number, but I—"

"You're still in here?" Paisley bursts in. She's a little surprised to see Bits in the room and pauses a moment, but when Bits doesn't say anything, she comes to the dressing table. "Aren't you done yet?"

"Honestly, darling, I'm shocked to hear such a thing coming from you..." I say, standing up. "We girls have to stick together with regards to preparation times."

"It's true, we do, but sometimes prep needs to be the short version. You look ready, though, are you ready?"

"Yes, I'm ready." Perhaps Rafe sent her. Bits shrugs a little, barely noticeable other than to the discerning eye, so whatever she was saying must not have been terribly crucial. I allow Paisley to whisk me away to a fairly normal dinner, with herself and Ned, Rosalie and her Paul, and Rafe and Gabe. The seating arrangement isn't the usual; Gabe is seated next to me, not Rosalie, though she keeps shooting me agonized little glances when Paisley has her attention elsewhere.

Finally, when dessert is cleared and we're getting up to go to the verandah and greet the soon to be arriving guests for the cocktail party portion of the evening, Rosalie catches my arm. "Your dress," she says, getting a little jumbled in her haste, I think.

"Yes? Paisley helped me pick it out for this evening." I smile; outwardly, I assume nothing has seemed amiss, but I'm unaccustomed to such surprises as I had this afternoon, and between that and Paisley's strange energy when we returned, and now Rosalie, I still feel quite ruffled.

This stops Rosalie cold, though. "I wonder why."

"What's wrong? It's one of my favorite dresses."

"Great-Aunt Gertrude detests pink," she says, and then Paul calls to her from the doorway and she hurries away, and Rafe comes to collect me.

"What's wrong?" he says, when he sees my face, and I can only laugh. What a ridiculous situation.

"I've been informed that Great-Aunt Gertrude doesn't like pink," I say, composing myself.

"I've never heard that," he says, frowning. "Though I guess maybe she wouldn't think to tell me something like that."

"No, I suppose not."

Rafe takes my hand, gives it a little squeeze. "Anyway, it's not like it matters, right? Nothin' to get worked up about. Though I appreciate you're taking it so seriously."

"You know, you're right. I just got so caught up." He smiles down at me, and I can't help but smile back.

"She isn't here yet, if you want to go change anyway."

"I do not want to go change, I love this dress."

He shrugs. "Then wear it." People outside are shouting his name. I'm given to understand tonight's party is a lot of rodeo friends, and some other local friends, both of the business sort and the high school sort. "That's our cue." He holds out his arm and I take it, and we walk outside to applause and a few whistles. Somebody pops a bottle of champagne, and then another, and tall glasses, sparkling in the faerie lights, are passed around. I'm more than accustomed to plunging into a crowd of strangers as though I belong, and these are exceedingly welcoming strangers, all eager to meet Rafe's very sudden lady love at long last.

Great-Aunt Gertrude has not yet appeared when Rosalie appears at my elbow with an umbrella drink. "Here, you're running low," she says. "They're Paisley's specialty."

"Oh, thank you, I need this! My throat is dry with so much talking." I take a moment to admire the colors. "A Tequila sunrise? Is it the wrong time of day?"

"It's sunrise somewhere, probably," one of the nearby rodeo people observes, and we all laugh.

"They're always really good," Rosalie says, as I take my first sip.

"It isn't my usual cocktail, but it is lovely," I say. One can't drink champagne all the time, after all.

"I really like them," Rosalie says, but she doesn't have one, and I wonder if the news that Bits was going to share earlier was a reason Rosalie would opt not to consume alcohol at this party. I see Paisley across the crowd and raise my drink to her, just a little, and she smiles and winks at me before returning to her conversation, and I return to mine.

They're telling me a very tamed but still hair raising rodeo story about Rafe when Gabe finds me. "Hey, R.J. just got the news, Great-Aunt Gertrude isn't coming tonight after all," he says.

"Waiting for Great-Aunt Gertrude, a sequel play by Samuel Beckett," I say, and giggle. He frowns and looks at me, cocking his head.

"What?"

"It's a theater joke, darling, it's all right." I set down my empty glass on a passing server's tray, and they don't even break stride.

He shrugs. "Sorry, not really my thing."

"Where *is* Rafe?" I ask. Am I speaking too loudly? I should probably have spent more time with him tonight publicly. But these are his friends, that is how parties go.

"Some of the girls wanted to see the baby ostriches, so he took them over to the nursery." I should have asked for that. But everybody here will assume I would have already been. Baby ostriches indeed, I'm certain they're horrifyingly ugly. Everybody here is about babies, it's so very odd.

Gabe goes away again while I'm woolgathering, and my rodeo people seem to have also disappeared, and I realize that the crowd and the fairy lights have become a multicolored smear as if I was back on the carousel. I am not drunk; I have not drunk enough for this, and this is not what drunkenness feels like, and there are many reasons I am not given to dwelling on the past, but it puts me in mind of my fairly recent private stay at an unnamed government facility, I take a few steps, but I'm not sure where I intend to go, and stumble into the little fence that surrounds the pool. This is embarrassing, I think, though I do not feel embarrassed. I feel as though the part of me that controls everything has detached, and the part of me that takes action is a floating balloon, and somehow I manage to coordinate the two and fumble in my bracelets and find my panic button. It doesn't make any noise when I press it. Did I press it correctly? It doesn't light up, either, but I suppose that would defeat the purpose of secretly having a panic button, if it had any outward appearance of such.

"Madison, honey, are you okay? You don't look so good." Paisley, sweet and far too solicitous, is at my elbow. It seems as though I can't really see her face. I wish I still had my glass, I was so foolish. It's because she sent Rosalie. It's because I was distracted from Lorraine earlier, or this never would have happened. Wouldn't she be shocked if I slapped her pretty face? But I can't organize myself or marshal my senses to do so, or to rebuff her, and just grip onto the fence with my wooden-feeling hands, like they're puppet hands, the sort where each finger has its own little joints all the way down to the tips. She takes me by the shoulders, gently but firmly, and says "Let's get you out of here." I can't let go of the fence, though, and don't think I should like to go with her, though I can't sort out why that would be. After all, hasn't she been so kind and welcoming? Haven't we had so many parties together already? "Madison, come on now." Her tone becomes more brusque, businesslike, and just like that, my hands fall open.

It's a little too abrupt, and I giggle as she staggers under my sudden full weight. Serves her right, is this her fault? I'm not drunk, I'm not. I don't know where the house is, but I'm also not convinced that's where she is trying to take me, and I don't want to go with her, and simply sit down right there on the pavement. It feels nice and cool, and suddenly I feel flushed all over, and so the next reasonable step is to lie down, pillowing my cheek on the nice smooth-rough concrete that glitters just a little in the party lights. It's more comfortable than I might have thought, but when, if ever, have I just laid on pavement? I think perhaps never.

Paisley tries again to get me to my feet, her tone complaining but her words have gone away somewhere, and then her voice sharpens, far too high pitched, and I don't like that, I can't abide high pitched noises. I can't seem to put my hands over my ears, so I squinch my eyes closed instead. There are other voices, all smeared like the lights were, and somebody gets me up off the pavement in a strong, sure motion but now that my eyes are closed I can't open them again, but I know that it isn't Paisley. There's no mistaking the feel of the skin on Dolly's fake hand no matter what any marketing material says. And she always smells a little like gun oil. I'm leaning on that arm that I can mostly ignore otherwise, and that I never mention, because I don't want her to feel bad, or to think that I think ill of her for having it. But I'm safe from Paisley, and that's enough for me.

Chapter Eleven

I wake up in that long blue hour of the morning before dawn, my mouth the driest it has ever in my life been, feeling as though, physically, my cheeks are just stuffed to bursting with cotton. They are not, of course. I'm lying in an unaccustomed way and shift on the bed, my skirt wrapping around my legs. Bed? Skirt? I have very blurry, sudden memories of the party, the pavement, and feel a surge of panic that whatever I was drugged with didn't properly let me feel at the time. Ketamine, probably. Funny, the law enforcement and animal husbandry overlap. I'm not used to fully panicking either, though, and don't quite know what to do with myself once I sit up, gasping. Am I about to cry? I examine the feeling with fascination.

In the gap between my action and reaction, Dolly gets out of the chair she was in, back against the closed door. I know she can move quickly, maybe even more quickly than I've seen, but she approaches me with surprising care, perhaps as one would a distressed animal. "Hey, Bristol, how you feeling?"

"Very thirsty," I say slowly, to make sure I can. My eyelashes are gummy with the mascara I didn't wash off last evening. My hair has come only partly undone, the very ends of it tickling my neck. My shoes are off, but otherwise I'm still dressed.

"Hold on a sec." She goes into the bathroom, runs the water. She hasn't turned on any lights, and I can't remember if she's had that dreadful eye surgery or not. Perhaps she's just always had good vision in different environments. "Here."

"Thank you," I say, and then would have promptly spilled the water into my lap if she did not reach out and steady my hand. My hands are very cold, it seems.

"Just take it easy," she says, taking the glass once I've drained it. "You should probably sleep more." Had I been sleeping? It could be considered sleep. I blink at her, not really knowing what to say. "I'm not leaving," she says, and that must have been what I was waiting for. I lay my head on the pillow and slip away once more, as she pulls a blanket up around my shoulders.

When next I awaken, it is much more calmly. The room is *very* bright. I only open my eyes at first, I don't thrash about or jerk upright, and Dolly remains slouched dozing in her chair against the door until I actually move. I do try to be slow and quiet, I imagine she did not get sufficient sleep last night, or at least not very restful sleep, upright in a wingback chair dragged over from elsewhere in the room. But she's too sensitive, something I did not anticipate, and is awake immediately.

"Morning, sunshine," she says, uncrossing her legs and sitting up.

"Good morning," I say. I feel oh so much better, my thoughts and actions in line once again. I hate that feeling, that detachment and removal from myself. That loss of control.

"I'll clear outta here so you can get cleaned up." She stands and stretches, and some unnamed part of her crackles. "Your phone was going nuts, but it can probably wait."

"I'm sure it was," I say, pulling the pins out of my hair, or rather, the pins that were left out of my hair. What a dreadful night. "Dolly, what—"

"Not now, go get hosed off." She moves the chair back to where it was and exits the room, whistling.

My phone does have ever so many messages, and I glance at them and then set it aside. It isn't necessary to face them immediately, and indeed, I would benefit from waiting. I ache all over, and a long and steaming shower eventually banishes that, as I use every potion, lotion, and ointment that I've got at my disposal. What a positively dreadful night. I wasn't sure of all that had happened; if I was, I would have an idea of my actions moving forward. As it is, I have nothing satisfying to concentrate on, just loose ends and partial clues, and I make an effort to clear my mind instead.

Towel-wrapped, I survey my clothing. The pink dress isn't too worse for wear, it just needs to be dry-cleaned. The dress I select for the day is light blue, patterned subtly with silver stars that shift in the light, appearing and disappearing. I dry my hair and pin it up sleekly, do my makeup lightly but with care. A single night sleeping in make-up won't do too much damage. I finish off the look with some min-imalist silver jewelry, slip into a pair of heels, and then finally I am ready to face the world, and go to join Bits and Dolly in the suite's sitting room.

Dolly is mixing up something at the mini bar, perhaps a hang-over cure. Never in my life have I needed such a thing, though this obviously isn't the usual sort of hangover. I check in with myself; I'm still feeling very bewildered, and exceedingly angry.

"What's the plan?" Bits asks after looking at me for a moment.

"Obviously, I want to know what happened. And then I want them to regret that. Most specifically Paisley."

"Apparently there's a long history of kidnapping the Sutter bride, as I found out when R.J. was bawling Paisley out in front of every-body gathered, and I was handling you." Dolly pauses a moment in her mixing. "It really was a sight, she wasn't ready for him to cor-rect her at all, much less in full voice and in public. I guess he'd al-ready told her in what he assumed to be no uncertain terms that they wouldn't be doin' the kidnapping thing with you, no way, no how."

"Kidnapping," I say faintly. Obviously, nobody here but Bits and Dolly have any inkling of what sort of effect such an event, however in fun, may have on me. I think I also still perhaps have some baggage to work through with regards to my recent experience, even though it is done with. It's so unfair, to still be emotionally caught up with it.

I take a deep breath, but before I can continue, Dolly says "Is it still kidnapping when it's an adult? It seems like that'd be sort of a champagne thing."

I look at her. Heaven help me, I somewhat grasp what she means. "Dolly, no, it's—"

"Like it's only kidnapping between the ages of nothin' and seventeen, and after that it's sparkling abduction?" She laughs loudly, and hands me what looks like a mimosa. She's still wearing her bodyguard clothing from last night, while Bits is more normally dressed. I can't help but also laugh. I take the drink and settle into a chair with a sigh.

"No, it's. It's still kidnapping," Bits says, eyebrows quirked.

"The woman is a jealous menace," I say, sipping the drink after a split second's hesitation that I push past. I can trust Dolly. It *is* a mimosa, though there's something else in it. Pineapple juice. It's lovely.

"She is," Dolly says. "So we gotta put the fear of god in her, then."

"It's probably the option that's kindest to Rafe, since ruining his friend's livelihood and portfolios is likely to distress him." Or worse; it isn't often that I in fact want to do bodily harm to a person, but it also isn't often that I myself am threatened with the implication of bodily harm.

"And he was willing to go to bat in your honor. If I hadn't whisked you away, he was gonna."

"He's very sweet," I say thoughtfully. "I do think he'll make some lucky lady very happy one day."

"But not you," Dolly says.

"No, not me. What, did you think I was actually falling for him?"

She shrugs. "Well, for almost anybody else in the world, the signs were there. But it's the job, and you're just always real convincing."

"Thank you," I say.

"So, a couple of things," Bits says, and I turn my attention to her. She's been waiting Dolly and I out patiently, as she so often does. "First, somebody, probably Paisley, talked to the gossip columns about last night, and they have an actual good picture of you circulating. Second, I don't know if any other members of agency X are in town, but Will got in last night. Third—"

"This is the one that's gonna be good news, right Bitsy?" Dolly asks, grinning hard and flinty.

"Paisley has been texting R.J. all morning and he's been ignoring her all morning. She's starting to threaten him now with pictures she says she has. I've had a look through her cloud and so far haven't found anything digital, but she takes a lot of pictures."

"Oh, they must be in the safe," I say. "There were a lot of envelopes."

"She just opened her safe in front of you?" Bits asks.

"Yes, it's in her little office or craft room, behind a painting."

"Would she really nuke her own marriage so the guy she broke up with a few years back pays attention to her?" Dolly asks, finally sitting down with her own mimosa.

"Maybe? She doesn't really seem very reasonable."

"I guess when it comes down to it, I'd rather be married to a cowboy than an accountant."

"Retired cowboy," I say.

"Yeah, can't forget the tragic backstory." Dolly laughs, then shakes her head. "Gotta wonder how fun and innocent this little kidnapping schtick was actually gonna be, if the ringleader was willing to open her safe of blackmail material in front of you."

"I'd been trying to avoid wondering," I say stiffly, and she frowns. "Sorry."

"There's no way any of us could have known," I say after a moment of taut silence. "And I suppose that I need to face Rafe sooner or later."

"You've got every right to just stay in bed today," Bits says. "I can just go tell him that you're okay, but resting."

"Thank you, Bits darling, but I do think I'd rather just face the world."

"Just make sure you hydrate," Dolly says. "Now, I gotta go get myself hosed off."

I'VE ONLY SPENT A HANDFUL of days here, not truly long enough to know where in his home Rafe might be found. I do try some likely places, the breakfast room, and his office, before I find him outside. He's talking to one of the employees who works with the ostriches, but breaks off when he sees me, meets me halfway across the drive. "Madison, I am so fucking sorry about last night, I don't even know where to start."

"It isn't your fault," I say, perhaps a little startled at his vigor.

"No, but I still feel like I should've known Paisley would pull something. She's always pushing boundaries, and doesn't respect what anybody tells her, and I know that. I just thought that she'd listen to me, about this. Or I should've warned you, but like I said, I thought it was settled."

"If she told you it was, you had no reason to doubt her. You've known each other a long time."

"We have. And after it didn't work out with us, and she married Ned, I thought that was it, we were friends, it was done. But I kicked her out last night, and she's not coming to the wedding." He pauses. "I might've told her that I don't care if I ever see her again."

"Rafe!" I'm definitely startled, and a little touched. "I'm sure you don't mean that. After all, I'm only here for a little while longer. You're paying me to do this. There isn't any need to—"

"Well that's just it. She doesn't know I'm paying you to do this. As far as Paisley is concerned, I brought you home after love at first sight, and I'm head over heels for you. And this is what she did."

"You're right," I say, after a pause. We're standing quite close together, talking quietly. I can feel his conflict, that he wants to comfort me, put an arm around me, and also doesn't feel like he should touch me. "You're right, she doesn't know the truth of it. I certainly didn't tell her."

"I just wish I knew what was going on in her head. What a stupid, reckless choice."

"How did she take being ejected from the party? And the invitation rescinded?"

"Oh, she got all doe eyed, and said 'R.J., you know you don't mean that! The wedding is the day after tomorrow!' And I told Ned to get her off my property and out of my sight, and tried to chase after you and your bodyguards, to help, but Darlene there isn't somebody to be tangled with." He shakes his head, rubbing the back of his neck. "What am I supposed to do here? Sorry isn't good enough, do you want a bonus, maybe? Anything like that?"

"I'll consider it and let you know," I say. It is such an impossible situation, but it is a comfort that he's so conflicted about it. Not that I thought he was the sort of man to allow his old friends and ex-fiancée to drug somebody he'd hired just for fun, but I did not expect his unilateral support on the matter. I assumed he would be cross with Paisley but also be inclined to forgive and move on. "Thank you," I say, after perhaps a bit too much time has passed, but he waits for me.

"You're welcome. I wish like hell it just didn't happen, but it did. You're okay? You don't need to go to the doctor or anything?"

"I don't think I need a doctor, no." The worst time to ask if somebody is okay is when they are not; the social convention is to say yes, even when it is not true. "She didn't give me too much, other than that it was without my consent, and I believe it leaves the system quickly."

He lets out a long sigh. "Okay then."

"I do think I want to meet with her, though," I say. "Not at one of our houses, at a cafe perhaps."

"You do? Why?"

"Perhaps to make very sure that she never does anything like this again." This will take some time and coordination, though, so that I have her engaged while those pictures are procured. If they truly exist. And then there's Will to think of, but he's a separate problem. Bits likes her programming puzzles, and I like my social ones.

"Well, you want to meet in public, so I guess I don't need to worry about what you'll do to her."

"And I'm not Darlene," I say, smiling sweetly. I wonder if Bits and Dolly have been listening; they've been notably silent.

"That you are not. Not that Darlene isn't perfectly charming, mind. You're just real different."

"We get on well."

"She's loyal to you, that's a fact." The ostrich employee, who had gone away, has returned and is standing at a polite remove. "I'm sorry, I probably ought to—"

"No, it's quite alright. Go about your business, and I'll let you know should anything important happen. Or alarming."

"Yeah, keep me in that loop." We laugh together, a little ruefully, and he lifts my hand and brushes a kiss across my knuckles. "You're a special lady, Madison, I'm glad to have known you."

"Thank you," I say, surprised and touched. "It's such good fortune we met at that party."

"Even after last night?" Oh dear, I do know that look on his face all too well.

"Even after last night, I'd say." I'm perhaps not being entirely truthful, but our relationship hasn't required that.

I return to the suite and devote time to my phone's messages and notifications. One from Marquis, saying to call them when I could. An apology from Rosalie. Other pings from friends who had picked up on the gossip and were shocked to hear of my engagement, and wanted to know if it was actually me. Bits is right; the picture the column has is better than ones they previously had, but still not crystal clear. I wonder if Paisley sent it to them. I've no missives from Paisley. A little short message from Lorraine, who I do not think has seen any fresh gossip column news, but who says it was unbelievably nice to see me again. And I think about how she said that the rodeos were fun.

"Bits darling, what were you going to tell me last night, when Paisley came and whisked me away?"

A brief pause, before she answers from the couch. "Hmm?"

"We were interrupted last night."

"Oh. What I said this morning, that Will was on his way and had motel reservations. He checked in not too long ago. I guess it's to our advantage that he wants to arrest you himself?"

That indeed shortens the post-wedding timeline, if not the pre-wedding one. We spent so much time lazing about, and now everything has come together in a final rush. "And Dolly is...?

"She said that if you didn't know, you wouldn't have to lie about it." Bits in general avoids eye contact, and right now is no exception. This would normally be very frustrating for me, Dolly going off-script once more, but I perhaps have an inkling of what she might do. I hope.

"Just so," I say, instead of any of the expected responses, and Bits' eyes dart to mine. "I'm going to invite Paisley out to a cafe, I think. I expect you or Dolly to send me a useful message at some point during that tête-à-tête, does that sound correct?"

"I'd say so, yeah."

"We understand each other, then." I send Paisley the message, even grandly suggesting that she might pick the establishment. I check my hair and my makeup, find them satisfactory. "I'm quite surprised you did not accompany Dolly."

"I slow her down," Bits says ruefully.

"Don't we all."

My phone chimes; Paisley has sent me an address.

Chapter Twelve

Because I prefer to be driven does not mean that I cannot drive, but Paisley still seems surprised to see me park in front of the cafe and walk to her table alone. "Surprised you don't still have your bodyguards," she says, a bit snidely. The implication being that they didn't help me all that much last night, except that they did. It really is testament to Dolly's restraint that Paisley is upright and able to maintain this attitude, I'm quite surprised and impressed. Dare I say proud?

"They're occupied elsewhere," I say airily. "I'll go order, and be with you directly."

"I thought about getting you something, but..." She smirks and sips her iced tea. The gloves are off, I see.

"Oh don't be silly, you'd have no idea what I want." I smile and sweep up to the counter, scanning the kitschy chalked menu as I go. I waver briefly between an espresso and an affogato, but it is quite warm out and I do think the affogato will be far more refreshing. And Paisley, indeed, regards my glass with obvious surprise when I return to the table and settle myself across from her.

"Well you made quite the scene last night," she says.

"I suppose I did; ketamine isn't my party drug of choice, I'm afraid, even if the drink you made me did taste lovely otherwise." I spoon up some of my espresso-drowned ice cream and regard her with the full weight of my disdain.

She makes a show of confusion, quirking her lips and furrowing her brow, setting her drink down. "I'm sure I don't—"

I cut her off. "There are tests for chemicals in drinks, I'm very certain you realize that. And when people very suddenly behave out of character, well..."

"You're a stranger, how would we know your character?" She says, not quite maintaining her lightness of tone.

"You made me feel so *welcome*." I shake my head, sip my drink. "And then do this ugly, awful thing. I'm not certain what your aim was, Paisley." I pause as though I want to hear her answer, and when she takes a breath to speak, I lean in just slightly and say "He doesn't want you, darling. He will never again be yours."

She jerks back in her seat as though I've slapped her, getting red across the cheekbones and white around the lips. "How dare you," she says slowly, and with deliberation. "You don't even know him. You waltz in here like you're hot shit, like you *belong* here, and I never even heard of you before last week. Never laid eyes on you. Never had the slightest notion that R.J. had somebody he was interested in, much less interested in *marrying*. And you want to be treated like you're family? Like we *want* you?"

"Truly, your opinion doesn't matter. We do not require your input." She's breathing in short, furious little bursts now. I must be careful to bait her only far enough, not into actually flinging herself across the table at me. Though I am confident I could handle her. I pause, and then soften my voice into a pitying tone. "Paisley, just be happy with what you have. I see how Ned looks at you. I'm not certain what you thought you still had with Rafe, but even though some flame was once there, it has long since gone out. You need to let it go. You can't possibly hope to go on like this." The change in her expression is exquisite. She goes from even more incandescently furious to smug again. Cat who swallowed the canary smug, just as I'd hoped.

Glowing now but happily, triumphant, Paisley says "Oh, but that's where you're wrong, *darling*. I have proof that R.J. still loves me, or is at least interested enough to do the deed. And we both know how he is, what a white knight. He won't be able to help but step in and protect me from Ned, who is sure to be angry, and jealous. There's just no telling what—" My phone chimes once, twice, thrice, and I smile, raising my eyebrows just a little before I look away from her entirely and retrieve my phone from my purse as it pings again.

I unlock the screen, to three photographs and a video. The photographs are of the open safe, Dolly holding an envelope marked "R.J. at the Point Inn," and a number of polaroids fanned like a hand of cards, of Paisley and a man, anyway, in flagrante delicto. The video is Dolly walking out of the office and onto the adjoining screened porch, lighting the photographs with the engraved lighter from Paisley's desk, and dropping them into one of those little metal fire pits once they've burned beyond recognition.

"What are you doing?" Paisley asks.

"You'll want to see these," I say, and she accepts my send request. She swipes through the photos, blinking rapidly, and gets very still when she comes to the video, her mouth growing very pinched. I finish my affogato as she stares at her phone in silence. Dolly really did time things just so, she must have entered Paisley's house not long after Paisley left to meet me here. Then she could crack the safe at her leisure, take care of the photos, and provide me with the grand reveal. We really do work well together, despite our differences.

What does one say, after their blackmail fodder has gone up in smoke? I do wonder who that man at the Point Inn was; it seems unlikely for it to have been Rafe. I *do* think Paisley is correct, though, he's the sort of man whose morality would not let a woman be ruined with such a claim. It would have worked. Perhaps they might have even been happy, after a fashion. Clouds are darkening the sky the longer we sit, rain suddenly imminent. Paisley still seems frozen, her castle in the air having crumbled apart before her eyes. I do think the fight has gone out of her; if she was going to come across the table at me, it would have been the moment she realized what she was seeing on her screen.

I dab my lips to make sure no ice cream remains there and stand; she looks at me a little blankly as my chair scrapes back. "I'll be sure your hair combs are returned to you," I say, and she gives a single dazed nod. I wonder if she will cry here, or in the car, or once she's home. I wonder if she'll ever tell Ned, and I wonder what she may have told Ned already, if she thought this was a sure thing.

The first raindrops patter onto the pavement around me as I walk to the car. There are people who talk about the scent of rain on the earth, but one of my pleasures is the smell of rain on hot pavement. I slide into the driver's seat and lock the doors, settle my purse on the seat beside me.

//It's probably not a crazy coincidence// Bits says //But Will is at the Point Inn.//

"Shall I drop in on him, while I'm out? I was going to wait but I'm not certain that's to our advantage."

//Bristol, the wedding is tomorrow. The rehearsal dinner is later.//

"Yes, and here I am with an unforeseen gap in my schedule." I recall having driven past the Point Inn during our wanderings, and am able to get myself there without much trouble. "What room?"

//17.//

I park next to his rental car and sit a moment, listening to the rain pattering on the roof and hood of the car, watching the pavement steam. I get perfume out of my purse to freshen up, the hyacinth scent that I like to wear when it rains, and that I was wearing when Will and I once sat down together in a very fancy restaurant indeed.

"Be sure to trap the security footage."

//I know how to do my job, Bristol.// Dolly is strangely silent, but it's possible she's also off on her own errand, and we will all regroup this evening after the rehearsal dinner.

I stand in the rain just for a moment, both to bedraggle my hair ever so slightly and also to make sure that the perfume is properly affected, then go and rap lightly on the door to room 17, wooden I think, and painted a pleasant marmalade sort of color. There's a moment of pause, then a shadow crosses the eyehole, and the door is flung open. "Madison," he says with deliberation, trying to mask his surprise. He's wearing the same category of suit that he was when we met previously, midrange, nondescript, dark navy. "Like the avenue, I assume?"

"You clever darling, you do catch on," I say, and he stands aside to allow me inside.

"I saw your picture in the paper," he says, closing the door quickly.

"You're being very generous to that gossip rag," I say, surveying the room for a moment. Two double beds, but only one of them is rumpled with the evidence of somebody having sat upon the bedspread to watch television, an overnight bag on the other. Only one set of toiletries laid upon the bureau: a comb, deodorant, cologne. I pick up the bottle and give it a cursory sniff; something peppery and department store, but serviceable.

"What are you doing here?"

"I was hoping for your help," I say, after letting the silence stretch between us, punctuated by the rain.

"My help?" I wonder if he imagined what our meeting might be like, when he finally caught up to me. He must have. How I would look, where we would be, what he would say. This abrupt invasion of his space is none of those things.

"You saw me in the paper," I say, turning to him now. "One of those dreadful people drugged me. If not for Dolly's help, who knows what may have happened. I might not be standing here talking to you."

"You seem very, uh, intimate with at least one of those dreadful people. He has no idea who you are, does he?"

I smile, slowly. "He doesn't. To be fair, neither do you."

"No, I guess I don't." He sits on the edge of the rumpled bed. "You might as well tell me a story."

Oh, the poor darling, his pride is still wounded. "The marriage is simply a business arrangement, I have no attachment to him."

"There's a surprise." He's had more training, or practice, at outward composure. He seems more self assured. I wonder if he has a gun.

"Do you really think I'm so heartless?" I allow myself to pout, just a little.

"I think that you're very business minded."

"I suppose that's fair." I sit on the edge of the made bed, facing him. There's enough space between that our knees do not touch, quite, but we're close enough that I can feel his warmth. "But of course not everybody was in on the arrangement, so the woman who was to stand in as my maid of honor, and who is also his high school sweetheart and ex-fiancée, thought that she was losing her final chance at happiness with him. Hence last night."

He laughs a little, in surprise or in disbelief. "You get into the wildest situations. Or is that the plot to the world's most popular soap opera, and I just don't know it because I don't watch soap operas?"

"It is a summary of the last week and a half of my life," I say.

"Heavily edited, I assume." I only smile at that, and he sighs and doesn't let the silence last quite so long this time. "So what help do you think I would give you? Oh, I could take you into protective custody, what about that."

"I'm certain you'd like that," I say, shifting my weight a little and holding out my hands, offering my wrists to him. "Do you need to cuff me?"

He reddens then, just like the Will I remember, pushes my hands away just a little and stands up, walks to the bureau to put some space between us. "No, I don't have handcuffs. I'm not going to handcuff you."

"Then why are *you* here? Were you just upset to not be invited to the wedding?"

"I've followed a lot of false leads, trying to find you. I admit, I didn't actually think it was going to be you, here." And neither did his higher-ups, is what I assume he isn't saying. He was free to come and investigate for himself, but they are done assuming that sightings are credible. "I kind of couldn't believe that a paper like that would be right."

"And yet here you are."

"Here I am." He smiles, laughs a little, like he can't believe it worked, and now he doesn't know what to do. He ought to call back-up, likely, though how long it would take them to arrive is something I don't know, and Bits would rapidly find out. "And here you are."

"Yes, that does make things rather difficult for you, doesn't it darling," I say. I've put my hands down, but am still sitting on the bed.

"Come again?"

"Well you allowed me into your room so willingly. And I'm not certain what action you are supposed to take, but clearly you haven't yet. There are timestamps on security footage, and there are protocols that agencies follow, even the sort that has you in its employ."

He shakes his head. "I see what you're trying to do. But some decisions are discretionary, nothing that you're saying is all that damning."

"Oh, I see." I don't know if I believe him, but he's still a bit flustered over the handcuffs business, and that might be muddying the waters. "Perhaps I'm on the wrong trail, assuming you want to arrest me anyway. Perhaps you're here to recruit me instead. Tell me that my skills would be well suited in your organization, and that you can offer amnesty for our past encounters."

"Is that what you think?"

I smile, tilt my head. "No, but it's a pretty story. And you did ask for a story."

"You're right, I did." Now that he's standing, he doesn't quite know how to position himself. He ends up leaning against the bureau. I glance at my watch.

"Have someplace to be?"

"The rehearsal dinner," I say. "If you aren't going to be arresting me now, I really ought to—

"I read your file," he says abruptly, like he's been holding it back this entire time.

"My file?"

"From when you were in Homeland custody." It's to his credit that I wasn't expecting that; I allow my reaction to play across my face before making a show of composing myself once again, and I see the shadow in his eyes. "I'm sorry that happened to you."

"Thank you," I say after a pause and a deep breath that I allow to shake just a little. "It was..." I don't finish my sentence, though; I drop my gaze and sigh.

"Yeah, so. Another reason for no handcuffs."

"I truly do appreciate that," I say, looking up at him, my voice pitched a little more quietly, and for the second time today, I see a certain type of look cross a man's face, and drop my eyes again. I sit very still and quiet, and allow him to assume that I'm struggling to keep composed after being reminded of my harrowing experience.

"So getting married as a business arrangement isn't illegal," he says after several moments.

"Does this mean you're letting me go?"

"I'm probably crazy but. For right this second, yeah, I'm letting you go. Plus I'm sure you have that video of me letting you in here." He gives a self deprecating laugh. "It wouldn't count as a clean arrest."

"I thought you said that some things were discretionary?" I say, teasing a little as I get to my feet.

"I think both of us say a lot of things." We laugh together, what a strange sensation that is.

"When will I see you next?" I ask, as he walks me to the door.

"Before you leave town, hopefully," he says. Not a threat, or a promise, from the sound of it. We have indeed both said a lot of things. He stands in the doorway and watches me get in the car and drive away.

Chapter Thirteen

At the rehearsal dinner, I catch Rosalie when she arrives to tell her that she's now the maid of honor. I hadn't answered any of her messages earlier in the day, and perhaps I should have. It's possible my silence would have prevented her from coming, but to her credit, she's here.

"Madison, I'm so sorry," she says before I can get any words out, and hugs me. I'm so very surprised that I let her, and after a moment, I hug her back. Though I've spent the last little while cultivating what she and everybody here thinks of me, I do wonder what she actually thinks of me. And I wonder what she'll think when I'm gone; will I fade swiftly from her memory, as if I was an imaginary friend or a character in a movie only partly paid mind to? Or have I left enough of a blazing impression that she'll think of me years and decades down the line, perhaps even describe one very strange spring when her friend suddenly brought home a fiancée that nobody had heard of, and just as suddenly, just a few weeks later, she was gone. Goodness, it does sound like a soap opera.

"It's okay, I know it was Paisley," I say. "It has been the entire time. And since she's no longer coming to the wedding, I need you to do a tremendous favor for me, and be my maid of honor."

"Of course I will," she says, pink with surprise, or maybe with the tears that I can see she's struggling to not let fall. I should have tried to spend more time with her, but she required less handling and active manipulation, and so I left her undisturbed.

"Thank you so much, darling, I knew I could count on you."

"Did you see Paisley?" she asks. "She said she was going to talk to you today and then stopped answering my messages."

Blessedly, Rafe calls me from across the room, and I turn to go to him. "I did see her briefly," I say over my shoulder. "I told her I'd make sure she got her hair combs back."

"You were gone a real long time," Rafe says in a low voice once I'm at his side. "Everything okay?"

"I do think so, yes. We're so close now," I say.

"So long as I'm married tomorrow, you won't have to worry about me anymore," he says, seriously because that was why we did all of this in the first place, but conflicted, because he didn't want there to be any kind of a harmful cost. The only thing we were hurting was the intentions of the trust-setters, placing this unnecessary marriage date restriction on his inheritance. I realize I've never asked who came up with that; his parents, presumably. Or maybe it's another tradition, like the kidnapping of the Sutter bride.

"By this time tomorrow, you'll be married," I say in a less confidential tone, smiling. "You're not nervous are you?"

He laughs, surprised. People near us look around, and smile at the presumably happy couple sharing a moment. "Nervous? Nah. I've ridden some of the meanest bulls in the world, and been thrown by some of the meanest bulls in the world. Marriage isn't going to match up to that."

"I'm sure you're right," I say.

"I know we're going to be busy tomorrow, so I guess I want to say this now, even though we're not exactly alone," he says, lowering his voice again. "But I think I'm really going to miss you."

"Rafe," I say, touched, and he brushes a kiss on my cheek and we get on with the rehearsal dinner, which is far more dinner than rehearsal. Everybody knows how to walk down the aisle, even if they've never done it before themselves. Gabe stands in for the judge, whom we'll meet tomorrow at the event, and we do a single short run-through there in the dining hall before the appetizers start coming out.

At one point, I glance up and notice Dolly standing in one of the open doors to the verandah. She's in the midst of lighting a cigarette, and as she snaps an engraved bronze lighter closed, she sees me looking and grins before wandering off so that the smoke doesn't get inside. Bits doesn't make an appearance, but I can assume that she's on the chaise in the master suite, keeping digital tabs on everything, and making arrangements for our imminent exit. There are digital footprints that we will want swept away, caches cleared, impressions erased, and the sooner she starts, the sooner we will be done. Besides needing to pay attention to the Agency X aspect of things now, though I do think Will shall be on very good behavior. I could be incorrect.

It's a fun evening, perhaps even more fun for Paisley's absence. Nobody asks after her, in my earshot; either they were at the party last night and saw the finale, or they saw the paper, or they were already informed by guests who are in the know. Though nobody but Rafe knows it, this is my farewell dinner here, and I circulate amongst the guests with a flute of champagne and make sure to speak to everybody at least a little bit. I'm not a person who exists here, not really, but I do still want them to think well of me when I'm gone.

At one point, Rosalie says to me "I honestly don't know why we put up with her. I guess we're just used to it."

"It can be hard, handling an old friend's habits," I say.

"Sometimes it takes a new friend to make you realize the way things are."

"Yes, I think it does."

As the evening winds down, and I think some guests have left already, Gabe stands up and shouts "I want to propose a toast."

Rafe and I look at each other from across the room, and he shrugs helplessly. He has no idea what his brother is about. Some of the guests say "toast, toast," surprised, but enthusiastic, and Gabe waits for them to settle down again.

"I know maybe I should save some of this for the best man speech tomorrow," Gabe says. "But what's a rehearsal dinner for if you don't get to practice stuff, right? I want to practice making a speech. I never made a speech before." He isn't slurring, but I do think perhaps he has drunk too much. He pauses, perhaps remembering that a toast and a speech are not the same thing, and weighing one against the other.

"To R.J. and Madison," Rosalie speaks up, holding her glass aloft.

"Hear, hear, to R.J. and Madison," Gabe repeats. Everybody holds up their glasses, and then takes a drink. "I don't know if I've ever seen my brother happier. Not as an adult. Being kids and getting our first cars is a close second." Everybody laughs, and drinks again, and the evening moves to a close.

"I thought we were in trouble there," R.J. teases as Gabe finds his way to us.

"Well, if I actually brought my damn speech notes, maybe you would've been," Gabe says, then laughs. "Nah, nothing bad to say. I don't need to talk about all the times we kicked each other's asses growing up." He laughs again. "Okay maybe I'm a little pissed I didn't see her first, but that ain't really appropriate wedding conversation."

"You're right," Rafe says, and Gabe looks at me.

"Sorry, Madison, I oughtn't have said that."

"It's okay, Gabe."

"See, she calls me the right name. Will you call him R.J. just once?"

I wrinkle my nose ever so slightly. "I fail to see why I would."

Gabe laughs again. "See, she's great. I'm so happy for you two."

Rafe laughs too. "Well thanks. Keep that energy for tomorrow, okay?"

"You know I will." Gabe punches him in the shoulder, gently, and ambles off.

Once the guests have gone, Rafe and I remain outside under the stars for a time. "I suppose we ought to get some sleep before the big day," I say eventually.

"I suppose," he says. "You know. You've been here all this time, and I don't think you've come to see the birds once. Do you want to?"

"See the birds? Certainly not, though I appreciate you've checked in to see."

"Anytime." I've spent just enough time with him, I can imagine his smile.

Dolly and Bits are both waiting for me back in the suite. "Will hasn't called anybody or sent out any messages," Bits says without preamble.

"Did we expect him to?" I ask.

"I didn't expect him not to, that's for sure." She pauses a moment, either parsing what she wants to say next or taking in the latest datastream, it's hard to discern which. "Paisley also hasn't done much. Went home. Screamed at Ned. Threw stuff around."

"Is that all? She's rather predictable, isn't she."

"That's cold, Bristles," Dolly says, but she's grinning.

"Did you take any other souvenirs?" I ask her pointedly.

"Maybe a coupla things. Haven't you always wanted your very own gold ingot?" She tosses it to me abruptly, though not so hard that it would do damage if I didn't catch it. I do catch it, and turn it over in my hands.

"Isn't it funny, how gold is so *heavy* when it's this size? It doesn't seem as though it would be." It's truly a marvel.

"Get yourself somebody who looks at you the way Bristles looks at valuables." Dolly laughs. "Anyway, this has been like a vacation for me. Using the gym, including a pro mechanical bull. I didn't even have to shoot anybody, or hit anybody, though it was real close with Paisley. So thanks, you two, for doing the heavy lifting."

"We all played our parts," Bits says judiciously.

"I somewhat regret that none of us hit Paisley," I confess. "Isn't that wicked?"

"Nah, it's human. Some people just really ought to be hit."

"*Dolly.*" But I can't help but laugh, and Bits is laughing too, and I've certainly never seen Bits strike anybody in our time together, so it is a truth. Some people just really ought to be hit. "So that's that, then. Just one little bit left and we've got everything neatly wrapped up."

"Yeah, just you gettin' actually married to a guy who seems more and more in love with you every day," Dolly says in an elaborately casual tone.

"You're forgetting we're leaving not long after, as our duty will have been discharged."

"What, no honeymoon?" Dolly asks in mock surprise.

"No reservations have been made," Bits says. "Somebody asked him the other night, and he said that there's too much going on with the farm right now, and they'll go to Mexico or something in the winter."

"Dolly, you're also forgetting that my real name isn't Madison and that I am actually not, in the eyes of the law, getting married to Rafe."

"Don't worry, Stephanie, I won't forget that." She grins at me, and I give a little sniff. "Hey, I'm supposed to be your bodyguard. Paranoia is good, right?"

"It isn't unwarranted. Though what exactly are you paranoid about? We knew this would burn one of my aliases. Do you think he will prevent me from leaving? Is there a basement he's planned to lock me into?"

"I didn't say that. I don't think he has a dungeon or anything, no." She considers a moment, and her expression is serious for once, I'll give her that credit. "I'm just surprised we don't have a contingency plan, is what I'm saying."

"Just in case of the double cross," Bits says helpfully, before I can react. "Which we absolutely don't assume will happen, but—"

I laugh, and Bits stops and blinks at me. "Oh, is that all?" I ask airily.

"What?"

"Darlings, I've already thought of our best exit, we've just been so scattered for the last couple of days, we hadn't discussed it yet."

"Bristol we are literally connected at all—"

"There are some things one prefers to say face to face, wouldn't you say?"

Bits and Dolly look at each other, and then Dolly laughs. "Well okay then. Care to share with the rest of the class?"

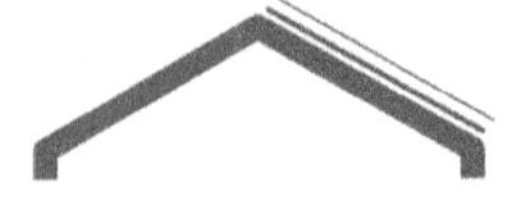

Chapter Fourteen

My wedding day dawns beautifully. It is neither too hot nor too cold, and the air and sky are clear, no clouds, no humidity. My breakfast arrives on a tray from the kitchen, to avoid the possibility of the groom seeing the bride ahead of time, and it is accompanied by a bouquet of beautiful, deep pink roses. No note; I can imagine Rafe wavering over that decision. Knowing what this day is supposed to be like, but also knowing the nature of our agreement.

"Tell me I was just in a fugue state when you took care of the flowers and stuff," Dolly says. "Because I don't remember it, but also can't imagine you forgetting."

"Yes, arrangements were made," I say. "You can't possibly be nervous? Honestly, Dolly."

"Just don't want anything to go wrong on your special day," she grins.

I prepare with care, of course. The dress is perfect, just as expected, though also what a relief due to the rush job. For my something new, I wear a perfume that I bought on one of my outings, honeysuckle and sandalwood. For my something old, I have the Sutter jewels, retrieved from the family bank vault and housed in a padded blue velvet case. For my something borrowed, I have Paisley's combs, though it is with mixed feelings that I slide them into my hair. It would be suiting for the Greek tragedy of her personal narrative, should they turn out to be poisoned, and I scratch my scalp with them and perish here in the cheery sunlight streaming through the window. I also have a pearl bracelet from Rosalie that I wear on the wrist opposite from my usual bracelets. And finally, my something blue is a nice pair of shoes that I can wear all day and dance in as necessary; the cowboy boots did seem as though they would be too much, on further reflection.

Rosalie knocks on the suite door when it's time to get in the limo and go to the church, and Bits lets her in. "Rosalie, darling, I'm so glad you're here," I say, giving her a quick hug. "Could you help me with my veil? The girls are indispensable, but this sort of thing..."

"Of course I can! You look amazing, wow."

"Thank you." We smile at each other in the mirror once the veil is settled. "And I love that dress."

"Thank you! I don't remember when I bought it, but I'd never worn it even once, and thought it was as good as any for maid of honor! I've never been anybody's maid of honor before."

"Not even Paisley?"

"No, she had her sister." Rosalie's smile falters just a little and I take one of her hands and give it a squeeze.

"I'm so sorry, I shouldn't have brought her up! Forget that I did."

"It's okay! I shouldn't be making you feel bad on your wedding day!" We both laugh, and the tension dissipates. "You don't think she might..."

"Show up to the wedding? I will say, Darlene wishes she would."

"I think she knows that." We laugh again.

"Are you riding with me in the limo, to the church?"

"I hope so! I told Paul I was, so he's already there by now."

I check the time. "I do think we are ready, and that now is the perfect time to go."

The church is one that the Sutters helped historically to build, and has weathered many years and many storms. It isn't ostentatious, but it isn't really a utilitarian settlement church either, it's mostly wood with some stone. I imagine the trees that they used were very

very old indeed, maybe some of the first trees cut down by colonists who came in. I allow Rosalie to get out first, and she goes inside to make sure everybody's in their proper places. Bits and Dolly came in the other car, and already checked to make sure, security wise, things were how we wanted.

//Will isn't here, if you were wondering// Bits says after Rosalie closes the limo door and walks inside.

"I was, thank you," I say quietly. The limo driver is unlikely to pay me any mind, but there isn't any sense in drawing undue attention.

//Or Paisley// Dolly says, with true disappointment in her voice.

"I'm so sorry, darling."

//I'll live. And so will she.//

Rosalie comes back to the church steps and waves at me, and I step out of the limo. One of the event people from the church comes out behind her, holding her bouquet and mine.

"Thank you so much," I say.

"You're welcome. Everything is ready for you, should I signal them to start?"

"Yes, please."

Rosalie and I smile at each other, and at the swell of organ music, she walks in ahead of me. We've truncated the process of coming down the aisle, as nobody is giving me away, and we know no small children about, so no flower girl or ring bearer. Just my maid of honor, and then myself. My groom and his best man already wait at the altar, with the judge, who is also the pastor here, which was an unusual and interesting thing for me to learn. When one hears judge, one does not think of a church wedding, and yet, here we are.

Rafe and Gabe are both grinning widely, and the faces of everybody as they turn to watch me walk up the aisle are so happy. Some bemused, but in general happy. I've met most of them by this point, through the whirlwind days of our supposed engagement. At the front is a wheelchair, and I meet eyes with Great-Aunt Gertrude at last, though ever so briefly. I can see how Paisley would have thought she was so formidable, and I regret her recent ill health. It would have been ever so interesting, getting to know her at least a little bit. As it is, I pause very briefly, and she very obviously looks me up and down, her lips pursed. Then she looks at my face, I raise an eyebrow, and she nods just slightly. I continue to the altar, and hand my bouquet off to Rosalie as Rafe steps over to take my hands, and the judge begins.

It is surreal, to be at a real wedding that you know in your heart is a fake wedding, to see all the expectant friends and family gathered, to have all of the trappings of a real wedding. What a delightful, delicious secret that we have. Though of course there is the final pièce de résistance, and when the judge, as rote, says, "And if there is anybody present who thinks that this couple should not be married, would they please—" a voice rings out from somewhere in the assembly.

"Me! I object!"

There are actual gasps, and I'm thankful for both the veil and the foreknowledge, that my reaction is both obscured and also I can take care to school my face into one of shock rather than amusement as we turn to face our objector. Lorraine, my oldest partner in crime, standing boldly amongst the seated guests.

Rafe, of course, was unprepared, and he gapes at her. I see again the flicker of recognition in his face that he had when he first approached me at the party that night, and I know now that Lorraine was at the local rodeo when he had his last, worst, accident. Did he see her in the crowd there, before his injury? It's possible. Will it make a good story? It absolutely will.

"And who are you?" the judge asks, a little grumpily. I don't think anybody actually objects at weddings, nowadays. I imagine it used to be quite the issue in the olden days. Or maybe it was a strange convention then as well, to ask. Some social rule about asking a question that you expect by rote to be refused, that everybody is party to.

"This woman isn't who she says she is!" She advances to the aisle. "I don't think she's intended any harm, but she's misrepresented herself."

Rafe tears his eyes from her to look at me, questioning, desperately confused. "She's the one you were looking for, the night we met," I say, firmly and carefully. He's a sweet man who deserves happiness, and Lorraine is my oldest friend, and deserves to be lifted out of the gutter. She's enough like me that, if he was genuinely as enamored as he thought he was, perhaps his affections will transfer. Perhaps not. But what a story this makes.

"Is she?" he asks, breathless, as though he can't believe it. Either he's a quick study, or all of my guesses have been correct. He turns to her, walks down off of the altar to look at her face. "She is," he says, louder and in a more sure tone. A part of me wishes that Will *was* here, in order to witness this ridiculous, over the top scene, which was so carefully crafted.

"What?" Rosalie says behind me, and I glance at her guileless face. She's in complete disbelief.

There's some indistinct whispering in the pews, and Lorraine walks up the aisle and Rafe walks down, and they meet part way. They speak to one another quietly for a few moments, and then he shakes his head and laughs. I can still see Lorraine's face, and she's smiling. He takes her hand and looks around the church, and then looks up at me. "Madison, I think you're right. I think I got so focused on some things that we made a mistake," he says.

"I do think it seems that way, yes," I say. Gabe, still across the altar from me, laughs.

"Well now what?" he asks. "What do you say, judge, can we just change the names on the marriage license or what?" Bless him. I look at Rafe, and then turn to the judge, whose face I would mostly describe as impatient.

"Yes, is that possible?" I ask.

He looks at his watch and sighs. He must have plans right after the ceremony that he needs to get away to. "There's no waiting period here between having a marriage license and the ceremony, so while we won't cross the names off, we can get a new one issued and proceed."

"Is that what you want?" Rafe asks Lorraine, and she smiles and nods, as though she's so overcome that she can't really speak.

"I'll make a call," the judge says, and walks off.

"Madison what...what just happened?" Rosalie asks, barely touching my elbow with the tips of her fingers. She seems quite shaken, actually, and I am sorry that I've been so disruptive to her little world. Though maybe, once all has settled, things will have worked out for the better.

"In a nutshell, I'd say that what happened was love at first sight, except Lorraine is who Rafe saw first." She nods, because she thinks that's what I've expected of her, but I'm not certain she quite grasps the story just yet.

It's then that I think to look at Great-Aunt Gertrude; she's of advanced age and has been in poor health lately, I do hope that this hasn't been too much of a shock for her. But she has a look on her face that is something like delight, as if this is the most fun she's seen or had in quite a long time. She sees me looking at her, makes eye contact, and then her eyes drop, very pointedly, to the Sutter jewels around my neck. I'd be lying if I said I hadn't considered making off with them, but their assessed value is such that it is far more important to me to pull off this social situation. The payment for that, and what Dolly purloined from Paisley's safe, are more than enough.

"Lorraine!" I call, not shouting, but pitched to cut through the murmur of the crowd. She turns to me immediately, and I beckon to her. She says something to Rafe, who bends his head to her to listen, and then sneaks a kiss. She's flushed quite prettily when she comes over to me. "I'm wearing the Sutter jewels," I say to her, and her eyes widen with the realization.

"Oh! Well we should…"

"Let's just go to the ladies room, and swap what we need to," I say. "Your dress is quite nice, but not a wedding dress." No matter her financial situation, Lorraine has always had a fantastic eye for fashion, and has also been handy with a needle. The dress is grass green, with an a-line skirt and ruched bodice. Maybe better suited for a cookout than a church wedding. We trade dresses, giggling a little at the thrill, and at how ridiculous this all is. And how familiar, like when we used to cram into a dressing room together.

"Am I really getting married to R.J. Sutter?" she asks, as I settle her veil and slide Paisley's combs into her hair. I pull the engagement ring off my finger, and hand it to her.

"You really are," I say. "If it's what you want."

She nods, taking the earrings from me, and turning around so I can clasp the necklace. "It is what I want. I don't really know when I got interested in rodeos, and when I started watching, but when I told you that I moved here because I could be poor anywhere, he was part of the reason. I just never dreamed…" She trails off, looking at herself in the mirror.

"You look beautiful," I say.

"You're not going to forget me this time, are you?" she asks, still looking at herself in the mirror.

"I already promised that I would not."

"You promise a lot of things," she says, and we both laugh.

"I confess, I've been caught."

There's a knock at the door, but Dolly doesn't wait for us to answer. "Are you about ready? The judge's clerk or whoever just got here and needs to see IDs and stuff. No blood test at least."

"We'll be out directly," I say.

"I'll tell 'em."

"Do you want my shoes?" I ask Lorraine. "I can't remember, are we the same size there as well?"

Lorraine looks at me critically. "We are, and yes, I'd better take them. Mine are new too, and that blue doesn't go with that dress anyway."

And with that, we are ready, and exit the ladies' room once more. Almost immediately, Lorraine is whisked away to Rafe's side, and embroiled in paperwork and general activity; most of the guests have remained seated or at least amongst the pews, though they're all speaking in full voice, trying to make sense of everything. Rafe looks up one last time, and I blow him a kiss before I slip out the door and walk to the car.

"You've made sure to pack everything?" I ask, even though we all worked together in the suite to do so the night before.

"Of course we did," Dolly says, sliding her sunglasses on and pulling away down the church drive.

"And Bits—"

"I started making sure you'd be a surveillance ghost from the second we got here," she says.

"So sorry to be so bossy, darlings," I say, settling back into the seat.

"Nah, it's fine, you're coming down from being the lady of the house," Dolly says. "We're lucky you didn't pull this with a prince or something."

"Maybe next time," Bits says.

Epilogue

It is not raining when Will next opens his motel door to me. I do not know who he was expecting to be here, but he's unable to hide his surprise when he sees me. "You wanted to see me before I left town," I say, brushing past him into the room.

"I did," he says. He looks pointedly at my bare hands. "The romance didn't work out?"

"It did," I say. "Just not for me."

"You're unbelievable."

"I've been told." His belongings are packed; the comb and things are no longer on the bureau, and his suitcase and briefcase are on the made bed. "I'm surprised you didn't try to make the wedding."

"I wasn't authorized," he says with a frown in his voice. "This was ruled not a credible sighting. It seems Bits does unbelievable work."

"I would agree with that, yes, she does. And after all, one blonde does look very much like another." I smile at him in the mirror and reach into my purse for my lipstick.

He moves to me quickly, catching me by the wrist. "We won't be kissing goodbye this time," he says. Regardless of what was said between us last time, he is reaching for his handcuffs.

Dolly says, if somebody has hold of you like this, to try and touch elbows. I do, opening his hand, and when I reach into my purse next, I pull out a bottle of perfume.

"I'm disappointed you'd think I would perform the same stunt twice," I say, smiling as I remove the cap.

"You understand my caution," he says. He's standing between me and the door, and still thinks he has the upper hand.

"Of course I do," I say, and spray him in the face with Dolly's surplus pepper spray. Then I scoop up his briefcase and step briskly over him to leave the room before I feel the effects of the spray too badly myself.

Run With the Hunted 5: Insert Coin to Play

Chapter One

"How long should this take?" Dolly asks after her second cigarette and I shrug. Bristol's entering our team in the game while Dolly and I wait in the parking lot, Dolly sitting on the hood of the car and smoking, me drinking my first iced coffee of the day or my final iced coffee of the night. I didn't mean to not sleep, it's just how it happened.

We weren't all in the same city when I floated the idea of the game for our next job, and after we got her from the airport, I had to make sure Bristol was prepared for the entry challenge. And then we had to make sure equipment we needed was ready to be packed in the car. Could some of it have been done this morning? Yeah but I was already awake.

"I'm not worried yet." After all, Bristol could just be chatting with and charming people, entry already secured. She likes socializing, and even though she prefers to be a little snobby, she likes to be able to talk to anybody. So practice is practice.

"Okay but when will you be worried? Can you set a timer or something?" She grins at me and I laugh.

"Nobody in there is going to have a gun or anything but the casino guards," I say. "And not all of them will."

"Yeah that's true. Hey, maybe I'm lookin' at this wrong, and it's the nerds I should be concerned about. They've never talked to anybody like Bristol, she'll eat them alive."

"That might be true." Granted, a lot of people haven't talked to anybody like Bristol. It's part of how she's so effective.

While I'm not technically banned from entering this game, it seemed like a good call to let Bristol be our point of entry instead, just in case. This isn't life or death. We don't even really need the money. A lot of games like this don't even *have* a prize, but in this case, the prizes are lucrative (cash, crypto wallet) and fun (a motor-cycle referencing a classic manga/anime that's so respected that there have been few remakes though many dreams, with a matching jack-et) and interesting (a 20th century IBM computer chip.) And it'd be nice to have a payday where we aren't necessarily risking our lives or breaking the law.

Not that breaking the law bothers us much, obviously, or we wouldn't keep doing what we do.

Due to the nature of the setup, I didn't put a wire or camera on Bristol before she went in. She even took out her earbud. If a thing like that was discovered, she'd be accused of cheating and barred. We don't even know what the entry challenge is, beyond the roll of ac-tual physical quarters that gets you through the door. If it's a puzzle or riddle or game or what. The challenges vary throughout the game itself, and the gamerunners aren't totally the same from year to year, adding some newer winners, dropping some past winners. Just the way these kinds of games work.

The automatic doors woosh open, and Bristol click-clacks out. I told her there might be locations in the game that she won't want to be in a dress and heels for, but she told me she'll do a costume change if and when it comes to that. We've seen her run in heels, we know she can, but she might not want to crawl in a faux dungeon dressed like that. Well. She doesn't want to crawl in a faux dungeon at all, but the game is the game.

"How'd it go?" Dolly asks, hopping off the car.

"They were both so sweet," Bristol says, with a particularly sharp smile. "And the entry test was a simple little logic puzzle that I just breezed through, thanks to your tutelage, Bits." She hands me a manila envelope. "One of them gave me his number in case we 'ran into any problems,' which I think perhaps he was not supposed to do. He said his name is *Ant*."

"No, I don't think so." He also wouldn't have given me or Dolly his number, so sending Bristol was the right call either way. I get in the back of the car and open the envelope, sliding out its contents. The welcome letter isn't anything to be concerned with at a glance, but I'll look at it under different lights later, just to be sure. We've got a team AR badge which is also a little GPS/RFID tag so that the gamerunners can keep track of the players, both for safety and planning. I'll look at it more closely later, but from the looks of it, it's factory, hasn't been popped open or anything. There's a cheap cell phone, for similar reasons, I assume. The gamerunners can always call or text a team, and the only number saved in the phone is labeled The Game. There's also, very generous of them I think, a rudimentary flatpack of lock picks, a utility knife, and a game-branded plastic case of band aids.

And, finally, a smaller manila envelope that points us at the first location. "I thought you were joking about the mineshaft thing," Dolly says, reading over my shoulder.

"I sent you the article about that one game." Years and years ago, and with every game anybody has run thereafter being even more careful and safety-aware, but still. It really sticks out in the narrative.

"Yeah I didn't read it."

"That figures." I though about 50/50 that she would. "Anyway this one is a cave so that they can pretend it's a dungeon crawl. Or that this portion is a dungeon crawl. So not a mine, technically. I guess." Dolly nods, but from her face, she doesn't really know what I mean by this usage of dungeon crawl.

"Shall we, darlings?" Bristol asks, settling herself in the front passenger seat. "Much as I love bickering in parking lots."

"It's almost its own sport," Dolly says, sliding into the driver's seat and starting the car. "Definitely a pastime."

"We're practically specialists by this point," I add, pulling up my VR headset. I want to scout the location and get a sense of the history of it, and I want to see if anybody else playing has posted on social media yet. They probably *shouldn't*, it's better for security, both to keep other players honest and also to prevent outside interference. But it doesn't mean that they *don't*, and during last year's game, or one of last year's games, I tracked the players pretty easily using that. It wasn't this duo's game.

The gussied up cave that we're going to is one that the gamerunners, or the Incorporated Entity of this Game™, bought years ago, and went through extensively, shoring things up and leveling things out and ensuring there were no horrible drops or too tight squeezes or way for it to unexpectedly flood. There are a couple of pictures online from past players, and I circle around local municipal websites until I find the one that it falls under the jurisdiction of, and then root around for the blueprints and permits that would be on file for the kind of work that the game's site describes in the most circumspect of ways. Is having that kind of information on a location cheating? I don't think so, and I don't think the rules speak against it anyway. Maybe it just takes some of the fun out of it.

It's listed as a theme attraction now, like it's part of a park with rides, which is kind of funny. It's got lots of ventilation, it's been checked over for hazardous materials, and is in general as safe as a short network of tunnels in the ground can be made to be. They aren't well lit, of course, but it'd be silly to expect that. Everybody who has a phone has a flashlight, anyway. Has for decades.

"So what do we think the first puzzle'll be?" Dolly asks while I'm doing this.

"Probably we'll have to find and open a locked chest," I say. That's one thing that past players did stick with: none of them posted any of the puzzles they found and solved online, or at least not in unsecured channels.

"Makes sense." I think all of us can lockpick pretty well by this point. Bristol is a quick study in nearly everything. "And you said we won't know how many teams there are?"

"Well not officially, during the game."

"Meaning..."

"Well they gave us this GPS tag which means every team has a GPS tag."

"Uh-huh?" Dolly glances at me over her shoulder as she backs out of the parking spot.

"Which means I can see if I can follow the signal back and then chase who else they're tracing."

"Does it matter, how many other teams there are?" Bristol asks.

"Not particularly." I have a look at our gametag, just with my eyeballs, and then I scan it. It's for both safety tracking and so that it can give updates about how far ahead anybody is, who's gaining on who, to ratchet the tension and competitive spirit, via an app on the provided phone. And it has the team's name. I thought they'd number or color us, but no, there's a name here. If I wanted to, I'm pretty sure it wouldn't take me long to figure out how to nudge our locations, but I don't want to. Yet, anyway. Instead, I mess around until I essentially find the lines of code that broadcast, and then chase that to the game's mainframe, which seems to be an actual mainframe and not just, I don't know, a laptop. A dedicated smartphone. Another thing to look into later.

They've got good security, it would be embarrassing if they didn't. They aren't unfamiliar with the kinds of device vulnerabilities that people (read: people like me, or people like the game participants, I assume) love to exploit when it comes to things like this, and internet of things devices, and the like. I set a dictionary hack to run in the background, and also work out a bit of code to notice when other devices of this type ping home. Then I become aware of Dolly chanting my name and I push my headset up.

"Bits Bits Bits Bits...oh okay."

"Dolly, one sec. Bristol, did they ask you to name the team?"

She smiles, slow and pleased. "They *did*, darling, and we hadn't discussed it ahead of time."

"That's true we didn't."

"Why, what'd she call us?" Dolly asks in a tone of mock horror.

"The Fashion Police."

Dolly brays a laugh. "Seriously?"

"I thought it was a fine name," Bristol says primly. "If we knew we were going to have to come up with a name..."

"No, no, it's fine." Dolly looks back at me. "Right?"

"Yeah, I don't care. It is funny." There was something else. "You were trying to get my attention?"

"Yeah, do you want food or should I just drive?"

"Just drive, I'm going to try and sleep. If you do a drive thru get me something that'll still be okay when I wake up."

"Roger that," Dolly says, sliding on sunglasses. I catch a glimpse of Bristol wrinkling her nose a little, as I lay down across the seats and pull my headset back down. It beats pretty much everything for blocking the light, even in the desert.

Chapter Two

Dolly wakes me up around noon, waving hot fresh french fries under my nose. "I tried to tell her not to, darling," Bristol says in a tone of amused defeat. "But she muttered something about smelling salts, which are not the same at all."

"Yeah but fries are salty, it's practically the same thing," Dolly says, laughing. I sit up and take the fries.

"I think I'm with Bristol on this one."

"Aw come on, Bitsy, did they or did they not work?"

"Not because of the *salt*." I check my programs; I'm not into the mainframe yet, but I did get a pingback on two other teams' game tags, another trio, and also a group of five. On the map, we're only a few miles away from the first location, at an improbable drive thru that used to be a rollerskate drive-in in the nineteen sixties, a non-chain called The Oasis.

"Everybody's against me," she says dramatically, and Bristol purses her lips and looks at the nearby cars to see if anybody is paying attention to us, I guess.

"Honestly, Dolly..."

"Bristles, you need to have some *fun*, okay? We're playing a *game.* Thing." She looks at me.

"It's a game," I mumble around a mouthful of fries.

Bristol sighs, maybe trying to decide which thing to hone in on. Getting Dolly to not call her 'Bristles' has been a losing endeavor, but it's probably the least bothersome of nicknames she could've picked. "You behave as though I never have fun ever," she finally says.

"I mean, no, but yes."

"Dolly, we all just have different kinds of fun," I say.

"With some overlap," she says.

"Okay, when's the last time you suggested something that you thought Bristol would have fun doing?"

She hands a milkshake back to me, but she does look like she's thinking. Bristol looks *very* amused, but waits. I stab a straw into the milkshake.

"We met at that museum!" Dolly says after a while.

"That was my idea," I say, and Bristol lets a smile slowly spread.

"Oh yeah, fair."

"Take your time," Bristol says and Dolly sticks her tongue out.

"Okay fine, we stole that Christmas tree and then went to Marquis' place to make up for—"

"Yes, what a *good* example," Bristol says, clasping her hands together. "What a lovely time that was."

"Best Christmas ever," Dolly agrees. "Are we ready? Bits, you want a burger or anything?"

"No, not right now. Let's go." There aren't many cars, even in the parking lot, and there's nobody around us for miles and miles even on the highway. And then we leave the highway for the first challenge location.

"So we should all three go in, right? Or just two of us?" Dolly asks, standing with her door hanging open. "Maybe we don't want to leave the vehicle. Or all be underground."

"I'll wait with the car," Bristol says. "Because I most certainly don't want to crawl underground if I don't need to."

"Fair enough." Dolly throws her the keys and throws me an I-told-you-so look.

"Vehicle sabotage is unlikely, even if somebody was around," I say. "In addition to being against the rules, it just isn't the tone of the game."

"You said you didn't know who's playin' yet."

"Yeah, that's true, but we're unlikely to be up against my black hat nemesis who can't wait to win by any means necessary."

"Oh, you got one of those?" Dolly's tone is one of idle curiosity, but her eyes sharpen. I can feel Bristol's studied disinterest but absolute focus. "We gonna learn about the seedy underbelly of the hackersphere on this particular road trip?"

"No, I don't have one of those, I was making it up for emphasis."

Dolly waves her hands. "You can't tell me that you hackers don't have any kinds of rivalries going on. I'm sure somebody'd love a chance to take you down a peg."

I blink at her. "Well yes, probably, but my code is all over the place. They wouldn't have to resort to real life situations."

Bristol laughs. "Goodness, do you mean to say that you don't even know who might want to target you, in such an event? Bits, you are a marvel."

I consider possible replies to that statement. "Thanks."

"Well okay, we're burnin' daylight," Dolly says, and heads for the trailhead. I don't bother reminding her that it was her delay, not anybody else's. "You really think these nerds'll use an actual treasure chest in here?" she asks when I catch up.

"I think I'll be disappointed if they don't." I look at the map. "Unless we're misunderstanding what kind of a dungeon they're talking about, and instead it's more like—"

"You know, we've gone a long time without discussing that kind of thing, and it might just be better that way," Dolly says thoughtfully. We keep walking, and then look at each other after a minute and snicker.

"You're probably right though." I don't want to talk about sex dungeons with Dolly. Or anybody, actually. And if it *was* a sex dungeon, we wouldn't be heading underground in the desert, we'd be playing elevator games in the middle of a city. Las Vegas was right there.

They've got a ye olde mineshaft looking entry, but it has a door instead of just being an open hole into the ground, and when Dolly pulls the handle it's locked. Of course it's locked. "Does our thingie unlock it?" she asks, even as she's swiping the badge. I'm about to say no, probably not, but the light on the door goes from red to green and Dolly pulls the door open. "Lookit, I'm a puzzlemaster too."

"See, I knew we'd all pull our weight," I say, and she gestures me ahead of her.

From the door, I almost expected a linoleum floored, fluorescent-lit hallway, but it is a dark tunnel. Dolly's got her flashlight out and on before I do. "Keep your hands free long as you can," she says.

"Okay?" I say, because it does make sense but also I want to know Dolly's reasoning.

"It's a dungeon, right? These nerds—" and then I hear an almost subaudible click as she grabs my shoulder. What looks like a spiky metal ball on a chain releases from the ceiling up by the wall and swings across the tunnel, and when it finishes its arc on the other side, one comes down from there too, and they both swing for a while before stopping. "See?"

"I think they're probably foam," I say. "But yeah, you're right. Obviously." I crouch down and find the place on the floor that triggered the trap, and then fiddle with the settings in my contacts until I find a spectrum of light that can see whatever otherwise invisibly lights up their sensors.

"Maybe they bought the setpieces from American Gladiators or something." The spiky balls have come to a swaying halt in the middle of the tunnel, and Dolly prods at one.

"That show's probably due for a revival again soon, right?" I ask as we move past. I look at the floors but also the walls; they probably won't have the same kind of trigger twice in a row.

"Yeah, hopefully. It's currently an untapped market."

"It might be unfair for you to audition for a thing like that."

"It would *absolutely* be unfair for me to audition for a thing like that," she laughs. "Completely. It'd be a Bristol level fireworks show."

"It's fun to swap roles sometimes," I mutter, stopping to look at a glowing spot on the ceiling up ahead. "Can you see that?"

"I don't think we're ever gonna have *you*...wait you mean...no see what?"

"Okay just wondered." I look at the ground under the spot on the ceiling.

"Would it be in poor taste if they drop us in a hole after what you told me about that historic game?" Dolly drawls. She sounds like she's turned around and looked back behind us.

"Yeah." I dig in my pockets for a laser pointer, pull out a red one first, consider, keep looking until I find my green one instead. I go a couple of steps closer for the better angle, and then flick my laser beam across the point in the ceiling. It stops glowing, and the whole place gets quieter; I hadn't realized that there'd been an ambient sound, maybe of running water, until it was gone. I think all of us have a certain level of static in our hearing at all times. Well, maybe not Bristol. Dolly probably definitely has tinnitus, I can't remember if we've ever talked about it. Or maybe she's never not had tinnitus and didn't realize. "Okay."

"What the fuck was that?"

"A water hazard? Maybe?" The noise doesn't restart, and we walk to the spot, and then through it, with no ill effects. I wonder if we're going to have to walk back through here, or if the tunnels will loop and drop us back at the entrance.

She laughs. "Hey wouldn't it be funny if one of the puzzles was just mini golf?"

"Be careful what you wish for. That'll be the kind of thing that Bristol just beats our pants off at."

"I dunno, I still think that'd be fun *and* funny. Don't you like mini golf?" We come to a fork in the tunnels, and she shines her flashlight one way, and then the other. "Flip a coin?"

"Sure, let me get out my lucky quarter," I say.

"The ecig machine gave me change in gold dollars for some reason. I guess it's kind of fitting here?" She gets one out, balances it on her thumb. I don't ask what ecig machine, it was probably when I was asleep. She had normal cigarettes this morning.

"Uh, heads left, tails right," I say, and she flips, catches it, slaps it on the back of her hand.

"That's heads but who *is* that?" Dolly hands it to me.

"Ida B. Wells?" She shrugs. "Civil rights activist and journalist."

"Oh cool." The left tunnel leads us down further, the air getting cooler and damper. "Hey do you think—" and then there's a click and the floor crumbles away and turns into a slide, shooting us down another hundred feet or so, the walls smooth, nothing to grab onto to slow our momentum. Then there's a short drop, just limbs flailing in the air, and we hit the ground, Dolly's elbow in my ribs, my knee in her back. Then her flashlight clunks down next to us, beam shining on a wooden treasure chest, a web of infrared beams around it.

"Are you okay?" I ask, rolling off of her and getting up. I feel okay, just startled. One of my elbows stings, and I brush some gravel out of it. She pops up too, grabs the flashlight. "I'm okay."

"Yeah, shit, that'll wake you up." She takes a step towards the box and stops. "Okay now what."

"Now I figure out how to disable the security on the box and we open the box."

"What's it gonna do? Shoot us with foam darts? Open spider vents on us? Fill the room with water and then drain us back out at the entrance?"

"We're lower than the entrance."

"I'm sure science could find a way."

"I know your point is that those are mostly funny, nonlethal things, but I do want to figure out the security."

I hear her shrug. "Suit yourself. Do you care if I smoke?"

"Ecig should be fine, sure." I don't know what it could hurt, it's water vapor in an already damp environment, and the vapor is unlikely to interact with the box anyway. The box itself doesn't look locked, so the idea is that somebody will reach unsuspecting through the security grid and then...what? I walk around it at a respectful distance, and finally in the back corner, almost against the wall, I can see where the dirt is disturbed just a little bit. I crouch down and blow on it a little, clearing a view of the power supply. I blow on it again, and there's the infrared transmitter. Or, one of the transmitters. I sit back on my heels and squint; at this angle, there's kind of a too-smooth square of dirt around the chest, that you also aren't supposed to notice, in your focus on the goal. Low-level electrical shock? Maybe? It would really be dampened by the soles of most shoes, though.

This trap isn't online in any way, which is interesting. Though I guess they wanted to make sure nobody caught it by seeing stray code in the air. The gamerunners would know to come reset it based on entry and exit of players. Wire cutters would be super simple. Or, no, I'll splice into the microcontroller, it won't take me long to just alter the pattern long enough to access the chest, then put it back how we found it, leaving the room still set, to all appearances. That would be nicer than making them rewire it, anyway.

I unroll my likeliest set of tools and get on my belly near the base of the thing. Dolly smokes her ecigarette and shifts her weight once in a while, but she's strangely good at waiting. I guess that comes from the sniper training. Or programming.

I've got a juiced up smartphone that's a good enough microcomputer, and after a while I've got things connected and figured out and peel the grid down off the box. "Okay."

"Bits, everything you just did is invisible. It's like the most complicated mime act."

"Oh yeah, sorry. There's an infrared grid that I think will light the floor up with a certain amount of voltage. But that's rerouted for right this second."

She exhales, putting her ecigarette away. "Yeah what's a little light electrocution amongst friends."

"You and Nicolai had a taser duel."

"Exactly." She comes over and opens the box, peers inside. I wonder what's going on with her flashlight, if both her hands are full, but it's hooked onto the front of her utility vest somehow. "It's a lunchbox?"

"There's a joke involved, I'm sure. Just grab it, and we'll figure out the next location back at the car."

"Copy that." She doesn't pick it up by the handle, though, she reaches in with both hands and pulls it out, keeping it level. She glances down at me. "Just in case."

"I wasn't going to say anything. Is there anything else in the box?"

"Not that I can see." Hmm, good point. I stand up and have a peek myself but no, nothing. No message on the inside of the lid, no hidden compartment inside.

"Okay, we're good I guess." I kneel down again and reset the grid, then carefully remove my connectors. You can see the slightly brighter marks, if you look closely, but all in all, not damagingly intrusive. I even scuff the dirt back into the right place. "Now what?"

"Judging from where the vapor went, the exit's over there," Dolly says with a jerk of her chin. I lead the way and we come to what seems like a rock face, but when I run my fingers along it, I can feel the thrum of electricity. Some patience and vectoring, and I find the catch that triggers the door to slide open, and we walk up what had been the righthand passage, and then walk out of the place, remembering to trick the laser on that one trap a second time.

Outside, Bristol's in the car with all of the windows open, flicking through one of her glossy magazines while talking on the phone. When she looks up and sees us coming, she says "Here they are, Marquis darling, I'm going to let you go. Yes, I did enjoy catching up. Yes, I *do* hope to see you next month in Venice."

"Glad you weren't too worried," Dolly says. She starts to put the lunchbox on the hood of the car then stops, looks around, and picks a nearby boulder instead.

"It probably isn't a bomb," I say.

"Can't be too careful."

"Is that a princess lunchbox?" Bristol asks, getting out of the car. "What happened? You're both absolutely covered in dirt! Like you were—"

"In a cave?" Dolly asks, smirking, and Bristol laughs.

"Just so."

"Super scandalous for the fashion police, right? Like, they'll come and take our badges away if—"

"No, the oversight for the fashion police doesn't issue physical badges," Bristol says smoothly, winking at me. "They can disable them remotely."

"Well I guess you told me, princess."

Chapter Three

I t *is* a princess lunchbox, not any specific character who falls under copyright, probably from a five dollar store or something. Inside is a half gallon sized, resealable silicon bag like you'd have for kitchen stuff, and inside of *that* is a notecard with the clue to the next location. I guess that water hazard can get out of control.

I check on my running code; two more teams, both also trios. The progress bar on the mainframe is almost full, but that can be misleading, that just means it thinks that it's getting close to what the password is, based on how many characters it thinks the password is (seventeen) and how much time has elapsed (five hours.) There can be one or more further layers of security that set me back, there could be two-factor authentication to try and figure out, the list goes on. I do know that people tend not to use biometric security, because it still isn't protected by the Fourth Amendment and is unlikely to be in our lifetime.

"Well okay, so what does this mean?" Dolly asks, handing the card to me. "Riddles aren't my thing."

"Far from the Magic Kingdom and too late for Burning Man, there's still enchantment to be found in the desert," I read out loud. "I don't know. There's a lot of desert. Maybe—"

"Honestly, girls, they mean the Seven Magic Mountains art installation." Dolly looks at her blankly, so she's got that part covered, and I look it up online instead and plot the route. Back the way we came, of course, and then further south still.

"See, Bristles, you've got *culture*, I've always said that we appreciate that about you."

"Have you?" Bristol smiles one of her particular smiles, but she is clearly pleased. If it wasn't weird I'd number and label them sometime, because a certain array of her smiles are practiced and calculated.

"Well not when you can hear me, that's not how that kind of compliment works."

"Of course not," Bristol says, still smiling. "Shall we, then? And we need to stop at a package pickup, I ordered more sunscreen. Somehow, I'd wildly underestimated how much I thought we would need."

"We?" I ask.

"If we're going to be driving around together solving riddles for an indeterminate amount of time while slathered in sufficient amounts of sunscreen, yes no matter how tan you are already hush Dolly, you will not do so while smelling like drugstore no-name brands. So yes. We." Dolly snaps her mouth shut. That might've been the first time Bristol has ever commented on either of our skin tones. Bristol looks at her, and then at me. "Does that seem fair?"

"I don't mind, I was just surprised." I could know how much Bristol's sunscreen costs in thirty seconds, but it's fun to imagine how much instead. Thirty dollars a tube? Or whatever the containment is. Fifty?

"Well let's hit the road then. This is a race too, isn't it? Plus we have to feed Bits."

"I had fries?"

"Yeah but usin' all that brain power needs more calories."

"Dolly, if you're hungry again you can just say so," Bristol says. "And we'll buy more water too."

"Sure thing, queen of the desert." For all their bickering, I think I've only seen Dolly actually mad at Bristol one time, and right now, we aren't even close. This is just recreational, and apparently how they communicate best.

WE GO THROUGH THE OASIS again, and again miss out on the rollerskating waitstaff experience, but their fries are really good, so I'm happy for the repeat. Bristol less so, but she's had lots of opportunity to add snacks that she deems acceptable to her sunscreen order. It's while we're driving to that package pickup location that she suddenly says, with suspicion, "How will we be arranging accommodations for the night, with all this bouncing about? We don't even know where we'll go after the installation."

"Well that's the thing about these kinds of events," I say carefully. "They're not officially serial all-nighters, that can't really be safely condoned, but most of the time nobody like, gets rooms or anything."

Dolly keeps quiet, checking me in the mirror occasionally, containing her smirk, while Bristol mulls this over. "And how long did last year's event run?"

I already know, but take a little bit of time, like I'm looking it up. "The winning team finished in 53 hours and change, and the final team finished in 78 hours."

"I see."

"Teams still bother to finish, after the first three?" Dolly asks.

"Well yeah. Wouldn't you?" I don't really understand the question. Yes, winning and doing well are important, but sometimes when you start a thing, you just have to finish the thing.

"Yeah, I guess I would. Sometimes you just gotta see something through to the bitter end." We laugh, even though it isn't really quite a joke, I don't think. She looks over at Bristol. "Just gotta add dry shampoo to your order, I guess." Bristol gives the slightest of shudders.

THE PACKAGE PICKUP location is an unstaffed, multi-purpose rest stop, a bank of car chargers facing a bank of vending machines and restrooms, asphalt in between, locked delivery boxes at the far end.

"Want to make bets on how long she'll last without stopping for a hotel or anything?" Dolly asks when I walk out of the bathroom. She's studying the canned coffee machine, already holding a snack bag.

"No. Bristol always finds a way to rise to an occasion."

"Maybe you're right." She considers, nodding, then pushes a couple of buttons on the machine and a coffee kachunks out for her. "We've still got laws about labeling right?" She shows me the can; Nitro Himalayan™ butter* coffee.

"Much as they've ever worked, yeah. What's it say when you chase the asterisk?" It's also weird enough to be tempting and I might as well try it, and she squints at the tiny writing on the can while I get my own.

"It's a plant-based butter, not authentically from yaks. Oh, *and* it's made with genetic engineering. That's a separate line, not the butter specifically."

"Ooh I love genetic engineering." I eye the QR code on the can until it scans and pops up all that info for me in AR, crisp and zoomable. Something about these cans almost always ends up weirdly overprinted, like they got sprayed twice just slightly offset, or somebody knocked the machine at just the wrong time. Maybe a hurricane passed over and the automated factory kept running because the wind didn't trip the sensors. Or the employees weren't allowed to leave.

"Right? It's our favorite." She pops the tab, waits a second while the nitro thing makes its noise, and then takes a swig, kind of tilts her head this way and that like Bristol at a wine tasting, and I laugh. "Well it's obviously not the real thing. Like really really obviously. But the nitro thing helps with the texture, I think?"

I pop the tab on my own and smell it. Smells like nitro and vegetable yak butter. "Have you had the real thing?"

"Yeah, haven't you?" She watches my face as I try it. The nitro and not-butter do combine to make that supposed-to-be-velvety texture but it also isn't quite correct.

"I've had what a cafe called bulletproof coffee, which amounted to the same thing. Plus I think it's normally tea that they use in—"

"Well yeah of course it is. But I've had the tea, is what I mean."

"In the Himalayas?" I only have the loosest of reckonings of Dolly's global travel. Bristol's, more so, because she'll talk about it in some detail with frequency. Dolly, you just get the occasional sporadic anecdote of taser duels and sturgeon fishing and cliff diving and now drinking Himalayan butter tea in the Himalayas.

"Yeah, one of my buddies was going to summit Everest and I went to see him off."

I take a moment to process that because again, one of Dolly's buddies could be any category of people from various job fields and locales. "Did he?"

"Did he what? Did he make it? Wow what a question. Yeah, he made it up. Back down off the mountain too, hardly anybody ever talks about that. That you gotta walk back down, after you summit Everest."

"You're right, they don't." I mean, they must. But I'm not into mountaineering, I've never seen even the most idle comment of coming back down off the mountain.

"Anyway he stuck around there and hooked up with one of those groups that does garbage runs, because people just fucking dump trash all over that mountain an' it's disgusting. There oughta be a law."

"Dolly, calling for laws? You feeling okay?" I drink more of my coffee and check out the snacks. One of the machines is ocean themed, weird choice for the middle of the desert or maybe not; dried shrimp, and squid, and seaweed snacks. Another one is cricket chips and corn chips, and cricket corn chips, and that's what Dolly's bag is from. Finally, there is a candy one, chocolate and fake chocolate and a surprising range of gummies. She keeps chattering about environmentalism of all things, and I get a bag of what claims to be up to* 100 gummy flavors but probably doesn't contain 100 total gummies so we'll see how that goes.

"What alarming things are you two getting?" Bristol asks.

"Do you like Himalayan butter beverages?" Dolly asks, holding out her can. Bristol looks at it, pursing her lips a little as she reads the label.

"Not in my experience, but thank you," she says.

"We're over here swishing our canned coffee for the bouquet and Bristol's all 'bestie, not even once,'" Dolly says to me in a confidential tone.

"I don't think they canned coffee with beans that Bristol would prefer," I say.

"Definitely not nitro canned coffee," Dolly says.

"Oh definitely not."

"Are you two quite through?" Bristol asks, but she's smiling. The curiosity has gotten the better of her, or it's something she's had before, and she's gotten a chocolate croissant from one machine and a bottle of milk tea from another. I saw her look at the sushi machine, but it very diligently has a date and time for when the contents were placed in the machine and the buttons are all dark; it wouldn't let you buy even if you wanted to.

Dolly chugs the rest of her coffee and tosses it into the recycle bin. "Yeah, let's get back on the road. We were waiting for you."

Bristol rolls her eyes. "Of course you were."

Chapter Four

While we're en route to the art installation, I do the VR experience to try and assess where I think the clue might be. It seems likely that it's in the retro museum tour headsets that are there for guests; it would be the least invasive thing that they could do. Interfering with the exhibit would be against the game's own rules, and probably laws too, if they were worried about that. I know that they're concerned with their rules, anyway.

According to the website, the installation hasn't always had headsets that visitors could use, in museum tour fashion, because it previously relied on smartphone apps. But thanks to a donor a few years back, they had them available now. According to the website, the installation has been maintained for many years beyond its original inception, and there's talk of leaving a virtual experience if it's ever physically dismantled. Bristol hasn't said if she's visited it before, but I don't think that's a necessary detail. The tour headsets will all look the same, or they won't. There will be an indeterminate number available, and we'll have to quickly get through them to get to the right one.

My phone vibrates; another team identified.

"Hey wouldn't it be funny if we were playin' against one of your nemeses or something," Dolly asks, as we pull into the parking area.

I blink at her. "One of my nemeses?"

"Yeah, isn't that a thing you nerds do? Have nemeses? Rivals? Competition?"

"Other than the competition we're in right now."

"Yeah." She parks, and exchanges a look with Bristol. "Nobody's coming to mind?"

"No. Are you hinting at something?" I look out the rearview window, in case somebody's standing there with a gun, wearing a t-shirt that says 'I'll get you, Bits!' but nobody's there. Nobody else is in the parking area, actually. I look back at them. "What?"

"I just find it hard to believe that you don't have anybody who thinks you're their nemesis or rival or whatever. If I search it online, do you think it'll come up?"

I laugh. "Dolly, you're ridiculous."

"She does have an interesting point, darling," Bristol says, and I wonder if that's it. Dolly's trying to keep Bristol engaged.

"Yeah, search it online, see if anything comes up. Me and Bristol will check out the tour recordings for the clue." Oh, I didn't tell them that part. "Because there aren't any guides or signs, they have record-ed material for visitors, and I think that's where the clue will be."

"Yes, let's," Bristol says. Dolly shrugs and runs her window down, digging out her phone with one hand and her ecigarette with the other.

"I'll let you know what I find," she says.

"Thanks a bunch, Dolly," I say, and Bristol laughs. We get out of the car, and she stops me, pulling out one of her containers of sun-screen.

"Hold out your arms," she says, and gives me a spray, top to bot-tom. "Rub it in on your face."

"Thanks." It smells lightly floral, I don't know what kind.

"You're welcome. Though honestly, Bits, I don't know how you can be so confident," she says as we walk towards the rack where the recordings are.

"Having a rival or nemesis or whatever wouldn't mean that it puts me in personal danger. It's not like if people just started showing up to taser duel Dolly or something."

"I think if people with a vendetta against Dolly were to appear, it wouln't be tasers that they wielded," Bristol says.

"You're probably right." I survey the tour headsets; they're made to look like tape decks, but nobody's made cassettes in a really long time. They've come back and gone out again two or three times since the early aughts. The headphones material is antibacterial, and there's a wipes and hand sanitizer station nearby. "Seven statues," I say.

"There aren't really statues, they're painted stacks of rock," Bristol says.

"True." But she's still talking and I'm counting the row of headset tours, and there are eight here, one and two doubled up on the same hook. I pick up the seventh in line, and then I pick up the eighth one, to spot the differences. Seven is heavier, actually, it's a metal tape deck spray-painted white to match the plastic of the others, and I slide the headphones on. I hear Bristol break off speaking abruptly, but I'm also pulling up my VR headset so that I can record whatever the tape says, in case it self destructs or we want to refer back to it or whatever.

Whoever recorded it clearly listened to the actual tour; it even starts the same way, but the voice is all wrong. Then they have a static effects noise, like a radio getting garbled between stations, and then the voice says "Good job, player, you've found the clue. The next location doesn't allow earthly visitors, but things are different if you're out of this world." The static plays again, with whistling noise layered into it, and then it's some more of the tour before cutting off to dead air.

"Was that it? Have we gotten the clue?" Bristol asks, when I pull the headphones off.

"Yeah, but I don't think you're going to know this one," I say. I pull one of the wipes out of the dispenser and swipe it over the headphones, then pull another and wipe down the body of the tape deck as I hang it up.

Bristol quirks her lips. "Well why not?"

"Let's go back to the car and I'll play it for both of you." I almost want to look around, to see if there's another component here, but I don't think there is. I think they think what they said was enough, and I'm drawing an immediate blank, but that whistling is familiar. And the person I associate with whistling most is in the car not far from here.

Dolly's still in the same place, which isn't to say she didn't get out and spy on us from afar while we were at the exhibit, but if she did that, she made it back to the car without any of us seeing. We get in the car, Bristol in the front and me in back. I seem to remember her saying something about never getting to ride in front, and I hadn't realized it bothered her. And especially on trips like this, I like being able to stretch out on the seat anyway.

"Okay, so what's the story?" Dolly asks. "Was that it?"

I pull up my headset and make it talk to the car's bluetooth. "Listen." I play the clue, then rewind it just to the whistle and play that again.

"Bits, I apologize, you are entirely correct. I don't know this one."

We look at Dolly, who looks thoughtful. "Play it again." I do. "It prob'ly won't change anything, but can you get rid of the static?"

"I think so?" I mess around with the recording for a little while and get the layers peeled apart, and play just the whistling.

Dolly nods. "The answer's gotta be Area 51, right?"

"Does it?" Bristol asks, eyebrows raised. I wonder if she knows what Area 51 is; it's hard to parse what I think is and isn't common knowledge, after a certain point.

"There's a real old show the guys used to watch, that's still too new for you to like it, Bristles, so no wonder you don't know it. But it was about government conspiracies, so it was a nice in-joke for us to watch episodes in our downtime. And that's part of the theme song. So, that plus the words and bam, Area 51." She starts the car.

Bristol's still sideways in her seat, and she looks back at me. "Do you agree?"

"I can verify now, anyway." I look up the show, listen to the theme song. "Yeah, okay." I run it through the car speakers.

"Excellent work, Dolly," Bristol says appreciatively, as she settles into her seat and fastens the seatbelt.

DRIVING BACK AND FORTH across Nevada gives some stark landscape, but also some pretty stuff. Almost alien in and of itself; it'd be easy to film a Mars movie out here or something. Or maybe a Mars landing conspiracy theory movie, wouldn't that be fun? I take some recordings, because every once in a while it's fun to tinker with video game engines and builders, even if I'm not all that creative. Plus, Creative Commons and stock photo sites could always use more available material.

Bristol hums to herself a little, occasionally, as she responds to messages and I think scrolls articles online. I'm not watching her, per se, I just know that's her typical habit. Who knew that 'being a socialite' was still a real thing, in this day and age? But that's what Bristol is, in addition to the whole heist and thievery thing. And running The Game, though I'm pretty sure she would never have done this if we didn't ask. It's social currency; she has a little bit of leverage now, if there's a job or whatever that she wants to do but we don't. I can understand that, it's fine.

"So what're we gonna do when we get to Area 51 and it's, y'know, a military installation that doesn't allow visitors?" Dolly asks.

"Well I don't imagine the gamerunners went to Area 51, Dolly, they probably went to the nearest bar," Bristol says without looking up.

Dolly glances at me in the rear view. "On it," I say. There's three to five near-ish bars or bar restaurants, depending on how you're counting, and only one of them has a menu online, so I put that in the GPS for Dolly. "Yes they have burgers."

"Oooh," Dolly says at the same time Bristol sort of sniffs.

"They do call the appetizers 'starters' if that helps at all, Bristol," I say.

"Helps *what*?" Dolly asks.

"That they don't call them something appalling like snackatizers," Bristol says.

"What's it matter? It's the same stuff. It means the same thing."

"It's an *awful* word."

Dolly looks at her for a little too long, frowning, before looking at the road again. "How can a word be terrible? It's just a word. It's not a slur or anything, it's a whatchamacallit, a portmanteau of snacks and appetizers. Snackatizers."

"It sounds vulgar."

"It does *not*, Bristles, come off it." Dolly's laughing now, though.

"Not vulgar like, shouldn't be said in polite company just. Crass. No, perhaps that isn't what I mean either."

"You mean low class," I say helpfully. "You mean it sounds cheap."

Dolly looks at Bristol's face and laughs again. "She's got you there."

"Perhaps I thought it was impolite to be so snobby," Bristol says primly.

"Sure, but ain't it what you mean?"

A pause, a test; if Bristol calls Dolly on 'ain't' she's even snobbier. "Yes, I suppose it is what I mean," Bristol says finally. "I do hope you're satisfied."

"*Quite* satisfied," Dolly says. "Can we order ahead, or should we wait until we're there?" she asks me. "To spare Bristol's sensibilities." It's very quiet, but I think I hear Bristol laugh.

"Probably wait," I say. "We'll want to find the clue first, and they're open late anyway."

"What a relief," Bristol says.

"Do we wanna guess what we'll have to look for? Skywriting? A simulated UFO crash? Blacklight on the rocks?"

"I think it'll have to be small," I say. "Or subtle, anyway. So no fiery crash reenactments probably."

"Ah well, a girl can dream, right Bristles?"

"Of course, Dolly darling."

WE DRIVE UP THE ASSUMED stretch of road and then back down again, and then Bristol points at a newspaper vending machine rack that's in a puddle of light at a convenience store. I guess it's been the whole day, I shouldn't say it's dark 'already' but it feels like already. "That isn't real," she says.

"Looks pretty real," Dolly says, but she's already pulling over.

"The paper that uses that coloring and masthead isn't called that, though," Bristol says. I take a screenshot and search, but she's right, and I get out to go investigate.

"Hold up," Dolly says, and hops out too, leaving the car on.

"It's out in the open, they can't booby trap it."

"Still." We both give it a quick visual once-over, and then she pulls on the handle and it's locked. "They seriously want you to pay for the fake newspaper?"

"Well I'm sure they *want* us to," I say, looking at the coin slot. I don't always carry around slugs of all sizes, but this seemed like a good time to have all my niche stuff on hand. I can also then just pop the lock and get my slugs back, and I feed them into the machine one by one, until the latch clicks. "Here." I hand it to Dolly and get out my lockpicks.

"How many newspapers do you think Bristol is like, familiar with at a glance. Is that weird?"

"We've all got our skills," I say, setting the pins and opening the lock without difficulty; if nothing else, I thought it might have rusted or something. It seems like an older model, a lot of them will take a chip now. "See anything apparent in the paper?"

"Not at a glance, but I'm not a newshound, so who knows."

"Even if you were, I think we're all up on different kinds of news." My slugs are the only thing in the cash box, and I take them and close the thing up again before opening the game app on the provided phone and texting the saved number that we got the clue. I wonder why they didn't create an app, it would've been simple enough. It might've also further fueled the competition, to see the progress bars of the other teams. Maybe they wanted to keep it just analog enough, who can say.

I stand up and hold my hand out for the paper, and when Dolly hands it over, something falls out on the ground. Another manilla envelope, and nothing is written on either side, when I pick it up and turn it over. The newspaper's real masthead, fake title matches the one on the vending machine, and isn't that interesting, that they printed a whole very short fake newspaper but didn't program an app. The title story is about declassified government documents about UFOs, as if that was big news and not something they've been doing periodically since the twenties.

We go back to the car and turn on the dome light. I open the envelope, which contains two pieces of paper that have pictures of regular-seeming individual keys on them. Dolly hands Bristol the newspaper to peruse and takes out her ecigarette. "What's that?" she asks.

"Somebody's house keys? I'm not sure yet."

Bristol pages through the paper. "These are all articles from online," she says. "Mostly about alien conspiracies. But there is an advertisements section in the back, perhaps that's where our clue is? Otherwise I'm at a loss." She hands the paper to me.

It feels like a newspaper should, they had it printed someplace pulpily authentic, but each article has its separate sourced website at the bottom of it. The ads also seem like very normal newspaper sorts of ads, used cars and a refrigerator and some personals. At first I concentrate on the personals, that seems like the stereotypical place where they put clues in old spy movies, isn't it? But there's almost no information there, clue-y or otherwise; I wonder if those are real or if the gamerunners made them up, and which would be worse.

"Okay I've got no idea," I say. "Other than that the clue is here." My phone pings; I've got all of the team information now. I close the alert, I'll look at that after we finish this. Then I'll be able to tell Dolly if I've got somebody who thinks they're my nemesis or not on an opposing team.

"How 'bout we get food before that place closes and maybe it'll come to us."

"A proper sit down meal. I'm not eating in the car with food balanced on my knees," Bristol says.

"You did this morning."

"My limit for that activity is once per day."

"Of course, princess, sorry." But Dolly's grinning, not put out by this really, and Bristol laughs.

Chapter Five

Dolly and I get burgers and fries and Bristol gets fish and chips. Our fries do all look the same, for the record. We also get a basket of fried pickle chips that she looks askance at, but does take a few. Dolly and I meet eyes briefly, but we don't say anything; we've never seen Bristol have so much fried food on her plate at once, and don't want to break the spell.

I entertain a brief mental fantasy that Bristol isn't Bristol, and has actually been replaced with an AI copy that they first engineered back when she was in detention at that black site, and then perfected the body over time, and finally thought it was time to deploy after she pepper sprayed Will after that wedding. Poor Will.

But it's an interesting thought; how would we know Bristol was really Bristol? Or any of us, for that matter. We've spent a lot of time together, but enough time to know the difference from computer generated copies? I guess depending on the copy. Depending on the person.

"Should we have come up with a pass phrase before now?" I ask, and judging from their faces, eyebrows raised almost the same exact way, that's nowhere in the ballpark of where the conversation had been.

"Maybe, Bitsy, but why complicate things?"

"I guess you're right," I say.

"Though we could do that, darling, if it'll make you feel better," Bristol says, folding her napkin and setting it on the table again. It's a paper napkin but she still does it.

"I guess we'll think about it. Maybe implement it after this." I appreciate that they just know we're on different trains of thought sometimes, it can be hard to reconcile.

"How do we think the other teams're doing?" Dolly asks after a few minutes have passed, and the waitress clears our things away.

"Oh that's right, I've got the lists now. And I could scope out how many clues they've each gotten."

"If we have any sort of a margin, might we be permitted a hotel room for a few hours?" Bristol asks in a very slightly wheedling tone.

Dolly shrugs. "I guess. If we're good enough."

I don't put on my VR headset in the restaurant, I just get out my phone and swipe through the data. I do see names that I recognize just from the hackersphere in general, but nobody I really know to talk to. No names that I have flagged, red or otherwise. "Looks like everybody else has done their second clue, and we're the only ones who've logged reaching their third."

"Seeing any overlap yet?"

"One other team has done our first clue now, as their second."

"Hmm," Dolly says, and Bristol glances at her pleadingly. "Okay fine we'll stop for the night, but we're up early."

"Of course, darling," she says.

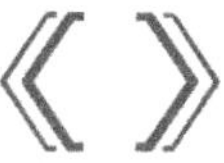

BRISTOL VETOES THE first motel option without even saying a word; Dolly pulls into the parking lot, looks at her face, laughs, and gets back on the road. The hotel we reach next isn't as bad, or is good enough, which are about the same thing I guess. We just get one room, with a cot, and while Bristol does her evening preening, I just sack out on the cot.

I check my messages to see if there's anything I need to pay attention to right away but it's mostly a lot of junk, no action items. I'm still not in the gamerunners' mainframe but that's okay, it'll be soon I think.

I look at the list of other teams now, ten total. Some of them have named themselves very obvious online gamer clan tag sorts of things, and one of them might be a band, they're named after a band. None of it seems particularly notable, and they're all miles and hours away from us, and I scroll through the team rosters, mostly handle-style names and not like, first-and-last, which makes sense, given the territory and nature of the competition. None of them look familiar, but that isn't really a surprise; even if you narrow all of the billions of people in the world down to just the hackers, there's still a lot. But it's been a long day, both physically and mentally, and I really need to sleep or else I'm really a hypocrite for saying anything to Dolly about it.

I leave the headset on, because I do most nights anyway, and as I'm drifting off, I hear Dolly drop her boots on the floor, and dimly hear Bristol take a call. From Marquis I think, but I'm only catching the occasional word in addition to darling.

The way she says darling to Marquis is different from how she says it to Dolly is different from how she says it to Will. I've got an ever-updating table of the situations where Bristol calls us, and other people, darling; it's got a vocal scale rating of 1-5. This was about a 2. She's kind of stressed, but in the way she gets stressed when in underperforming accommodations after being in the car with Dolly all day. But there's a way she says it when she means it, to people she ostensibly cares about, and there's a way she says it to people that she wants to think she cares about, and the nuance is very slim. It's been an interesting pattern to observe and track. She'll say darling when she wants to smooth things over and want somebody to not be mad at her, or when she wants people to feel as though they're in her confidence and soften towards her. It's only rarely that I've heard somebody snap back at her, don't call me darling. Or, I never have, actually, thinking back. But it has to have happened, I think. It's almost impossible for it to not have happened.

I don't dream anything, or if I do, I don't remember. Dolly's quiet when she gets up, but I wake up anyway when she turns on the shower. Bristol doesn't move until she starts whistling, though. She moves, maybe to check the time, and sighs a little before sitting up. It's 5:30; Dolly did promise early, and I don't know if she's like this because she's just always been like this, or if it's from the secret super soldier training program or a combination of the two. It's probably a combination of the two; she mentions brothers often enough that we'll probably meet them sooner or later, and I'm sure they'll be the same way. Though I think some of them were also in the program, like Butler, so we really will never know.

There's a rustle of paper, and I sit up and pull my headset off. Bristol is flicking through the pages of the clue newspaper again. She looks up at me and asks, "Are these real estate listings genuine, or fake?"

I get up to come look, and there's a grid of houses on one of the pages. None of them have any more page space than the others, and they all seem normal enough. I don't know anything about real estate in the area, but I don't really need to. A couple of quick seconds searching, and these are all real addresses, on realtor websites. I find one of those real estate aggregate sites that lists them all on a map and look at it; one of them, while still in a neighborhood, seems to have more land surrounding it than the others. A long driveway and more tree cover.

"This might be it," I say, tapping on the paper.

"Kinda risky, isn't it?" Dolly asks. I didn't notice her come out of the bathroom, but she's toweling her hair off and watching us.

"Maybe one of them is a real estate agent," I say. "So they've got the keys to all these places."

"We've already established that many of *us* don't need keys," Bristol says.

"No, but when they've already made it so easy, why not go along with it?" One of us threw a coffee can in the wastebasket and I take it out and go to the bathroom to rinse it. "Plus, they might have tried to set up trappy protections against people using picks, as an elimination tactic."

"Do people normally get eliminated from these games?" Dolly asks.

"Once in a while. It's all supposed to be sportsmanlike and in good fun, but also this one has the rewards it does, so..."

"It may have attracted an unsavory element?" Bristol asks. She's getting out her toiletries and who knows how long that'll take. I'm sure her 'drive around to play a clue game' skin care and makeup routine is a little less involved than it would be for going out to an art gallery or a date, but I also can't reliably tell the difference.

"Something like that." I've got tin snips in my toolkit, and they both watch me in silence for a few minutes.

"You done that before, Bitsy?"

"Yeah, have you?"

"Not successfully, just screwin' around because somebody watched a video online." Hair dry enough, apparently, Dolly's scraping it back into a ponytail. Bristol watches her but doesn't say anything. I'm sure Bristol has fashion plates ready to go, mentally, with how she'd do us up given the opportunity. The closest she's come so far was being able to tell us to have suits to be her bodyguards when she was playing rich fiancée, and even then, I'm not sure how necessary the suits were after all. Like, she was sure in danger at least once, but it wasn't anything the suits helped with.

"How else would one solve that particular bit of the clue?" Bristol asks.

"There are places online that you can give a picture of keys and they'll send you one, but it takes at least a couple of days, I think. I've never done it. I guess you could also use a bump key. Without seeing their setup, if we even take the time to look at it, I don't know if a bump key is more risky than picking or less. I don't know if any of it is risky, and that's probably part of the game."

"Probably, yes," Bristol says, and goes to the shower.

BRISTOL DOESN'T WEAR heels today, and Dolly and I somehow don't say anything about the boots she's wearing instead. I'm also not sure if what she's wearing is a dress or a romper or what, but that's not my business. She's also got her hair in a ponytail but then I think she also curled it or something. Bristol's hair in a ponytail looks different from almost everybody else's hair in a ponytail.

To her credit, she only gives me and Dolly the slightest of despairing looks as we get in the car and swing through a drive thru on the way to the location.

"How are the other teams lookin', Bitsy?" Dolly asks when she hands back my iced coffee and cardboard tube of little hash browns.

"No more clue successes have been logged since last night. Also, I don't think any of them is my nemesis."

"Aw, dang."

"Dolly, why are you so keen on Bits having a nemesis?"

Dolly shrugs. "I just figured that with such a niche thing, there had to be rivalries, right?"

"Perhaps. Do *you* have a nemesis?"

"Oh yeah, I did."

"You...did."

I catch a glimpse of Dolly's grin in the rear view as she glances at Bristol. "Well, yeah. It's not like I could let it keep going."

Bristol waits a few minutes, I think, but Dolly doesn't continue, and she sighs. "Dolly, darling, you simply cannot dangle a story like that and not tell it."

"Well yeah I can, it might upset your delicate sensibilities." Bristol sighs again and Dolly laughs. "Okay fine, it was one of our kind of neighbors, before any of us kids joined up with the program. I say kind of neighbor because he didn't really *live* there, he was a rich guy from the city who had a vacant property most of the time and then once in a while came out to get drunk and do stupid weekend shit like drunk fourwheeling, hunting outside his property lines, generally makin' himself a nuisance to the locals."

"If you were so young, was he really your nemesis?" I ask.

"Maybe not by the dictionary definition, I dunno. You look it up if it bothers you so much. Anyway, his disrespect for property lines was personal, he absolutely wanted everybody else to respect *his* property lines, whether they were kids or not, or hunting or not, and there was one genuinely scary time when he ran us off that it seemed like maybe he was gonna do more than yell about it. So I went back that night with a roll of fishing line and put it across one of his four wheeler trails."

"Dolly, you didn't," Bristol says, horrified but rapt.

"Sure did. And he broke his fuckin' neck, coming down that trail at high speed. But if you wondered, breaking your neck doesn't automatically kill you, so he was out there yelling for a while before anybody investigated because, you know. Property lines."

"Jesus Christ, Dolly," I say, when she doesn't keep going.

"What? Oh, we didn't let him like, suffocate to death out there. Somebody went out to check on him eventually and he got airlifted out. Sold the property the next year; the new neighbors were nicer."

We're all quiet for a little while. "Well that's good," I finally say, and Dolly nods, loudly rattling the ice in her cup.

"Yeah, real nice folks. Had dogs, fit in good with the neighborhood. Such as it was. More like a vicinity, not a real neighborhood like you prob'ly grew up in, Bristles."

"I wasn't—"

"No, I know, but it helps paint the mental picture, doesn't it?"

"Yes, darling, it does."

We drive through what Dolly probably calls a real neighborhood, and go past the driveway once, taking a long loop back so as not to draw attention, but I don't even see a single curtain twitch. Surprisingly, this neighborhood is also short on those little yard signs that tell you what kind of surveillance cameras they've got on the front porches, which is probably something the gamerunners also noticed and took into consideration when they picked this location.

No other cars are in the driveway, and when I do a scan, I don't see any active device in the vicinity. The thermostat inside is a smart one, but that's it. Nobody's surveillance around, unless it's offline, no rival teams who hid when we pulled up, nothing. There's even birdsong when we get out of the car.

"How the other half lives," Dolly says, as though we haven't had more money than we know what to do with for a couple of years now.

"Dolly, do you ever think about settling down and starting a family? Perhaps with Butler?" Bristol asks, as we get out of the car and go up the front walk. There's a real estate lockbox on the front door handle, and I guess that's one of the alternatives. If you don't know how to make a key, can't take the time to order one, you maybe know how to get around one of those digital locks to get the house keys from inside.

"With *Butler*?" Dolly almost shriek-laughs, and I blink at my coffee can keys, trying to choose which one is for the doorknob and which is for the deadbolt. "Bristol what the fuck?"

"Well he's clearly smitten with you," Bristol says primly. "But whomever."

"Are you just sayin' that because he wasn't all over you? Are you *jealous*?"

"I am not jealous."

It's kind of funny that this kind of bickering is almost the only way that Bristol and Dolly communicate, but also it works, so who am I to judge? I let their conversation fade in my perception as I get out a penlight and peer into the keyways, look at my keys, and make my choices.

When the locks click and the door swings open, Bristol and Dolly cut off behind me, and I think all of us are looking for an alarm panel to be disabled, but there isn't one. No alarm sounds. The house has that cold bleachy smell of a place that's air conditioned and cleaned regularly, but that nobody's living in. There was a while right when I was getting started with all this that I'd spoof reservations at condos and stuff, and this is what they'd smell like. They'd look like homes, or movie sets of homes, waiting for people to be in them.

The entry hall leads straight back to one of those kitchens with the island, marble countertops, and the refrigerator is hidden as one of the wood-paneled cabinets. I think Dolly once called this a lemonade lady kitchen, when she was describing something. The island has a bouquet of flowers in a vase on it, and an accompanying card. I look back at Bristol and Dolly, and Dolly shrugs but Bristol's the one among us most accustomed to getting flowers and she goes to the bouquet and examines it briefly before picking up the card. Actually, I've never gotten flowers. I can't speak for Dolly.

"Won't the flower means something?" Bristol asks. "I don't think they do in a language of flowers way, I think that might be too involved and get us off track. But do you know anything about desert flora?"

"We don't really need to know about desert flora, we have the internet," I say. I snap a picture and search; the top results are about Death Valley superbloom. I show Bristol and Dolly, who shrugs, and then ask, "What does the card say?"

"It's called the most dangerous eight seconds in sports, but don't worry, we'll cushion your fall." Bristol shrugs a little. "I'm certain it's—"

Dolly laughs. "Are you two kiddin' me?"

"What?" I look at the flowers again, like there's something obvious there, that Dolly sees but we don't.

"The most dangerous eight seconds in sports is *bullriding*," she says. "And those're Death Valley flowers, you said? So that's where we're going and that's what we're doing."

"We are *not* bullriding," Bristol says, blinking.

"Well probably not a *real* one." Dolly looks at me, and I shrug. "Well okay come on, we've got ourselves pointed, anyway."

Chapter Six

We stop to charge the car again. This time, it's in an outlet mall parking lot, and Bristol abandons us for air conditioning and the promise of coach bags and a new bottle of perfume. I check on the other teams. Could I be noting their locations, to make our time easier? Probably, sure, especially since only a couple of them have pinged where we've been so far. Do I want to actually play the game fair and square? Also yes. That probably won't be the case for everybody, but also none of my levels of digital security have been breached yet. I'm not counting the gamerunner tag in this consideration; it's certainly vulnerable, I clocked that immediately. But it won't allow a leapfrog into any of our devices.

That doesn't mean I shouldn't do a scan, now that I'm thinking about it. I've always got security running, of course, and nobody's breached my firewall yet but that doesn't mean it'll never happen. And there's no reason to think that I'm the only one, out of all these teams, doing any kind of hacking up the chain.

At least we don't have to worry about the car. This is one that Dolly and I have worked on, and the engine and security systems are separate from anything that's online. It's still got the GPS sure, but to the outside observer, it looks like a phone GPS or a dedicated unit, it doesn't tell you anything about the car. Some makes and models have a remote killswitch that the cops can subpoena on the fly for, but Dolly will not drive one of those unless it's an absolute emergency, no matter my confidence that I can work around that. I haven't done it on the fly before, in a real police situation, but I've done it stationary, just me and the car and the connection.

It isn't that Dolly doesn't trust me; she doesn't trust the machines. Or not the hackable ones. She trusts her left arm, for instance. It isn't connected to the internet, or connectable to the internet, and she knows that it isn't. If it was, she would've gone with a more obvious prosthetic, just for the security. Like how she always uses analog guns.

Bristol is interesting, because she can appreciate the need for security most of the time. She trusts me, us, most on *device* security, and lets me scan and tinker with her devices as needed. I think she realizes that I'm already on the honor system with regards to reading her stuff, and has never even tried to swear me to secrecy. Either she has to trust me, or she can't trust me, and she made her decision I guess. We wouldn't be a team if she didn't trust me, and Dolly, implicitly.

Trust is a funny thing. If you'd asked me a few years ago who the people I trusted most in the world were, a socialite and an ex super soldier were not the list. Before I left home, it was my family that I trusted the most, and I didn't leave because we had a falling out, I left because we decided that it was best to split up and spread out so that the government didn't come and pull a Waco on us. Well, Waco wouldn't be right, we weren't a cult or a religious institution, we were a family minding our own business and being as off the grid as possible while also separately still tapped into shortwave radio and satellite internet. I guess Ruby Ridge might be a better comparison. There've been others, of course, because there are always other stories like that. It's not something I talk about much, my upbringing, and I think with separation, some of my family has grown more paranoid than others. We check in every once in a while, via throwaway emails and dead end websites, and message boards for innocuous niche topics. But never for very long; not long enough that somebody with a podcast could put the pieces together.

It would be funny, if one of my brothers was on one of the other teams, but that would be too much of a coincidence, and also too splashy of an event. None of them would ever do something like this, and probably would've tried to discourage me from doing it. But, I always have to have my projects, and right now, this is it. It seemed fun enough and lucrative enough, and Dolly's always up for a road trip. Bristol turns up her nose at some things, but she's also always looking for new experiences to further calibrate her social intelligence. It's like how she first met Dolly in a bottom-rung bar; she wasn't there for fun or because she thought she'd like it, she was there to educate herself.

That's a thing that I really respect about Bristol, she knows her strengths and works for potentials. The only time I've ever seen her even a little off balance was when her old friend Lorraine showed up when we were doing the fake engagement job. Well okay twice, but anybody'll be off balance when they drink a cocktail spiked with ketamine, you can't plan and educate yourself around that. I don't think you can even acclimate yourself to it, like cyanide or whatever. Arsenic? Maybe there's a few things.

Bristol comes back with some shopping bags and Dolly pops the trunk without comment. Dolly also stops at the next convenience store without comment and says "If we're going to Death Valley we need to bring water." She goes inside for seven minutes, and comes out with two flats of bottled water.

"Do you think that will be quite enough?" Bristol asks.

"Probably, but it's better to have too much than too little, right?" Dolly winks at me as she slides the water into the footwell I'm not using in the back seat. "Hey Bitsy, lemme know when we get to one of these that somebody else has done already."

"We haven't yet," I say. "But I'll keep that in mind." She's got sabotage on her mind, which makes sense. We don't know any of the behind the scenes details, how closely they're monitoring anything. If and how they would interrupt, if somebody decided to pull something. I wasn't thinking about a double cross; I'm glad she is. Really, we should always be thinking about a double cross. So few jobs go totally straight.

"We'll have to soon, won't we?" Bristol asks. "How many more of these can there possibly be?"

"We all started at different locations and had different first clues," I say, and then Dolly interrupts and says,

"You're the one who likes logic puzzles, Bristles."

Bristol bites off whatever she was going to say, and then in a brighter tone says "I think Dolly assumes I need to keep occupied, Bits. How many other teams are there? Did you end up finding out?"

"It's ten," I say.

"I didn't *say* you needed to keep occupied," Dolly said. "You just seem to like it best when you have a job."

"Mmm," Bristol says, and I can picture the look on her face, one of her stock masks of serene tolerance.

"How many of 'em do you think are familiar with bullriding?"

"It's an easily searchable phrase," I say, shrugging even though neither of them is looking at me.

"Seems on the nose, though," Dolly says. Her ecigarette is in her mouth but she's not smoking it and I don't know if it's because she forgot or she's out of the juice or what. She probably isn't out.

"Are you suggesting we're being sabotaged? Or sabotaged already? By somebody somehow familiar with our past escapades?" Bristol asks. I can't tell if she thinks Dolly's being ridiculous or not.

Dolly's the one who shrugs. "I'm saying it's possible. Because when they planned the game, it's not like they even knew that you were going to sign up, right Bitsy?"

"That's true, they didn't," I say. Is Dolly being paranoid or is this reasonable caution? I pretty much never think that somebody's suspicions are paranoia. It isn't paranoia if somebody's really after you. "So either it's a coincidence, or a team actually did get that clue ahead of time, and left us this one as a fake."

We drive in silence for a little while. "I think it's ridiculous to be so worried," Bristol says. "The worst case scenario in this instance is that we lose some time, I suppose. It isn't as though Death Valley is uninhabited and unnavigable, after all. And if you're really so concerned, you can simply call the gamerunners. Or I could, since I have the private cell for one of them."

"Nah, don't do that yet. It's probably fine. You just know how trains of thoughts go."

"Many people's, yes. Yours, Dolly darling, almost never."

"Perfect." Dolly looks at me in the rear view mirror and winks.

FINDING THE MECHANICAL bull isn't hard; there's even a hotel here called The Ranch. It all seems very easy but also how hard can the clues be? Somebody comes out from the front of the place when we park near the bull, carrying a remote key fob and an envelope. They've got a game lanyard around their neck with a name tag hunt on it that reads Liam.

"I need you to show your group tag before I turn on the bull," they say.

"I've got it here," I say, and they scrutinize their phone screen for a minute.

"Good, okay," they say, and click a button on their fob.

"We aren't your first group, are we?" Bristol asks. She's wearing both sunglasses and a hat with a broad droopy brim, and they look at her like she's got to be a movie star

"Well I'm not really supposed to say..." they trail off as Dolly takes stuff out of her pockets, depositing it in the driver's seat of the car. Then she stretches until her back cracks, looking at the bull, and picks up a handful of desert sand driveway, rubbing it between her palms.

"Neither of you want to do this, right?" She asks, pausing suddenly. Bristol wrinkles her nose, just a tiny little bit

"No, thank you. I'm quite satisfied to leave it to somebody more practiced."

Dolly nods. "Bits?"

"Also no. I'd never deprive you of the opportunity."

"Fair enough, I didn't want to hog it without even thinking about it." I'm not sure how many bars Dolly has gone to with mechanical bulls, even before we spent time on a bona fide (former) bull rider's ranch, but the number is more than zero.

"You're not. Just be careful "

"You two worry so much," she says, never mind that she's the one who introduced the idea that another team is sabotaging us already or intends to.

At a glance, the mechanical bull is completely normal. The thing that powers it is even normal, not remotely operated or anything like that. The keyfob was to unlock a protective housing that had been put over the controls, I guess for added security. On closer inspection, it isn't just set up in the middle of a dirt parking lot, the immediate surroundings are foam that were painted to blend in.

"This isn't at the hotel all the time, is it?" I ask Liam and they give a slightly nervous laugh.

"Oh no, not at all. This is just for the game. I'm also not a hotel employee, I was hired by the gamerunners."

"That makes sense." I look back down at my phone, because it's a more normal gesture than staring straight ahead at my HUD to see the things I'm keeping track of, my messages, our timer in the game, where the other players are. It would be interesting to know where the gamerunners also are, and where the mainframe is, since they're clearly using it remotely. My progress bar on that is full but I'm still not in yet.

"Did they call you Bits?" Liam asks hesitantly, and I blink and look up at them, remembering hazily the way that Null acted when we met, and how Dolly crowed about how I was famous and didn't even know it. I guess it makes sense, that my name would be known; I can think of a couple of other famous and/or notorious hackers, even people I've messaged with occasionally.

"Yeah, I'm Bits."

They look around a little, but it's just Bristol and Dolly and I out here, and Bristol and Dolly are talking just slightly out of earshot at the mechanical bull. I can't imagine what they're talking about, Dolly could've been done by now. Liam leans in a little and says "I'm Smog."

For a second I think oh no, I'm not going to know this person's handle, but my brain fast cycles and it clicks. They did a credit card/crypto hack a few years back. "Hey! Nice to meet you. That was a good job."

"Thank you." They also were afraid, I think, that I wouldn't know who they were, but they stand up a little straighter with the praise. "If you need any help with this, I could..."

"Oh, no, that's okay. Thank you I mean. But we want to do it fair and square, this is just for fun." Is it rude bragging, to say playing a game with prizes like that is just for fun? Bristol would be able to tell me. "Dolly is very enthusiastic"

"I can see that," Smog says, with something like wonderment.

Bristol backs off, shaking her head, and Dolly gets up on the bull and gets herself settled before giving the thumbs up, leaving her left hand in the air and holding on with her right. Smog gives a nod, then reaches down and hits the switch, and there's a brief pause and then the bull grinds to life. I can only assume the desert environment isn't super great for it, and it's been out here for a couple of days at least, as the gamerunners got everything set up.

I remember Dolly once telling me that there's only so many patterns that mechanical bulls have, and that a lot of the ones she's ridden have started out with the 'head down' buck and spin, and that's what this one does. I don't think I ever asked Dolly how many mechanical bulls she's ridden; the number's more than zero, and so that's already more than I've experienced. The control panel has a running digital counter, and as the bull bucks and spins, and then changes direction, Dolly stays on, stays upright even, though I can almost hear her teeth clack together during one of the direction changes. She gives a whoop when it hits eight seconds. I don't know how she knows it was eight seconds. Smog hits the button again and the bull settles down into its hibernation mode again and Dolly slides off.

"Piece of cake," she says, breathing a little hard, but not too much, and Bristol claps.

"Brilliant performance, darling."

"I've ridden that model before, if not that specific bull. I think there's only so many of 'em, y'know?" She looks over at Smog and me. "So we got the next clue?"

Smog gives kind of a start and fumbles with the envelope they've been holding all along. "Sorry, sorry, here."

Dolly briefly gives me a short eyebrows-raised 'what's with them?' sort of look and I shrug. "Thanks Smog, we appreciate it," I say.

"You're welcome. Good luck! I think you're doing pretty good, right? I think you have—no you wouldn't know, I shouldn't say."

"Nope," I say with a smile, and Dolly laughs.

"No cheating!" she says.

"Is it really cheating?" Bristol asks. Smog looks at the three of us, just unprepared to handle the reality of us, I guess. I wonder what they know about us, or think they know about us. But they've got intel on all the teams, are they going to be like this for all of them?

"I don't think it's cheating to tell us if we're in the lead or not," I say after a pause. "It wouldn't be able to affect our performance, right?"

"That's right," Smog says. "You're in the lead, and the next team after you needs one more to tie."

"Which means we gotta get going, right?" Dolly asks. "We have the clue?" I raise the envelope. "Perfect. Hey, thanks a lot!"

"You're welcome," Smog says. "Good luck!"

"Thanks," I say, and we go back to the car.

"What's the clue, Bitsy?" Dolly asks, checking her mirrors as she backs out, eyeing the charge on the car.

"I didn't look yet, hold on." I open the envelope, plain manilla like the other ones. I pull out the index card and read the careful lettering. "From Sea to Shining Sea."

Silence in the car, and then Dolly laughs. "What the fuck does that mean?"

"I don't know." I search it, and it's a line from a really old patriotic song. Okay. "Bristol?"

"Yeah, Bristles, culture us? It's obvious a certain kinda guy is the one making these clues, maybe the same one who gave you his number. He knew you were snooty, and wants to woo you with obscure shit."

"I am not *snooty*," Bristol says with a little sniff, and then laughs. "Oh dear that sounded very snooty."

"Point," Dolly says.

I click through a few things, half listening to them. Patriotic song lyrics referencing what? Cool, great, Manifest Destiny. Okay but also referenced in stuff about the transcontinental railroad, which went through Sacramento and eventually was finished up in San Francisco. But Stanford is where there's a museum that has the golden spike (one of the golden spikes?) that they drove when the building effort from the east coming west and the building effort from the west going east met. "They wouldn't want us to steal that, right? That would be weird." I look up, and Dolly looks at me in the mirror and Bristol has turned around halfway in her seat to look over her shoulder at me.

"Gotta tell us the rest of the thought, Bitsy."

"The golden spike from the transcontinental railroad is in a museum at Stanford. Well, one of them. There's also one in a museum in San Francisco."

"I imagine they don't want us to steal anything," Bristol says. "This isn't a scavenger hunt, it's a puzzle game."

"You're right, this is just the first thing that's come up that seemed really like, mobile."

"Well and there's only the one in the world, so you probably assumed Bristol'd want it for her very own, to keep with that egg or something. Make a li'l shadowbox."

"I guess they made four?"

"Four egg shadowboxes?" Dolly's grinning, and Bristol sighs.

"Four golden spikes," I say.

"Even better, that's one for each of us and then one that the museum can keep."

"I do not want a golden railroad spike, personally, but thank you," Bristol says.

"More for us," Dolly says. "So...Stanford?"

"I guess? I don't know if one makes more sense than the other."

"I dunno. Is one on the way to the other?"

"No but yes. Stanford's first, if we do this route." I send it to her GPS.

"I'd just like to leave Death Valley, please," Bristol says.

"You just object to the name, Bristles, look at all the natural splendor around us. How can you love Morocco and not Death Valley? Is it just the PR or what? You're smarter'n that."

I expect Bristol to have a sharp or even huffy comeback, and instead there's thoughtful silence. "You know, maybe you're right," she says after a few minutes, as we drive through one of the areas that's carpeted with wildflowers. There's a superbloom this year, is what sites said when I'd searched the flowers. Whatever a superbloom is. Well I mean, we're looking at it. "It is very lovely, it just has a bad name."

"There, see. Not so bad?"

"No, not so bad."

"Good, now I can give you the bad news," Dolly says and Bristol sighs.

"Oh goodness. What is it?"

"It's like eight hours to Stanford and we gotta stop at least once to charge."

"It isn't as though I'm disused to travel, Dolly darling."

"Well there, good, she took it better than I thought," Dolly says to me.

"Yeah, she took it really well."

Bristol laughs. "You two are ridiculous."

"That's us!" Dolly agrees, taking out her ecigarette.

Chapter Seven

Of course, the museum where the golden spike is also happens to be at Stanford University, which isn't like, where the internet started per se (that was ARPANET at UCLA), but it received the first internet message, so the story goes, and was a hotbed for early internet culture. A lot of slang that gets used among hackers is still Stanford stuff, even though some things are so many times removed that it just doesn't make any sense anymore. Like talking about dialing a phone when the last rotary anything was manufactured more than a hundred years ago. So it makes me wonder what else we might have access to, once we're on the campus. What's still online? What's laying around, disused, in storage rooms? I'll keep an eye out for student credentials and how they work, for future exploration.

There's also a history of computing museum at Stanford. Or there are exhibits throughout the computer sciences building? I didn't take the time to really look at first, because of the job at hand, but now I do. There's both, now, a museum and also things in the computer sciences buildings, because there are also more than one now.

We're almost to Stanford when I sit up in the back seat and paw the headset off my face. "This is too easy."

"What now?" Dolly asks, in a tone that says my sudden movement behind her flipped all the 'time for violence already?' switches that she's got. To her credit, she only swerved a little bit and corrected immediately.

"We aren't perfect trivia puzzle riddle solvers, this has been too easy." God damn it, I should've been the one to sign us up, so I could look those people in the face. Not that I don't think Bristol can't do a logic puzzle, that isn't it. "Like the hardest thing is how many times we've had to drive like, eight hours. And also the bull thing I guess."

"The bull thing," Dolly repeats, laughing a little.

"Bits, darling, this game was your idea. Why would you suddenly mistrust it so?" Bristol turns to look at me, and there is real concern in her face. Whether it's concern about my concern, or whether she's worried that I've got something wrong with me, I can't tell.

"Well I'm not sure I ever trust anything entirely," I say. "But I don't have proof I guess. It's just a feeling." I pull my headset up for a second, check my HUD. "Oh and I'm still not in their mainframe yet, that's something. That's been bothering me."

"Well just try Will's agency credentials and see," Dolly says in a hard-edged, fake cheerful voice that says she's fine with this turning more serious than our little family road trip.

"They wouldn't leave anything that was on that laptop active," I say.

"Mmmhmm?" Bristol isn't even sure what to ask.

"Okay yeah I wrote a program to use everything on Will's laptop to see if they left a channel still open to try and trap me."

"That's our girl," Dolly says.

As I'm pulling my headset on again, Bristol says "Girls, aren't we being the teensiest bit paranoid? You said there are other teams and you can see their movements. That would be a *very* elaborate trap just for us."

"Ain't paranoia if somebody's really after you," Dolly says. "Which we know they are."

"Yes, but—"

I think of Smog back in Death Valley, knowing who I was, and try to compare it against Null knowing who I was, back when we were getting Bristol out of custody, but I can't make it match up right. My mental video from that time isn't really reliable. It makes sense for a hacker helping in a real life puzzle game to know who I am; it makes equivalent sense for a government agent inserting into a real life puzzle game to have been briefed on who I am. Who we all are.

My mainframe hack is at the same percent which means either their security is that good, which it can be, we're all hackers here, or they've got a countermeasure stalling it, and I cut that connection. I should've thought of this sooner but I was familiar with previous games of varying sizes and there were no red flags. Maybe this is paranoia but I think in this business paranoia pays. Especially if we're merrily driving around in the U.S. knowing damn well that there's at least one unnamed government agency that wants its hands on us.

In VR, nobody else is around the mainframe that I can see. They've made it look like a casino building, flat-topped and round, all flashing lights running around it in a pattern. I set a program recording and parsing the pattern because there have been dumber things than people putting the key right there on the outside of the thing that's locked, physically and virtually. Sometimes people think a physically locked thing is very secure, but I've seen Dolly open a hotel room keypad safe with a spoon, so security is an eternally variable thing.

I circle around it, look at the different angles and potentials. I sort through the credentials that I skimmed not from Will's laptop, but from the connection that I used it to follow back to the Agency, in as subtle and thorough a smash and grab as I was able to perform before he called it in and access was pulled. Which was a very successful smash and grab, actually, as I've been able to spoof other agents' connections when I wanted to have a little walk through every once in a while, to try and see if they'd pinged us lately or added to our files. When Dolly returned that laptop to Will, she said that he about dropped dead the second he saw her. I know that level of intimidation was part of her goal, even as keeping him sympathetic and intrigued is part of Bristol's.

This doesn't appear to be an Agency mainframe, though, as nothing matches up. Maybe they're independent contractors, there are any number of bounties for us and other hackers who would've been drawn in by the promise of challenge and reward. Or maybe they are just who they say they are, their own team of hackers having some fun. Is anybody who they say they are? It's hard to tell. Bristol absolutely tells you who she is, if you're paying attention. Dolly too. And I mostly try to say nothing at all.

My program pings me, tells me that there is deliberately not a pattern in the lights pattern, which means it's absolutely a security thing, just like the wall of lava lamps that's been at a particular encryption company for decades now, and I wonder briefly about how long an individual lava lamp will keep functioning. No wonder my auto hack stalled out.

Thing thing about security is that the flaw is nearly always human. A potential vulnerability here is one that I already thought about; the geotags. They should've thought of it, these things absolutely shouldn't create a vulnerability to the mainframe if they indeed go back to it and not just a dedicated laptop or whatever, but bigger things have been brought down by less, historically.

I sort through the lines of code I have around me, find the geotag for the Fashion Police, and yup, follow it right to the mainframe, and into the mainframe. There's a partition for these so okay, that's smart. But there's only so many ways to partition access like this, and I think of Dolly with the spoon again, as I feel out the edges, metaphorically but also literally via code, and I do find a vulnerability. If this was a real room that the geotags all connected to, what I find is essentially the wire that connects from the other side of the wall and leads to the rest of the building. That's probably a bad metaphor, but that's how I picture it. Phone cords and motel rooms.

The concept of the mainframe is maybe an antiquated one, or maybe it's just audacious now, *extravagant*, to think of using a physically large computer for large computing things, when computing has gotten *so* small and portable. They put men on the moon with less computing power than Dolly's vintage robot dog, and now I'm in VR using something that fits into what is to all appearances a toy. You can buy low-grade VR headsets in line at the grocery store and play a bunch of built-in games, or walk through a bunch of premade experiences, for fifty bucks. Mine cost more than fifty bucks, but I think my point is clear.

The mainframe here, that I'm referring to, is a big computational machine. I think physically large, in addition to being powerful, which again makes me think this is an agency project. Do the gamerunners know? Do they just think they're using generous corporate sponsorship for computational power, and that's the shell the agency is using? Questions for later, I need to figure out the goal here.

Slowly, carefully, I move through the data, look at the geotags, scan electronic signatures. I'm not super worried about being detected; at my level, I've spent years creeping around people's data architecture not touching anything and most of them have never known. Targets large and small, because sometimes you get curious.

I copy stuff as I go, that I think might be of interest, but I keep going because I want to know who the owner of the mainframe is. I don't have proof yet that it isn't the gamerunners, I just have that feeling that it isn't. Their tech startup wouldn't have a thing like this, they're clustering laptops and phones and headsets. Again, they could've leased computing power, but why do it for a silly thing like this? It doesn't add up, unless this is a rich kid with access to their parent's company or something like that. That's the most innocuous flight of fancy I can take, I think. Maybe I'll come up with more later.

It's isn't unusual, that they've got it set up so I need to be deeper in the data architecture to find ownership. Hanging your name out front can make you a target, for attacks serious and recreational. Arguably it's also a trap, but since they're already tracking us as game participants both via the phones and the geotags that they gave us, they don't really have much to gain by knowing who I am and that I'm here. And of course I'm proud of my own security, but if it goes untested, it gets static and stale. Then I get too lazy and full of myself.

On cue, I get one of my own security popups. I'm not securing a whole mainframe, so it's perfectly reasonable for me to have several layers of security. Ablative, almost. I think Dolly would appreciate that I know that word. And, for instance, I know that our dragonscale armor *isn't* ablative, but that some of the heavier stuff she has is. Though speaking of dragonscale...

//We should swap to riot gear when we get the chance// I text Dolly. She can handle bickering with Bristol about it.

//ten four// Dolly says, maybe a little too quickly. Did we park? I'm not in full VR immersion but I'm also not paying attention to my physicality. It isn't a good plan to split my attention right now.

The attempt at breaching my security was barely an attack, just a packet ping that my systems rebuffed. It might even just be an auto-response to my connection, but it's sure to draw a human response, and I set a stopwatch running for fun to see how long it takes before we make contact, and I stop being such a tourist and get to more serious business. Really, they should've assumed I'd do this, maybe they just thought it would be way earlier in the game.

Though that reminds me, while I can take advantage of the mainframe power, I do a scan of the other team's geotags, and then search for nearby vulnerable cameras. Traffic cameras, Rings, whatever, I don't care. Are the other teams real, or are they digital packets to make me think we're playing a real game? Is that why the game is *so* widespread, so it makes sense that we wouldn't run into other teams right away, and not wonder about it until it's too late? But what's the too late here, what's *their* endgame? They could've swooped in with black helicopters when Smog had eyes on us in Death Valley, if capture is the goal.

My security pings me again, then a second and third time quickly. Not human yet, though, stopwatch still counting up. I get to what I assume is the ownership credentials that I'm looking for and of course there's more passive security here as well, it'd be laughable if there wasn't but I'm getting antsy. I know this is low risk but also my alarm bells are going off even assuming what I'm assuming. Maybe I'm just making things out to be worse than they really are.

But I run my utility of the Agency credentials that I've gleaned and by its very nature I don't know *which* one unlocks the files for me to grab, but one of them does and then in my HUD I get confirmation that I can have eyes on just one other team and isn't that interesting. I take a screenshot, then break the connection with my stopwatch still counting upwards, and then power down, just in case something did get in under my radar. I sit up, pulling my headset down so it hangs around my neck.

We're parked on the side of the road, Dolly and Bristol both turned around to look at me. Nobody else seems to be here, no other cars are around us.

"I don't really know how yet," I say. "But this is probably a trap."

Chapter Eight

"Okay, so let's get this straight," Dolly says, another thirty or so miles down the road, when we're all sitting around a table at a diner, eyeing the holo menus. "The new working theory here is that the agency is running this shindig and there's really only one other team? They spoofed the rest of it, right down to the gamerunners?"

"Well those guys could be in the agency and just nobody knows," I say. "Or they could've been strongarmed into it as part of a deal. That's the theory I'm betting on, actually, since we know the agency makes deals." I look at Bristol, who smiles briefly. If this was an anime, she'd have just one single sharp tooth bared for that fleeting second.

"But, darlings, if the game is a ruse, then what is the goal? Why such a farce?"

"Well I don't know yet," I say, and the waitress comes by right then. I blink at the menu some more because I haven't thought about food in hours, as in, it hasn't occurred to me that I might want food. Because why not one team but two? Why actually set up clues in locations? What benefit could come from fooling multiple groups of people like this? And there's no way to trust the payout now, the winner isn't getting all of those prizes. There's no reason to expect them to honor—oh the waitress. I look up and she's gone again, and I look at Dolly.

"I got you chicken fingers and fries," she says with a laugh. "It seemed like a burger might take too much processing power right now."

"Thanks." I blink some more but she's right. Bristol now has a tiny wine bottle and what must pass for a wine glass in this place. I can't keep track of what kinds of diners you can expect to be able to drink at and what ones you can't. I look out the window and it's actually later than I would've thought. I have connection to clocks of course but what is time. "Okay I guess they must never have intended for anybody to find out that this is anything but a game?"

"So they're really ponying up all that cash and stuff?" Dolly's eyebrows show me just how doubtful she is.

"I don't know. It seems impossible, right? But that would be on the gamerunners, and tarnish their reputation in the community. So maybe that's just doing double duty for them." A narrative is starting to form for me, and I don't know how right it is, but it *feels* right. "Okay, let's say the agency caught the gamerunners doing something, what it is doesn't matter. Caught, interrogated, got to the 'let's make a deal' portion. The agency needs access to something that they can't legitimately request or access, and their people can't handle it. Maybe the gamerunners can't either, and that was part of their initial plan."

"So they need more people with particular skills to do the job," Bristol says. She doesn't look too pleased with her wine, once she sips it, but I know she likes having a prop in her hand.

"Exactly. So they lured us and the other team in with the promise of the game, and they set up the game for real, so that we wouldn't know anything weird was going on."

"It'd be funny if they still made those nerds do most of the work," Dolly says, leaning back for her burger to get set in front of her.

I laugh, surprised. "I guess they'd have to, right? Other than pointing us to a particular geographic location."

"Do you think Stanford has whatever prize they're after?" Bristol asks. Now she's eyeing her food dubiously. We already knew that the roadside diner experience is not what Bristol is into, it's a wonder she agreed to this at all. I think it all looks okay, but my food opinions and Bristol's don't always match up. Don't ever match up, from her perspective.

"Maybe, but I'd be surprised if we get to the endgame so soon. Even though I'd love to just spend a month at Stanford, probably."

"How come?" Dolly mumbles with her mouth full.

"Computer history stuff. Internet history stuff." I shrug. "Nerd stuff."

"Figures."

"Should we try to contact the other group?" Bristol asks. "To see if they've noticed anything?"

"Bristles, that's real sportin' of you, wanting to compare notes with the competition."

"While it might benefit us to keep them in the dark, it is worth inquiring if they know anything, wouldn't you say? Are they very near to us?"

"No, they're still in Nevada." From the data I skimmed, none of their clues so far had any overlap with ours.

"Maybe it's not a trap," Dolly says. "Maybe it's recruitment."

"That's still a trap," Bristol says, making a little face.

"Tomato, tomahto," Dolly says, finishing her burger. "Some people never had the chance to go legit and would jump at it if they could."

"I do suppose that's true." Bristol looks at me. "Have you seen any indication of that?"

"Of what, that this game by these gamerunners could be a government agency recruitment tool?"

"Don't make it sound so silly, darling."

"I'm not, I'm making sure I've got it straight." They wait, and while I think about it I run a search, but nothing comes up. "No, they always seemed legit. Not legit. Or I mean, not government plants. So either it's recent or it's how they've always been, but on the face, nothing has changed, nobody's seen any red flags or raised alarms. Unless I'm in the wrong whisper networks, which is always possible."

"Whisper networks?" Dolly has her ecigarette on the table in front of her, but seemed to remember just in time that she couldn't do that in here, and she's lightly tapping it against the tabletop, end to end, while we wait for Bristol to finish eating, and to pay. Or maybe they already paid and I was distracted.

"Yeah, like. Backchannels to warn people about stuff when it isn't necessarily safe to just broadcast it." Bristol nods; Bristol knows.

"Gotcha," Dolly says. Maybe she's less mystified or maybe she's just never heard it called that. "Okay, we ready to roll? That golden spike isn't gonna drive itself."

"We aren't—" I start, and she laughs.

"I know, I know."

Bristol folds her napkin, and we go out to the parking lot, where in the street lights we see that the car has a flat tire. Dolly crouches to examine it, vapor trailing above her head. It isn't completely flat, not a rubber puddle surrounding the rim, but it's at-a-glance obvious.

"Did we pick up a nail?" I ask, and she shrugs.

"Hard to say. Doesn't look like a knife, anyway," she says cheerfully. "Or a screwdriver."

"Were you expecting sabotage?" Bristol asks, eyebrows raised.

"Yeah, always. I'm surprised you're not." Dolly stands back up again and goes to trunk, feels around for the mechanism. "One reason I like jeep-shaped things, they hang the spare on the outside."

"Does this even have a spare?" I ask, leaning inside and popping the trunk. Some cars have a voice activated password for that. There has to still be a physical mechanism, right? Maybe not.

"Well it's got a donut and I put a full sized one in here too. Besides having a patch kit, of course."

"Of course," Bristol says. I'm not certain she knows what a donut is, in this context. I don't think I would, with her background.

Dolly pulls a little jack out, hands it to me. "You can handle that, right Bitsy?"

"Sure." In a bigger vehicle no, I'd have no idea where to put the jack. The bumper? With this car, though, I know I can put it in the space between the doors and that'll lift it up the right way. I crank the crank, and the car lifts up enough that the tire hangs straight again, and then so it's high enough that Dolly can pull it off and trade it out. I don't see a screw or anything from my vantage, or other obvious punctures. And the other team that I *know* is a live team isn't anywhere near us, so sabotage wouldn't have anything to do with them. It doesn't have to mean anything. Is this the first flat I've changed with Dolly? I think so. Statistically, it was bound to happen.

"I've somehow never done this before," Bristol says, watching us work.

"Will you be insulted if I say I'm not surprised?" Dolly asks, spinning the tire iron on the bolts. When she gets the tire off she rolls it in the light, examining the surface. "Here, look, this big chunk of metal got in it. Just something off a truck or something, probably, that was in the road." She wiggles it out and drops it at our feet. "Or maybe it's off one of those thingers the police drop in a car chase. Hole might be too big for the patch, but it can cure in the trunk."

I'm a little surprised when Bristol crouches and picks up the piece of metal; she doesn't typically volunteer to touch dirty things, or anonymous sharp things. "It *does* seem innocuous," she says thoughtfully, looking from it to the other cars in the lot. At least a couple left after we got here, but they were just normal-seeming diners, that I could tell. Normal civilian devices and vehicles.

"But now you don't think so? Uh-oh, Bitsy, nothing's more dangerous than a new conspiracy head." Dolly's letting the jack down again already, the new tire screwed on snug.

"We are well aware of the existence of the agency," Bristol says primly. "It's hardly a flight of fancy to suspect them, once we've already started suspecting them."

"Yeah, if the shoe fits." Dolly checks the patch, then tosses everything back in the trunk and slams it. "This is what we get for thinking we'll profit off of a little fun."

"Dolly, you always have fun."

She grins at me. "Well, yeah. But you two don't."

"Point."

"I don't know what you girls are talking about, I find our work highly amusing." She pauses, perhaps running a couple of historic mishaps through her head. "I typically find our work highly amusing."

"That's the spirit. Bitsy, does this change our plans at all?"

The ten million dollar question. "No, I guess it doesn't. We don't know anything, so we don't have anything to go on."

"And if we ditch now, we'll never find out," Dolly says, once we're all in the car.

"We simply must find out," Bristol says. "Either we genuinely are so skilled that we've outsmarted the gamerunners and will tidily win, or it is the agency again, and we'll know what measures to take next."

"Leavin' the country's always a nice start," Dolly says, and Bristol sort of hums in response. I know it's been a while since she's been back to Morocco, and also that she doesn't consider that location burned for some reason.

No, I know the reason; she considers Will to be on the hook already, if not outright compromised. I think he's compromised, but he doesn't know it yet, which makes him still dangerous. But Bristol makes survival decisions first, so her decisions regarding him have been shrewd and airtight, even when taking the occasional risk. Whomst among us doesn't take the occasional risk? Deciding to do the game was a risk. Being in the States at all is a risk. Some days, breathing is a risk, it's just how it is.

That sounds dramatic, but it isn't. When you're wanted by un-specified shadow government agency or agencies, it's easy to want to go far far away and hole up somewhere. When you learn that that agency or agencies operate across international borders, even in lim-ited capacity, well. You might get tired of waiting to get caught and just keep living your life instead.

Assuming agency involvement, there's a few reasons for two live teams instead of one. In case one of us fails, the other can still get whatever target the agency won't go after themselves. Or they want to reassure us that we aren't a target and that the game is real, with multiple teams. Or we're the bait, to lure in the other team and assure *them* that this is all on the up and up.

I worry it in circles long enough that it becomes impossible to worry about in a tangible way. It's either too big for us to affect or the things we would do to affect it are the things we'd do anyway as standard operating procedure. We just know to be on our guard now, which we typically are anyway. I think Dolly most out of all of us, but maybe I'm wrong. By her very nature, Bristol is hard to get a read on, other than how she wants you to perceive her.

The other live team isn't as diversified as we are, they're mostly hackers and one gearhead, if I'm remembering right. Cars and mo-torcycles and anything with an engine, really. That might be my in with them, now that I think about it. I pull up a recent article on the 3D printed helicopters that Dolly's friend Butler and his busi-ness partners were making and marketing, and then root around for a public source of contact information for the gearhead, who's listed in the game signup as "Cortina" and that makes me wonder if he is a she or a they maybe and I genuinely don't know, but I trace that name to a forum post that seems like something I could've stumbled across and send off the message.

I get an almost immediate response. It's almost funny how fast it is, but I'd probably do the same thing, if an internet big deal suddenly messaged me out of nowhere, and I didn't know they knew I existed. Well. If I worried about things like that, it's kind of confusing to think about. I can't be responsible for how people think of me; I can only be responsible for the things that I do.

//Is this real?// is all the message says, and I wonder over it a little bit like. Which part? That it's from me, or that the helicopters are 3D printed.

//Yeah, almost like any other helicopter// I send back. //Lighter weight, maybe a shorter range.//

//No, I mean is this really Bits. Sorry, in a situation right now.//

//Sorry. Yes, it's really Bits.// There's a long pause, and I can only imagine they're all conferring with one another. //You're in the game, right?//

//.....yes?//

//I'm not trying to cheat or get answers from you or anything, just wanted to give you a wave and make sure things were going okay. We just got a flat tire so I was killing time.//

//Bad luck. Things are good, are we supposed to even have contact?//

//Probably not.//

"They don't seem to think anything is weird but me reaching out," I say to the front seat.

"They meanin' the other team?"

"Yeah."

"Perhaps they're safe then, at least," Bristol says.

"Very magnanimous of you, Bristles," Dolly says. "We can imagine you have a heart."

Bristol gives a sniff but lets that ride. "Should I call Ant?"

"Who now?" Dolly asks.

"The gamerunner who gave her his number."

"Fuck, I forgot about that. So many men felled wherever she goes..."

"Now who's dramatic," Bristol sighs, but I can hear her smile.

"Well is he cute?"

"By whose standards, darling?" Dolly shrugs. "And am I calling him or not?"

"To be a super spy and get him to spill the game's secrets to you? Didn't you need more relationship-buildin' to get to that stage of wrapped around your finger?"

"Relationship building, like...texting throughout the game?" Bristol asks sweetly.

"Sure, like that." Dolly gives her a suspicious glance. "You holdin' out on us?"

"Perhaps I am."

"Bitsy, did you know about this?"

"Given the constant stream of contacts that Bristol gets at all time of the day and night, no, it's not my business unless she makes it my business or we're looking out for something in particular. Bristol, did you really?"

"I did, yes."

"So it'd be weird if you suddenly called him instead, huh?"

"I do think it would, which wouldn't *particularly* bother me, but you know how these things go."

"Yeah, sure," Dolly says, in a tone that means she absolutely does not.

"No, I get it," I say. "Especially if you haven't been talking about the game."

Bristol laughs. "We absolutely have not been, why would we."

"Why would you," Dolly repeats, a laugh in her voice but not laughing. "*Obviously.*"

"What have you been talking about?" I ask.

"Oh, nothing terribly important, darling, just getting to know you chitchat. He hasn't traveled much and would love to do more, so I recommended him the best credit card for the rewards points to interest ratio."

"You did what?" Dolly says.

"Is it really so odd?"

"I guess not." Dolly laughs, looks at me. "So, keep on target?"

"Keep on target," I say.

Chapter Nine

The Stanford campus is like a city within a city. It's weird, how little time I've spent on college campuses, any of them. I think it'd be easy to blend, and I'm keeping that as a back pocket solution for the next time I or we need to immediately hide out from prying eyes. Dolly parks by the museum and I look at the cars around us to see how the parking credentials works. Students have etags of course, more temporary visitors have holos for their windows with a little addition to their car code, and museum visitors just need to feed the meter.

Quick quiz, how do the three of us deal with parking meters?

Bristol enjoys the esoteria of coins, and even though most people don't carry cash modernly, and especially not coins, she does. Though Bristol also hardly drives herself anywhere, and even more rarely has to deal with something like a parking meter.

Dolly lies to them with a paperclip. Why paperclips are still an item that exist in the world and are manufactured every year is not a question for me to ask; some industries are still paper-driven. Some countries, too. She has other tools she can use too, but paperclips are small, and flex right but have the right stiffness.

For me, it depends on the meters. Some are genuine antiques, only mechanical, and I'll pay them in coins or slugs, whatever the de-tritus in my pockets gives me. I can do the paperclip thing, or I can also use other tools. If it's an internet device, I can fool it with a magnet or a fake RFID debit card or by hopping onto its network and lying to it.

The museum wouldn't normally be open this late, but there's some kind of additional exhibition opening and reception, and there are enough people around that it's clear school is also in session. Unless they're all just here for the special event. I have kind of a funny thought, that at least we're not actually racing nine other teams now or whatever, we can just act pretty normal. Visitors are expected here, even if we wouldn't hold up the illusion of being students, since we haven't prepped for that. But the pressure is different. I see Bristol looking at sleekly bearded maybe-professor types, and when I look at Dolly quizzically, she rolls her eyes. Oh, it's that kind of looking. But she's also making eyes at the nearby sculpture garden, that we have to walk past to go into the museum, and that I understand.

Plus, on a job or not, I never went to this many museums and things before I knew Bristol. It just wasn't within the framework of my existence. When museums were mentioned in my childhood, they were described as housing items stolen from their rightful owners and cultures, which is true and not true. The Elgin Marbles, in Europe? Yeah. The Golden Spike, at Stanford? No. But nuance is hard with prepper mindsets.

The statues outside here are interesting, but not fascinating to me, and maybe sometime I'll ask Bristol to recommend some art. She has to have something in mind that she thinks I'd like. That's the kind of thing Bristol seems to do, catalogs things in her head as they relate to people that she might be called upon to interact with. She can talk to anybody about all kinds of things as a result.

We get into the museum, past ionic columns that look weird to me for reasons I can't describe, and Dolly says "Okay, where're we going, Bitsy?" once we're inside and I blink at the marble entry that we're looking at, staircases going up to arches, and then look around for a sign. I step out of the trickle of foot traffic and find a QR code to scan, holding my headset to my face to look at the virtual guest welcome, the map of the museum.

"Well it's not one of the exhibits, it's..." and then I trail off because there are collections and exhibitions and those are two different things so then I just search the spike and it says it's on display but not *where*, like why can't I just select it and have a place on the map light up? Well there's only so big this place is, it'd be in poor form to go tearing into their network because I'm frustrated by visitor UI. Oh it *is* an exhibit, it's just about Stanton and not specifically the *railroad*. I was just asking my question wrong.

I lower my headset and Bristol is earnestly saying to somebody in a suit jacket and a lanyard with a dangling name tag "Oh, she's quite all right, she just gets these *headaches* sometimes, it's the light I think...There, see? No intervention required." They look at me with a small, dubious frown, and look back to Bristol.

"We will be closing soon, but, if you need further assistance—"

"No, no, it's fine. But thank you so much." She doesn't say darling, I add that to my mental catalog. A college student wouldn't say darling, so she doesn't say it to this random campus person. She also didn't change into riot gear; I'd brought it up, but we'd immediately moved on, and she looks exactly as though she belongs here, in her romper dress thing and sandals.

"Ready to roll?" Dolly asks.

"Well I didn't—"

"That's okay, Bristol gathered some information when it seemed to the casual viewer like you were havin' an episode of some kind."

"How would what I just did be so weird on a college campus?" Or anywhere, really. VR having become as ubiquitous as it is, stepping aside to pull your goggles up for a second isn't really so different from walking around looking at your phone.

Dolly shrugs, nodding at Bristol so that we start walking. "Hell if I know."

"Every setting has its own rules," Bristol says, as though it's readily obvious how I broke any social rules.

I know enough program languages that I could write like, a neutral social interactions protocol for myself if I wanted to, with prompts in my HUD. If this, then you can do/say this. I'm not going to, though. Most of the time I don't draw notice, and if I wasn't here with Dolly and Bristol, I wouldn't have done that, not just out in the open. I would've used my HUD or I would've gone to a bathroom or something.

It's another indicator, I guess, that the game isn't a real game. They haven't had wild-eyed weirdoes running in here looking for the golden spike to find the next clue. Everything's business as usual. My focus was elsewhere, but now I can just load my 'how to behave in a museum' program that I didn't write because who needs a program for that?

I follow Bristol and Dolly through the halls, playing the 'where's Dolly's gun hidden?' game, though also I guess it depends on *which* gun because sometimes she's got a really little one that she's trying out and those go up sleeves pretty easily. In addition to the kind of small-but-normal-sized gun she can holster in the small of her back and with riot gear you absolutely can't tell. And because Dolly herself is a weapon, whether she's carrying something additional or not never changes her bearing. She stands up straight enough for Bristol's tastes most of the time, at least.

I was for some reason under the impression that Dolly's gun would be the only one present, but then I glimpse a security guard and his holster. Okay then. I guess mass shootings being what they are, most places opt for armed guards. Were there even metal detectors at the doors? Not that I noticed, and actually with all of the tech so many people carry at all times, just a regular metal detector would have too many false positives, so even if they did have them at one time, they probably had to take them out. You can't have them going off for people's cybernetic limbs and other implants and personal webs of phone-watch-tablet-eye stuff, it's just too much.

The golden spike is behind plexiglass, of course, and then in another separate box of its own. My leap of logic to 'do they expect us to steal it?' didn't make sense, obviously, because that isn't what the game is. But it is what the agency might expect of us, if they thought we might have a buyer, god knows why we would. I'm sure enough people, modernly, are obsessed with the old time railroad days and maybe have the money to be esoteric collectors of the stuff, but even then, most of them wouldn't want something out of an active museum display that they couldn't show off to their other railroad enthusiast friends. Plus there are really good 3D scans of this online, and you could print a reasonable copy for display, just so that you had it aesthetically. Even with the slow rise of high-speed rail in the states, I don't know if anybody's capitalized on that aesthetic, but really that's probably for the better, what with the marginalized labor and all. They don't want to call attention to historic wrongs while perpetuating current ones.

There aren't any paper brochures in the room, and we sort of mill around looking at the exhibit without looking at the exhibit.Well. I'm not really looking at the exhibit, I think it's very possible that Bristol is and equally possible that Dolly isn't. I look at Dolly and she's looking at a set of bull's horns that are mounted on the wall above the door.

I go and look at the spike itself. For something gold driven into the ground, it looks pretty good actually. It has some dings where I assume the hammer hit it, and The Last Spike is engraved on that end. The length of it is also engraved, with names and things, but I could've seen that online in its picture, or by reading the articles about it, coming here wouldn't have been necessary. There's a more normal looking railroad spike tossed in there too, bend near the sharp end, and I wonder if they drove that one first to make room for the ceremonial gold one. It would make sense.

"San Francisco, then?" I ask. This room is painted red on three walls where there aren't exhibit cases, and that bothers me in a way I can't quite put my finger on. The other wall is a big painting, and that's what Bristol is looking at, her head cocked as though somebody's telling a story and she wants them to know that she is listening, enchanted.

"No, darling, I think the clue is where this painting was. There's an odd little video that explains this scene, and then describes how to get to its setting through the campus and nearby buildings."

"Well ain't that something," Dolly says. Now she's looking at the plaster death masks to our right. Bristol looks at her, and then me, and shrugs minutely. I scan the code for the video and watch it myself.

"This is in the virtual tour, though, we didn't have to come here."

"I haven't the foggiest idea otherwise," Bristol says. "It seems as though it's the closest possibility, that we should try before driving further."

"Yeah, I'm not arguing that. I'm just confused, I guess And confused that I'm confused."

"We takin' a walk, then?" Dolly asks. She's apparently not worried that I'm confused, so okay. It's fine. I'm confused because I'm distracted and I'm distracted because I've got so much stuff happening in my systems to try and chase down the gamerunners, and see if they match with the agency, keep an eye on surrounding security systems so that we get maybe any kind of warning if somebody decides to move on us, the list goes on.

"I *did* want to see the outside sculptures," Bristol says confidingly. "And since the video says that we must walk through them..."

"Look, we got nothing but time," Dolly says, grinning at her and winking at me. "Right Bits?"

"Yeah we've only been doing this..." I check *that* timer. "39 hours."

"Oh is that all," Bristol says, a little faintly.

We go back out the way we came, before that guard comes to find us and kick us out, or we have to talk to any other security, and hang a right through the sculpture garden. I didn't expect to feel one way or another about this but I don't like it, actually. Nothing against the statues themselves, I don't think, but standing among statues instead of looking at them well-lit in an exhibition hall is something that makes my brain try to play the Uncanny Valley game. Are these people? Did that one just move? Are they about to move? A lot of them are on pedestals, and some are laying down.

One of them is a giant set of closed doors that the local map guide helpfully tells me is called The Gates of Hell before we have to walk through some vertical trees, and I can see that something about this is bothering Dolly too, maybe not the statues, but the walking through the suddenly kind of empty college campus, when not too long ago there were a lot of people. There are a lot of wooden benches here, scattered under trees and on the gravel or whatever this is, all vacant. Somebody left a bouquet of blue flowers in front of The Gates of Hell, at the feet of the statue labeled Eve, and Bristol stoops to examine them for a second, picking something up and tucking it in her pocket.

"Bristol, what—" She shakes her head, her tight smile telling me that she's caught my mood.

We pass between the straight trees or bushes or whatever they are, they remind me of pictures from the Roman countryside, and it's darker over here as we walk towards the road that we'll take to where the painting was set. Except it doesn't really quite exist as such anymore, that I can tell, but if there's a clue it can be taped to a light pole for all we know. Maybe as one of those advertisements with the little pull-off tabs; you can make those that are flat little USB drives, and not that most of us would just plug a random USB into an unsecured device, but if you were participating in the game you might.

It's a relief when Dolly asks, "Does it bother anybody else that we're walkin' down quarry road?"

"I thought you'd never mention it, darling."

"Bits?"

"Yeah but I don't see a problem yet. Which might be the problem." I sync up my scanner app with the local law enforcement networks. Their chatter is boring and minimal, nothing indicating that they're gearing up/have geared up for anything unusual or interagency.

"It's quiet, a little too quiet?"

"Yeah."

To our left is just hospital buildings, a whole hospital compound, and to our right is more museum or campus property, a cactus garden, the map says.

"Do we think they can hear us?" Bristol looks around without looking around, something we're all pretty good at by now.

I shrug, because it's always possible. "Maybe."

//We're gonna have to scatter, I think// Dolly says in our earbuds, using the subaudible system.

//Not too early// Bristol answers, and I nod.

//Bristol, power the game phone off. Do we all have our cloaking devices?// I ask. Mine's in one of my pockets, I don't know if Bristol's is in her purse or not. Who knows what Bristol has in her purse. I also assume Dolly's got one in a pocket.

//I do, yes.//

//Sure do. Drop a marker on a meetup, Bitsy.// I look at what's nearby on the map. A fine dining restaurant that all of us but Bristol would get kicked out of, and I light that up for her as possible scatter location. It would be predictable to the agency though, so who knows. A coffee shop. Further, more museums, all of them closed. A couple of hotels or motels. A lot of shopping centers, all of them closed for the night. Some residential neighborhoods. The mall might be good; there'll be overnight cleaning staff, maybe, but probably it'll be automated. Organizations like automating. And I can take care of entry.

//The amount of time we spend physically running...// Bristol says, trailing off with a sigh, taking out her active camouflage device, and that's when we hear the sudden approach of engines, pushed a little faster than we'd normally expect on this little back road, no sirens so it's not ambulances for the hospital. No headlights reflect off the street signs; they're running dark.

"Now," Dolly says, and we split, Dolly directly to the right across a short open expanse and into the trees, or I assume into the trees, because she disappears as she moves, the active camo doing its job. Bristol and I break left across the street, keying our devices, and I hear her taking stairs that hook up behind a bus shelter, me running straight into a little foyer ahead of closed hospital doors. This might be a mistake, I think, I'm good at doors but am I *this* good at doors, these don't have *handles*, but a narrow line of light is visible between them and I scrabble my fingers at the gap and pull one open, slip in, knock the wadded plastic out of the latch that kept it from closing. Maybe this is the door employees slip out of to smoke. Maybe this is the door family members use to come in after hours, I don't know, and I'm sorry I can't leave it the way I found it right now but it's better if it closes right now.

No visible cameras, and nobody in the hallway, and I jog up it as quietly as I can before turning down the first hallway that I see, and then the next. This is not the patient or visitors part of the hospital, this is definitely staff realm. I even pass somebody pushing a cart full of supplies and they pause like they hear me and so I pause so that they don't, and they walk on. I find a bathroom to go into and decloak, then wash my hands and walk out like I'm supposed to be there visiting or whatever. It's better to save the battery, for when I leave and cross all of those streets and parking lots.

I haven't spent a lot of time in hospitals, luckily, but there's so much interesting equipment networked here. I sign onto the public network just with the phone I've been using, and then backdoor into the broader connections, and I'm floored by all of the stuff that they have online. Lots of sensitive information systems, lots of sensitive medical equipment. The wrong person could do a lot of damage, even accidentally. Granted, *most* people won't even think to do what I've done, they just want to be on social media to talk to people while they're here, or they want to stream their shows, or whatever. But it was easy for me to get in and it was easy for me to plug in, and that's something I think about for later. The records systems probably have more layers of protection that I don't see because I'm not touching them, they must. Their security people have to know better, right?

But it's not my problem, I can't make it my problem right now. I stop at a water fountain to catch my breath and drink. I always need to drink more water. //Check check// Dolly says quietly into our earbuds, and it's about when I thought she'd check in, and check on us, but I'm so relieved all the same.

//Check// I say.

//Check// Bristol says, sounding out of breath still.

//Holding pattern?// Dolly asks.

//Yes, alright// Bristol says. She's gotten to the restaurant, I think, and I imagine she's in the ladies' room taking the five magical minutes she can use to look unruffled and put together.

//Understood// I say, and look for a waiting room.

Chapter Ten

We stay apart for a few hours, long enough for Bristol to have a light meal, and have several drinks paid for by men at the restaurant, and for me to watch our parking meter run down and our car get towed away to a nearby impound lot. I don't know what Dolly does; she's active, and she checks in periodically, but doesn't narrate or enlighten us. She doesn't like that I want to go to the mall first, but I want to be sure of the security systems letting us in, and I've got active camo too.

I leave the hospital maybe a little earlier than I say that I was going to, because there's only so comfortable I feel milling around a hospital in the middle of the night. If I could focus on just that, it'd be one thing, but I can't. I've kept an eye on the entrances, remotely, when I could, to make sure no agency sweeps came in looking. That I can tell, nobody out of place did, other than me. Maybe I saw some homeless people sneak in but, no I didn't. Absolutely not my business.

Once I'm out of sight from the hospital and am in an intersection of shadows, because of signs and trees and low buildings, I activate the camo. It's interesting, because I can't see myself either, and it's best not to think too much about that or it's easy to get really tripped up. I'm sure we all had some really funny private practice sessions, getting used to these. Or maybe it was part of Dolly's super soldier training, who knows. Well, I could know, I have her files. I only look at them when she asks me to, though, not just because I wonder about something.

It's possible I don't need it, but also I don't want to walk across a big huge parking lot alone in the middle of the night when people are actively after us without it. I wonder what made the agency jumpy, that they wanted to reel us in now. Or maybe they've been working on this since Bristol's wedding, or since Dolly had her little meeting with Will, and it took this long for the request to pass through committee and the plan to be planned. I probably should've keyed in sooner, like at the mechanical bull. Or when there was literally a bouquet of flowers for a clue.

Were the blue flowers at the sculpture garden meant as warning, or were they just a coincidence? I search blue roses while I walk, and the internet consensus seems to be that they're meant to signify mystery. I'm sure Bristol knows that, she mentioned flowers having meaning.

I get to the mall entrance, and of course the automatic doors don't open. I have a look for infrared sensors, motion detectors, all of that, and find the panel for the security keypad. A pretty standard, widely used model, and I hold down the two buttons that'll give me admin access and type 1234#, and the panel flashes green and I hear a click of the door releasing.

Slipping inside, I'm not really sure this mall is currently functioning. A cursory glance at the website had recently updated hours and tenants, but looking at it again, not all of the indoor stores are still functioning, and the most recently updated store only has outdoor access. Even better, for us. It's clean in here, no debris on the floor, no graffiti, but it smells dusty and empty. It's unbelievably quiet; the HVAC must not be on, I realize after a while that there isn't the ever-present, almost subaudible hum from that.

//It's clear// I say.

//I'll be arriving in a few moments// Bristol says in less than five minutes, according to my stopwatch. The silence from Dolly stretches out. She heard me, I know she had to hear me. She doesn't always answer right away, depending on positioning. This isn't outside of normal Dolly parameters.

The time keeps ticking up and I'm about to go looking for Dolly's electronic signature, which I'd held off on doing so that no local surveillance would notice extra packet traffic, when she says //Gonna be a little while longer, just sit tight. I'm okay.//

//Understood// I say, not understanding but isn't all of this a trust fall, and I go to the door to let Bristol in.

"What is she *doing*?" Bristol asks in an alarmed, loud whisper. Her eyes are taking in the abandoned setting as I trip the manual lock on the door again. She's changed her clothes, into her couture version of riot gear finally, though I don't know how she had all of it in her bag. It's a big bag, that's the only answer I need, I guess. One of those purses that's a big leather tote bag.

I shrug as we move away from the doors again. "I don't know. Dolly things."

"Very helpful, Bits darling." She sighs and then looks at me. "I'm so sorry that isn't fair. None of us are Dolly's keeper. I just worry that she's doing something dangerous, to keep the two of us safe."

"I do too. But we have to trust that she isn't. I don't think we're to that point right now." The only time, before, that we had been to that point, Bristol is the one who led away the hunters while Dolly and I, incapacitated in various ways, got to help and then safety. We're canny quarry, if nothing else. Plus, if you ask any outsider, they would say that they absolutely would not believe that Bristol would do such a thing.

We wait in what had once been a hallway for vending machines that led to public restrooms, near the doors we'd come in but not visible from them. There's holes in the wall for water fountains, but they're gone now, and their pipes. Uninstalled, or stolen for scrap. Which means the bathroom fixtures are probably also all gone. I look at the vending machines, dark-faced but their glass intact. Canned coffee and tea and energy drinks, bottled water, snacks assortment. Normally, because we live in a society, I wouldn't have the opportunity to just walk up to one of these things and use the vending machine key that I have, in a bundle of universally available keys if you know the right stores to buy from, but this is absolutely that opportunity and I need to distract myself for a few minutes, and I'm getting really tired actually and if there's still canned coffee or energy drinks in one of these, it might still be good. Or might not be poison, anyway. How 'bad' can coffee actually go? I'm not really sure.

"Bits, darling, what are you doing?" Bristol asks when I swing the first machine open.

"I know you just had dinner, but I could use a snack," I say. The first one's empty, well, beverages-empty but full of spiderwebs, and I shut it again. The second one has cans, dusty but brightly colored, and I'm reaching for one when Dolly comes in on the earbuds.

//Okay, I'm inbound, come let me in.//

"Thank goodness," Bristol says. She looks at her phone. "Oh, Ant has been texting me. I think that perhaps I shouldn't answer?"

"What's he saying?"

"The usual are you okay sorts of things. He does seem quite worried."

"You can tell him you're okay, if you want," I say. "You're using the app that—"

She smiles; Bristol's frivolous socialite façade makes it easy to forget that she's actually always as in control of herself and situation as she can be. "The secure one you make us all use to run our messages through, that scrambles our location in the occasion somebody attempts to trace it? Mais oui."

"Good then. Yeah, it's fine. It'll probably keep him from doing something stupid." We go to meet Dolly.

"Surely we'll stop somewhere to sleep now?"

"Probably, but it also should be like, a safehouse and not just any old hotel. Given our alert level."

"Oh yes, of course," she murmurs, only the slightest layer of veneer over her disappointment.

Bristol hangs back and I unlock the door for Dolly, who has Bristol's overnight bag, and her duffel, and mine. "I went and got our stuff from the car," she says, as I'm locking the door again.

"You're such a sweetheart," Bristol says, at the same time I'm saying, "Dolly, what?"

She grins, looking between the two of us. "Well they just had local law enforcement tow the car, and nobody looked at it right away. I don't know if they have agents coming in later or tomorrow or what. So I trailed them to the impound lot and then hopped the fence. I know how attached Bristol is to her shoes, I didn't want to owe her another pair."

"Darling, you know that wasn't actually your fault, and I've more than forgiven you by now."

"Sure, yeah, fool me once..." Dolly says, still grinning. "There isn't much creepier'n an abandoned mall, huh?"

"Cemeteries, I would think," Bristol says after a slight pause.

"Nah, they're not empty."

I laugh, surprised. "Jesus, Dolly."

"Well they're not!" I shake my head and sigh, and it turns into a yawn. "Okay, what's the plan? We crashing here tonight?"

"Heavens no," Bristol says, even more horrified than when I opened the vending machines. "Absolutely not, I would rather turn myself in."

"Aw, you don't mean that, Bristles," Dolly says, but she does look a little repentant. "Anyways, getting our next ride'll be easy enough, there are plenty of targets. We probably can't rent anything on account of the surveillance dragnet and all."

"And then where will we *go*?" Bristol asks.

"Well I assume back to Vegas to kick some nerd ass, but I'm open to suggestions."

"A hotel first, since Bristol doesn't want to sleep under a bridge or whatever, but maybe near the airport? Or further? And then tomorrow we'll have Bristol call that number Ant so nicely gave her, and I'll trace his location and devices and then we'll track him down and get some answers." It's already tomorrow, but tomorrow is after you get up.

"Couldn't you find him anyway without..." Dolly trails off.

"Yeah, but I want him to lie to her one more time, knowing what we know." I don't like catching people in crossfire.

"Atta girl."

"An airport hotel is the best idea, I'd say" Bristol says. "So many comings and goings, we'll be all the more unobtrusive."

"You've never wanted that in your life," I say, before Dolly has the chance, and Bristol gives a little laugh.

"We all know each other so well, don't we?"

We walk towards the exit at the other end of the mall; we'd already had so much activity at the doors I cracked, I'd rather circumvent security again than rely on that working out one last time. "Still think it's creepy," Dolly grumbles.

"But there's so much space!" Bristol says brightly. "You could turn cartwheels or rollerskate or..."

"Now Bristles, I didn't know you knew how to turn a cartwheel."

"Doesn't everybody?" She turns to me. "Bits, you can do a cartwheel, right?"

"Yeah," I say. It's been a while, but is that a thing you forget? I stop and put my bags down, look at the floor to make sure that I'm not about to put my hands in broken glass, and run the motion through my head, raising my hands and then bending to the floor before I could overthink it. Kind of sloppy, but I do it. Bristol claps, delighted, and Dolly laughs.

"Well okay, everybody can do a cartwheel. Supposedly." She does one too, and then when she lands does a backflip. "Sorry, gotta show off sometimes right? You understand, Bristles."

"Of course, darling," Bristol says, laughing and clapping her hands again. She hands me her bag."I'm afraid I am more at Bits's skill level." It isn't often that I think Bristol isn't telling us the truth; this might be the first time. Her cartwheel doesn't seem at all rusty, it's comfortable, like she's done them for her whole life or maybe practiced a lot. Maybe it's just that Bristol doesn't like doing anything unless it seems like she's good at it.

Dolly claps too, and I think it's maybe one of the first times all three of us have stood around laughing together like a group of friends doing friend things. We work really well together, and have for a couple of years now, but friendship is a thing that can be both weirdly narrow and really encompassing all at the same time, and we just don't always connect like that. Maybe it's mostly Bristol that keeps everybody at an arm's length on purpose; I've thought Dolly and I were actually friends versus colleagues for longer. But did that mean we didn't try harder, with Bristol? Or were we just letting her come around on her own terms? Well, if it bothered her, we'd know.

We all brush off our hands because even though the floor isn't fuzzy with dust, there is some, and Bristol offers around hand sanitizer. I wonder again about the cleanliness in here; I really think that it's probably robot vacuums or whatever but still haven't seen any stations for them. They could just be down a janitorial hallway, an off-shoot like the vending hallway Bristol and I were in for that little while.

I yawn hard and long enough that my eyes water before I get to work on this door. I'm tired enough that it takes a little more time, disengaging the security, manually clicking the lock, but I get there without tripping any other systems, defensive or cleaning or anything else, and we're back out into the night, and after I kind of do a general sweep of network chatters and police type vehicles, we risk a rideshare that's driving by with its lights hopefully on.

"You girls are out late," the driver says, eyeing us in her rear view mirror. "It's good you're all buddied up like that."

"Of course we always practice safety in numbers," Bristol says. She's sitting in the front seat, looking at her phone.

"That's smart. Wish I could do that driving, but I can't."

"You could get a robot dog," Dolly says, gives me a look of wide-eyed innocence when I elbow her. "What? You can charge them at charge stations and some of them are *specifically* for security."

"Too expensive," the driver says. "I just have a gun instead."

Dolly laughs. "Yeah, that'll do you."

They chatter about guns the rest of the way to the hotel, Dolly leaning between the front seats, and I reserve a room for us at the hotel, running our payment through and getting three days. We won't stay the whole time but that gives us a landing pad that we can use while we're here, and then as a decoy if we need to. It's an automated hotel, so no staff to contend with other that the maintenance staff who periodically come around, but they won't be there when we are, and they won't care about who we are.

I also check my messages, check on the other team's map location. New Mexico. It really is two different games, a real one, or real-adjacent anyway, and a trap one. I really did want that IBM chip, I think ruefully, but that's what they were counting on. I'll just have to find a tech dump or something, comb through satellite photos for likely candidates. The prizes were just too fine-tuned for our interests. Well, they took a gamble on Dolly caring about the motorcycle I guess. Or Bristol. Wouldn't that be funny, if it turned out that she was just really into 20th century anime? Nobody would expect that.

But if it was necessary, with some study, she could make pretty much anybody believe it.

I organize my files of the teams that aren't real teams, and flag the names that I thought I recognized. Then I run a search on the names that I don't recognize, across as many platforms as my crawlers can reasonably reach in a short time, and one by one, a lot of them come up dry. Some are real, and I run location traces on all of them. Most of us, 'hackers' us, run layers of location foiling, VPNs and redirects and all of that, but I just want approximate hits, I neither want nor expect genuine and accurate real time home addresses. I just want to confirm that they aren't actually clumped in teams in the Western half of the United States.

While that's running, we get to the hotel, and get our stuff out of the car. Our room is on the third floor, windows overlooking the road. Once we're inside, I take Dolly's phone for a minute and sign it onto the hotel wireless; I want to see how many people are locally active, and that's the simplest way without adding another thing to my systems, which can handle it, but I've got so many windows open, I don't want to shuffle them around again. It's a weekday, so our potential neighbors are pretty sparse. Only four other rooms are occupied, and there are two on the first floor, one on the second, and one on the fourth, good.

We walk up the outer ramp to our floor, and I copy those device markers and hand Dolly back her phone. "What're we looking at?" she asks.

"Only a few other people here, and we're alone on this floor." It's possible there are people here who aren't online, but almost everybody has at least one device that hops onto available wireless whether you want it to or not. I check my scanner app. "Nothing on the scanners."

"Just means they didn't involve the locals. Plus, the car was just a normal expired meter tow, not special fancy impound."

"Do you mind if I take a bath, darlings?" Bristol asks.

"No, go for it," I say. The room is long, railroad car style, with a little entry hall that's got a closet space, then a room with a big tv and two double beds, and then the other bedroom, with a king sized bed and huge windows that Bristol walks briskly to and pulls the shades on.

"I'm starving," Dolly says. "Anybody want anything? Gonna see what's on the hoof in the vending machines. Maybe at that 7-Eleven we passed on the way in."

"I'm just going to check on some stuff and I'm passing out," I say.

"Okay, but if it's dawn and you're still awake, I'm gonna take your toys away and put them in a tinfoil box."

"You won't know if I'm still awake," I say, laughing.

"That's what you think." She makes the 'eyes on you' gesture, then takes the keycard from me and goes out again.

I kick my boots off and crawl across one of the double beds. "7-Eleven," Bristol says with a sigh, as she closes the bathroom door.

"She likes 7-Eleven."

"Trust me, I am well aware."

Chapter Eleven

I'm still awake when Dolly comes back, but I'm finishing up with the fake team data and not really paying attention until I hear Bristol laughing. I've got a long list of people that don't seem to exist other than sockpuppet accounts with stock image avatars, and a short list of people who very much do exist and who are flung across the globe and country and don't seem to be in this area of operation. Though that also gives me a list of people to check agency files on next time I slip into their systems, and it's a list of people that need some kind of a warning.

I check the time; I definitely dozed for some of the time she was gone. I think. It's hard to tell sometimes. I push my headset up and blink at them. I can still see steam on the bathroom mirror, so I guess it hasn't been so long. Bristol is in one of the plush hotel robes, but her hair is dry. Already, or still?

"They had pairings on the shelf tags!" Dolly's saying in protest, but also laughing. "Is that wrong?"

"No, darling, I very much appreciate the thought."

"Then what's the problem? I brought choices. Pinot and grapes, rosé and watermelon. I assumed the fruit was like, the least adulterated thing I could get there, so you might eat it. Because I could've gotten the single-serve carton of chardonnay and their shrimp skewers."

"Thank you for not purchasing shrimp skewers for me at 7-Eleven," Bristol says in a careful, measured voice. "Sorry, Bits, did we wake you?"

"No," I say. "But it's not late enough that Dolly's going to take my stuff away. Early enough."

"It's gettin' there," Dolly says with her mouth full, shaking her fist.

"Then why are you making so much noise?" I ask, blinking at her. That surprises her, and she suddenly ceases all movement, trying to see if I'm joking or not, and I crack a smile as I put my headset on the bedside table.

Bristol cracks open one of the canned wines and sniffs it hesitantly. "Just a nightcap," she says, as though we're watching her judgmentally.

"Is it to m'lady's taste?" Dolly asks, and then shudders. "Hah, forget I said it like that."

"Yes, let's."

"Bitsy, I got you canned cold brew for when we get up, not now."

"Thank you," I say. It's funny, how much she's scolding me. She's the one who woke us up at 5:30 a.m. to get on the road. Bristol absolutely would not have picked that time. I wouldn't have picked that time.

They go into the room with the king sized bed to eat and bicker, and I get changed, wash up in the bathroom, then actually lay down to sleep, not even putting my headset back on. We hit all the activity high notes today, driving in the car for hours, and then physically running, interspersed with a lot of VR and other hacking type activities. I fall asleep before 5:30 a.m. at least, so I didn't stay up for a full twenty four hours. I've done it before, and I'm sure I'll do it again, just not today. Before I drop off, I reach out for the room remote and paw the controls until the door chimes that it's been set to Do Not

Disturb, and then I fall asleep before I'm able to put the remote back on the bedside table.

I come partway awake once, when I hear my phone vibrate with a notification, but Dolly and Bristol are clearly sleeping still, no noise from either of them, and I just roll over and figure the notifications can wait. We don't do anything until we're all rested, at this point, unless something dire is happening, and if something dire is happening, my phone will buzz more than once. More will happen than my phone buzzing.

I *really* sleep after that, waking up when Dolly stumbles to the bathroom and turns the shower on. I hope it isn't 5:30 again; I roll onto my back and stretch, check my HUD. No, almost noon. It's a miracle.

She put one of the cans of coffee next to my phone and headset as she passed by; my fingers graze it when I reach for the phone, and come away cold. I've got a bunch of notifications, a lot of them in the spam filter, which I always check because sometimes it's interesting or at least funny. Rarely useful, though. The buzz right as I was falling asleep was the flag that I have on Will's biometrics. He can change devices, but with his clearances, he can't change his fingerprints and retinas, they're in the system. What system? All of them. They're not always labeled the same way of course but the data is the data.

He didn't land in the airport we're sleeping next to; nope, he's in Las Vegas, which is still where the gamerunners are. I assume we'll fly there, I don't think Bristol is eager to get back in the car for another eight hours. Should we run away from Will instead of towards? Yeah probably. But they also won't expect this. And probably don't expect that we know what's going on. They can't not underestimate us, apparently, and I wonder why that is. We sat in a room with Will and his supervisor and we all signed contracts and then Marquis is the only one who kept to it. And yet the agency is still just shocked, shocked at the state of affairs regarding us. Do they just think Will is particularly bad at this? Do they think that, because they got the most important diamonds and data back, we aren't worth pursuit? It's true that while we stole those diamonds on purpose, we didn't steal the top clearance intel on purpose. It's also been true that Will, at least, is still after us, but hasn't been good enough on his own.

I sit up and grab the coffee, pop the tab before I notice that it says to shake. Typical. I take a sip off the top, and then kind of swirl the can in my hand like it's a glass of brandy. I can't tell the difference between my next sip and my first one. Shaking the can might be a scam, or at least with this brand.

Bristol sighs and rolls over when Dolly starts whistling in the shower. "Good morning," I say, and she kind of hums. "Do you want one of my canned coffees that Dolly got?"

"Thank you, darling, but no."

"You won't want anything at the airport."

"No, but if we fly first class, what they have will be suitable."

"If we don't?" Should I have reserved flights already, or did one of them do that? We were so tired.

"We are in the business of solving problems, aren't we?" She stands up and stretches luxuriantly, then twitches apart the curtains to look outside. "Oh, I'd forgotten the airport was our view."

"Sunrise over the tarmac," I say, and we laugh.

The shower cuts off and I drink my coffee and scroll through all of my notifications and updates. The other team is doing pretty well; they won't beat last year's winner on time, I think they've got more than one clue left. Maybe they don't, who knows. Two games diverged in the desert, and we took the ones planned by a government agency, question mark. In a not-really way, our time is much better than last year's team; we already figured out that the game is rigged.

I don't realize they're talking to me until Dolly hits me with balled-up foil. "What?"

"I was askin' if you got us flights already or if we need to do that."

"I wondered the same thing," I say.

"For heaven's sake," Bristol says, but she's smiling.

"Okay, so we need tickets to Vegas so we can kick some nerd ass. Unless we want to drive to Vegas?"

"No, thank you," Bristol says at the same time I say, "Probably not."

I check into flights, and Dolly makes coffee with the room's coffee maker and complimentary bag of grounds, reading the package with surprising concentration. "So I'm skeptical that people are growing fair trade coffee in North Dakota, that's weird, right?"

"I mean, it's probably in green houses?"

"In quantity to be robot hotel supply coffee?"

I shrug. "Maybe it's a selling point, it's this hotel exclusive or something."

"Or it's a lie."

"Just the fictions of marketing, darling," Bristol says, breezing through to the bathroom with her makeup bag. "First class, if it's available?"

"If it's available," I say, clicking through. We can check in at 1:30, which is soon but not too soon I don't think, be wheels up at 2:15 and in Las Vegas by 4:15.

"Nice to have the leg room, even on a short flight."

"Really short flight," I say, organizing my records of the IDs we're using on this trip, running the reservations and then doing the pre-flight check in once the notifications hit my inbox. I do the mental math quick to make sure I'm not forgetting, but we won't have to check any bags. "Dolly do you need firearms clearance?"

"Nah, I'm good."

I look at her. "You haven't had a gun this whole time?"

She grins, and the brew cycle gurgles to a finish behind her. "I didn't say that."

"But—"

"I can make a drop and then pick up somethin' new on the other side, I do it all the time." She pours a mug of the coffee and sniffs it before she takes a sip. It smells like pretty normal coffee from here. "Tastes like coffee," she says with a shrug.

"It smells over roasted," Bristol says from the bathroom.

"Lotta people like that. Or, they emperor's-new-clothesed themselves into thinking they like it."

"There's probably a less awkward way to say that," I say.

"Yeah, prob'ly." She takes another sip. "Wanna try?"

"Sure." It tastes okay, I guess; not burnt. I forget that Dolly drinks her coffee black, even though I just watched her make it. "Oh hey."

"Hey yourself," she says, taking the cup back. "What's up?"

"Will is also in Las Vegas."

"Since when?" Dolly asks, and Bristol comes to the bathroom door, holding her uncapped mascara.

"Late last night slash early this morning. After we went to bed. Well, after I went to bed, I don't technically know when you did."

"Wonder why," Dolly says.

"It's probably easiest for Will to work with the gamerunners in person at this portion of the operation," Bristol says thoughtfully. "And he doesn't want Bits to be privy to their conversations, should she be listening to them electronically."

"Will does have a healthy respect for Bitsy's prowess, that is true."

"And he thinks you're a cold-blooded killer without a shred of humanity."

"I mean, I am," she says, offering Bristol the coffee cup. Bristol shakes her head and goes back to the mirror. "He ain't the first one I've had that effect on."

"I'm sure," Bristol says.

"Anyway, you like it," I say, tossing my coffee can in the wastebasket.

"Of course I do, he isn't any use to me in the traditional way. Too goddamn wholesome."

"Right." She gets the other canned coffee out of the little hotel fridge and I nod when she waggles it at me. "So what's the actual plan for Vegas?"

"What, we need more of a plan than kicking nerd ass?"

"With Will present, we do," Bristol points out.

"I can kick his ass too," Dolly says cheerfully.

"Okay, but I mean, are we gonna steal the stuff that was supposed to be the prizes?"

"Yeah we could do that," Dolly says. "If it's real."

"They've still got one live team playing a game, something is real."

"There's something so sad about that," Bristol says, zipping up her makeup bag and coming out again. "They're doing the work and losing sleep, thinking that they're in a viable competition but they're only competing against the illusion of other teams."

"They know that we're in it," I say. "But not that there's like. Game/real game dynamics."

"Aww, poor buddies," Dolly says. "We can kick 'em some cash if you want, Bristles."

"I didn't say—"

"You didn't, but you also feel bad for people so rarely, we gotta reinforce that right?"

"Honestly, Dolly darling, I—"

"And I'm the one Will thinks is cold blooded," Dolly says, winking at me, but I'm chugging the second can of coffee to avoid having to say anything. I didn't shake this one either. Bristol, smiling fixedly, finishes packing her things.

"We all have our roles," she says after almost exactly a minute. Fifty five seconds.

"True, we do. So where are we going and what're we doing?"

I start digging in my kit; I should've been thinking about this and slept instead, but also in my defense, some of last night was spent sprinting and that's not a normal part of things. "Before we leave the hotel, we're going to have Bristol call the personal number she was given, using the game burner phone, which we'll leave here and go catch our flight. I'm making a clone now, though, so we don't lose access to that number and connection. She'll say that since we're unable to continue the game, we'll have to bow out, and thank them for the good time. Implying that we're skipping town, skipping the country, whatever. We'll see what they say from there. We know Bristol's good at improvising."

"Thank you, darling."

"We packed, then?" Dolly asks, then surveys the room, which other than the unmade beds looks like we just got here. "Okay."

I hand Bristol the phone, and she dials the number into it from hers. She leaves her earbud in, so Dolly and I can hear the whole conversation. Ant answers on the third ring. "Hey, what's up?"

"Good morning, darling, I'm afraid I have some bad news."

"What is it? Are you okay?" Dolly raises her eyebrows at me; he does sound genuinely concerned, I'll give him that. Some of that probably has to do with our team geotag just being in one place in the hours since the car was towed. Maybe he doesn't know, he's not the partner who's in on it with the agency. But he has to be, they can't possibly not all know that most of the teams are fake.

"It would seem that we are unable to complete the game, as things stand, so we will have to regretfully bow out. It is *such* a shame, this was great fun."

"Unable to complete...what happened out there?" There's muffled talking somewhere near him. Other gamerunners, Will, whoever Will brought with him expecting us to make contact. It might be Null again, that would be awkward. Theoretically.

"We just ran into a teensy snag and then didn't get the next clue and now we need to leave town without having done so, much to our deepest regrets. We thought we were doing so well and now disaster!"

"Yes, you were the leading team, yeah that's a shame. Are you...okay? Do you need one of us to come get you? From somewhere?" He still sounds pretty genuine, and I wonder if this got set up in part as a test case for Will, so he could see somebody else just helpless in Bristol's hands and maybe not feel so bad about being as smitten as he is. Seems possible.

"No, no, there's no need for that. We're fine, we're probably even safe. We're simply between a rock and a hard place."

There's rustling on the other end of the line, and some short, hushed argument, and then a new voice comes on the line.

"Did something really happen, or can you just not figure it out? You'd rather lose the whole game than ask for a hint?"

"Now that isn't very pleasant, is it?" Bristol says mildly, rolling her eyes.

Dolly mouths *Good nerd, bad nerd* and we all smile.

"It's unusual for an all-female team to try something like this."

"You'd be amazed at how often we run into comments like that, darling, it really isn't as original as you must have assumed. We needn't try to twist this into a women's issue, when really, you're trying to obfuscate the actual problem with your little game." She looks at me and Dolly, questioning. I check the timer and then hold up my thumb and forefinger: close to when she should hang up and we should leave. She nods.

It was the right thing to send this guy off, though. "Our *little* game? You mean our very successful game with big prizes that you volunteered for, if you're forgetting."

Bristol smiles, as though he can see her, and then says softly, indulgently, "Oh, darling. We know there are only two teams." She hangs up on his startled exclamation and drops the phone on the bed, as it immediately starts ringing.

"He had to know we knew, right?" Dolly asks, looking at the bed.

"It's hard to say," Bristol says. "But he's certainly upset about it, either way. Plus that female team nonsense. These men need better peers."

"He was probably trolling on purpose." I pick up my bags.

"In my experience, people who like trolling never got the assbeatings they deserved."

"Maybe not," I say. "But there's a first time for everything."

We go out and get a rideshare to the airport, visible from our hotel but of course not walkable. I check out of the hotel as we go, then check our pre-check for the flight and that's all smooth sailing. Security is even less of a pain than it could be about our equipment, the reinforcements in our clothes that are clearly visible on their scans, my computer stuff. I think sending Dolly through first, and the Bristol, is the right plan. That way they see Dolly's cybernetic arm and smell the money and class coming off of Bristol, and by the time they get to me, they have a plausible narrative that they told themselves.

Chapter Twelve

We reserve a hotel for a few days and stow our luggage, and Bristol and I go to a diner off the strip and get coffee (me) and sparkling water (her) while we wait for Dolly to take care of some business, as she said. I get nachos for the sake of having something to pick at while I chase the connections that the gamerunners have locally, to see how many people it's likely that we have to worry about when we go confront them. It doesn't seem like they expect us to be here. I could be wrong, but it doesn't seem like it.

The waitress does entice Bristol into some sort of pastry by the time Dolly arrives; apparently this place has a French-trained pastry chef for some reason. I guess I shouldn't say for some reason, people end up all kinds of places for all kinds of reasons. Maybe they're from here and went to France to train and bring it back right here. I'm not going to go interview them for a profile.

"Sorry that took so long," Dolly says. She doesn't seem out of breath or particularly ruffled. It didn't really even take all that long.

"It's no matter, darling, it just means we'll be able to see the sunset from the high rise hotel that they're in."

Dolly laughs. "Yeah you're right, it'll be a real romantic backdrop to the proceedings." She looks at the table, looks at us. "So are we ready?"

"I guess."

"Of course."

We go outside and I check one last time where the gamerunners are, crosschecking them with nearby devices. Then I do the same for Will. Still the same place. There seems to be just the three of them in the room, and while I don't know if that's really true, I just have to trust that we can handle that many or more. Mostly Dolly, but...

We walk up the street, cut a block over, and then walk through a hotel lobby to the elevator. "Okay, once we get up there, let's all use our camo so that we can do the 'knock on the door but the hallway looks empty when somebody looks out the keyhole' thing, I've always wanted to do that."

"Jesus Christ, Dolly," I say, but I can't help laughing. "Sure, yeah, we can do that. Right Bristol?"

"It will be very cinematic," she says thoughtfully.

"We watch different movies," Dolly points out, and then I shush them both, because we're two floors away and I don't want anybody to hear us talking. I text them the room number.

We activate our camo before the elevator opens; the hallway is empty, which is good. We try to avoid collateral damage. We go down the hallway to the door, and the floor is pretty quiet, either by happy accident or by agency/gamerunner design, it's hard to guess and I don't want to take the time to investigate right now. I stop to the side of the door, and assume Bristol does the same. Dolly knocks, shave and a haircut, and we wait.

There's a pause; I hadn't been aware of people talking in the room until they stopped. I watch the peephole, and a shadow passes over it when somebody looks through. Another pause, and Ant mutters, "That's weird, there's nobody there." He's got the bolt off and the knob turned when Will says

"No, wait!" but then the door flies open, coupled with unmistakable sound of a boot sole flat on wood. Ant stumbles back a few feet and then falls with a grunt, and I catch the waft of Bristol's perfume as she moves into the room and I go in too, closing the door behind us and bolting it again.

The guy on the floor gets invisibly dragged into the sitting room of the suite, like a horror movie, and the other gamerunner is just frozen in place, either through surprise or fear or Bristol tased him, and Will has his arm back for his holster but he's frozen too, his head tilted back just a little, and I realize no, that's where Bristol is, so I go to the other gamerunner and take the phone out of his loose fingers.

//On the three-count// I text on our network, and then we drop the active camo.

Dolly has her boot on Ant's chest on the floor and her arm straight out with her gun pointed at the face of the other one, and yeah, Bristol is standing next to Will's gun arm, with her hair down and one of her slim hairpin knives just against where his jaw meets his neck.

"Do we have to explain anything, or do you fellas understand how this is gonna go?" Dolly asks, grinning. Bristol unholsters Will's gun with her free hand and tosses it to Dolly. The way the other three flinch as she catches it is audible.

"What do you want?" The standing gamerunner asks. Trace, that's his name. He's the main face for the whole thing.

"An explanation, so that we know if our guesses got close, and the prizes would be nice. This is a version of winnin' the game, ain't it?"

"Uh, sure, yes, it is."

"This is almost disappointing," Dolly says to me in a confidential tone, but not really any quieter. "Too easy. What else do you have planned, Will? Is a helicopter gonna pull up and hover out that window?"

He clears his throat. "No helicopter."

"Good." She glances down at Ant on the floor. "You gonna behave if I let you park on the couch?"

"Yes," he says, immediately.

"You?" she asks the other one and he nods. From the look on his face, he's never looked down the barrel of a gun before. So few of us have, honestly, before our association with Dolly. "Okay, I'm gonna take three steps this way and let you two be honest and go straight to the couch. Got it?" They both nod. "Good." She takes three steps back away from them, one gun pointed at each, and I back off too, away to the side where there's a table full of takeout bags, so I'm out of her muzzle sweep.

"Get Ant's phone too. And Will's," I say. Dolly gestures with her gun, and Ant reaches slowly for his phone, tosses it towards me. It thumps onto the plush carpet and I go pick it up. Will rolls his eyes to Bristol, who nods.

"Go on, darling, give Bits your phone," she says, just as comfortably and easily as if we were sharing around pictures at an event. He gets it out slowly, and I wonder what he's thinking. How to disarm Bristol, maybe. If he can do it and get to Dolly without being shot. What I'd do in the meantime. He hands me his phone. "He can sit on the couch with the others, can't he, Dolly?"

"Hmm, I dunno."

I go sit at the table with their phones and the one I've been using. "If he has a panic button, he already hit it when we came through the door. It's probably fine." I don't think he has a panic button, I think this is his project and he's here solo. Just like when he was chasing the story of Bristol's wedding. He was absolutely certain it was her, and desperate to have backup, but the timing just didn't work out for him and muddied the waters enough once we left that the system files he has on us still say it's a dubious situation. I was even able to delete evidence of the original wedding license, so just the one with Bristol's friend is the only one that exists. I'd assume this means Will's learned his lesson about getting screenshots, but maybe not.

I set the gamerunners phones with a dongle that I have to crack their passcodes, and when I go to unlock Will's phone, it wants a fingerprint. I blink at it, and look over at him; he's watching me at the moment, which is a surprise. He always only has eyes for Bristol, which is I guess part of what the problem has been. I take the time to smile at him, because yeah, I can get around it, but then I get up and bring the phone over to him. He doesn't need to know that I can spoof his fingerprints.

"Unlock it, please," I say. He reaches out to take it and I shake my head. "Try again." His jaw tightens, but he nods and just presses his finger to the place. I watch the phone, and its connections, but no alarm is triggered, no timer that he has to do a puzzle for or anything. "Thanks." He just frowns.

"So are there prizes, or were you just gonna ghost on the other team?" Dolly asks. The game runners look at each other uncomfortably, and look at Will.

"The other team was going to be informed that they won second place and be given a smaller monetary award," Will says after a moment of clear deliberation. He doesn't have an earbud in, but that's earbud behavior. Maybe he was hoping to think of something else in that gap.

"Easy enough to do mockups of the motorcycle and stuff for online viewin'," Dolly says in a drawl, maybe to make Bristol frown, which she does. She's sitting on the arm of the vacant couch, putting her hair back up.

"Honestly, Dolly."

I go back to the table and copy the data off Will's phone. There isn't any point in ghosting it, it'll be cut off as soon as we leave here. Unless they assume I've ghosted it and leave the connection open as a trap or data point, but it's so obvious. Much like the game. Oh well, maybe we can do a real one a different year, that's way lower profile. Or, like Dolly auditioning for American Gladiators, that just isn't fair. I sigh.

"Is everything all right, Bits darling?"

"Yeah, unrelated," I say. They've been talking, I should pay attention. I try to run it back in my head, and yeah, it's what we expected. The gamerunners got caught red handed at something, and Will offered them this deal. "Give them the deal anyway, it's not their fault we knew."

"How *did* you know?" Trace bursts out. "Everything was compartmentalized."

"It was too easy," I say, blinking. "In some ways, the first and second clues were the only normal ones."

"You didn't get the clue at Stanford," Trace says.

"'Cause we were runnin' from Will's people, have some sense," Dolly says.

"Anyway, we were on our way to it, and I'm certain that right now, taunting us is not something you'll want to pursue." Bristol uses her phone to check her hair, then slips it into a pocket. "Now then, what shall we do with you boys?"

The gamerunners hadn't considered this, and Ant goes pale while Trace goes red. Will had considered this, but has to date been unable to predict our behavior, so why would now be any different?

In the pause, I say "I'm sending out a message to the other team's phone, that we won at 58.25 hours, but that second prize is still within their reach."

"Givin' them the money, Bitsy?" Dolly asks.

"They didn't know they'd be involved in this kind of stuff."

"Fair enough." I look at Bristol, who also nods.

"I agree, it's what's best."

Trace's phone is the one with the prize wallet, and I set up the contingency. When the other team finishes, it'll send their registered credentials the prize. "Done."

Ant says, faintly, "We're sorry about this, if that helps."

"Gotta save your own skin sometimes," Dolly says. "You about ready, Bits?"

"Almost." I give Will's files a quick scroll; pre-game, he's got a file of reported sightings of us, and I look at those one by one. We can't be impeccable with our security at all times, I can admit that, but only two of them are actually us. One is Bristol, in London, and the other one is Dolly in Mexico City. The other ten aren't, though, and Will's notes for each sighting are equally even handed, he talked himself out of being convinced on each one, but also saved them as the best ones, in case he was wrong.

While he's still got a connection to the agency, I put on my VR headset and follow it back. For a while now, a few years, I've been beating my head against how many staff the agency actually has, what they're a branch of, what their funding is like. They're smart, and I am only myself, so I'm slowly getting the picture but things are at all times changing. Will's clearance is pretty good, and I look at his profile's immediate connections. A few coworkers, Null included; even from looking at a bargain basement mocked up headset a couple years ago, I still recognize her style. The supervisor, of course. Their casework is varied; international thieves and hackers like us, some muscle, though Butler doesn't seem to be on their list or at least not this node's list. Nicolai is, but that's to be more than expected; I think he's on multiple agency lists around the world. A couple of Bristol's other friends are in a small watchlist, Marquis and some baroness and an art dealer. I copy all that to look at later, in case warnings are in order. Nearly everybody's on some kind of watchlist, anyway, you get there by breathing.

"Look, you don't benefit from hurting any of us," Will says.

"Unfortunately, darling, we would," Bristol says, and the look he gives her is more surprised than it should be. "I do think that removing you would remove our main pursuers." Dolly seems surprised too, tilting her head in Bristol's direction just a little bit, when she hadn't been before. The room is very still, the sunset now blasting it with orange light, throwing our shadows against the back wall.

"Is that what we wanna do?" Dolly asks the room.

"I don't know," I say. Okay, so I'm surprised too.

"You know that if you kill me, the agency will look for you based on that alone," Will says in a very composed voice.

"That is true," Bristol agrees, getting up off the couch and stalking over to stand next to Dolly. "And without your relentless focus, they'll have even less of a chance of finding us."

The gamerunners aren't made for this kind of movie bullshit, and their composure is cracking. "We didn't want anybody to get hurt," Ant says unsteadily. "That goes for him too, can't we all just walk away from this?"

"Surprise support, Will, ain't that nice?" Dolly asks. "They wouldn't be in this mess without you."

"I think it's probably shoot them all or let them all go," I say, stuffing phones in my pockets and wiping things down. "And we should do it soon."

"All or nothin', interesting Bitsy. Bristol?"

"This is a gambling town," she says slowly. She looks from Will over to me, and I'm not sure I quite understand the question in her face, but I think that I do, and I nod. "The choice is yours, Will. Come with us, and everybody walks away. Decline, and only we three walk away."

"I don't understand how—"

"Clock's ticking, Will Scarlet," Dolly says, thumbing back the hammer on the gun in her right hand. She's told me that you absolutely don't in general need to do that with guns anymore, but that it's one of those movie things that always produces an effect, like racking a shotgun, even though you'll lose a round.

He looks back at Dolly and I wonder what he's thinking. Then he swallows with an audible click and says, "I'll come with you." If the gamerunners weren't absolutely petrified in place, they would fall over with relief.

Bristol claps her hands once, and everybody on the couch jumps. Dolly smirks but doesn't laugh. "Excellent, darling." She looks around the room. "Do you have any luggage you need to collect?"

"The rolling suitcase there," he says, gesturing with his chin.

"Well get it, let's go," Dolly says. Will stands up, hesitantly, and walks to his suitcase in a daze, grabs the handle so it telescopes. "Gentlemen," she says nodding at the gamerunners. "It was fun while it lasted. Don't call the cops, if you know what's good for you." They nod in unison, like puppets.

I walk out ahead and call the elevator. I don't know if Dolly has a car lined up already, or if that's something we still need to do. We all stand in the elevator and watch the numbers go down. I don't know where Dolly disappeared Will's gun to, but it isn't in her hands anymore and it isn't in his holster again either.

"I cannot believe you told me your real name was Will the first time we met," Bristol says when we're still around the third floor.

"That was my baseline lie," he says, with difficulty.

Bristol reaches over and settles his collar where it got rumpled. "Well, it suits you."

We cross the lobby together, and Will behaves. He doesn't even look towards the front desk in a silent plea. I wonder what he's thinking; he's either too calm, or he's in shock. There are no sirens, even as we're out on the sidewalk again, the sun almost entirely gone. "I know a place we can get a car," Dolly says, taking out an ecigarette. "Prob'ly better to get our stuff and put this place behind us before we crash for the night and get some deprogramming done."

"I'm not—" Will says, and Bristol takes his arm.

"Hush, darling. There isn't anything to worry about right now."

"I wish I could believe that."
"If wishes were horses, then beggars could ride," I say.
Dolly huffs out a cloud of vapor laughing. "Bitsy, what?"
"Just an old saying."

Epilogue

After everything else, it really was only like six more hours in the car to get across the border to Mexico, and we do that before we get a hotel. The agency works globally, of course, but distance is always good.

Will is quiet for the drive, quiet in general. Probably thinking about his career, his family. It'll be interesting to see how the agency pursues this, if they want to recover or terminate. Maybe they already thought he was compromised; nobody ever said that outright in any of the files, but I think anybody who'd seen him and Bristol in the same room for any amount of time might have a sense of that. So, his supervisor definitely.

We get a suite in one of those all inclusive resort hotels that puts a wristband on you and makes it so easy to not leave, or at least not stray very far from its walls, beyond the kayaks they offer, the scuba adventure they'll take you on. Otherwise, lay out by the pool, and eat fresh chips and salsa daily and refill your daiquiris as needed, virgin or alcoholic. All of us speak Spanish, which make sense, but is nice to confirm.

Cortina from the other team messages me to congratulate me, hoping to keep the contact, I think. Which is fine, it's nice to have connections far and wide, at all levels. You never know when you're going to need somebody, and if you're smart, you never forget what it was like when you were just starting out.

Like Will is now, in fact. I'm pretty sure Bristol isn't going to let him far out of her sight for a while, but she'll have to eventually. Though also, the suite has enough beds for all of us, and everybody seems to have been sleeping in their own beds, so who knows. Dolly hasn't started making comments about it yet, which means it's serious.

Run With the Hunted 6:
Burned Asset

Chapter One

The thing about countries that don't have extradition treaties with the U.S. is that they might still do it anyway. Especially if they got somebody they wanna trade, or at least something else to leverage. We only stayed in Mexico for a week or so, time enough to arrange transport to Morocco by way of Hong Kong and picking up Butler as additional insurance, just in case Will's usual terror of me wasn't enough to keep him well behaved during global travel.

He was fine, though. Docile, maybe stunned by what the fuck just happened to him. We didn't even drug him this time. Butler's happy enough to be along for a trip, though, and I more'n like the idea of having him for backup in case the agency comes for Will in force. Bristol can handle herself surprisingly well in certain situations, and even Bits is a great shot, but they've never been operators. If we're going to have some movie siege in Bristol's Moroccan hotel, I want somebody else who's done exactly that kind of thing more than once, from either side of the map.

I want more than just Butler, but once we land in Morocco and get to Bristol's hotel, all of the stress about what just happened and how we have to plan and anticipate moving forward just...melts out of her pretty little head. It's wild to watch, I look at Bits to see if she's catching it, but she's distracted and I don't want to break her concentration.

Bristol links arms with Will, chattering about the renovations or restorations or something that she did to the building.

"Bristles, we gotta set up a war room," I say, and she smiles at me over her shoulder.

"It's too early to even consider anything a problem yet, darling," she says.

"Way I see it, you're walking next to the problem and he's about six feet tall."

"Mmm, indeed. Tell us, Will, when were you scheduled to check in?"

"What's today's date?" he asks, sounding like a sleepwalker, and she shows him her watch. "Three days from now."

"See? No problem yet "

I look at Bits again, who is paying attention now, though who can say when she started. "Bristol, that's—" she starts.

"Let's just all get settled in," she says, and she click-clacks off with Will in tow.

"I guess she's never had a pet," Butler grumbles, and I laugh.

"Just. Fuck," I say, and light a cigarette.

"You know she—" Bits says.

"Yeah, yeah, I know." Bristol takes bad things that happen and puts little protective coatings around them, like an oyster making pearls. Who doesn't, right? But this isn't a bad thing that happened, this is a lull in an ongoing situation. "I'll call Nicolai, anyway, she can't object to him."

"I mean, she can." Bits pops the top on a can of coffee and looks around at the parking lot courtyard area. A couple other cars here, staff and whoever else Bristol just lets stay here. What was her friend's name? Suzette. "I think she likes him though."

"How can you tell?" Butler asks, sarcastic but not.

"She added him to her phone," Bits says.

"That's just a thing you do when you meet people," he says, and Bits blinks at him. "She didn't add me to her phone?"

"No."

"Well." He seems genuinely surprised and I laugh. "I think we're getting away from the point."

"I think we're all too tired to know what the point is," I say, dropping my cigarette butt and stretching. "Which is a problem."

"I'm good, if you two want to sleep," Bits says. "And I'll message Nicolai. And keep an eye on Will and Bristol."

"Thanks, Bitsy." I'm sure Bristol isn't about to put us all at more risk than she already just did, but takin' Will with us was kind of an elegant solution. Even though he's an agency asset, assets tend to be negotiable. Maybe they'll make a deal and cut their losses, cutting him loose. He was why they kept after us, mostly, and Bits said he was the one most into it.

Or maybe they'll come for him, with whatever black ops they got, and we'll have to assume that if whatever happens here gets written about on account of the explosions and whatnot, it'll be written off as a gas leak or something else equally un-noteable on an international scale.

Or we'll fake his death and set him up with a new identity or somethin', maybe she's got a plastic surgeon we can fly in, and that'll make this all real easy, no lead poisoning required. I like that one, honestly, maybe I'll float it at brunch or whatever. Over mimosas.

We've been here at the hotel before, not long after Bristol bought it, or more like after Bristol paid it off and before all the renovations after we took the money and ran way back when. The first time we came here, she was almost embarrassed, and called it 'shabby chic' even though it still seemed awful nice to me. Of course now, seeing the restored tiles and fresh paint and window dressings and other folderol, I can see what her problem was. But it was still nice the first time.

It isn't *really* a hotel, like strangers can't make reservations and stay here, but if you know Bristol, and Bristol knows a lot of folks, there's kind of an invite system I guess. Bits made sure of the tech security and all that, the discreet cameras and places where things need to be locked right and all of that. Much as Bristol wants to show off that fucking Fabergé egg, it can't become public knowledge that she has it, and she's smart enough to know that.

"You okay?" Butler asks, as we wander through the place to where I assume Bristol'd like to keep us.

"Hard to shake the idea that this is a mistake."

"You ran your options," he says. "I'm sure it'll be a ride, but we'll come out okay."

"Probably," I say. "You still got your lucky rabbit's foot?"

He laughs, and I realize we've been checking doorways as we passed them, even though neither of us is carrying a weapon at ready. "Surprised you remember that."

I shrug. "I remember a lot of things."

"Sometimes you don't act like it." Oh this again. Well what did I expect, I guess.

"Mmm," I say instead, knocking on and then opening the door to the room I had last time. I don't want to assume that I have a 'my room' at Bristol's fancy personal hotel for her fancy friends, but it doesn't look like a whole lot, if anything, changed in here. There's a tented card on the dresser, like a place setting, that says *Dolly*. That's Bristol, always prepared. "Well this is me."

Butler kisses the back of my neck. "Want company?"

"I want *sleep*," I say. "Maybe company in about sixteen hours."

"You'll never sleep that long." He's still very close. This is very tempting.

"Maybe not." I turn around, standing in the doorway. "She probably put you across the hall there, if you wanna check. If she didn't, you can stay."

"It amazes me that she'd even take the time to what, message ahead? To assign us rooms?" He goes and checks. "Yeah, I got a card in here too.

"It amazes me that it amazes you," I say. "See you later."

"Sweet dreams."

Tempting as it is, though, to just drop my boots on the floor and lay down in that nice clean bed, I go into the bathroom first, and of course the shower is stocked with shampoo and conditioner and perfumed soaps and all that and suddenly a hot shower and a cold beer is what I want first more than anything in the world and while I'm not sure that Bristol is exactly sold on the notion of shower beers, there is a mini fridge in the room, and it does have beer and canned coffee and water in it, so I'm all set.

I stand in the hot spray for a while, just letting the travel dirt rinse away, drinking my beer and trying to relax. It's funny the way that kind of long haul travel makes you tired and wired, even without the added bonus of stealing an agent from an unnamed shadow agency. It was pretty clear he was done the second he saw Bristol in that hotel room when we stole the diamonds, but it's sure been a slow burn. Hard to blame him.

I finish the beer, then soap up and rinse off. There's a robe hung up in here that seems like it's probably worth more than cars I've driven. Not bought, mind you. But driven.

I get from the bathroom to the bed and that's what I remember for probably a good eight hours, which isn't enough but it's a start. I haven't spent enough time in Morocco to be able to tell what time it is from the light coming in the window and I slap around at the nightstand until I find my phone. Lots of messages but none of them dire; in addition to usual sorts of spam and people checking in from afar, Bits gave a couple of updates. No local law enforcement contact, no relevant chatter on the Agency network yet, that she's seen, Nicolai inbound probably tomorrow. Marquis also inbound in the next few days, which really just confirms my worries. Or is that a brilliant smokescreen, for Bristol to get the party started here, the way she normally would? No idea. Maybe it's both.

//I'm up, if you wanna turn in// I message Bits.

//I napped// she says.

//Liar// I roll out of bed and pull one of the coffee cans out of the fridge. If this was a real hotel, my tab would already be horrible. I chug it, then paw around in my clothes until I find both a tank top and pants, and get dressed. I jam my feet into my boots, then pause at the door, go back and put a bra on too. I don't need to have that conversation with Bristol first thing.

I wonder if Bristol's gonna want to pull some kind of designer bodyguard nonsense, like at the wedding gig. We'll get to it I'm sure. She's probably got a tailor on the way already. Or on staff. I open another canned coffee.

Chapter Two

When I listen at his door, Butler's still snoring, so I just leave him be and go wandering through the halls, savoring that canned coffee instead of shotgunning it, listening to my lace-ends clatter on the floor. Thinking about how this place has good, thick walls; we might not actually be fucked, if we have a siege.

There'll be fresh-brewed coffee, probably even the Turkish stuff Bristol loves so much; I think she keeps somebody on staff just to make that, and then read the grinds when you're done. She's quirkily superstitious, but also pays actual traditional practitioners of things, so I guess that's the way to do it.

As if summoned by my bootlaces, Bristol finds me. She already redid her manicure and pedicure, and whatever she does to her hair that makes it all sleek. Never in my life has my hair looked like that. No travel weariness evident here. "Really, Dolly darling, those laces are *awful*," she says, but smiling, like it isn't criticism.

"Sorry Bristles," I say, craning my head back to finish the coffee.

"You aren't."

"No," I agree. She plucks the can from my fingers before I can even look around for a bin. "That was one of yours, it's not like I brought contraband canned coffee from a convenience store that's under your minimum acceptable price point."

"I know it's one of mine." She rakes me over with an appraising gaze. "I assume we'll want to meet? Have a plan? Can that be soon?"

"Got someplace to be?" I make a show of looking around. "Oh, you wanna do it while Will is still snoring."

"I assume he's still sleeping, yes," she says stiffly.

"Oh don't be like that, I didn't mean you spent the night with him. I know from that experience that Butler snores, but I can hear him from the hallway. Unless, of course, he recorded it to fool any onlookers and then went for a walk."

"So far as I know, he did not. Security would've alerted me."

"You've got a team?" News to me.

"In a manner of speaking." She smiles, happy to have a little secret.

"You can brief us in the meeting," I say, watching her face. Ah, Bits knows. I won't worry too much then. "Feed us, too."

"I expected you'd say that. Do you remember where the breakfast room is?" She's still smiling; she knows I remember how to get anywhere I've been.

I laugh. "I'm sure I can find it."

"Splendid, we'll meet in ten minutes." She looks at my untied boots again, and then swans off with my empty can. I don't know if what she's wearing is her version of a bathrobe or a beach coverup or if it's an outfit itself, layers of gauzy stuff that manages to never actually be transparent, more's the pity.

That look meant she wanted me to get changed, in addition to tying my boots, but I'm not doing that. What else am I gonna wear? //Bitsy, where you at?//

She doesn't answer right away, and I'm debating between being worried and assuming she actually finally fell asleep and then she says //Shower, sorry. //

//Meeting in the breakfast room in ten with Bristol.//

//It was that easy?//

//Yeah, but I'm also gonna assume no.// The vibe is off, I don't know. I go find a courtyard doorway to stand in on the way to the breakfast room and smoke my ecigarette for a few minutes. I'll pick up more real cigarettes later or tomorrow, probably. Sugar cookies ain't gonna cut it.

A couple things are true at once; if Bristol wasn't attached to him, it would've been easy to put a bullet in Will's ear a long time ago and maybe we wouldn't have this problem now, but also I don't regret taking him. It might've been Bristol's long game all along, not like she shared it with the rest of the class. I sure was surprised in Vegas when she said shoot him or let him go. Well, meaning bring him with us. There were more players involved at the time, of course, but Will was the one who mattered.

I go the rest of the way to the breakfast room, where coffee is out, and also what looks like a full English breakfast. Bristol click-clacks in not long after me; even her sandals have heels. "I assumed you would be absolutely ravenous," she says.

"Always am," I say. Bits comes slouching in and blinks at all the food.

"I wasn't expecting all of this," she says.

"Eat what you'd like, it doesn't matter," Bristol says, waving her hand as she settles herself at the table. "It won't go to waste, I mean," she adds, looking at Bits again. I didn't see Bits's face change at all, but that's Bristol's specialty.

"Okay," she says dubiously, adding sugar to her coffee.

"So Bristol, you got a plan, or are we—"

"Dolly, we've hardly had coffee," Bristol says serenely.

"Speak for yourself." But I watch her add her cream, and sugar before I try again. "Plus, if we're banking on finishing this conversation when it's just the three of us, we need to get to it before our, uh, guests are awake."

"We won't be interrupted," she says. I glance at Bits, who shrugs just slightly.

"Trained Suzette in the art of distraction, did you?" Bristol's got so many little party people, that's the only name I can remember, other than Marquis of course.

Bristol waves a hand. "Oh, Suzette's in Paris right now. She'll be back tomorrow, though."

"We're gonna be expecting a lot more than Suzette pretty soon," I say. "We got two more days before Will is supposed to check in and then—"

"And we just spent three days doing Bits's little game," Bristol interrupts. "And now we will spend three days my way."

"Bristol, I don't think that completely unplugging for three days is a great plan," Bits says. "Like, it's not a matter of whose turn it is to choose what to do? We're against a clock here, and right now we're the ones who know it's running, which is great. We need to take advantage of that."

"Once Will misses his contact window, they'll have a plan that goes into immediate effect," I say. "He's got clearances that they just can't let walk."

"Bits did a very good job covering our trail, I'm certain of it. Didn't you, darling?"

"I did my best, anyway," Bits says.

"And your own contingencies will tell us when they're getting close, won't they?"

"Well, I hope so. But—"

"See? We have time to relax and unwind, and come up with something. And then it will be Dolly's turn for us to do what she wants." Bristol pushes away from the table, smiles at us, and click-clacks away again.

Bits and I sit there looking at each other for a minute, and then she drinks some more of her coffee and I start in on the breakfast. "I guess I expected that," I say eventually.

"I didn't but I did, if that makes sense?"

"It does. I'd say I don't know what was wrong with her, but I think that she reaches a point where everything gets piled up and she just puts it down someplace and walks away. Like she doesn't want to think about commandos coming here to gun us all down or whatever, so she just doesn't."

"Bristol's smarter than that," Bits says cautiously.

"Sure she is, but..." I think I have more eggs than Bits and that can only be on purpose.

"But she does set really hard partitions between some things."

"Yeah, that's more it. She never expected to have to like, *work* here, so. She isn't." I kinda wave my hands around to express the nothing.

"Yup."

I drink some of my own coffee. "Oh, so what's going about security here? She was giving me smug, knowing looks and I figured you had it handled."

"It's almost totally surveillance and electronic things," she says. "And a couple of local kids who aren't trained, really, but are in love with her. A supervisor."

"Everybody's in love with her," I mutter. "Okay so that's a project. Or, I'll run 'em off so we aren't getting any nineteen year olds killed here. They're fine for off-season work." I think a minute, as Bits pours her next cup of coffee. "What do you mean, electronic things?"

"Cameras, of course. Some ingress/egress failsafes, if we're in a panic button sort of situation. Then some other things I've been messing with, like drones. Oh, and robot dogs. Not like your kind, the kind that don't have faces."

"Leave it to Bristol to have the robot dogs that *don't* have faces. How many are there?"

"Three." I nod, thinking about the property. That's an okay patrol amount. It's enough to overwhelm anybody who doesn't know how to handle them. "Anyway, I'll set the clearances so you've got full run of all of it. Will Butler want anything like that?"

"Probably a good idea, but god, how he hates robot dogs." I grin. "Both kinds." Bits laughs.

"Noted."

"You wanna come with me to get cigarettes before we bunker down?"

She pauses long enough that I think she's figuring out the best way to tell me that isn't the saying, or no and I shouldn't go either, but then says, "Yeah, let me find a place that actually sells cigarettes."

"I wasn't gonna make you do that." It's smart, though, I was just gonna drive around but I also know that we should minimize our off site activities.

"I know, but there isn't a 7-Eleven, so this will just make it easier."

I laugh. "Am I really that predictable?"

"Mmm." She finishes her coffee. "Okay, I found a 24 hour one."

"Bitsy it's like, nine in the morning."

She gives a little huff. "I know, I'm just saying."

"I'm pulling your leg, that's good to know. " I get up, slapping my pockets for keys like I need 'em.

"Should we touch base with anybody?"

"Butler's sleeping, and I don't care about Will, so, no."

TRAFFIC'S OKAY BUT also I don't remember what day it is so don't know what to expect. Is it even tourist season? Is there a lot of 9-5 business here? Who knows. Bits seems to be actually looking at the sights out the window, and it is a nice day, blue skies, hot already. They got both city buses and slick looking cable cars here, so that probably cuts down on passenger vehicles. Plenty of pedestrians and people on motorcycles with no fear of man or meeting God, but where don't you see that, really?

Lotta places are still shuttered, which makes Bits's comment about the 24 hour convenience store make more sense but it could just be the approach I took, these are places that open and close later. I notice surveillance, but it's heavier in some places, nonexistent in others, and that's interesting.

We pass a smoke shop and a vape shop, but really, I prefer convenience stores and so does Bitsy. I also eye a McDonald's but we did just eat. We try to be unobtrusive in the convenience store, or, well, I try and Bits just *is* unobtrusive. I browse around the snacks, the baseline for chocolate is always higher quality when you're not stateside. The cigarettes have less advertising on them and bigger warnings and I wasn't gonna get a carton but then I think about the situation and I get a carton.

The guys behind the counter are doing the shift change and I wait, watching traffic out the window. Bits comes up with an armful of silver energy drink cans and when she drops one I catch it before it gets too far. "Power Horse?"

"I've heard of it but never had it."

I realize the guys behind the counter are now looking at us, either because of our accents or because of how fast I just moved. It's too early in the shift for one guy to see wild shit, and too late for the other one, the thresholds are all wrong. They ring us up and as I realize I don't have any local currency, Bitsy produces a Moroccan bank card outta nowhere and taps it. The morning guy puts our stuff in paper bags, wordlessly, and the night guy doesn't say much of anything, just runs the register, and I manage not to laugh at them until we're back in the car again. It's not a big deal, it's not their fault. They should be thankful that they didn't have to mop up Power Horse this late in the morning and/or this late in the shift. I sure didn't want it on my boots.

Chapter Three

When Butler opens his door, he looks disappointed that I'm dressed and happy that I'm holding a coffee pot and a mug. Bits offered Power Horses for him, and myself, and I respectfully declined. "You let me sleep in."

"Girl talk," I say, shoving the mug into his hands and going into the room past him.

"Of course, what was I thinking." He closes the door and follows me. "We got a plan?"

"Of course not," I say and he does an honest to god double take. "What?"

"Well, because we were just doing the game because it's what Bits wanted to do, Bristol is now taking her turn to do what she wants to do."

He rubs the back of his head. "What?"

I sit on the edge of the bed. "So, the security here is a coupla local kids that we either need to furlough or train up, and Bits has the surveillance and stuff all sewed up."

"I would expect nothing less." He drinks his coffee, watching me.

"Oh yeah, and robot dogs."

"I fuckin' hate robot dogs."

"Yeah, I know, it's fine. You won't have to deal with them." He stares at me, then drinks more coffee.

"Dolly..."

"You think I don't know? Anyway, they've never yet traced Bristol here, that we know of, and Bits erased and overwrote and threw off our trail best she knows how, and she's real damn good."

"She is, yes." He holds out his mug and I refill it. "You're not worried? You don't seem worried."

"When do I ever seem worried?"

"Point, I guess."

"Bitsy'll be able to give us an advance warning, even if all it looks like she's doing is stargazing. She'll know what to expect when, and we can shore up here but expect to cut 'em off someplace else."

"But we won't know what to expect? You've been dealing with these guys for a few years now."

"We've been having a mostly-cold shadow conflict for a few years, anytime we've dealt with them after the first time, it's really only been individuals. Will. That hacker once. The only time we ever saw anybody en masse was for the submarine and—"

"The *submarine*?"

"I told you about the submarine." I reach over and put the coffee pot on the dresser. "Anyway we're not really sure of numbers but the numbers've never been big. And they always try to be covert, because anything they're doing seems to have always been extrajudicial. They're not gonna want official local involvement."

"Well, as long as nobody accidentally tips off anybody to the pretty blonde rich lady who owns an entire fucking oceanfront hotel that she parties in..."

"Exactly, simple stuff." I grin at him, and we both laugh. "So we do a perimeter and make our shopping list if we need a shopping list and Bits keeps on keepin' on. Well we did go get cigarettes and weird French energy drinks so we're probably set for shopping. Nicolai gets in tomorrow."

Butler finishes his second cup of coffee, sets it down next to the pot. "Can we assume he'll bring some goodies?"

"When hasn't he?" I nod at the duffle bag Butler brought. "Though why don't you show me the goodies you brought?"

"What makes you think that's anything but a tuxedo so that Bristol doesn't skin me for being within smelling distance of one of her parties?"

"Heard the gunstocks clackin'."

"No you didn't," he says, grinning, but he puts the duffle on the bed next to me. "That's the nice thing about private flights with rich women, you just get out on the tarmac and can bring a small arsenal."

"Sure is a perk." I run the zipper back and give a peek inside. I know he's just got his handgun strapped, so do I, but he's got a couple little ones too, I recognize the lockbox. A couple of the stocks I see are 3D printed and I raise an eyebrow at him; he knows what I think about 3D printed guns.

"Wasn't sure what we'd need, and figured it'd be fine enough in the environment short term. Takes 7.62, easy enough to source."

"Wouldn't it be funny if the rest of us are buckling down like this, and Bristol's the one who's right to just cut loose and not worry about it?"

"It'd be nice," Butler rumbles. "But—"

"Not holding my breath, don't worry about that." He's got optics in his retinal replacements, no need to worry about packaging scopes so they don't get knocked around too bad in transit, that was always such a bitch.

"What're the boys doing while you're gone?"

"Finishing up a chopper for customer pickup. They wanted a custom paint job, which Meatball's great at. He does people's street racers too, they fly him out everywhere for that."

"Well that's nice." I know that look he's got on his face; he doesn't want to talk about Scooter and Meatball. He almost doesn't want to talk about guns, which sure is a thing for us. No, I'm pretty sure he's gonna propose again and is picking the time. Which is fine, it's not like I don't love him, but the timing ain't exactly great. I think I'm the one who asked the first time, and he'd been smart enough to know we were way too young. I don't think he'll do it this morning, anyway. I'd bet on it being within a week, except I'll probably keep the suspicion to myself so I don't have anybody to bet with. "Want to take our walk now, or do you want breakfast?"

"Haven't been up long enough for breakfast, let's have a look at the place."

THE NICE THING ABOUT party lights being strung up in the courtyards and gardens and whatnots is that it doesn't actually leave many shadowy areas for covert insert. At least not en masse; I'm thinking it'd be fun to try to do it, just to see if I can, without the active camo. I don't think they're liable to have it, what with budget constraints and all. Of course, they might get some inter-agency action if they admit that they lost an agent and want him back. Or maybe they'll just send somebody to kill him. I like thinking on the possibilities, and know if Bits sees anything she thinks is concrete, she'll share. Calm and thorough, Bitsy is.

We meet Bristol's local security team when we're looking at all the entry points, like actual gates, in the wall around this place. It *is* a pair of nineteen year olds, maybe they're twenty, maybe they're cousins. I've seen an older woman around too, so I'm not sure what *her* deal is yet. If she's a guest or another member of Bristol's staff or what. The staff largely make themselves invisible, which is a little weird. I guess this might be a cushy place to work, make a couple meals a day, eat what you want, keep your mouth shut. I know Bristol tips good, I'm sure she pays good too.

"I'm Joker," the first one says, holding out his hand to shake. I do, but he must've seen something in my face, or been used to getting questions. He's got a good grip, and he's surprised at mine; they always are. "Like from a deck of cards. Bristol said we should have work names."

"I'm Floyd," the other one says. They both really want to be taken seriously, but have different ideas of what seriously is, I think. They're about the same middling height, dark hair cut shortish, in pants and polo shirts, that Bristol must've designated as uniforms. "We already talked to Bits."

"Did you now," I say. They're both carrying, and I'm itching to know what they've got and how many, if any, range hours they have. "Range hours" in the loosest sense of the word, I want to know about *experience* and also I want to just send them home and I can't do that without pissing Bristol off and really damaging their confidence. We might not need them, it might be fine, but also the idea of having a pair of the greenest of the green to have to maybe watch my back isn't great. "Did she tell you that you might see some action?"

"She did," Floyd says, and before he can continue, we're joined by that older woman I'd seen.

"She wasn't able to tell us what kind of action or how much," the woman says, holding out her hand. "Marge. I know you're Dolly."

"Sure am. This is Butler." She shakes, and I grin when we match grips. "You're also on security?"

"Head of security, such as it is." She glances at Joker and Floyd. Her hair is short, iron gray, and her accent is Dutch maybe. "What *are* we looking at? On a scale of, say, Waco to—"

"Nah, Bits wasn't bullshitting you, we don't know yet. She's got fingers in pies they don't even know they have." Well that metaphor got away from me. "Once they're moving anything, anybody, we'll know. I know it sucks, we're not happy about it either." Pretty sure that I know better than to hope for a non-response. It'd probably hurt Will's feelings, anyway, unless they *are* just a 'disavow' agency and we didn't have that piece of the puzzle. I'll bring it up.

"When I talked to Bristol, she just laughed and waved her hands and said 'we're having *parties*, Marge, you've always been able to handle those' and walked away."

It's a good Bristol impression, and I laugh. "Yeah, sounds right." She seems old enough to know better than to get caught up in Bristol's bullshit. Or maybe that's exactly it, she sees through it, sees something there that she wants to protect. "Sorry about all this."

"At least it pays good," Marge says, a little grimly. She's strapped too, of course, and the kind of comfortable with it that me and Butler are. Well okay, if she's been in charge of these boys, she's made sure they're trained. Maybe.

"I don't suppose the princess told you when the first party is," Butler says.

"Didn't she tell *you*? Tonight, of course." Marge doesn't roll her eyes but I think we understand each other. "Anyway, let me know if you need anything, you've got run of the place of course. Bristol said that too."

"Glad you understand," I say, and Marge matches my smile.

"Even if I didn't on her say-so, I would after meeting you." She gives Butler a nod and saunters off.

"That make you feel better?" he asks me.

"No, but sorta. Havin' a crystal ball would make me feel better."

"Those burn people's houses down if they're not careful."

I give him a shove, but I laugh. "You know what I mean."

"Much as anybody can, yeah."

"I'm an open book."

"Sure." We're at another gate, looking at the beach, and I picture our own ridiculous mini Normandy. Well, us as the defenders. I think it's more likely it'll be like, a six person team who inserts, from what we know of their style. They'll probably even use one of those goddamn parties as their cover, it's hard to imagine otherwise actually, and I gotta assume Bits is vetting guest lists as soon as she can get her digital fingers on them. The way Bristol's parties go, though, Bits'll have her work cut out for her, haring off after every friend of a friend who gets the word passed that there's an event. Bristol always wants too much attention. Every job we've ever done, Bristol wants too much attention.

It wouldn't be a bad approach, if we coordinated it that way. Having a series of glitzy, internationally attended parties could be just the thing, seein' as how the agency presumably can't just go barging wherever it wants, interfering with everybody. This'll make them have to work harder, which is smart on Bristol's part. Again, if it's intentional. Thing is, Bristol is always up for a party.

"Well, we've always been good at reacting," I say. "The more involved the plan is, the more there is to forget."

"True enough," Butler says, watching me. "Priority is you three first, and then Will."

"Well aren't you sweet," I say.

"Am I wrong?"

"No." We keep walking, come around to the parking lot again. Bits has all kinds of cameras set up, and I'm pretty good at spotting them, but I know there are a few I've missed. Good, that means other people will miss them too. "Right, so the plan is there is no plan, which I'm not in love with."

"It is what it is. We've come through tough spots."

"Sure have," I say. Thinking of my fancy replacement arm. Thinking of 'training' situations me and Butler and the rest of the guys were in, in the program, that were clearly real to everybody else involved. Some of those details are hazy, that's what being decommissioned and then illegally deprogrammed'll do for you, but live fire tends to stick with you. "I'm not used to second guessing myself. You think that's enough?"

"It'll have to be." He hesitates, and before he makes up his mind to do whatever he's thinking about, Bristol appears in the entryway. I think she's already wearing different clothes from this morning.

"Would one of you darlings mind going to get Marquis at the airport? Their usual car service is having troubles and the wait is just *so* long for the other ones, without advance booking."

"Yeah, I don't mind," Butler says.

"Let me take your picture, so they'll know they can trust you."

"I'm not sure I'd go that far," I say, laughing, and Butler laughs too.

"Trust is just one of those things," he says. "Where's Prince Charming, anyway?"

"Will is having breakfast," Bristol says, smiling in her particular, magnanimous way that shows she isn't stooping to our level. "Should I have somebody bring out coffee for you, to take with?"

"Nah, I already had coffee service," he says, looking at me, then goes and gets in the car.

"If you see Nicky, grab him too," I call after him, and he waves a hand over his head without turning around.

"Dolly, don't yell," Bristol says, and disappears back into the hotel.

Chapter Four

With Butler gone for the moment, I go over the property again. Not with any specific, directed purpose, I just pick a direction to wander in. It's not a big enough place to get lost in, with or without built in direction sense, but I want to see if there's anything I might've missed, that I might notice if I'm not paying hard attention. It's hard to trick yourself into seeing a place new again, and it might not work, but still I try.

My bootlaces are still untied and I don't take particular care with other noise I might make besides, and the staff uses that to make themselves scarce ahead of me. I only hear one person scrambling, and don't laugh out loud at them, but it is funny. It's like belling the cat, I guess, but I belled myself.

Then I take a second to wonder, how *are* they making themselves invisible so easily? I stop and duck into a random room, one of like ten that're filled with plush furniture and gauzy curtains, and tie my boots. Then I get out my active camo box and turn the gadget on. It's always wild, watching my own self disappear; Bits always describes it in video game terms, like seeing pixels, and that's probably the best way to describe it, honestly. It's not environmental camo, like a ghillie suit or a tiger, it's something else.

I go creeping through the halls now, in the direction I'd heard that sudden scrambling, keeping my ears open. All is still as I reach a hallway junction and look down. Empty. But then, behind me, there's a click and a framed, full length mirror slides to one side, and one of Bristol's staff peers around and steps out. She looks youngish, maybe in her twenties, and is holding a tiny vacuum cleaner with an attachment at the end that almost looks like a feather duster. Makes sense, all these details and knicknacks, you need something like that I guess. Satisfied nobody's there, she moves further down the hallway, heading towards the room I just tied my boots in. There's another click, and I slip into the passage as the mirror slides back into place.

//Did you know this place has hidden goddamn passages?// I text Bits.

//No, I could never find blueprints. The records office had a fire ten years back.//

//Convenient.// Like, it's probably a coincidence, but...

//Wait why, where are you?//

//In a hidden passage, I thought that'd be obvious.// The floors have thick, plush carpets on them that look like the ones out in the hallways, and isn't that a Bristol-ass thing to do, have luxury fittings where the fewest people are likely to see them.

//Dolly.//

//It was behind a mirror. I was thinking about how funny it was that Bristol's staff were all making themselves scarce and then I was close enough to actually hear one making herself scarce and I took a second to wonder what was actually going on.//

//And then...//

//Well I tied my boots and popped the active camo and here we are. I'll wander around and get my bearings so I can draw you a map.//

She's quiet for a long time, and I start walking. There isn't any light in here, really, except what comes lancing through from cracks in the walls or whatever. I keep looking for peepholes that I think will be in a portrait, but then I realize that I don't think Bristol's got any portraits hung. Isn't that interesting. //Well we can use it to our advantage, anyway.//

//That's the idea.// I find a slightly glowing panel in the wall and stop to have a look. It's just a toggle switch, not a keypad or biometric or anything. Weird that Bristol would've kept this even from Bits. She has to know, though, it'd be even weirder if she didn't. Right? //She has to know, right?//

//What??// Oh maybe I left too much time in between there.

//Bristol has to know there's secret passages.//

//I assume yes.//

Fair enough. I listen for long enough to be sure nobody's outside wherever this hidden passage door will lead and toggle the switch. The click is very quiet, and the panel slides, and I'm looking at one of the guest bedrooms. This one doesn't have a little name card on the dresser, and the windows're still closed, so currently unassigned. I wonder if the passages lead to *all* the rooms, and I step out to have a look at the wall. There's gotta be a switch here too, or else what's the point?

I have to stop the panel from closing twice before I find it; it isn't on the other side of the wall from the switch in the passage. No, it's in the molding at the top of the bathroom door, which is about four steps away. Five if you're shorter than me, three if you're way taller. There aren't seams, it isn't really a *button*, it's just a place where when you touch it, it engages the mechanism. Somehow. Maybe they're all bluetooth or something. Magnets. I peek out the door to get my bearings; not the guest wing that me and Butler are currently housed in, but I think I'm oriented. I return to the passages, wait for that panel to close behind me.

A couple of times I hear staff and one time I press myself against the wall as an older guy with a toolbox comes past. He doesn't even miss a step; I won't call the passages roomy, but they're not tight either.

I wander around long enough that Butler gets back with Nicolai and Marquis. I've got a pretty good map of the place in my head by then. Map within a map. Not all bedrooms have the secret passage panels, which is good, because wow is that both creepy and dangerous. I don't want to accidentally merc one of Bristol's maids in my sleep. Kitchen, yes. Her Fabergé egg chamber, yes. I even find a panic room off one of the powder rooms by a main party area, and that makes me weirdly relieved, honestly. I take pictures of those controls and things and send them to Bits, who I assume has been tracking my movements through the depths of this place anyway.

I pop out into a hallway by the pool and saunter 'round to the front to say hey to Nicky. Marquis has already, I assume, gone to find Bristol and do air kisses and whatnot. Why there's a pool when the Mediterranean is right there, I'll never know. You'd think Bristol'd be horrified about the tolls that chlorine takes on the skin, but also the only time I've ever seen her swim was the time we took a header off a bridge in Macau. It's all, always, about appearances.

Nicolai and Butler are smoking cigarettes in the parking lot, Nicolai gesturing with his cigarette and speaking rapid Russian, Butler nodding. It takes me a second to catch up with what he's saying, I haven't thought Russian in a little while, but it's about caviar prices of all things, and sturgeon sustainability.

"Nicky I learned something about caviar lately, you'll be proud of me," I say in Russian, sidling up and taking Butler's cigarette to have a drag.

"I'm eager to hear it," he says.

"See, I didn't know caviar was like champagne, and it only meant wild sturgeon from *certain* places, I thought all sturgeon eggs were caviar. And then I heard that certain caviar was not only wild sturgeons from the Caspian and/or black sea *but also albino* and also a certain age. Fuck I forget what age." I give Butler his cigarette back. He takes it, but then he gives me a new pack of my very own. He must've done some duty-free shopping at the airport.

"I am...very proud," Nicolai says, and we all laugh.

"Did you get into the business? Bristol will be wild to hear it."

"I've got a share in a fishing vessel now, yes. I wanted to see how it might turn out. We do not fish the albinos, though."

"Still, diversifying the portfolio, good call."

"Thank you." He tilts his head and looks at me. "I think there might be cobwebs in your hair?"

"Better not be, Bristol would be horrified," I say, bending into one of the car mirrors to check. "Nope, just a thread." Must've been from one of the wall hangings or something.

"I thought it was your first gray hair, and I wasn't going to be the one who said anything," Butler says.

"Everybody always throws Nicolai under the bus," Nicky says with elaborate woe. "After sticking by each other through trouble and hardship."

"You're fine, buddy." I clap him on the shoulder. "Anyway, first party's tonight, are you excited?"

"I am, and also I must say, I'm proud of you for waiting this long before you asked what I brought you."

I grin at him. "Well that's for when we get inside. You had cigarette left."

"Dolly, you are always so kind," he says in English.

"She's right behind me, isn't she?" I ask, still in Russian, right before Bristol click-clacks out the front door and down the long low steps to the parking lot. Anyway, I can't hardly keep track of what *I* speak, much less what Bristol speaks.

"Nicolai, darling, how good of you to come!" she says, doing the partial embrace air kisses with him. He looks at me over her shoulder in silent desperation.

"How could I not?" he says smoothly. "If I missed this opportunity, you may never invite me again."

"Nonsense, darling, you've been *such* a good friend." Maybe she means that; Nicolai was the only help I could get when me and Bits had to spring Bristol from federal custody. If Butler was stateside, he would've come. If Bits had been in her right mind, she maybe could've had people to ask. Maybe not; those hacker types aren't always physically helpful.

Another presence behind me, Bristol's friend Suzette, who is much less stealthy. "Bristol, the wine delivery is here," she says. I look out at the parking lot; there is no truck.

"Thank you, darling, I'll be right there," Bristol says. She lays her hand on Nicolai's arm for a moment. "Just wait until you meet Will, I do think that you two are going to get along well!" and then she turns and breezes back past me, and I listen to her and Suzette's heels recede into the hotel.

Nicolai looks at me, and I shrug. "Will's pretty inoffensive," I say. "And probably needs deprogramming."

"That is outside my expertise," Nicolai says, and Butler laughs.

"I'm sure you'll take to it like a duck to water," he says.

"That saying does not make sense."

"Sure it does, Nicky," I say. "Much as anything else."

Chapter Five

Deprogramming Will is where Bits has been. He said from the get-go that he didn't have any programming, but that's the bitch of the posthypnotic suggestion shit of which our government has become so fond; sometimes there's stuff in there, walled off, that they made you forget that they walled off to begin with. We all got programming. We just don't all have government clearance programming, some of it's just the normal sorts of things like who goes at a four way stop and holding the door for the person coming inside behind you. Dolly, you might say, that's just living in a society. Maybe it is.

It's easy to assume, when you're in the club, that they aren't gonna do anything to you. It's also easy to sign employment-type contracts that you don't read or understand every word of, no matter how hard you try, your eyes glazing over, and then you figure, well, other people signed it, what's the worst? That's how you get yourself programmed. It's also, sometimes, how you get yourself out of whatever poverty rut your life was otherwise gonna take. Would I have signed up for that little secret government super soldier project if I knew what-all it was gonna be? Maybe not. Did the fact that I had brothers and friends who'd already signed up ahead of me nudge the needle? Sure did.

I don't *really* regret it; I don't think it changed who I am as a person, who I was going to become. And it's sure helped me out; if I didn't have my pain senses rescrambled, my adrenal systems and what have you adjusted, I never would've made it out of there, gotten to the doc to get a cybernetic arm put on. I would've just gone into shock and bled out on the spot when my original arm got blown apart. So no, I don't regret still being here.

It's a nice room, they're all nice rooms, this one big and open and with doors or windows or windows that're doors looking out at the beach, long gauzy curtains blowing in the wind, cushions and art with a capital A all over the place. Will was looking pretty relaxed until he realized it was me who'd come in. He seems almost comfortable around Bits, which I guess makes sense. He's a puppydog for Bristol and has been since first sight, and he's scared of me, he can't hide that. But Bits, he isn't physically scared of or physically attracted to, he just knows that she's one of the best hackers in the world. And if she isn't one of the best hackers in the world, then we're *all* in trouble.

There's a pitcher of iced coffee on the low, carved table between them, with brass fittings on it, and cups on a tray on the table. Cups that're too small for Bitsy's particular coffee habit, but we must have appearances for appearances sake, in Bristol's realm. "How we doing?" I ask. What *is* the prim 'n' proper thing to say, when somebody's getting their brains preliminarily unscrambled? Well, I'm not being fair; any work Will had done to him was a light touch. He came primed eager to save the free world, after all.

"I think it won't take much more for us to be okay," Bits says, and Will blinks at her. "It's lucky I've got your files, it really made this easier, knowing the kinds of—"

"You didn't even do anything," Will says, as I plop down on the couch, which creaks warningly, and reach for an empty cup on the tray, and the coffee pot. Bristol's furniture is for show, not rough treatment, good to know.

"Sure I did," she says. "It's just hard to know what I changed, because you didn't know what was there in the first place."

"So you could also just be making this up to push me away from the agency and gain my trust," he says.

"I could," she agrees. "But what would be the point? If I was going to manipulate you, I'd just change your posthypnotic suggestions to not be able to hurt us or whatever. Betray us?" She looks at me, frowning a little.

"Yeah, that sounds a little too supervillain," I say. This coffee is black as tar, I don't know who made it or how they got it that way. There's no spoons on the table, maybe because they all dissolved. Will watches us, his face schooled blank. Bristol has him dressed in resort clothes somehow, linen pants and a short sleeved button down shirt that's just the right blue for his eyes. Unless he already had that packed in his luggage, but I've seen how Will dresses himself, and this ain't it.

"You can't claim you're not manipulating me," he says, in a meter that says he's trying to be honest while choosin' his words carefully. "I'm not really here voluntarily."

"You mean you didn't want an all-inclusive luxury getaway with the woman of your dreams and her accomplices?" I ask with a grin.

"That isn't—"

"Relax Will, Jesus. We're all Bristol's puppets, it's fine. Like yeah sure we've held you at gunpoint a coupla times, but she does really want you to want to be here, and that's the truth." The coffee's strong enough to knock you on your ass, and it takes a lot for *me* to say that. "Bitsy, should this be watered down or something?"

She shrugs and makes a noncommittal noise, frowning into the middle-distance at something. "What do you know about Bristol's friend Warrington?"

"Is that his first name or his last name?" She doesn't say anything. "Nothing, sounds like a British prep school old money guy."

"That's what I thought too. Just socialite things." She blinks again, looks at me. "You don't like the coffee?"

"It tastes fine, I just think it's maybe concentrated jet fuel that isn't meant to be drunk like this."

"Oh maybe." She looks at the pot, considering. "Anyway, Will, you're probably tired for the day?"

"I didn't assume I would be off the hook so easily," he says.

"Bristol wants to parade you around, if I exhaust you too much for that, she'll be upset."

"Parade me around?" I watch the realization dawn on Will's face. He's as aware of her proclivities as he can be, which means he knows about Bristol's party people. He knows about Bristol's parties. And he's just now considering the implications of his involvement in one of those parties. "Oh."

I laugh. "Yup," I say, tossing back the rest of my coffee. "Yeah, Bits, you really shouldn't be drinking this straight."

She shrugs, looking at something else again already, I'm sure. "It's fine. How's Nicolai?"

"Also fine. Brought us goodies, mostly of the not-online type."

"Just the way you like it."

"Exactly." Will's still sitting there like he doesn't know exactly what he should be doing; leaving to find Bristol, still talking to us, what. "Buddy, you got a question?"

He takes a beat and then kind of laughs. "I'm just lost," he says. He's cute, I'll give Bristol that, but also those corn fed good looks gotta hide a level of unexpected duplicity or else the agency never would've had him on in the first place.

"Yeah, that feeling'll probably be around awhile. Uh, let's see. I dunno how much to tell you about everybody, we're operating under the assumption that somebody'll come and try to steal you back." I'd also assume sooner rather than later, but so far we've got clear skies.

"It makes sense to keep things need to know," he says. Maybe he thinks that'll limit his culpability, if we don't just introduce him around to Nicolai the arms dealer and whoever else. He already met Marquis, back when.

"Glad you see it that way." Maybe he just thinks I won't put a round in the back of his head once things start to slide sideways, if he behaves. Might be I won't. "Anyway, let's bring you to find Bristol." We gotta talk about him being supervised, at our next meeting. Providin' there is a next meeting.

Bits pours another cup of jet fuel. "I'll be here if you need me," she says.

"I figured you were about due to become furniture," I say, and she laughs. "You flyin' anybody in to help us out?"

"I reached out to Lockhart but he's pretty nailed down still. Same with Charlie. I've got friends in other time zones who can help me keep track of things, though."

"You're just saying that so I assume you sleep at all."

"We don't lie to each other."

"Yeah maybe, but we also don't always tell the truth." She gives me a wry smile, and I laugh.

"You aren't kidding."

I could ask her where Bristol is, but it's more fun this way. I lead Will off down the halls, and he has the good sense to walk next to me. If there's a party tonight, Bristol probably won't have a real lunch planned, but there might be finger food someplace. Brunch. I dunno, sometimes she seems to exist on champagne and gossip, and I know that isn't true.

"One thing we've never been able to figure out is how the three of you came to work together," Will says abruptly, like he rehearsed it but couldn't figure out a better way to say it.

"Hoping to get some counterspying in?"

"At this point, no. So I'm just giving in to curiosity."

"I admire the honesty." Well he did just watch Bits and me talk about that; I wonder if that's new information for him, that we don't lie to each other. I wonder how he *feels* about it.

"Obviously you were in a program, but Bristol and Bits just come out of nowhere." He pauses and I wait; he's fighting that conditioning, and maybe surprised that he even said that much. "And don't take this the wrong way, but you and Bristol…"

"Don't seem like the type to associate?" The tips of his ears turn a little bit pink and I laugh. "First time I met Bristol, we got in a bar fight."

"You *what*?" This place's echoes are interesting, if you get enough volume, which Will just did.

"She was putting a team together." And I thought she was gonna get herself killed. I guess that remains to be seen.

"I guess that tracks." He doesn't believe me. Do I care?

"Why, what was your guess?"

"I don't know. Maybe that Bits found each of you?"

"Okay, not a bad thought." Bits *did* find us, but after we'd already hooked up. Met, I mean. Agreed to work together. "But no. Shittiest bar Bristol's ever set foot in before or since, I'm sure. In heels, with her hair up in the knives." I tip a grin at him and he frowns. "Bet that was a bad surprise."

"That whole situation was a bad surprise." He's quiet again and a few steps later, Bristol's laugh floats down a hallway towards us.

"There she is," I say. He's perked up already and probably doesn't even realize it. "Look, I need to know that you aren't going to fuck us," I say, grabbing him by the arm and keeping my voice low.

"Even if I wanted to, I couldn't," he says, going *very* still, which means he doesn't know if I have a weapon, if it's out already behind him, whatever, and has maybe thought about this a lot. "I'm almost certainly disavowed and all my points of contact shut down. But I…I don't want to. I'm not happy with how this happened, but I'm starting to feel glad that it did."

He's gotta be a better liar than he looks. But still, I believe him, and I let him go. "Maybe you'll regret that, but I hope not." I hope none of us regrets this more than we already do. It's kind of Bristol's ultimate triumph, now she's got that Fabergé egg *and* the handsome man she made take her to dinner in the middle of the diamonds disaster.

Chapter Six

I find some paper and draw a rough map of the hotel, and then a rough map of the secret passageways. Bits can screenshot it and then I can give it to Butler to memorize. Hell of a thing, for Bristol to have secret passages she didn't bother to tell us about. It's fine, she'll know we know eventually. We just won't mention it until it matters. Or until it's the funniest.

I figure none of us are invited to the party tonight except maybe Nicolai, so I'm not gonna worry about what I'm wearing, I worry about where I'm gonna be instead. Can't overuse the secret passages or that'll be a secret that gets unsecret real fast. I can hang out with Marge and the kids, get a sense of how they do things, and how they run the robot dogs, or not. Could've asked earlier, but I'd rather see it than have 'em explain it cold.

I hear the smear of voices as more people arrive, singly or in twos and threes, Bristol I'm sure going to meet each of them. She doesn't put any of them in rooms down here by me and Butler, yet. Bits is probably in this wing too, I haven't asked. I should. I'm starting to feel like a sheepdog that doesn't know where-all the flock is, and clamp down on that. Bristol's got that panic button she wears now. Bits is a literal thought away from communicating with us at all times. It's fine.

When I decide the party is in swing enough that I can insert in the fringes and it'll be fine, I open my door. I heard Butler go back to his room a ways back, I assume for a nap; he likes doing that for night ops, when he can. He's not long after me when I head down the hall, though. "Hoping to scrounge some dinner?" he asks.

"Bristol always has the best horse divorce at these things," I say.

"What."

"It drives her nuts if you say stuff like hors d'oeuvres wrong. Horse divorce. Canapes as canopies is another good one. Car shootery."

"For...charcuterie?"

"Got it in one. Now don't overdo it, it'll ruin the effect."

"Your secret's safe with me," he says, sounding mystified, though I don't know how he can possibly be surprised that I think it's fun and funny to needle her.

I give him a sidelong look when we get to the door, terrace full of Bristol's party friends just outside in the twinkle-lit darkness. "Anyway, where's your tux?"

"Gut told me tonight's not a tux night." He gives that slow sly grin that keeps me on the hook.

"Well fine, how 'bout your gut gets us some plates while I go see Marge."

"You got it." He steps outside and blends through the crowd, a hell of a thing for a man his build and stature to do, and a treat to watch every time. I don't know for sure where Marge will be, but I can guess where Marge would be, because it's where I would be, and I slink my way over there. Bingo.

"Is this about what you expected?" she asks once I'm standing next to her and we've surveyed the scene a second. Bristol's party friends are all physically beautiful, and either wearing lots of sparkle that you just know is expensive, or the kind of simplicity that you know is even more expensive.

"Pretty much exactly, yeah." I can't see Bristol in the crowd, but I can see the crowd's movements around her. "Maybe less people than I expected, but it's only the first day."

"Debating whether to let the dogs out to patrol," she says. "Outside the walls, not in with the guests."

"I think it's probably a good call," I say. "Mind if I come with?"

"Please do."

I can't even remember the first time I saw one of those robot dogs, they've just been a fixture in law enforcement and military and whatnot since before I was born. Bits has shown me some of the early videos, the stuff they used to worm it into the public consciousness, to charm them out of stopping and thinking, *wait a minute. What is this for? Why would this be for that?* I wonder if the people who invented, engineered them, whatever, ever regret it. They thought they were making like, agile hostile environment investigative equipment, not crowd control toys to put in the hands of some of the worst people.

I've seen them stored a number of ways; folded up like a suitcase and racked, not folded but stacked, or stabled, like how Marge has them. Easy access, I guess, and space isn't an issue. "How do you tell them apart?" I ask and Marge frowns at the robot dogs and then at me.

"Would I ever need to?"

"Well do you refer to 'em by number when they're loose or what?"

"We refer to them by area of operation."

"Oh that makes sense." It does. She's still looking at me and waiting, though. "Why don't we name them, and give them different patrol behaviors. That way, nobody's learning their patterns, but also won't expect deviations from normal programming either."

"How are we going to do that? Do you know how to program them?"

"A little, but Bits'll have that covered. Might already, actually."

//I'm working on it, but you'll have to name them, I'm bad at that.//

"Bits says we'll have to name them," I say to Marge, who nods impassively. Just confirms what I already assumed, that she's seen a lot. "Anyway, just throwin' a tablecloth on one of these is enough to keep them from messin' with you, unless they're modified." There's a moment where none of us say anything, and Marge shrugs. "Bits, are they modified?"

//Just the one. Uh.// One of the robot dogs stands up taller on its four legs, like it's stretching.

"Got it." Marge nods, looking from the robot dogs, to me, back towards the party. "Fill me in later on what I need to know."

"Will do." It's hard to tell if she thinks I'm fucking around, or if she's happy to be relieved of the robot dog responsibility. Both can be true.

WE KIND OF KNEW IT would, but the evening passes without a hitch. I don't know who the attendees think Butler is, but they're weirdly charmed by his tall, dark, and handsome, and he can tell war stories and talk about helicopters, so he fits right in with some of the personalities Bristol's collected. I don't talk to many people but Marge and the boys; Bristol's guests are the type to assign a person to scenery pretty easily, and I don't want to dissuade them of that unless it's absolutely necessary. For that first party, it isn't.

At the end of the night, some guests split off to assigned rooms, and I'm sitting at a patio table sharing a bottle with Marge and Butler when Bristol wanders through. We'd sent Floyd and Joker home probably an hour ago, and I'm surprised to see Bristol; I thought she'd be having an even smaller party in the parlor or something with a whittled down chosen few.

She sits with us, though, and when I offer her a glass she nods. She seems tired, but pleased.

"A success?" I ask. Actually, I wonder what about her makes me think she seems tired. Might be useful to catalog.

"Very much so, thank you. Will Bits be joining us?"

"I think so." On cue, Bits comes through one of the open doors with the designed to be billowy curtains. "Yeah."

"Hi," Bits says, and Butler laughs. Bristol glances at him, smiling quizzically.

"It's just funny seeing you three mesh."

"We are a well-oiled machine," I say, sliding a glass over to Bits too, even though she'll probably only just sip it a little for the fellowship. She looks tired too, maybe she'll actually sleep for once. "Oh, speaking of, Bristles, we named the robot dogs. You don't mind, do you?"

She gives a little laugh. "I entirely forgot that I even *had* them, why would I mind?"

I shrug. "I dunno. People get a certain way about naming things."

She takes a sip from her glass, maybe thinking about that, maybe a million miles away, and then says "What did you name them?"

"Loki, Snorri, and Mr. Squeak but it's a girl."

"But...it's a girl?" She sets her glass down. I wonder if she practices frowning in a mirror, so it doesn't wrinkle her up too much.

"Yeah, I found a bow someplace and glued it on. Gives her character."

"To review, as I've forgotten...these are the patrol and security style of robot dog? Not the type that yours is?"

"Yeah, that's what they are."

Another pause, and then Bristol nods. "I understand, darling, thank you."

Marge laughs. "I told her I thought you'd like the bow," she says, finishing her drink. "I ought to be going, though."

"Thank you, Marge," Bristol says. I'm not sure if Marge is just eager to turn in, or if she's feeling Bristol close that loop of help versus not-help.

"Sure you don't want to hang around longer, trade some war stories?" I ask, grinning.

She hesitates, glancing at Bristol, who arches a brow. "I could be persuaded."

"I'm not so sure war stories are a good idea," Butler says.

"Oh yeah?" I ask.

"Yeah. Either Marge'll just cement her confidence in us as operators, or decide the best thing for her hide is to get away from us."

"Aw, I don't know about that," I say.

"Perhaps you *should* share a story, Butler," Bristol says, in a deliberately circumspect tone. "Dolly tells us so little about herself, and you."

"You never ask." I top off my drink, hold the bottle up, and Butler moves his glass over. Bits blinks at us like she can't decide if she's asleep or awake.

Butler clears his throat and looks at me; I shrug. I have no idea what story he has in mind. "So we're drinking whiskey, not tequila, but why don't I tell you a story about tequila," he says. Oh, this one. I knock back my glass without comment, and for some reason, that makes Bits look more awake. "Okay, this was when we were still in the program. Double black ops, even the secret projects don't know about us secret project, super soldiers in a base in Mexico. What are we doing in Mexico? I still don't know. Weren't supposed to be there, definitely. But we're in Mexico, on fucking dry base. Bored out of our minds, whole team just climbing the walls. Whatever action they had planned for us just wasn't happening."

Bristol is *very* intent; I have definitely never shared any detailed stories from the super soldier days. I'm not sure she'll love the payoff of this, though. "And what does a secret super soldier who isn't where they ought to be do in such a situation?" she asks. Bits smirks a little, but she doesn't know either. The level on her glass is lower than I expected, though.

"We're all on active duty, could be in the shit at any minute. Concertina wire, helmets, full armor. A million degrees down there in the jungle and we're sweating it out every day all kitted out. Maybe it's just a training exercise, and central is running some kind of test on us?" He pauses, just a little too long. "I guess technically everything they did was a test."

"But that's neither here nor there," I say, in my imitation of Bristol's voice, and she gives me a rueful look.

"You're right, it ain't. But so we hear stuff about the little town that's nearby, because what else is there to talk about? Not that the guys that are actually stationed there talk to us *much*, but they did enough that Dolly hears there's a special kind of tequila that they make here. Some bullshit magic mushroom tequila that I think they put scorpions in, instead of a worm, to scare the gringos."

"Do they even have scorpions, in Mexico?" Bristol asks.

"Mexico has lots of scorpions," Bits says. "I think the most in the world? No. The most *biodiversity* in scorpions in the world."

"...oh."

I look at Marge to see how she's taking all this in, and she's got one of those little smiles on that says she knows that this is a for fun bullshit story, and nothing too serious. Good. "Get to it, Butler."

"I'm setting the scene," he grumbles. "So Dolly goes, *solo* mind you, over the fence. Through the concertina wire, down to that town, where the bar is like, in some old lady's kitchen. Dolly, in her best Spanish, which is pretty good actually, asks for a bottle of magic mushroom scorpion tequila. The lady looks at this random American in her jungle and asks..."

"Plata or un año," I supply.

"Right, silver or one year. And Dolly, acting like she knows what the fuck this lady is talking about, says one year. Because, she reasons, older booze is better booze."

"I'm not wrong." Actually, looking at the label of this bottle of whiskey I've been so liberal with, it is not cheap whiskey. Bristol, to her credit, has not commented on that. Not that she tends to, actually. She hates to waste things, and sometimes wasting things is hoarding them away where nobody enjoys them. What's the point of liquor nobody drinks?

Butler laughs. "No, you're not, but I'm telling the story."

"It's not a very good story, really," I say to the table, and Bits laughs. "You're going to be underwhelmed. In fact, we might as well—"

"I want to hear it," Bristols says primly.

"Well. If the lady wants a story..." I light a cigarette, offer around the pack. Marge takes one, accepts the lighter.

"So she gets what, five? Six?" I nod. "Seis bottles of mezcal escórpioin un año, and starts her walk back out into the jungle, because that's always been a thing about Dolly, even before the super soldier stuff, she never gets lost. She'd taken her jacket and body armor off once she was outside of the fence, stashed them in a tree that was like, older than the world, so she wouldn't look like partisans or something coming out of the jungle. She gets back to the tree, and I'd say no sweat but like we mentioned, it's a bajillion degrees out, and as she's getting back in her jacket, she hears a noise."

"A noise?" Bristol asks, when he pauses for dramatic effect.

"A noise." He nods. Quite the storyteller, our Butler. "See, one of the guys there all the time, he tried to get us all spooked about chupacabras, but Dolly just wasn't having it. But in the middle of the jungle in the middle of the night, after maybe sampling some old lady's hallucinogenic tequila, you wonder. Dolly's checking the perimeter, making sure she's clear to sneak back in the way she came, but the noise is getting closer, and then she hears a radio nearby, an honest to goodness walkie, tuned way down low. And the action we'd all been waiting for, it was creeping up on the base right then."

"Well shit," Marge says, suitably impressed already. I guess it makes sense; I'm still here, right?

"So Dolly figures she needs to cop to what she's done because this is a bigger problem, messages the CO, but now these guys are between her and the fence, and she's got only a sidearm but also the drop on them, and *is* a secret supersoldier. But then Dolly feels something on the back of her neck."

Everybody looks at me, as if on cue. "I froze, because God knows what I've just encountered, and then I felt something on my arm too. It was fucking scorpions, because apparently where the scorpions in the tequila came from, for generations, was that super old tree. Dunno why. I don't know anything about scorpions, except apparently they love armored jackets when you give them the chance. Or loved *my* armored jacket, on account of how sweet I am. I didn't know how poisonous the things would be, what would make them sting, nothing. If they were real because yeah, I did get a sample of the tequila." I drag on my cigarette, shudder. That night had been beyond surreal. And ridiculous.

"So figuring she has nothing to lose, she whips off her jacket again and throws it over the head of one of the guys in the back, shoots two others, and then hit the dirt and prayed, I assume, as the lights on the base fences come on like the fucking sun and the teams assembled open up. Fucking bloodbath."

Bristol looks from Butler, to me. "That's the story?" she asks.

"I mean, I took a couple of rounds. I said it wasn't actually a very good story." I start to blow a smoke ring, but the breeze off the beach is a little too much. "One of the scars was in the arm I don't have anymore and the other one was fixed by Uncle Sam during one of the other surgeries. But no scorpions stung me, anyway, so jury's out on whether they were *actually* real, biodiversity or not."

"It's a great story to let people know how you are," Butler says.

"Sure it is, except there were shorter ones you could've employed. Like that time in Germany—"

Marge finishes her drink. "It's a fine story," she says. "I am going to turn in now, though."

"It is *very* late," Bristol says apologetically. "Much as I'd like to hear about Germany. Did that one also involve substances?"

"Nah, no hints," I say, before Butler can answer. I reach over and take his glass, finish the little bit he's got left. "Shuteye for all of us then, we'll leave the estate to the hounds." Mr. Squeak comes by on patrol at that moment, to illustrate my point. We all watch her go, the strings of lights glistening off the sequins on the bow I found. Marge gives her a little tap as she goes past; I wonder where she lives, actually. "I think she's a keeper," I say, once she's out of earshot.

"I'm very fond of Marge," Bristol says. "She does very well here, for me."

"Well good," I say, standing up and stretching until something in my back cracks. "Butler, shall we?"

"Sure," he says, a look of watchful intent in his eyes. He doesn't want to misunderstand.

"Goodnight, everybody," Bits says, and I grab her mostly-full glass before I go. I should've asked where Will is. Bits absolutely knows where Will is. Sorry he missed storytime, though.

Chapter Seven

The next morning, me and Bits sit down at the breakfast table but there's no place setting for Bristol, not even for coffee. "So much for the debrief," I say.

"You can't be surprised."

"I'm not surprised, just disappointed," I say, poking at the bowl of sliced fruit. Figs and melon and blueberries, and I wonder if Bristol okays a menu every day for the kitchen or what. Probably. I can't really imagine her just letting anybody else decide, this is her playground. Like how I'm sure every plant on the property has been examined and signed off on by her, not that I think she's a gardener, but because of the aesthetic vision.

"At least everything went fine last night," Bits says.

"Bitsy, you don't gotta try to make me feel better, I'm a big girl. And also we're still in the window of 'Will's people might think everything's still copacetic' so..."

She shrugs. "I know."

I squint at her. "*Do* they still think everything's copacetic?"

"Yeah, they seem to think so," she says, without hesitation.

"Have you *slept* since we got here?" It isn't fair to expect her to do round the clock crisis digital surveillance, we should've talked about this before we got here, or when we got here, or yesterday, or—

"Yeah, don't worry about it. I've had Speckle and Nautical Deborah doing dedicated tradeoffs, and a couple of others doing broader surveillance."

"Okay, good." We eat in silence for a few minutes. "Nautical Deborah?"

"She's in an oil platform squatter community." Bits is doing that look off and to the right thing, her eyes scanning just slightly, and I leave her be a little longer, chewing on that intel along with my breakfast.

"Is there a....what, Landlocked Deborah? Do you also have Zeppelin Steve?"

"No, I don't think any perpetual aerial communities have lasted long enough for anything like that," she says, then blinks and looks at me. "It's not that weird a name."

"Not really, and that's part of what makes it so weird, I think." Perpetual aerial communities. Sure. What do I know. "Anyway, I think we've in general hit the more normal end of hacker names. I haven't run into a whole lot of Zorgoth the Destroyers or whatever, and honestly I'm disappointed."

"Naming conventions shift every few years, there's still time."

"I would never make fun of Nautical Deborah to her face," I say.

"Well no, we'd have to go out there, and—" she looks at me, blinking more. "I know."

I laugh. "I think you need more sleep than you got."

"Probably, but..."

"Yeah."

Somebody's approaching from down the hallway, and Bits and I both look to the door as Nicolai appears. He glances in as he walks past, then stops and backs up. "You're up early," he says, a bit sheepishly.

"Nicky, you disappeared last night," I say. I saw him circulating early on, maybe right after we named the robot dogs, and then not after. "Coffee?"

"I had to take some calls," he says, coming to sit. "And then when I returned, I met a very nice woman who shared my interest in caviar."

"Your passion maybe?" I ask, and he smiles again.

"Maybe," he agrees."Such things are a flash in the pan."

"I don't know if that's—" Bits starts, and I cut her off.

"Yeah, they can be." Nicolai is very judicious about his one night stands, but they're always one night stands. Good for him, really; comin' from a big family like his, it's hard to guess if he's gonna abruptly settle down and have a million kids, or just be a perpetual bachelor. Or maybe that's what his caviar business is supposed to be, a nice, close to home step down from the arms dealing.

"Won't she be at the party tonight, though?" Bits asks.

Nicolai shrugs. "Maybe. And maybe we will again pass the time."

"Don't poison Bitsy's mind with your Casanova ways." I'd offer him some of my breakfast but I ate it. It's fine, I'm sure there's a nice buffet Bristol has for the real guests, like an all-inclusive resort.

"My apologies," he says, and she shakes her head.

"Dolly can't decide if I'm impressionable or not. We're all grown ups."

"Sure we are," I say. She isn't mad, just mystified. "Anyway, hear anything interesting on your end of things?"

"No, just normal party things. Not even a business lead. Most of these people Bristol has surrounded herself with are entirely careless. Without responsibility."

"Kinda like how Bristol herself wants to be," I say. "For one more day, at least."

"I beg your pardon," Nicky says.

"It's only fair," Bits says, and we laugh.

"I do not understand the joke."

"It's okay. Just keep your eyes peeled and your hands wandering, I guess." I push back from the table and stand up. "I might take another field trip, want anything from off site, Bitsy?"

"Not if it has scorpions in it," she says, and the face Nicolai makes is a combination between pleading and horrified.

"I'll tell you some other time, bud," I say. "Or actually, ask Butler, he tells it better."

"Maybe stay here, though," Bits says as I'm leaving the room.

"You might be right. Don't wanna trip the global surveillance network and give Nautical Deborah too much of a hard time."

Before I'm out of earshot, I hear Nicolai say "I know you aren't speaking in code, but it does not make it any more understandable."

I RUN OUR PERIMETER again, what else am I going to do? Maybe I should be resting up. Once ops kick off, there isn't going to be much opportunity for that, why not just enjoy myself? But I actually don't trust that; I don't think Will was lying about his three day check in window, I think he believes it. But I think things're gonna be in motion tonight or tomorrow and if I'm wrong that's fine and if I'm right, nobody made any bets with me anyway.

Butler comes out to join me when I'm staring at the beach through one of those doors in the wall again. "Missed my coffee this morning," he says.

"Sorry, got distracted."

"Understandable." He's good at not smothering me, I appreciate that. "Any news?"

"Nothing. It's driving me nuts."

"It'd be a hell of a thing, if they just never came for him."

"Wouldn't it though? We'd never be able to trust that, though. Disavowed, or double cross?"

"Are you ever gonna trust him anyway?" He lights a cigarette, offers me the pack, and I take one. I finished my pack already and didn't feel like going back to my room for more.

"Point." I let him light my cigarette. "Anyway there's only so many of these parties are gonna happen before something goes south. Maybe it's a miracle that we even had one good one."

"Probably." Gotta hand it to Butler, he has the good sense not to give empty reassurances. Or contradict me for the sake of it. Maybe he feels it too, that sense that while nothing's *wrong* yet, maybe, it isn't right either.

He walks with me, and as we pass the pool, which has some early-morning sunbathers in bikinis with their mimosas, I hear one of them say "Did you notice one of the robot dogs is wearing a bow?" and I manage to not laugh my head off and make it so we have to interact or something.

Most of Bristol's party people are not early risers, though, like I know for a fact that we won't see Marquis before noon and that might even be noon Eastern Standard Time, so when we see her and Will inside, they're alone. "Still enjoying the honeymoon period?" I ask, and Will flushes and Bristol smiles tightly.

"Actually, Dolly, I'm going to need your help with something before this evening's festivities, if you wouldn't mind."

"Mind? I'd be honored," I say, thinking it's a mistake that I don't ask 'help with what' but also I guess I can still say no later.

"Perfect, darling, thank you. Around six, say?"

"Oh, we're havin' an early bird party tonight?"

"I'm making an effort to strike the balance between our night owls and early risers," she says. She tilts her head just slightly, looking at me critically. "Must you always carry that gun?"

"It's almost like you forgot what's goin' on, Bristles, did you get a knock in the head that I forgot about?"

Her smile doesn't falter, but her eyes sharpen a little. "It's making my guests uncomfortable."

"Now, that's a thing to choose to lie about," I say, grinning hard, keeping our eye contact but in my periphery, I see Will react just slightly. He's a fast learner, he remembers what me and Bitsy said yesterday. "Not a single one of them has the sense to know what they're looking for, and if I'm making them uncomfortable, that's just by merit of my scintillatin' personality."

Butler has the good sense to stay out of this, and so does Will, and I watch Bristol run her social calculation which is not normally something you really see behind the curtain on, and it only takes a split second and her smile changes, apologetic now. "You're right, darling, I'm so sorry. What a silly thing for me to do, after all we've been through together. Can you just forget I said anything?"

"Sure," I say easily. "We're all under a lot of pressure." I wink at Will. "Anyway, at least one guest knows I'm strapped." I literally just mentioned a double cross, but I was talking about Will, not Bristol. It never occurred to me to worry about Bristol. Should I be?

"Splendid, thank you. I'll see you at six, then." They split off and go off towards the pool.

"Gonna go talk to Bits," I say to Butler, and leave him to go find her.

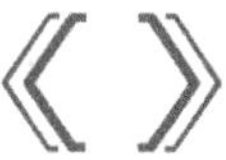

"I DON'T KNOW WHEN SHE would've had the chance to talk to anybody," Bits says carefully. "I don't *think* Bristol would want to double cross us. It doesn't make sense."

"No, it doesn't. But I wanted to actually say it and have you tell me that." I take a deep breath, let it out. "I'm not used to things like 'the strain getting to me.'" I make elaborate air quotes to get her to laugh.

"The price of giving up your cybernetic supersoldier programming, I assume," she says.

"We did that *ages* ago."

"Yeah, and have had various stress levels since, but I think not this kind of sustained level of anticipatory stress."

"Keep talkin' sense to me, Bitsy, we might be getting somewhere." We're in the same room where she was deprogramming Will. Wonder how many more people Bits will get to deprogram; two already is kind of a lot. I should ask Butler how he got his done; is it weird that we haven't already talked about it? I know he has, though. He doesn't whistle anymore.

"It makes sense to be jumpy, and it makes sense for you to double check your impulses. Nothing you're doing is wrong." She's got her headset pushed up on top of her head, her hair going every which way. "There has been a lot of chatter on the agency network today. If we hadn't done such a good job undermining Will's credibility, we'd be in trouble already."

"It's nice of you to say 'we' when you're the one who did all the heavy lifting."

"We got here as a team," she says, reaching for her glass of coffee. I look at the pitcher on the table; the same jet fuel, I think. I chew on my lip instead of saying anything, she's a grown up. "But also I think they've got people on the way, if some aren't here already. They're being very circumspect."

"I ever tell you that in the program, they put us in VR and tested our precognitive abilities."

She raises her eyebrows at me, but finishes drinking first. "No, you never talked about it."

She read my file from front to back, of course. I know that, she knows that. "I was awful at it. But there was *one* time I was sure about the test thing and I was right." She blinks at me. "I guess it was bound to happen sooner or later, with enough repetitions of the test."

"Some of the program separated off the people with what they thought were demonstrative precognitive abilities," Bits says. "With you, the notes said that you're able to rapidly put together context clues, which sometimes makes it seem as though you've had a precursor indicator but really you're just very good at subconsciously reacting to the environment."

"Well we knew that." I mean, I didn't, when I was a wet-behind-the-ears kid in a cybernetic supersoldier program, but we sure as hell know that by now.

"Sure, but we can really leverage it at times like this." She frowns. "I mean, in theory. Not like I know how to turn *up* your situational awareness."

"More's the pity." I wonder if the program that trained precognitives kept going somewhere, or if it got mothballed too.Wouldn't that be funny, if they were still operating somewhere, givin' world governments a nudge here and there. "Anyway, I hope the real action kicks off soon, before I end up putting one of Bristol's guests against a wall."

"Are you worried that you'll do that?"

"Not really, but this many fancy people around, there's no telling what can happen."

"Maybe you should do some more laps. Or go in the ocean, did you do that yet?"

"Maybe that's a good idea. Get some beach time in before six."

Her eyes move to the side, I guess checking an AR calendar. "What's at six?"

"I dunno, Bristol asked me to help her with something then."

"Dinner's at seven, according to the kitchen calendar."

"Well who knows, maybe she wanted to get me alone for some reason." I wiggle my eyebrows at Bits, who frowns first and then laughs.

"I'm sure."

Chapter Eight

Going out to the actual beach and into the little waves does actually do me some good, I think. Everybody has the good sense to leave me alone, even Butler, and none of the party people come out to the beach when there's a perfectly good pool right there. They've got music playing, not too loud, and sometimes voices get raised loud enough that I can kind of hear their echo, but they're not particularly *rowdy* party people. I've seen worse, and I'm not even talking about my military experience.

I rinse off and throw clothes on and get to Bristol's door at six sharp. She's wearing yet another one of those silky, gauzy robe things when she answers, and her hair and makeup are already done. I think. They look done, anyway. "What's up?" I ask, and she all but pulls me inside.

"This is going to be such fun, you'll see," she says, her eyes actually twinkling.

"Bristles, your idea of fun and mine don't have a lotta overlap."

"Mmm, true," she says, shutting the door and then bringing me into her room's little living room. I guess it's a suite, that she's got. There's a hassock or footstool or whatever in the middle of the room, and a couple of spray cans on the coffee table.

"Is this something you could've asked Marquis for?" I ask, and then realize I only saw Marquis last night, and only for a little while. Not today.

"Oh, Marquis was called away to Paris, to assess the legitimacy of a painting."

"I didn't realize Marquis did stuff like that." The cans look like too-tall spray paint cans and I can't see any writing on them from my angle.

"They have degrees in museum studies and have worked in galleries and facilities all over the world," Bristol says. "And so it falls to you, as Bits isn't tall enough and Will would not be appropriate to ask."

"Suzette?" This is making me weirdly nervous and I don't know why. Maybe because she hasn't said yet what the help is.

"Busy with her own outfit for tonight. Really, darling, it's quite simple, you—"

"Bristol, how am I gonna be *outfit* help?"

"Honestly, Dolly." She picks up one of the spray cans, which rattles, and hands it to me. "I'm going to stand on this stool and you're going to go around me and spray my dress on, and I'll adjust as necessary. I want you to walk around so that it'll drape like fabric cut on the bias."

"Spray your dress on." I turn the can over in my hands. It says, essentially, "dress in a can" in French. A designer name, I assume, and an ingredients list. Silk fibers, synthetic, suspended in stuff I don't really have the vocabulary for because they aren't food words or violence words.

"Yes, so you understand now?"

"I guess. At least you've got more'n one, for if I fuck it up."

"You won't, I'm confident you'll do fine." She picks up her phone and shows me a picture, like I'm gonna be able to spray a dress on her that looks like that. "Just start behind me, on my right shoulder, and like I said..."

"Yeah," I say, squinting at the picture and rattling the can. She pushes the phone in my hand and drops her robe, stepping up onto the stool. I pop the cap and look from the picture to her and stop again. "*No* dragonscale, Bristles?"

"I simply cannot be armored at all times, Dolly, it's impossible." She looks over her shoulder at me. "Besides, it isn't as though *you* did either, when you were swimming this afternoon? Be reasonable."

"Fair enough." I guess the camisole or whatever would ruin the lines of the spray dress the way bra and underwear don't. What do I know.

"Oh it's cold," she says when I start spraying, a laugh in her voice, her skin rippling gooseflesh.

"Should I stop?" Watching the spray turn into fabric is wild, like magic. It's white; it's interesting, how often Bristol wears white. Just strikes me as impractical.

"No, no, it'll be fine." There's a mirror across from her, of course, and a door to the secret passages behind it. She watches the fabric form in the mirror, making adjustments a couple of times, and I do my best to concentrate. I'm not an uncontrollable horndog, but Bristol's charms cannot be overstated. We've gotta work together, I made the decision a long time ago not to even try to pursue.

The can is starting to sputter when I'm at the hem and I say, "I guess that's it."

She's looking at herself in the mirror, critically, and looks down at the skirt. "Do you have a knife?"

"Yeah." I pull a folding jackknife and a combat knife and hold them both out to her. She rolls her eyes, but she's smiling just a little, and she actually picks the combat knife and traces a slit up the skirt.

"Hold that taut?" I do, and she makes the actual cut, and the fabric pulls apart and then the edges roll over and sorta heal themselves instead of fraying. She hands the knife back and then fiddles with the straps, pulling them out a little bit and laying them down so it's more off the shoulder. "How is the back?"

I clear my throat. "I'm not exactly a neutral audience," I say. Our eyes meet in the mirror.

"Thank you for your help, darling, I don't know what I would've done without you," she says, stepping down and going over to her jewelry table. Her sandals stand at ready over there too.

"No problem," I say, stowing my knives again. "I'll see you later." For a second I think about how funny it would be to exit via secret passage, without saying anything, but I take the door instead. I go back out onto the beach, drop my clothes in the sand, and dive into the surf again.

WHEN I GET OUT OF THE shower, Butler's in my room. "What's up?" I call, toweling off.

"How'd you know I was here?"

"Smelled your cologne." Is that how, or is that my flash-in-the-pan precognitive abilities. I look at the mirror, and a heart drawn there in the steam makes me smile. Guess he must've done that last night. "Where've you been?"

"Talking to Will."

"What, really?" I pull the bathroom door open, sloppily wrapped in a towel. The towels here, or in my room anyway, aren't the terrycloth loop kind, and I feel like they don't actually get me dry, just kinda slick the water around. He's sitting on the foot of the bed. "About what?"

"We're both in love with difficult women." He pats what he can reach as I go past.

"Isn't everybody? What, you got a club?" I grin at him and rummage in my clothes. I should do laundry at some point, before we're likely to start bleedin'.

"It's part of what we were hashing out, bylaws and shit."

"We've all been spending too much time *talking*," I say, throwing my towel at him and wrestling into my clothes. "At this point I'd rather somebody just shot at us."

"That bad, huh?"

"Asshole." I sit next to him to put my boots on. "Sorry."

He puts an arm around me and kisses the top of my head. "It's fine. I'd rather you go swimming than go lookin' for hallucinogenic tequila," he murmurs against my hair.

"You don't really get a say." I stay leaning into him for a little while, though. He always smells good.

"I know." He kisses me again, then lets me go and I finish putting my boots on. "Waiting isn't good for anybody and they're probably doing it on purpose."

"It's possible we're already fucked, honestly, but we gotta just find that out for ourselves."

"That's more like it." He laughs. "Anyway, it's also giving me time to train the kids."

"With Will?"

"He's a good shot, and steady enough when you aren't around." I laugh. "No, really."

"No, I believe you. And can't help but think how smart it is that you're tricking him into making connections with people here other'n Bristol."

"Don't know if I'm tricking him," Butler says with a shrug. "Anyway, he seems comfortable enough with Bits."

"Bits isn't the kind of existential threat that makes him nervous." I flop back on the bed. "How's it going with the kids, though? Tell me. Should I be helping?"

"It's okay to do what you're doing," he says. "They're taking it seriously, which is more than I can say about us when we started."

"Excuse yourself, I took it very seriously."

"Sure you did." He lays next to me, props himself on an elbow. "You've always wanted to make sure the big dogs know you're a big dog too."

I move my gaze from the ceiling to his face. "Well I am."

"I always knew it."

And he always acted like it, too. "Sorry I lost my belt buckle," I say after a few minutes. He looks surprised and his eyes drop to my belt. Then he smiles, leans down and kisses me.

"It's just stuff. We'll go back to the old swimming hole sometime and you can find another piece of something to use. For the next one."

THE PARTY IS THE SAME. The robot dogs patrol outside of the lights, Marge and Floyd and Joker and Butler and I hover around at the edges of things, very occasionally engaging with Bristol's guests. I watch Nicolai and Suzette make eye contact from across the room and little by little get closer to each other as the night progresses, until finally he makes the first move, snagging two glasses of champagne off a tray and going to offer her one. I'm sure they'll make beautiful babies. Or, have a torrid, no-strings affair and come away from their time here having made a new hookup friend. Whichever. Something good coming out of this mess. In theory, more good'll come out of this, but we gotta get there. It's not like the agency's been persistently causing us *that* much trouble. Actually, it's kinda funny how little overall impact they've had on us.

I didn't get to see Will's face when he first saw Bristol in that dress, but just like last night, she keeps him near her most of the time, and I do see the glances he keeps giving her. Suzette's outfit doesn't look like anything special to me, but who knows, maybe she had to iron it or something.

//I think we're okay tonight// Bits messages me at one point. //Airport and actual ports are quiet, agency chatter is about normal level. If they're smart, they'll fly in somewhere else and drive over.//

"If you say so," I say.

//You sound disappointed.//

"Bored. Anticipation fatigue."

//I get it.// Bits knows better than to tell me to try and enjoy the party. //How are Floyd and Joker?//

"They've got the basics. They've seen zero action, so who knows how that'd shake out. But they've been okay for this, they're eager to please, and Marge is good. Plus, Butler and Will have been working with them. Both to save our hides and also for something to do." One of the robot dogs trundles past me; Mr. Squeak, it's got the bow. And an empty can of Power Horse on its back. "Have the dog patrols ever noticed anything weird?"

//Like recently, or in the history of ever?// A pause, and I wait, because I know she's checking. //Yeah, the Loki designate tased somebody three months ago and they ran off before Marge could get to them. Mr. Squeak, no, and Snorri had somebody put a bikini bottom on it just this afternoon. Yes, I cross checked the cameras, it was one of the invited guests.//

"I don't know if I should say poor Snorri or lucky Snorri."

//Dealer's choice.//

I laugh, and one of the guests walking by carrying her heels looks at me and I wink. She giggles uncertainly and keeps walking. She's the Crayola heiress or something, I'm sure. I saw an invite list, Marge had it, but I didn't exactly commit it to memory. None of these people interest me, other than threat mitigation. "Hey, is Marquis really in Paris?"

Another pause, I assume while Bits recalibrates. //Yeah. Why?//

"It seemed like they left awfully soon."

//They got the call this morning.// I hear Bristol laugh, and from where I'm standing can just get a glimpse of her on Will's arm, but not who she's talking to. //We can't do this. Second guessing each other.// I can imagine the look of careful concern on Bits's face.

"No, it's bad for business." But then, so is going to your private hotel and filling it with a rotating cast of mostly-strangers right after stealing some kinda double-hush government agent. "Plus, it's good for Marquis not to have more contact with the agency. They got when the gettin' was good the first time around."

//That might've contributed to their early departure.//

"Makes sense. Plus Paris is like, right there." It is and it isn't. Everything's closer together here than stateside, anyway. "It'd be better for the agency if they didn't have more contact with us, too."

//I'm sure they don't see it that way, that's not how government agencies work.//

"Yeah, I know. But it'd be nice, right?" Wishing it wasn't going like this won't change anything, but if wishes were horses then beggars could ride.

Chapter Nine

When things go wrong, it's so quick and clean that we almost don't realize at first. We're tipped off pretty quick, but that's a combination of one robot dog going dark, Mr. Squeak tasing somebody, and Bristol hitting her panic button. I almost get to her in time. Bristol hits that button and Bits shows me a blip of where on property she is, and I take the shortest way to it. Of course they hear me coming. I'm not careful. I don't think about like. Stealth.

I get a glimpse of Bristol's face and the flip of her skirt, disappearing around a corner, as I come out of one of this place's long dark hallways and something, somebody, hits me in the middle of the chest and slams me to the ground on my back. I hear a sound that I know is my head hitting those nice shiny tiles but I put that away for later, I'm hyped up enough I can do that. I kip up onto my feet, slapping for my knife, because everything is still so fucking *quiet,* I don't want to bring gunplay into this just yet. I still think that I can stop them here.

I tag the guy twice in a stab vest and then once for real, I feel it land and hear him grunt, and then he catches my wrist and gives a yank and a twist, meant to disarm me, which it does, and break my arm, which it doesn't, because it's my cybernetic arm. I see his face then; it's Clancy, the pile of muscle they had doing security when we ran that diamond job where we all got so cozy. Guys like that really take it to heart when you make 'em look bad, and it's on me that he surprised me. I'm running those thoughts in my brain separate of all my combat-reaction-space; times like these, I understand Bitsy's data deluge.

He's still got my arm and doesn't much like it when I head butt him but he isn't letting *go* and I grab on with my other hand and let him hold me up while I plant both boots in his stomach-ribs-crotch area. He lets me go then, because he throws me, and I clip off the corner at the end of the hallway, my air woofing out, and thump on the floor again, curled around my poor ribs. I use the wall to drag myself to my feet, and he smirks, and then the wind of a suppressed round passes over my shoulder. He isn't hit, but he puts a finger to his ear in classic comms pose and then goes off the way I saw Bristol get taken.

I take a step to follow and stagger instead, catching the wall again, getting that next breath finally. My head's trying to spin and I can't tell yet what's happening in my ribs and back. "Woah hey, Dolly, hey," Butler says, holstering his handgun, stopping short of touching me. I know that gentled-down tone of voice he's using. Haven't heard it in a while but I've heard it a lot. "Stop, take it easy."

"No, they went—"

//They're offsite// Bits says. //Time to regroup.//

"Dolly, look at me." Butler's in front of me, trying to catch my gaze as I'm bending to pick up my knife. I wipe my nose with the back of my hand, blink at the blood. I'm pretty tired of breaking my nose, actually. Wonder if I can get a cybernetic replacement. I laugh, and Butler frowns. "How many fingers?"

"You know that doesn't happen with us, they fixed that," I say, brushing his hand away. I forget what part of the permanent supersoldier suite negates, or tries like hell to negate, concussions. I cracked my head bad enough for one, whatever, no arguments there. But for us it doesn't mean anything. "We gotta go get the one they left and see what we can get out of him."

"Sure, but—" While we're standing there wasting time, one of the little mopping robots whirrs out and starts cleaning blood off the tiles. Mine or Clancy's, I can't bother about it right now.

"Please, Butler." He shuts his mouth and we go. He watches me, but I can breathe and I can walk.

Snorri is the robot dog that went dark, and that's just because it got a sport coat thrown over it, and Marge has to get Loki to stand down, because it went and covered Will once the other robot dogs activated. Part of the special other programming that Bits did without really laying out in detail for the rest of the class. I listen to that chatter as Butler gets the agent zip tied and drags him by the tuxedo collar to a nearby non-guest-occupied room to further secure him to a straight backed chair. I pull the curtain tiebacks off their hooks and let my hands remember the right kind of knot.

We, well mostly Butler, give him a quick patdown, take his handgun and take a keycard that he's got tucked into his shirt pocket. How the party's still going, I don't know. It started even earlier today, four instead of six, or maybe it never really ended last night, just some people went to bed and other people didn't and it's like partying by shift work.

Marge brings Will in while I'm still deciding if I want to wait and hear what this guy has to say, or if I'm gonna just break his neck and go get Bristol, no matter the sidelong looks Butler's giving me. Loki clatters in behind them, which is fine, but what I really want is for Bits to get in here.

"Shit, I'm sorry," Marge says. "I did what I could but—"

"We all did, and it wasn't enough. The kids okay?" I know they are but I gotta get her refocused.

"Yeah, they checked in, they're fine. Didn't see anything either. The guests are still happy."

"That's fine. Don't feel bad, and don't let 'em feel bad. Just you three do business as usual, this is very much above your pay grade." I remember how to put a smile on. "It's why the whole gang is here."

She looks at my face, looks at the guy in the chair. Looks at Butler. She wants to protest, she wants to help, and I just need her out of my way. It isn't that I can't trust her, it's that we need to keep the party going, keep up appearances, and get this fixed behind the scenes. Bristol's got too many people here from too many walks of life for them to know that anything just went down. "Understood," she finally says. "You tell me if you need me for anything."

"Thanks Marge. Really, it's appreciated." She stalks off, leaving Loki, and the second she's out of earshot, I whip around and chokeslam Will up against the nearest wall. "Did you know this was going to happen?".

He, well, he can't answer and I let up just enough. I know my own strength, I know what I'm doing. "I thought they would come for *me*," he says, in a gasp.

"Did they decide they want her instead or is she bait?"

"I don't know, I have no way to know." I think about choking him again, he's always expected me to hurt him, and I drop him instead. The guy in the chair hasn't come around yet so either he's faking or Mr. Squeak got him worse than a normal taser and we're wasting *time* and then Bits comes in, with Nicolai, and I'm glad to see that. Nicolai's good to have at your back.

"What're we lookin' at, Bitsy?" I wipe my nose again. Bleeding stopped.

"They want to trade."

"How do you know that already?" Will's still backed up against the wall and I'm still way too close to him for his comfort, but I turn to her. Her expression doesn't tend to give away much in the best of times, and right now ain't exactly the best of times. Them taking

Bristol, out of all of us, is the worst thing they could do to her, after everything. And they *know* it.

"They called Will's phone."

"And you talked to them?" That's not the question I mean. I hard blink to refocus. "What did they say?"

She'd been starting to answer, stops, blinks. "I answered, and they said to bring Will to an address, and texted that address. It's a hotel by the airport, pretty touristy and busy. They don't have it emptied, that I can tell, from records and street and security cameras."

"They're assuming collateral will protect them." The guy in the chair makes kind of a snoring noise, then snorts and the chair creaks, so I guess he's awake now. "Hello sunshine," I say. He looks around the room, looks up at Butler, then looks over at me, and at Will. He tries to get up, realizes he's attached to the chair he's in, *and* zip tied, and sets his jaw.

"I don't know what you think you'll—"

"We don't really need you, I just kept you for funsies," I say. "Did they even mention this guy, Bitsy?"

"No," she says. If the guy was going to say anything else right then, that shut him up. I wonder if he's got any comms equipment on him, but if he does, that's Bitsy's territory. My territory right now is getting Bristol back.

"Will, what's the play here?" I step back, give him some breathing room.

"What? I—" He looks at my face, gathers himself. "We...the agency hasn't had to deal with this particular situation before. I assume the goal is asset recovery. And/or damage control."

"Bits, gimme his phone, and an alternate address."

"What kind of alternate address?" She hands me the phone, slowly, frowning.

"It can still be populated, if that's what you mean. We want them to think that we're changing addresses to assert a sense of control over the situation." It'll also mean making Bristol go through getting moved more'n once but maybe they're just in a holding pattern driving her around town right now. Actually. "Where *is* Bristol?"

She pauses, looking. "In a car, moving. Sort of towards the hotel, but like they're taking the long way?"

Oh this is fun isn't it. "Pick a mall or something. A market." The guy tied to the chair takes a breath like he's gonna say something. "Will, can you put the fear of God in him, I ain't exactly got the time right now."

"Um," Will says, and I can't help but laugh, which has an ugly edge to it, all things considered.

"Do you even know each other? Are you *colleagues*?" I ask.

"We've met," Will says stiffly. Oh he's feeling his deprogramming now. I wonder if he doesn't even know the secret handshake anymore. That's gonna fuck him when we hand him over. Guess he's probably already fucked.

"Well you've met, and you're the only agent who takes us seriously, so make him understand that I will kill him and not care. You get that, right?"

"I get that," Will says. The other agent is listening silently, resentfully.

"Actually, wait, you. What's your name?" He looks at me. "Nevermind I don't care. Tell me what your plan was." Still silent. "What was the *operation*."

"Why would I tell you?" Welp.

"So I don't break every bone you got." I get behind him and start with his pinkie, that one's easy and won't really mess up his life too much. If he lives through this. If you've never had somebody break one of your bones on purpose, it's a very unpleasant surprise, both how easy it can be and just how much it hurts. Bones aren't typically brittle or dry, so if you've ever tried to break a green stick of wood, you know how there's a *flex* first, it's got *give*. It bends before it breaks. When it's flexing, he's doing a clean inhale through his nostrils; maybe he's broken a bone before. When it goes, though, he lets out a guttural noise. I'm watching Will as I do it, and he's got on a brave face but I'm not so sure how his stomach is, and there's a way he flinches around the eyes. "Hope you're not right handed." I move in to his ring finger, and as it's flexing, he says,

"The op was to extract Will Scarlet, but we had a timer. If it was getting too close to time and he couldn't be extracted, one of you three was the next option. If that was also unattainable, then we were to pull out. No wetworks."

And try again for another party. God damn it. "There, see how easy that was?" I wink at Will and let go of the guy's hand. "Remind me to rough you up a little before all this is done, so they can't tell you caved immediately. If you think your devices're recording, no they aren't." He must've looked at Will, who nods. "So they always wanted you back, Will Scarlet, ain't that sweet." Or they want to kill him themselves. That seems likely.

Nicolai rattles ice in a drink, reminding me about the rest of us in the room. Tunnel vision sure is a thing. "Dolly, what is the play?"

"We get Bristol back, obviously. And she's the one who wanted Will, no offense Will, so I don't really give a shit what happens to him." She isn't a helpless maiden, maybe she stabbed one of 'em and then took out the driver and is on her way back here on her own. She'll come clacking in, her hair down around her shoulders, and laugh at us for worrying. I look at the door. She doesn't do that.

"No offense taken," he says carefully. "I agree with that plan."

"Good, super simple." I glance around the room. Butler and Nicolai each have a drink and are just waiting for me to call the shots, good. Except Butler's watching me like he wants to bench me and he can't do that. I guess he's the closest to somebody I'd listen to, but we don't have that luxury and I'm not so bad off. Mildly concussed, a couple cracked and or bruised parts, mostly ribs, I'll sort it out later. Chew some excedrin. Bits has that faraway look on her face that means she's tracking more data than I can even conceive of; maybe listenin' on Bristol's devices while looking at agency chatter. Seems like a good guess. "Ready for me to make this call, Bitsy? Picked a place?"

"I picked a place. There's supposed to be an open-air market by a French import shop. Kind of open, not really crowded right now but not no public, good approach and egress vectors."

"Good, so we can put Butler and Nicolai up with rifles."

"Maybe deploy a robot dog," Butler says. "Keep them from circling in on us with more personnel."

"Never thought I'd hear you say that," I say. "That's what we call growth. Yeah we'll give Snorri the chance to get payback."

Butler sighs, just slightly, and finishes his whiskey. The picture of calm control. "I forgot you named them."

"They're good names." I redial the number that called Will's phone last. It rings six times and I assume the call will dump and then Harding says, "I assume this isn't Will."

"Got it in one," I say.

"Is there a problem with the arrangement?"

"Yeah, we're changin' the venue. Hopefully you can accommodate that. As Bristol would say."

"The ever-charming Bristol," he says, in that combination of frustration and admiration I know well from every other goddamn person in the world who has ever had to deal with Bristol as anything but the party girl. He wants me to be mad, though, he wants me to react, and I wait. I think about lighting a cigarette but don't. I could use a cigarette. I could use non-broken ribs. "Of course we can accommodate a change of venue, if you're amenable to the rest of the agreement."

"Yeah I don't give a fuck about Will, you can have him back. In one piece, even."

"That's very nice to know. I don't suppose I can speak to Will."

"I don't suppose I can speak to Bristol?" A pause. "I figured. So yeah, not at this time." I hope to Christ they didn't drug her.

"Understandable." There's a pause, where he muffles the phone. "I don't suppose you've seen another of our misplaced agents?"

"We only stole the one," I say. "But if you can describe the agent, we'll keep an eye out. As a professional courtesy."

"Noted. Maybe we'll belay that for now, since we're so chummy."

"Suit yourself." Interesting that the agent, who is not gagged or anything, is also not trying to communicate when I'm on the phone. Guess he's a quick learner. "Okay, so by the French import shop, there's an open air market. I figure that'll do us."

"Is that so." He's deciding if he wants to fuck with us more and we both know it. He's deciding if it's worth it, and I hope for his sake and the sake of the two agents in the room with me that he makes the right decision. "We can make that happen. See you in an hour?"

"An hour sounds good, roger that."

"I'm glad you're being reasonable, Dolly. There's no reason this can't go smoothly."

"Agreed, Harding. You're a real sport." He hangs up. "He never described you," I say to the other agent. "Didn't know you were on his shit list, huh?" The guy doesn't say anything, just stares at me sullenly. "Oh, don't pout, I might start crackin' fingers again to see if there's anything else interesting you might have to tell me, like how many of you were on site tonight and how many're in town total. We know you've got a small operation. Did you come here in the sub?"

"The sub is mothballed," Will says.

"Aw, that's a shame. We all liked the sub, right Bitsy?" She pulled on her headset at some point, and kind of makes a noise at me that might be an assent.

The other agent doesn't say anything, and I shrug and go back to his fingers. I get to the pointer before he grates out, "Four of us came to the party. Ten total came to Morocco. Plus Harding." The pain of betrayal doesn't stand up to the pain of broken fingers, I guess. They used to build 'em stronger. Or I shouldn't have made fun of how easy he cracked the first time.

"Atta boy, thanks." So ten left. Could be a hundred and could be just Harding, for all it matters, if we play nice when we trade. They wouldn't do all this if they were just gonna frag Will and dump him in the desert. In theory. I don't fucking know. "Anyway, Butler, Nicky, get goin' and we'll see you on the other side. Bits'll give you the location if she hasn't already, and cut surveillance for you to get in position, if she hasn't already." Guess we're solidly in "what Dolly wants to do" territory, sorry Bristol is missing it.

"I'm sorry about all this," Will says, maybe to keep me from breaking his fingers too. Maybe he is actually sorry about all this. Sorry for Bristol, anyway.

"Sure you are," I say. "Butler, you really gonna take one of the robot dogs?"

"Might as well. Or two. Like I said, be nice to have something watching our backs when you're doing the heavy lifting." He gives me a long look.

"I can drive a car and do a handoff," I say. More true than guessing at how okay I feel.

"Okay."

"What about him, though?" Nicolai asks, not exactly *nervous* but not really comfortable with letting it go either. We all look at the agent in the chair.

"Good question," I say. He's extraneous, he doesn't have anything to do with the leverage or negotiations, he just got his ass tased by a robot dog and we found him before he got himself together enough to leave again. "He's not really worth anything to us."

"Meaning?" I close my eyes a second, feel the world try to spin, and then look at Butler.

"I guess blindfold him and leave him in an alley someplace and they'll pick him up after this is done." Nicky looks dubious and Butler looks surprised. "Look, you got a better idea, go for it. We wanna zero out the ledgers here." I dunno if that's exactly the saying I mean, but it gets the point across. What's a few broken fingers amongst uneasy truce-holders?

"Okay then. Looks like you're coming with us," Butler says, and pulls the knot I used; my hands remember, his hands remember.

"I don't—" the guy starts to say, and Butler give him a shake, like a dog with a rope.

"Trust me, you want to get away from her. And your agency'll pick you up. This is a good outcome for you." The agent doesn't say anything else.

Chapter Ten

We get to the meetup, Bits using her active camo in the back seat, so it looks like it's just me and Will. The other end of the market, Harding comes out of a car, alone, which makes me check rooftops. //Clear// Bits says in my ear. //No idea why. Butler and Nicolai didn't run into anybody to clean up.//

"Is it possible they're *actually* just doing a clean handoff?" I ask Bitsy but also for Will's benefit. I don't ask where they dropped off the other agent. Maybe a hospital, what a courtesy that'd be.

"Maybe?" Will says. It's interesting how calm he is, actually, commendable. Maybe he still trusts the government. Wonder what that's like; even when I was in the program, it wasn't the government I trusted. It was the people I knew that were also in the program. It was the promise that we'd all come out the other side better off.

//Loki's giving the all clear too. And Snorri. Well. Snorri scared a stray cat or something but then it was all clear.//

"Reassuring." I look at Will. "Okay, you ready? Any last words?"

"I don't think that's necessary," he says.

"Suit yourself." In a movie, I'd be checking my handgun again before getting out of the car, but I already did that back at the hotel, this isn't a movie, I get out of the car and raise my hand to Harding. Wonder what, if anything, Clancy told him about our meeting.

There are people here, going about their lives, browsing the market, whatever, but after a moment he sees me and nods, goes around to the passenger side of the car and opens the door to hand Bristol out. They start walking our way, which is, I think, a real show of good faith on his part.

//Target acquired// Butler says in my ear. //Let me know if you need me to take the shot.//

"Understood," I say, and go open Will's door, though he's been a very good boy and not required any kind of extra handling. Really, we picked him at just the right time, plus the deprogramming. I don't look at Bits, don't look back at the car as we start walking to meet Harding and Bristol, and neither does Will. Am I starting to feel bad about this? Shit.

Bristol's face changes a little when she sees that it's just me and Will, the mask slipping for a heartbeat. She returns to her serene neutral expression almost immediately, but I wonder what she hoped for. I wonder what she thought we were doing. When we're close enough, she breaks loose of Harding's hand on her arm or he lets her go, and she flings herself into Will's arms. He looks at me over the top of her head, and I can see that conflict there too, in his wide eyes, that question too. What did she think this was. What don't we know, that she does. They didn't drug her, though, her movements are normal, her eyes, when I saw them, were clear.

I could give Butler the signal, but this is too open, and then there'd still be nine agents left, and we'd have to Whac-a-Mole back to the hotel and even then, what? Have Floyd and Joker and Marge pick them off? Plus local law enforcement. No, if the agency's playing nice we have to play nice, there are too many civilians here.

"Well, Mr. Harding, I wish I could say it was a pleasure," I say. He's also watching the embrace, and I also can't read the look on his face.

"In another life," he says, maybe poetically, maybe regretfully. I can only assume he's read my file by now, or a file about the program, such as Bits left available for him. Probably that's part of what she's doing in the car right now, erasing us. Erasing this. She spends so much time erasing us. Maybe at some point, Harding had visions of what it would be like, to bring us over. Maybe that's why he entertained the notion of extracting us.

Will turns to me, his arm still around Bristol's shoulders. "Dolly, get her out of here."

"Sure thing," I say, because yeah that's the plan, and at the same time Bristol says,

"Absolutely not, what could you possibly mean?"

"Please, Dolly," he says, as she's twisting to look up into his face.

"Will, *no*, I'm not some damsel to be handed off and *protected*. We'll—"

But I see what's in his face, and I understand, or think I understand. He's got a plan too, and he made it with Bits, I assume. Or I hope to Christ he made it with Bits at least, maybe Butler and Nicolai too, and they didn't tell Bristol and they didn't tell me, because they needed this to be real. And because he knows I love her too.

"Yeah, we're going," I say, and Bristol whips around to me.

"*Dolly*." She's furious, she's heartbroken, and I take her by the arm, gently, and she tears her arm out of my grasp and dodges back a few steps as I grab for her again. "Dolly, we are *not* letting him do this!" This is the first time I've ever heard her voice break. I see at least one glance from shoppers, but everybody is very determined to mind their business this time of night and in public.

"Bristol. Come on." Bristol does not come on. Will shifts behind her, getting nervous, needing us gone. He's got a sense of a timer that I've only just become aware of. If they did this while I spent all that time being bored, it'll be worth it. If we can pull it off. If he lives through it. If we all live through it. "Bristol, I don't wanna hurt you."

Bristol lowers her voice, her eyes electric. "Dolly, if you do this, I will never forgive you."

"I'd rather you be alive than forgive me," I say, and she turns around to Will, to do I don't know what, and I grab her around the waist and haul her off, and she *yells* at me, the prim and proper princess yells and struggles and she's always been stronger than she looks, but not strong enough. I grit my teeth and acknowledge and then ignore the pain in my ribs, shoving her into the car. She tries to open the door again the second I close it but Bits keeps that door locked. Nobody tries to stop us, but there is distinctly less crowd now, people filtering out of the thoroughfare.

I slide across the hood and get behind the wheel, even as Will and Harding are walking back to Harding's car, and Butler and Nicolai cover as we get out of there and drive to Bristol's hotel. It would make sense to do it in a circuitous way, but they've known where we were the whole time. So I don't do that. She stops trying to jump out, once we're moving. Buckles her belt, even. She pulls out her phone but then throws it on the dashboard in disgust, Bitsy coming through once again.

The parking lot is still full, and the party music is still floating out of the windows, up from the back patio. I park, and turn to her to say something about cleaning up and getting back to it, distracted by whatever my back is doing, and she shocks me by slapping me full across the face, hard enough that my eyes water.

"How *could* you?" The world is see-sawing and I can't see her face. My friggin' *nose.*

"Bristol, I—" She slaps me again, putting her all into it, and I manage to catch her wrist before she connects on the third one. She twists away and gets out of the car, slamming the door. She never acts like this, never. She must really think they're gonna hurt him. Like, worse than a mindwipe agent reset. Or she thinks they're gonna kill him. But also she'd be horrified if anybody saw her like this. I get out of the car, lean on the roof, and call to her in my best 'everything is normal' tone, "Bristles, come on. Party's still going." She stops, her back to me, completely rigid, and I watch her flex her hands. Then I watch her give her head a little toss, and I can imagine her pulling the composure back over her face, her whole self. Somehow, she doesn't have a single hair askew, I didn't notice that before now. And then she goes back inside to her party, the rhythm of her high heels steady and normal on the tiles.

Bits gets out of the car next to me, her VR headset hung around her neck, blinking against the now-setting sun. "Sorry," she says

"Tell me there's a plan," I say, once I don't have to lean on the car anymore, getting out my pack of cigarettes and lighting one.

"There's a plan." She rummages through her pockets, comes out with a battered, rattling pill bottle, and she shakes out a couple to hand me.

I exhale the first lungful of smoke. "Thanks." I dry swallow them without even checking what they are, drag on my cigarette again. "You need me?"

"I will." She's looking at me, really looking, and I avoid her eyes. Think about how I'm breathing. "You're—"

"Everybody keeps asking if I'm okay, and somebody's not gonna be."

She gives a nod, looks at her phone. "When Butler and Nicolai get back."

"Understood." Bits goes inside too, leaving me alone with my thoughts, which was kinda the opposite of what I wanted but that's life I guess. I'm gonna have to apologize to her for that. It wasn't too bad, but also is probably the worst thing I've ever said to Bits.

I'm sitting on the hood of the car, my boots on the bumper and elbows on my knees, up to my third cigarette when Butler and Nicolai park next to me. It's a position that doesn't so much hurt, gargoyled over like that. Butler cuts the engine and then pops the trunk, and the robot dogs climb out and skitter back into the hotel. Even without faces I can tell Snorri from Loki and I'm not sure if I could explain why without thinking about it harder than I've got the capacity for right now.

"That's one of the roughest easy times we've ever had, huh?" he asks, pretend casual, coming and leaning against the car. I offer him my cigarettes and he takes one, leans over to light it off mine.

"Sure was."

Nicolai comes over too, offers a flask. I take it, then look at him and laugh, and he looks hurt. "What?"

"You just climbed up on some roof to maybe-snipe somebody in a suit."

"Oh, well yes. Why would I have gotten changed?" He watches me take a swig, glancing at Butler.

"You're right, silly me." I take another swig, hand the flask to Butler. "Where'd you drop the other agent?

Butler shrugs. "By some museum that wasn't open. Funny they don't teach any of these people how to get outta zip ties, isn't it?"

"Sure is." I remember that from our brief encounter with Homeland. "You'd figure it'd be standard by now."

"You'd figure," Butler agrees.

"So you know about Bits's further plan?" He hesitates. "Butler."

"Yeah. We were operating on hypotheticals, but yeah."

"Fair enough." I drop my cigarette, check the time. Not an hour, but whatever, Bits can tell me to wait or she can tell me the plan. "I'm not mad."

"I didn't say you were." He looks at Nicolai, who takes his flask back.

"I will see if Bits is ready for us or not," he says, putting his hands in his pockets and walking inside.

"You okay?" Butler asks.

"Let's not start that again," I say.

"I meant the obvious but also, I guess you probably don't even feel the cut under your eye." He reaches out and rubs a thumb along my cheekbone gently. It stings then; it didn't register before though. Too much else going on.

"Bristol must've caught me with a ring or something," I say, and let him sit with however he wants to think about that statement.

"I guess she must've," he says, and Nicolai reappears in the entrance and waves. "He could've texted."

"Nicolai likes the personal approach, clearly." I hop off the car. Proof of concept, I can move like normal. "Plus he's probably on his way to raid one of the mini bars for our war room."

"Can't tell if that's a great thought or the worst thought."

"Right? Every time." I grin at him and we go inside to find Bits. The curtain ties are still on the chair, and it feels like we were in this room both thirty seconds ago and three years ago at the same time.

Nicolai has just poured a drink, and Bits has a fresh pitcher of that fucking coffee, and looks up at Butler and I for a second. "You both have retinal upgrades, right? From the program? Does it let you see AR?"

"I mostly keep that part of it turned off," I say. "Except for your texts, and if I need to snipe." The letting me see in the dark part has been the most useful.

"Well turn it on so I can show you the hotel where the agency is." I do the blink pattern that makes that happen. There's not a lot of ambient AR here in the hotel anyway, Bristol's old fashioned like that. It's not like when you walk down a city street and get popup ads for businesses and government weather alerts and whatnot.

The hotel is I don't know how many stories tall, but what Bits has illuminated isn't up past the first floor; it's the entrances, and then it's sublevels, done wireframe style so we can see the rooms and things. I never took much time to think about whether there were many basements here, commonly, but I'm pretty sure it isn't common to have multiple sublevels. "Shit," I say.

"Stairs and an elevator," she says. "I think Miller was telling the truth about how many agency members are here, they don't have the area super populated, and it could be that a couple of allied agencies sort of share this office space. Maybe British too? French? I don't know. But there are eleven people now, so that's Harding, the nine other agents, and Will."

"To be clear, Miller being the other guy?" I ask, nodding to the now-empty chair.

"Yeah."

"How do you know how many people are in the espionage basement?" Butler asks.

"The wifi." He looks at me and I shrug; Bits sighs. "You can use the signal to see people in a room, essentially. Easier than looking at every device location, once I've got the network."

"Fair enough," he says.

"Whiskey?" Nicolai asks, and Butler nods and I shake my head, looking at the hotel.

"Okay, so the back here is employees? And that leads to the stairs that go down-down?" I sort of trace the path with my finger.

"No, the employee entrance doesn't. The guest stairs do, here." Bits blinks it. "So if you go in the front lobby, and then past the desk and the elevators, you can take the stairs down like, a half level, before they've got a smart lock on it, which I know you know how to handle. Or you can take the elevator down, I think I've got a set of keys for that model, but—"

"But I don't want to ding on the floor and let everybody know I'm there," I finish. I look at the floating hotel, look at the flights of stairs. Nine agents, plus Harding. How surprised could they possibly be, right? Hotel full of civilians upstairs. Very full, actually.

"What's with the crowd, all vacationers?"

"There's a bachelorette party, a couple of families on separate vacations, some kind of sightseeing tour that's got a bus parked nearby, and..." Bits trails off a second, still reading the check in log or whatever, I assume. "A group of five U.S. Army on furlough from Spain."

"Actual Army, or Agency under another name?"

"Actual Army, as far as I can tell. Their records aren't this-week or even this year new."

I nod a little. I reach over and take Butler's drink and knock it back. "Okay, so I can't go in dressed like this, then."

"Why are you acting like you're doing this alone?" Butler asks. He's smart, he doesn't ask me why I'm acting like I'm doing it at all. The cost of stopping me, or trying to stop me, outweighs the benefit. Or it doesn't; Butler doesn't give a fuck about like, Bristol's happiness. He never met Will before three days ago or whenever. He wants *me* to be okay. So we kinda daisy chain those motivations together.

"We insert two people, that means we need to get three out instead of two."

He frowns. "Yeah. Obviously." That's how math works, Dolly, he doesn't say.

"If you weren't here, I'd do it alone." Well, I'd do it with Bristol holding the entire hotel ballroom in the palm of her charismatic fucking hand but I ain't exactly got that option right now. She's got too many people out there jockeying to spend time with her to just take her away again, mysteriously, and then have mysterious shit go down at a hotel downtown. She needs to keep the party people occupied.

"But I *am* here and so's Nicolai and—"

The door opens, and Suzette walks in and stops short with a look on her face that she didn't expect *anybody* to be here, much less all of us. But then her eyes hit Nicolai and she just lights up. "I've been looking for you!" she exclaims. "Is this where you've been hiding the whole time? With Bristol's friends?" She hesitates a little over friends; she doesn't really understand why Bristol has us here. What we are.

"I got caught up in conversation, I did not mean to abandon you," Nicolai says.

"De rien, but it's almost dinner, you must come." She walks towards him with her hand out, and he looks at Butler and then me apologetically, and I give him a nod.

"Go enjoy," I say. It'll be good to leave him here, embedded in the party. Worst case already happened, with all of us on deck. I'm gonna have everybody's attention in a little while here.

"If you need anything from my room, you are welcome to it," he says, as Suzette pulls him out the door. What a romcom-ass thing to happen.

"Dolly," Butler says, when the door closes behind them again.

"I'm going to need you, yes, but I need you outside to extract me, us, if I need backup. We'll only get one fuckup on this. Maybe. And I'm gonna need you to help me get ready, so if you've got this map committed to memory, meet me in my room in..." I think how long it'll take me to get from here, to Bristol's room, and then back to mine. "Fifteen."

He's still just looking at me and I can hear the seconds ticking away on a cosmic level, and then he sighs, which says everything that he's leaving unsaid. "Okay."

"Dolly?" Bits asks, frowning.

"You too. I'm just very aware of how not-private this room is."

Chapter Eleven

I grab two of Bristol's spraycan dresses in case we fuck up the first one, and because my sizing and hers ain't exactly the same, we'll need the extra for my height at the very least. I look at her shoes for a second, but we're not the same size in those, I'll just wear my boots and like, put a belt on, and it'll be fashion or some shit. I also take one of her dragonscale camisoles; I might not be doing this in an armored jacket or with a helmet, but I'd like *some* protection for my insides. I think about grabbing some of her makeup, but learning how to contour a broken nose isn't something I really got the time or interest for.

As I'm leaving, I notice the water glasses that she has with a pitcher, and something about their size and shape makes me take one. We'll see if it matches up with what Nicolai brought.

I go back through the secret passages to the opening nearest my room, listen to make sure it's all clear, and then step out. Mr. Squeak is trundling past and pauses to give me a once-over, but I pass the sniff test and she keeps going.

In my room, Bits is sitting on the bed up near the pillows, and Butler put down towels and then laid out guns and a few other fun things. "Just like Christmas," I say. I throw an eye on them, but there isn't anything I'll be able to covertly take. I could just use the active camo to get in, but that'll be better served on Butler for his covert positioning, and Bits for hers if she comes with, and while I happily stole Bristol's spray cans I can't make myself borrow her active camo.

I'd spend the whole time catastrophizing about what if something happens while we're doing this cowboy bullshit and she needs it and doesn't have it and then it's like an even sadder ending for Gift of the Magi.

"What the fuck is that?" Butler asks, jutting his chin out at the spray cans. He's digging in his bag for something else.

"A dress, once you're done with me," I say. "Bitsy, avert your eyes or whatever." She shrugs and pulls her headset on again.

"A *dress*?"

"Wild, right? I did it for Bristol last night, which means it's pretty idiot proof." I search on my phone a couple of times, trying to imagine what words she would've used, and come up with not the same picture but a similar one. I don't need to fuck around with sleeve straps, I would like a slit in the skirt for mobility, but if Bristol can get it done with a combat knife, I guess we can too. I drop my clothes on the floor, pull on the dragonscale camisole. "You can do that right?"

"Pull that up, I want to wrap your ribs first." He's got a roll of compression stuff, that's what he was after in his bag.

"I didn't say anything about my ribs."

"You can't hardly stand up straight."

"God, are you and Bristol gonna bond over my posture?" But I pull up the camisole to give him access, stand myself up straight as I can, then the rest of the way, hissing as I do it. He frowns, and I wonder if he's gonna pull something to keep me from going after all. He doesn't, though, he just wraps me up good and careful, and I'm glad he does it, I'm breathing easier once he's done. He pulls the camisole down over it, then picks up my phone to look at the picture I found.

"Stay still I guess," Butler says dubiously, shaking the can. I laugh, because I know exactly how he feels. Well maybe not exactly; he and I have a history of relations. Bristol was right though, it is cold coming out of the can, and it's funny to feel my skin ripple and goose-bump the way I saw hers do. I stay as still as I'm able, which is pretty still actually, with my enhanced sniper training, and when he gets down to right after the camisole hem he says, "It's leaving a line there, does that matter?"

"Go over it again to make it look on purpose or something, and I'm gonna wear a belt." I've seen Bristol wear a belt over a dress, it's fine. He kinda grunts as he keeps going. The can peters out not very far past my hips and he shakes the next one.

"This is like actual witchcraft."

"Ain't it, though?" He glances up at me and I grin down. Funny it's the dress in a can that makes me and him nervous, not wound care. "Alright I guess right at the knee, to at least kinda hide the gun. Don't suppose you can do pockets?" The *look* he gives me. I pull the knife, picture how Bristol did it, and have him hold the skirt taut while I cut the slit. I roll my shoulders a little, gauging each pain as I feel the fabric curing against my skin.

"Fit okay?"

"How the fuck should I know?" I do a slow turn in front of the mirror; I guess it looks okay. I feel like I'm looking at a weird copy of myself; Bristol will be sorry that she missed Dolly-dress-up. A white dress, Jesus. I put my boots on, and especially with the compression bandaging can bend just fine, like it's real clothes, the only limitations are my own. I put a belt on and I can't tell if it looks bad, but I need to keep my extra mags somewhere. It's been a good long time since I've strapped a gun to my thigh, and even then it was because I was wearing shorts and test driving the principle, but with the length the skirt is, it's pretty hidden. I lean into the mirror, to do my signature short work with some eyeliner. I should've iced the nose. "Oh goddamn it, my hair." Maybe I should cut it. No, I don't want to take too much more time.

"Need me to watch a video on that too?" Butler asks, joking but serious, we're in ops mode. He's snapping a little first aid trauma kit on my belt. It'll have those foaming things in it that plug up bullet holes best, probably a couple of painkiller slap patches. I think about starting with one of those going, but it's only gonna get worse. I'm good, but fully expect to get shot at least once.

"If you can." I'm mostly joking, and he's picking up my phone again. "No, I don't have pins or anything, I'm just gonna twist it back into a bun and that'll be good enough for government work."

"Okay." He looks at the guns he laid out, and packs up one of the 3D printed sniper rifles that he brought from Hong Kong. I didn't look at it enough to say what makes it different from factory, but we've all got our gun particulars. Some of what's there is what Nicolai brought, and it takes three seconds for me to find grenades. They're flashbangs, but a compact kind that looks enough like a normal frag grenade that I think it's going to work with my glass trick. I put one in carefully, just to see, and yeah, it's the right shape that the crenellations on the glass will hold the hammer even after I pull the pin. So I can wander through that lobby looking like I'm holding a drink, take the stairs down, and make my entrance. Of course, flash bangs are loud, but if I had to guess, the secret sublevels of a hotel used by secret government agencies are probably real damn sound proof. We'll find out together. "Here, I've got something else that'll probably be useful," Butler says, voice a little gruff, pulling me out of my focus.

"What is it?"

He pulls a square leather case out of his duffel; it looks like one of the jewelry boxes that Bristol uses for a necklace, broad and a couple inches deep. He opens the lid and holds it out to me, and I put the glass down to look. It's an antique derringer, big enough for four shots, small enough to drop into the top of the dress and not be a bother. Smooth wooden grips, bronze frame, you can even still read Colt etched into the top of the barrel. "It's perfect, it's like you knew," I say, picking it up and turning it over in my hands. There's an inset in the case, for a little box that's rattling with rounds, and I load it and then take the ammo box too. It's bad luck to assume you won't be able to reload.

"Just had a feeling," he says, elaborately casual, and of course I know there's more at play here, but we don't have the time.

"Thank you," I say, and kiss him. He kisses me back, but doesn't know where to put his hands, resting them on my hips after a sec. Then I load the derringer and drop it between my boobs like a dance hall girl. Alright, one last thing. I take a deep breath that's got two and a half hitches in it. "Bitsy, gonna need you to reactivate me."

She yanks her headset off and stares at me for three seconds too long. "Dolly, no." I've never heard her sound like that either. What a day of firsts this is.

"I know I said that I didn't want the full array ever again, but if I have to wade through ten or more people like a video game level, I need that buffer." Some of the super soldier programming stuck, is just permanent, like how my pain tolerance is almost completely rewired, like how my reflexes are better, but the other stuff, the stuff that we went to decommissioned bunkers looking for because it was only on paper…it's past what I can achieve just naturally, which is part of the point. It's only gonna be nine or ten people, if I get down there the way I have it pictured in my head, but that's still nine or ten *people*. That's more than I've handled, post-deprogramming. With or without another fresh injury.

"Dolly, think about how they'll consider that you've done that. You don't want them to use a codeword and turn you against us."

"That's always been the risk, right?" I grin at her. Behind me, Butler's slapping a mag into a handgun. Too bad we don't have one of their choppers, that would and wouldn't help with this. The possibility of air support tends to be nice. "You said you changed it, though, so we've got failsafes?"

"I mean, of course I have, but we haven't tested anything to see if it would work. What if I'm wrong, and nothing changes? It just textbook reactivates your super soldier suite, controls and all, and that's that?"

"Then I guess I need earplugs too."

"Dolly, I don't want to do this."

"It'll be worse for me if you don't." I can do it anyway, I think. This ain't my first rodeo, first blood, any of that. It's been us and them for so long, I can do it. Maybe I won't have to kill all of them, maybe the flashbang will be good enough and I can move fast enough. But if I don't, then we're back at square one, with the agency still knowing where we are and wanting to stop us or control us or both.

I watch her process this, watch her eyes move as she's reading stuff in AR. Doin' the math, I guess. Potential unfriendlies, how much ammo I can carry, how much psychological damage any of us might have to reckon with...it's a lotta math, but Bits is good at that kind of thing. I am very aware of the passage of time, of all of us breathing, of the party people outside. Finally, she says, "Okay. Okay earplugs over your earbuds, so you can still hear me."

"Of course."

"I'm going to reactivate you, but I'm also going to program the new failsafe word, just in case what we did to remove the control command didn't work."

"Good, yes, do it." I'm glad Bits is being careful, really I am. That's a worst-case, that Harding takes control and gives me an attack dog kill command and I take everybody out. We never wanted that possibility to exist.

It's kinda the nature of activation/deactivation that you don't really know it's happened. You don't remember those couple minutes surrounding the key phrases, as the posthypnotic suggestion comes online, or shuts down. We saw it with Will just a couple days ago, and even though I think that I'm watching this time, I know what to look for, no I don't. Butler's shrugging into his armored jacket and he's got a keffiyeh that I know messes with digital surveillance, and I check my ammo, shove a knife in my boot, and pick up the glass with the grenade in it. Bits is watching me closely, as worried as I've ever seen her.

"I feel okay," I say, and I do. This is the right choice, the right move. Hopefully no civilian collateral. That lobby full of partyers worries me. Hopefully our team all walks away from this, plus Will. I guess I gotta consider him our team now, we wouldn't really do this for anybody else. Our side, anyway.

"Butler has your active camo?" I don't remember talking about it. Butler nods, though. He isn't frowning but I recognize his deliberately-not-frowning face.

"Let's get this show on the road," I say. "They don't need too much time to either plan their exit or think about if we're coming for them."

"They have to expect we are," Bits says. She looks at Butler, who shrugs.

"Not if they think they already won."

"Hmm," Bits says, but we go out to the car. Nobody sees us, or says anything. I half hope Bristol does see us, wants to know what we're doing, wants to come along, but actually I'm glad to not have to worry about her more right now. If they think they won, then Nicolai, and Marge, and Floyd and Joker and the robot dogs are enough. And if this goes well, then for a little while anyway, we really won't need to worry about more. If it goes bad enough, I won't be worrying about anything anymore anyway.

WHEN THEY DROP ME OFF in front of the hotel, other people are also getting dropped off, so it's easy for me to fall into the loose groups walking into the automatic doors, keeping my eyes peeled as I cross the lobby. The people at the front desk are looking at everybody who enters, but not in a way that bothers me, they're just keeping general track of the crowd. It's gotta be hard with all that's going on, to try and mark who you think is *supposed* to be here, who you think is gonna be a problem, all of that. I bump one of the bachelorette partygoers, or more correctly, she's blasted out of her mind and bumps me. She doesn't even look at me, just kind of exclaims something and moves in the opposite direction. Some of those girls are carrying on, or trying to, with what looks to me like some of the army guys, who've somehow been on base long enough to forget what partying girls like this look like. Or maybe they didn't know before now, and their horizons are being abruptly broadened.

Then one of the army guys backs up into me, as the story he's telling gets too big for the space he's in, hard enough that I let out an involuntary gasp and come real close to dropping my grenade glass. Good thing the pin's still in, but it'd still fuck the situation for that to go spinnin' across the floor.

"Sorry, oh god sorry, I didn't see you there," the guy says, the kind of red-faced and pale-lidded that says he's both sunburned and also drunker than he feels yet and both of those are gonna suck come morning. He grabs at my elbow and there's too many people I still need to get past to do anything so I let him do it, keeping my glass in the other hand away from him. I can barely hear him but it's fine, I can read lips pretty good by this point.

"It's okay it's really crowded," I yell, grinning hard and blinking a lot. Can't say I've ever wanted to pretend to be drunk before.

He lights up like it's Christmas. "You're American!" Oh come on.

"Yeah! But I have to..." He's still got my elbow, is trying to explain to his friends that he found another American, and I look 'em over real quick. One is stone cold sober and hates this, but he must hate leaving people unsupervised worse. The others are also very drunk, maybe with some other additives, and they forgot him and his story the second he broke the circle and ran into me. He can't get their attention back, but the sober one looks at me. Thank Christ for the bachelorettes, he's mentally prepped to think I'm one of them, or in that category, and not anything more interesting. Or more threatening, if Harding tagged him as some kind of frontline here. Interagency cooperation, son, just need you to keep a casual lookout. Maybe that's why he's sober, maybe not. He's strapped and the other ones aren't. But his eyes slide off me and my spraycan dress without registering.

"Kevin, you asshole, you can't go grabbing random girls, I don't care where she's from."

"Shit, I'm sorry!" Kevin looks at me again, wide-eyed, and I hold up my free hand.

"It's okay! Have fun!" Kevin says something else that I can't hear, as I weave into the crowd away from him. Nobody else takes particular notice of me, and I tell myself it's because I did this stupid dress thing to blend in, instead of coming in here actually geared. Probably it's what kept the sober Army guy from keying in. I changed my silhouette to not look like an operator.

I wait until I'm in the stairwell to pull the pin on the grenade and settle it back down into the cup. I just wear the ring on my thumb, I might get a chance to wave it at somebody for intimidation purposes. I might just drop the glass as my opening sally. We'll see.

The smart lock is no trouble, it's not one I can slap, but it is one that has the manual bypass right there and visible under a little rubber plug, and I shim it quick and am through that door and pulling it softly closed behind me in under a minute. Some vulnerabilities just never get fixed.

This flight of stairs goes for a while. Down, turn at a landing, down. Extra secure, extra quiet. No, upstairs isn't gonna hear this grenade, or any gunshots. Another reason not to take the elevator, though. They're finicky, and return to a ground floor and then open and lock and that's that, if a fire alarm goes off or whatever. Maybe I should've pulled one on my way in, but that's also the opposite of stealthy ain't it.

The door at the bottom of the stairs has a keycard reader and a number pad, I guess so you can use either. I run the card we took off that other guy. Miller? If they're smart they would've deactivated it. The reader goes green and the door clicks. Or it's a trap. I don't pull the gun yet, I just inch the door open and have a peek. Nothing, nobody. It's so quiet down here that if I'm not careful I can hear my rough-edged breathing. My fingertips are zinging, I'm so hyped up. I close the door behind me quiet as I can, listening to see if anybody reacts to the click. Nothing. There's a camera in the hall here but I can't think about that, gotta trust that Bitsy has it in hand. She always does.

It's too quiet, maybe they cleared out already. Or they're used to the quiet and waiting. Or it's the fucking earplugs but I made a promise and I do my best to keep those. Nine Agents. Harding. Will. One of them's gonna be Clancy, so I guess we'll get a tiebreaker. I run the map in my head, of where people were when Bits showed us, and clear the first two rooms I pass without anything and then the third has a guy in a vest and BDUs and those yellow sunglasses and he was ready for me but also he shifts right as I get to the door and I hear his belt creak.

Ready or not, I'm faster than a normal guy like that can be, and I clear the gun from my thigh holster, pop the door the rest of the way open by stomping right next to it, and put a round in the space between his collarbones before he's finished drawing. He looks surprised; they often do. I get the rest of the way into the room, swing the door half shut again, fade back into the corner, crouch, wait. The sound of a firearm should be unmistakable to these people. There should be immediate response.

And there is. They're methodical, they've gotta assume this guy is already down. I hear their boots and can envision them funneling out of the nearby rooms to come to this one, giving a hand signal to hold outside, then somebody presses the door open with a rifle butt and I throw my glass past them, so it hits the wall across the hallway, and I close my eyes and duck my head under my forearm. The glass breaks, they startle, the flashbang goes off, they give muffled yells. One fires, I think they just involuntarily squeezed off a round, and one staggers in front of the doorway and I drop them. Another, in a crouch, comes to check them and I drop him too. Then I leave my corner and enter the hallway, shooting the woman who's still standing, first in the shoulder, then in the chest.

There's one on the ground against the wall, face bloody from sprayed glass looks like, and he shoots me in the belly twice before I steal a breath and put both hands on my gun for the first time and headshot him.

Then it's quiet again. Four Agents. Harding. Will. Nine rounds left in this mag, maybe that's enough and I won't need to reload. Maybe I should reload now, to be sure. Decisions, decisions.

I check myself; something cut one of my arms, maybe just fragments, not a lot of blood, doesn't hurt. My stomach hurts but the dragonscale caught the rounds for me. If that one had a rifle it would've punctured, I think. It'll bruise up nice later. Join whatever my ribs are doing.

//Are you okay?// Bits asks. It must've cost her a lot to break silence.

It feels like it's definitely me having that thought, but it's behind glass, like me and my actions are over here, and everything that I think and feel and remember are over there. I don't remember this feeling; the first time I got programmed, I was then in boot, and didn't have time to think and feel and remember.

"Yeah," I say, so quietly I can't hear myself. Butler doesn't say anything but it's like I can *feel* him listening.

I stalk down the hall, posted up, ready. I gotta assume the four agents left are the gold star ones, because if what they sent first was the front line, then they should already be surrendering or they just got a death wish. I gotta assume that Harding is no slouch. I guess he could just be an ROTC-officer school deskjockey, but I'm not so sure that's the case. I know now that Clancy's an operator. The hallway empties into a bigger, open room. Empty. Stairwell door across the way. Wishing I brought a second flashbang. The glass was a good trick, though. I drop mag, reload. If the next ones have more consistent armor I'm gonna need more shots.

I edge the stairwell door open and it seems clear all the way down. No noise, no shadows, no gun oil other than what I brought with me. I go down, step by step, keeping my back to the wall. They could circle around on me, probably, using the elevator. I don't think they will. I get to the next door, and it's propped with a plant, like somebody wanted air. It's almost funny, maybe it's funny. I can feel the weight of people in the next room and I stop, wait. They know I'm here, if I were them, this is where I'd have a rifle set up.

I breathe, clear my thoughts, shed my tension.Then I tuck and roll low into the room, come up on a knee and snap my gun into place, get one guy center mass, probably his vest took it, and the one with the rifle takes the shot a little too soon and it goes through the bicep of my left arm. The cybernetic stuff is sorta self healing, to a point. One round is fine. That arm's more than paid for itself today. I feel the shockwave, but it doesn't *hurt* and now that I've seen the rest of the room I can duck to the side for cover, such as it is, behind one of those movable cubicle partitions. The guy I shot is grumbling about his vest and the woman with the rifle tells him to shut up and

I listen to their voices and decide that they've for some reason decided not to move and pop out again, double tap the guy I shot the first time, and risk taking my time aiming up on the woman with the rifle before I shoot.

We fire at the same time, and her round grazes right past my face, and my round hits her scope. She drops but I'm not sure she's down and I cross the room in the blink of an eye and kick both their weapons away. Yeah. Good enough.

Why am I not picking up weapons as I go? I want to do this fast, and I don't want to make the mistake of relying on anything one of their hackers can turn off on me, since these are all smart guns. Actually, since they're all smart guns, they might not even work for me unless I talk to 'em with a paperclip or wait for Bits to jailbreak them and I don't have the *time*.

Two left, then Harding. Will.

Chapter Twelve

Another set of stairs, this time they've got a tripwire set that I spot just in time, quarter way up from the bottom. I back up, consider. I look over the railing, gauge the distance, and just go over that and drop down. I land okay, but I'm also not the most stealthy and one of them rushes me, gets me in the sternum with his shoulder and runs me into the wall under the stairs. Unfortunately for him, closer isn't safer, and I ride the momentum, yell-exhale on impact, then stomp his instep when he goes to reposition. The angle's bad, I don't think I broke anything the way I intended, but it doesn't feel good, and he jerks back and bends a little and I grab a handful of his hair and use that momentum to introduce his face to my knee, let go to let him stumble back in shock and assess his body armor, and put a round in his thigh about where I think the femoral is. The fountain tells me I'm right.

This dress isn't so white anymore.

As this is all happening, he's conveniently blocking his friend's shot, and as he's dropping I spin away to get to the side of the door-way and take cover, and the rifle coughs and clips me in the calf. I still make it but I need to handle that right now. I grab at the first aid kit, pop out one of the foam things and I break off the end of the tube as I'm shaking it, get the nozzle against the wound and the button pressed. I can hear the rifle reloading and I wonder how many shots they took, that they only got me with the one. Maybe they've just got the reflex, like when you're playing a shooter and want to be ready to fully mag dump at a moment's notice. This doesn't hurt too bad but it does hurt a lot and that guy hurt my ribs again or more or whatever and it'd be stupid not to use a pain patch, so I take the time to slap one of those on too.

I hear the scuff of a boot; are they really coming closer? They had to hear me use the foam, it makes an unmistakable noise. I look at the bright pool of blood from the other guy, tilt my head so I can see the lights going down the hallway reflected. A shadow of movement. Yeah, they're taking the time to reposition, probably if only so they're not in the same place I saw them last. That's okay, a breather is good. Let the painkiller go to work. Another boot scuff, the slightest shadow reflected in the edge of the blood. They're still a ways down the hallway.

I throw an eye over my shoulder at that tripwire to see if it was attached to anything but no. That's smart, wouldn't want to use mines or an IED down here, too close.

I'm not gonna get another hail Mary shot down somebody's scope and we're both ready for each other and I guess I just need to get a move on. I look over at the dead guy, but he's no use to me, framed in the doorway. Trying to take anything off him would be a waste of time and just get me killed.

I've still got the grenade pin on my thumb and I think about that. If the person with the rifle is like me, they know very well what the sound of that ring on concrete sounds like. Maybe it'll buy me a couple seconds. I drop the pin, do a silent three count like I'm cooking a grenade, then throw my handgun clattering down the hall, follow when I hear "Shit," and scrambling.

They didn't move very far up the hall, they were cautious, but they switched sides and now they're crouched with their back turned, so that tells me they're wearing a ballistic vest too and hoped it would save their ass. Literally. But the grenade doesn't go off, and they're turning back around as I get *almost* to my gun and I yank the derringer out of my boobs and shoot for where I see skin, clipping their wrist, and I recognize the wince and jaw set *very* well, this person was also in the program, or in *a* program and they get the rifle around and hipfire it as I dive for them and this camisole doesn't cover shit, I can't believe we let Bristol wear it for as many ops as she has but also nobody 'lets' Bristol do things.

But that pain patch is singing through me and getting shot'll put a delay on you but I've already got the momentum, so when I collide with them the rifle clatter-slides across the floor and I jam the derringer up under their jaw with my left hand and pull the trigger the three more times. Then I sit back on my heels, drop the casings, reload, my hands working without thinking, even though I can't really feel my right fingers right now. Good thing I was ambidextrous even before the program.

Despite the pain patch and the programming, it hurts enough that I'm not sure exactly where I'm hit as I jam the derringer behind my belt, pull and prep another foam thing. Right shoulder, further from my neck rather than closer, so that's good. Doesn't seem to have broken my collarbone or anything. There aren't really any good safe places to get shot unless you already got replacement limbs or unless you were wearing better protection than me, but I'll live through this one anyway, and probably not need much. I can still move the arm and flex my fingers. I think the round went clean through, I feel the foam drip down my back before it hardens. I pick my gun up off the floor, give it a quick check to make sure nothing bent or broke. It's fine.

Just Harding and Will left now.

I'm surprised Bits hasn't checked in again but maybe I don't have a good enough signal down here, can't take the time. I move down the hallway again, quiet as I can, except I think I might be leaving bloody boot prints. I can't bother about that right now. Miller told the truth about personnel, at least; I clear every room on my way to the final room, the conference room or office or whatever they did there. No sign of anybody else.

No, where's Clancy?

As I get closer to that room, I hear Harding, though. He sounds like how the Chief did anytime he dressed us down for not running a scenario right, or for being goof offs. I never think about Chief; funny what surfaces, sometimes. The doors're thick as the walls down here and the sound is dampened, but that's Harding's tone of voice, no doubt, and Will isn't saying anything. Is Harding dressing Will down? Is Harding on the horn yelling at backup that isn't coming in time? Only way to find out is to go through door number one.

I kick it open, and they're sitting at the conference table, or Will is sitting and Harding is standing and talking to him while using a knife hand instead of pointing. Pointing's bad. Will flinches less than I would've expected, guess he's learning, and Harding full body reacts, but in a way that tells me that yeah, he isn't just a deskjockey, and he turns to me like he's at ready, but he doesn't have a weapon and I don't take the shot. He made the choice to be here, and to not bar the door, and to not have a weapon. We look at each other across the expanse of the room; it can't really be all that big, but my perceptions are understandably going a little screwy right now. Still operable, just affected. I can feel the little shock-tremors that the programming just lets me ignore.

He says "Steel magnolia," and even after the gunplay and grenade and earplugs, I hear him a little too loud and clear and let out a breath, but nothing changes. This is only my third or fourth time seeing Harding, so I can't really track nuances of his expression, though I'd say 'put upon' fits the bill, at the very least.

"Are you takin' the time to dress him down before you kill him?" I ask, half laughing with disbelief and maybe delirium, and then I see the shimmer in the corner of my eye and almost turn fast enough to put a round in Clancy instead of the opposite wall. Guess Clancy isn't technically an agent, shouldn't've trusted Miller's estimate of how many agents. Wonder how Bitsy's wifi trick didn't see him though.

He knows he hurt me before, and he knows using his bulk is the best bet, and he tries to run me into the wall and I've had about enough of that today and get a grip on whatever part of him's touching me, drop to the floor, which I've also had enough of today, and use his momentum to put him up and over. We're far enough from the wall still that he doesn't hit it, but he comes crashing down on the floor, and he must've landed on his active camo box because he glitches back into sight, fades out again, then comes back for good in the time it takes me to get back to my feet in a much sloppier kip up then the one I did like an hour ago. I hear, or feel, the spray foam that I put in my leg crack. That's a new one.

But it doesn't suit my needs to give Clancy a chance to get back up again, and I reach back for the derringer because damn if I know where my other gun got to and somebody, Harding, fires a round into the ceiling. "Enough."

I back up a couple steps, slowly, with my hands visible, so I can keep an eye on both him and Clancy. Will's still in his seat, though he has turned to watch. He knew I was deprogrammed, knew Bits knew some of the nuts and bolts, and didn't warn Harding. Fucking steel magnolia indeed, come the fuck on. "Time to negotiate?" I ask. There's my gun, partway between me and Harding. He isn't holding his weapon on me, that's interesting. He's holding it on Will.

Clancy climbs slowly to his feet, leaving a puddle of plastic shards on the floor. He's frowning, looks at me, looks at Harding.

"The last time we had contract negotiations, things fell through," Harding says. "The only one who honored their agreement is Marquis."

"What can I say, somebody takes you someplace on their submarine and surrounds you with armed guards, you sign a contract that's put in front of you." I can't get over there before he shoots Will, if that's his actual intent.

"We treated you people very well."

"You did." He doesn't know what to do with that, and Clancy fidgets. I wait; I'm not the negotiator, for one, and for two, I'm not really sure what kind of compelling argument I can offer him after killing a bunch of his personnel. Plus I hate talking with earplugs in. I think Harding is doing the extended math. He might be able to shoot Will before I can do anything about it, but I'll definitely shoot him before Clancy can do anything about it.

Harding nods like he's made up his mind, or maybe he's got his directives from higher-ups, who knows. Bits has stayed out of it, which is probably for the better. "Will Scarlet is no longer a member of this agency. He was lost during an operation in Morocco. His parents will receive a letter commending him and thanking him for his service."

"That's good, his mom's real sweet. Makes good cookies too." Maybe now ain't the right time to taunt him but I also feel pretty put upon. From the swallowed-frog look on his face, he didn't know I interacted with either of his folks that night I gave his laptop back, once Bitsy was done with it. I pop my earplugs; I don't think I'll need 'em anymore. I could be wrong, but also just suddenly couldn't stand the feeling. He won't have a different codeword that works.

Harding holsters his gun, and says, "His remains will be signed over to them as well."

"May he have a comfortable afterlife or whatever," I say. My adrenaline's starting to come down, and that means a whole lotta hurt is starting to surface. Even with the pain patch and the reactivation. The painkillers Bits gave me earlier.

"As a result, his case files are being cleared and closed. We see no further threats to national security in any of his personal projects, he was simply doing his due diligence and had some bad luck."

"Could've saved us all a lotta grief," I mutter. I'm unwilling turn my back on Clancy, who seems like he'd just as soon pick up where we left off.

"Hindsight," Harding says, weight of a judge's gavel in his voice, and Will flinches, just a little. I'm sure he was also real broken up anytime his parents said that they weren't angry, just disappointed.

"If I hadn't made it to this room, would you be having the same conversation?"

"Yes, because I also wasn't interested in being on the receiving end of whatever retribution your global friends network would bring down upon us. You can have Will, he is no longer of use to us. You are clearly capable and dangerous, but in a way that does not have overlap with our jurisdictional concerns."

"Wish I had clarification on what those are, exactly," I say. I glance at Clancy, who's just shy of pouting.

"I'm sure your friend Bits can fill you in," Harding says dryly. "Now get the fuck out of my area of operation."

"Roger that." I look at Will, who's still sitting, and he's got a pretty priceless look on his face. "Take a picture, it'll last longer," I say.

"Sorry." He pushes his chair back, stands. "Mr. Harding, sir—"

Harding holds up a hand. "Get out of here, son. I hope your little blonde is worth it." I laugh, which ain't exactly the kindest thing, but also ain't that the heart of all of this. Harding gives me another onceover, again with that look on his face that speaks of missed opportunities. He actually kicks the handgun over to me. "I look forward to never seeing you again, miss."

"Right back at you." I pick it up, then stand aside to let Will go out ahead of me, before backing out of the room. I give Clancy a salute before pulling the door closed. "You want a blindfold or will you be okay?"

"I'll be okay," Will says quietly. "Thank you."

"Don't mention it. And watch your step at the bottom of these stairs." We make our way through the floors, up the stairs. I keep flexing my right hand, just to make sure I can. I haven't been hurt like this since the job where Bits got her brain scrambled. Hard to say if I'm in better shape now or not, but no that's dumb, of course I am. I'm not cruising for any limb replacements this time and my blood stayed mostly inside. I lost some, got a couple extra holes, but it's fine, we'll get that situated soon.

I slip a little, stepping over one of the bodies, and Will actually reaches out to steady me, and I let him. It's a nice impulse for him to have. Then we're in the last staircase, the first one, the long one, going up and up.

"I don't know how you're going to walk out of here looking like that," he says to me at one point.

"Yeah, good point," I say. "Hey Bits?"

//I'm here// she says. //Butler can come in and meet you at the stairs?//

//Got it covered// Butler says. I don't know what conversation they had when I was down there, but I'm glad they did, and I'm glad they left me to it. This could've been worse. Could've been better, but could've been far worse.

"Thanks," I say. Fuck, I'm thirsty. "Bring water too?"

//I remember.//

"Butler's meeting us," I say to Will. "You probably got that."

"I did." He's got kinda that dazed look that he did when we left Vegas but it's different, just a little. Like he's got a freedom now that he didn't know he wanted and doesn't know what to do with. Well. He'll figure it out. Him and Bristol. "You're going to laugh at me, but are you okay?"

"I'll need medical attention, but I think I'm unlikely to drop dead." I look down; I'm not still leaving bloody footprints, anyway. I reholster my handgun, and put the derringer back in the top of my spraycan dress, which all things considered, has really held up to what I just put it through. Other than not being white anymore.

We reach the ground floor, and the door to the outside world, and Will has a look through the little wire-grid window. "He's there," he says in a voice of strange relief, and pulls the door open. Even after all I just did for him, Will doesn't want to spend one on one time with me, which is fine. Butler pushes in, gives a short, hard sniff when he looks at me, and sheds the jacket he was wearing to put around my shoulders. It doesn't cover all of me, but it covers the worst of it, and since I foamed the leg wound early, maybe that's explainable to a casual observer as I fell and got scraped up on pavement.

Then we open the door, and cross the lobby at a leisurely pace. It's even more crowded now, and dark out now, which for some reason made the lobby lights get lowered and some kind of flashing party lighting happen. I don't really have an explanation, but it sure suits our purposes. The army guys aren't there anymore. Butler left the car right out front, and a hotel employee is standing there with a look on his face that says the car shouldn't be there and he doesn't want to have to deal with it. "I'm moving it now," Butler says, too loud, too cheerful. "Have a good night."

"Shotgun," I say, and Butler laughs. He opens the door for me, and then stands back in between the hotel door and me, but I get myself into the car without too much trouble. I got time left on the pain patch.

At first, we don't make a whole lot of conversation on the way back. Once we're away from the hotel, Bits drops the active camo and Will about shits himself, and that's pretty funny. Other than that, he keeps his own counsel back there, and Butler keeps looking at me.

"Dolly, you need a hospital," Bits says at one point. She doesn't think I'll agree, but has to try, I get that.

"We know a guy," I say. "We'll figure it out." I can't remember where that guy might be right this second. Maybe Dubai, maybe Portugal. Portugal'd be better for our purposes. "Too bad we don't have a chopper."

"Sorry, it wouldn't fit in my bag," Butler says.

"That's fine, what you brought me was real good."

"When I saw it, I knew it was for you," he says.

I find his cigarettes in the jacket pocket, light one on my first try, so I think I look worse than I am. I missed the opportunity to mention that the blood isn't all mine.

Finally, we're back at Bristol's hotel, and Will gets out of the car almost immediately but then just stands here, like he isn't sure he's fine to go in.

"C'mere." I hold my cigarette in my teeth and straighten Will's tie and pat him on the shoulder. "Go on back to her now."

He'd been looking towards the hotel, but actually makes eye contact for once, startled. "You're not coming in?"

"Nah. Seems like I should skip it. 'Specially with the state I'm in. She'll get mad about the rugs." He looks at me a minute longer, frowning, then turns and walks across the parking lot, through the side gate. I listen, as though I'll hear Bristol see him, greet him, but the smeared murmur of voices and laughing and music mask that, of course.

"She'll forgive you," Butler says, taking the pack out of his/my pocket and lighting his own cigarette.

I shrug. "Yeah, maybe." Bits finishes extricating herself from the car and just looks plain exhausted. "When's the last sleep you got, Bitsy?"

"I'm fine," she says. "But—"

"It's all that jet fuel you've been drinking," I say. "I said you were supposed to dilute it."

"Dolly—"

"It's fine. We'll see our guy, and then I'll head back to Hong Kong with Butler, stay there awhile. You always know how to find me."

"Yeah, that's true," she says. She still looks worried. *And* exhausted. "Let me deactivate you again first?"

"Oh yeah, true, good." I take a breath. "This is gonna suck so bad."

"Maybe come in and—"

"Butler, can you pack our stuff?"

"Yeah, I'll get that squared away, and call Doc. Can you wait until I'm back at least?"

"We can wait," I say, and he saunters off. "See, that wasn't so bad?"

"I'm not validating that," Bits says, shaking her head. "We shouldn't have let you go in there alone."

I laugh. "I don't think 'let' enters into any of our decisions." She still looks dubious.

"It's just not how we typically do things. I know I won't change your mind, especially since it's already over with."

"Exactly, now we're on the same page." I let the car door hang open and sit back down on the edge of the seat, my legs dangling out. I know it's hot out, but I hug Butler's jacket around me anyway, to smell him, and in anticipation of what it's gonna feel like when Bits drops my programming again.

I finish my cigarette, and kind of whistle aimlessly and tunelessly until Butler comes back out with our duffles. "Leaving most of the arsenal for Marge," he says, "So I took a minute to let her know. We can always just print more. Said goodbye to Nicolai too."

"Oh good. We know how he worries." Bits makes a noise like an outraged sigh. "You ready Bitsy?"

"The question is if you're ready. Did you already call your 'guy'?" she asks, turning to Butler.

"Yeah, and he put me in touch with somebody in town, so we can go right there and get her stable and get the good drugs. Get some sleep. Then make travel arrangements."

"I can do that part," Bits says.

"Sounds good," I say.

Bits puts her finger in front of her face, between us, and has me focus on it. There's a tone that she plays in my ears, I remember that, and then there's other parts that I don't remember, and then those pieces of glass keeping things separate fall away, and all the pain is a brief roaring haze and maybe I'll just black out but no, I get my breathing under control and push it down some. Those pain patches I already slapped on make that possible, I think. I blink and look around. Bits is still standing there, still frowning. Butler's crouched in next to me, though, like he wants to comfort me somehow but there's no good way to go about it.

"Okay, all set," Bits says.

"Thanks, Bitsy, you're the best." I manage a grin at her, and she quirks her lips and shakes her head.

"Just try to be careful, okay?"

"I do what I can," I say. "That sounds like I'm lying, I'm not lying. Anyway, I'm sure I'll see you in a couple months. It won't be long."

"It probably won't be long, yeah." She stands there long enough to watch Butler help me sit right in the car and buckle me in, and then she turns and goes into the hotel.

He gets in the driver's seat and starts the car. "You're unbelievable," he says.

"If you're gonna get on my case about—"

"No, I mean, what you just accomplished. You could've been killed and instead you're...well you're in rough shape but okay. And all for Bristol?"

"Friendship is like that sometimes," I mutter.

"Right, yeah, the power of friendship." He doesn't roll his eyes, but he might as well have.

"Fuck you."

"Not now, but once we're back in Hong Kong you'll probably be up for it again."

Epilogue

Butler proposes on the ferry over to Hong Kong. He doesn't have a ring, but that's not a surprise. Neither of us is in a hurry for a degloving accident. That's what the derringer was for, a pretty little thing, if somebody was inclined to get me in particular something that's pretty. Plus it is *very* functional, and what more could a girl ask for.

"Last time, it wasn't the right time," he says. "Maybe it isn't now either. I even did it right, I went and talked to your parents first."

"My parents love you," I say. We're alone on the deck, of course, because he's got a lick of sense. Between the guys we knew, I got pretty well patched up in Morocco and still have some pain but it's manageable without hard drugs, even. "That sounds like I'm hedging. I love you."

"But?"

"But...hell, I don't know. I just want to understand, I guess? What do we need to be married for, if we understand each other? Just want to stake your claim?" I knew this was coming, or suspected it was coming, but I still have to ask.

"Would that be wrong?" I wait and he laughs. "It could just be for the hell of it, could be so I can legally leave you all my assets, if I die in a terrible 3D printed helicopter crash."

"We don't need to be married for that."

"I suppose not." He reaches over and takes my hand. My real hand. He's maybe the most serious I've ever seen him and we've seen some serious shit. Recently, even. "You're the person I want to spend my days with. That I never get tired of. That I think about all the time."

I'm not surprised. I can't possibly be surprised. I've told him no or put him off every other time and still he waits and then asks again. To be fair, it's been years; since before I started working with Bits and Bristol. And we've spent a lot of time apart over those years. And a lot of close time together just these past couple days, and every time, it's like we pick up exactly where we left off. "Butler, I don't know."

"You already said that." He glances past me, just a split second, but I turn and look; members of the ferry crew are suddenly acting very casual.

"Did you pick here to propose so that the captain would marry us?" I ask.

He hesitates. "Maybe."

"Bristol would be furious if she missed my wedding," I say, as if I think that bridge isn't burned. Maybe it isn't. There's only so mad she stays for so long. Plus, we fixed it. There'll be another job, soon enough.

"Is that enough to get you to say yes?" He grins.

"It'd be shitty for you if it was," I say.

"But?" He knows. He knew before he asked, this time.

"Yeah, let's do it."

Butler gives the crew the thumbs up, and the ferry blares its horn. Wait 'til I send Bitsy the pictures.

Further work by Jennifer R. Donohue

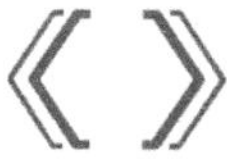

Exit Ghost
Learn to Howl
The Drowned Heir
Between the Blood and the Sun
Other books in the Run With the Hunted series
Run With the Hunted
Run With the Hunted 2: Ctrl Alt Delete
Run With the Hunted 3: Standard Operating Procedure
Run With the Hunted 4: VIP
Run With the Hunted 5: Insert Coin to Play

JENNIFER R. DONOHUE grew up at the Jersey Shore and now lives in central New York with her husband and their Dobermans. A member of the SFWA, she works at her local public library where she also facilitates a writing workshop. She is the author of the Run With the Hunted novella series, and her debut novel, Exit Ghost, released in 2023. Her work has otherwise appeared in Apex Magazine, Escape Pod, Fantasy Magazine, Gamut, and elsewhere.